The Caves of Kurazi

Finding Earth Book 3

N. R. Tucker

ISBN- 978-0-9907163-9-6

Map of Kurazi

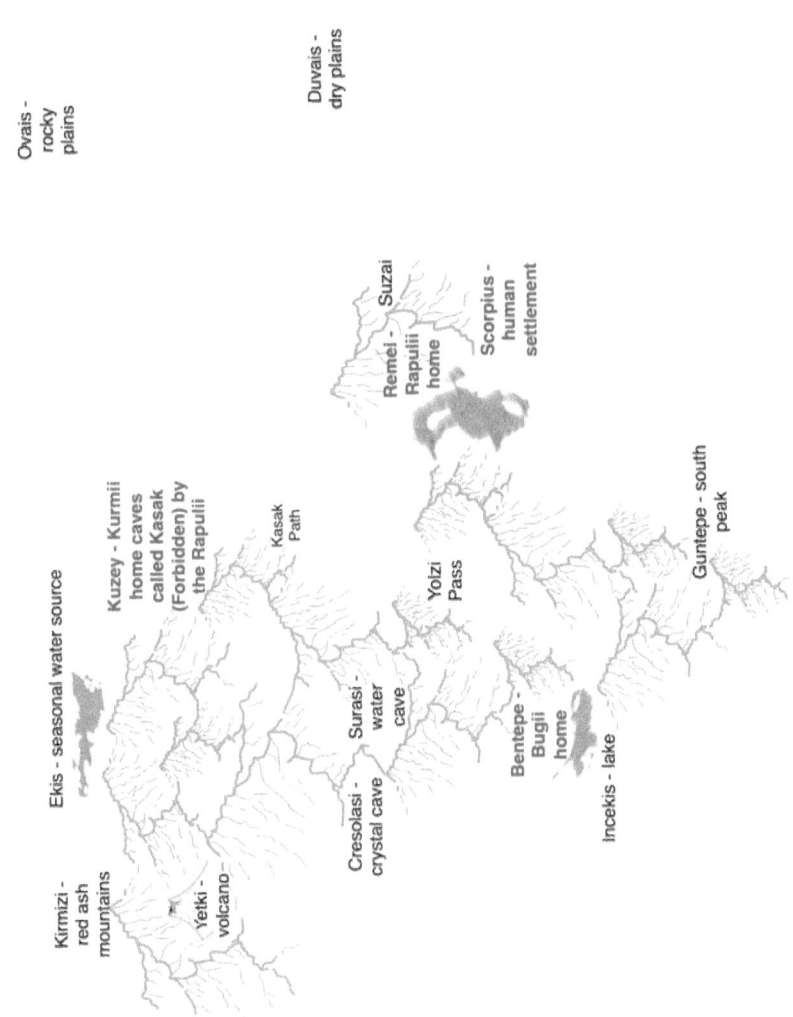

Ovais - rocky plains

Duvais - dry plains

Remej - Rapulii home

Suzai

Scorpius - human settlement

Kuzey - Kurmii home caves called Kasak (Forbidden) by the Rapulii

Ekis - seasonal water source

Kasak Path

Yolzi Pass

Guntepe - south peak

Surasi - water cave

Cresolasi - crystal cave

Bentepe - Bugii home

Incekis - lake

Kirmizi - red ash mountains

Yetki - volcano

Chapter 1

Lieutenant Embry Porter rolled out of the bunk, pulled on his pants and shirt, and tilted his head to the side. "Computer, F2 Status."

"F2 status is green." The computer's non-emotional reply did not match Porter's relief. Aside from the crew, all of whom he met when assigned to the *Scorpius*, he knew exactly two people on this ship of five thousand: magistrate Jacey Rees, in status pod SP0050 and her son, Ish, in SP4613. Porter had served as aide to Jacey before they left Old Earth. She would be the civilian leader once they made landfall on a suitable planet until everyone was awakened and general elections could be held.

"What the heck is F2?" Ensign Katz asked as he rolled out of bed and grabbed his pants. With only a skeleton crew awake, the two junior officers were the only two people in the four-bed chamber. "You ask every morning."

"Just a status." He wouldn't tell Katz why he checked every day. It sounded needy. Porter focused on making his bed. There would be no inspection, but his mother had taught him to always make his bed, and he performed the task every day in memory of her. Besides, the room was small, with just enough space for two sets of built-in bunk beds, wall monitors for work or play, and room to stand up, barely. Porter was glad he shared the room with just one other person.

Katz ignored his messy bed and opened the door to the corridor. "Don't think so. I checked. There is no F2 status, and the computer said only you are cleared for that data. What gives?"

Katz's digital beeped and its computer voice said, "Power fluctuation in Level 3, Section Delta."

"Later." Katz ran down the corridor. A previous power fluctuation had destroyed some of the crops in hydroponics, reducing food stores. Now Katz ran to investigate every fluctuation, no matter how small.

Porter headed for the mess hall, relieved he had been spared the need to answer. The *Scorpius* had been in transit for many years. All total, Porter, along with the rest of Alpha Crew, had been awake for almost ten, rotating duty with Beta Crew. He had anticipated that being an awakened crew member, searching for a planet to populate, would be more exciting than the repetitive nature of failure: possible world identified, investigation, insurmountable issues, and moving on to another world identified as a possible.

The spaceships were designed to travel through Einstein-Rosen Bridges (ERB) and could travel at three-fourths the speed of light outside an ERB. Currently, they were in a star cluster, not having much luck. The search, interesting at first, was now a desperate hunt for a habitable world, and it was proving to be surprisingly difficult to find.

Entering the mess hall, Porter grabbed his breakfast, consisting of some type of stew or soup and an apple. He flashed his wrist, the one with the embedded ID, in front of the monitor and the steward poured his daily allotment of coffee. Porter took a sip and sighed. Coffee stores were low, in part due to the power issues in hydroponics, and everyone was now restricted to one cup per day. Turning to face the room of tables and chairs, Porter made his way to the only occupied table and sat down.

"What I wouldn't give for a nice steak." Despite his words, Petty Officer Third Class Weber ate his stew with gusto.

Hiding his smile, Lieutenant Porter dug in, finished his meal quickly, and bit into his apple. The chef was excellent and at first the meals had tasted wonderful, but stews and soups, while an efficient use of the food grown on the *Scorpius*, were getting old. Ten years was a long time to eat the same thing, or near to it, shift after shift. Regardless of what the chef called it, every meal was the same: stew, soup, chowder, or gumbo. "At least the fruit from hydroponics is good."

"You could always ask for a plate of raw veggies and fruit." Saber Isles, civilian head of logistics, joined the table with just such a plate.

"Once a week is all. Just think of it. A thick, juicy rib-eye, pink in the middle, with a side of fries." Weber put down his spoon, picked his bowl up, and drank the last of the liquid.

"When did you ever have steak?" Porter asked. Only the ultra-wealthy could afford meat on Old Earth, and the cost was exorbitant. PC Weber was a brilliant technician, but he always looked for an angle to make his own life easier or better. No way would he waste a year's salary for one meal.

"Only once, lieutenant," Weber admitted. "I rescued a rich kid with more money than sense and his family sent me a voucher for a steak. It was grand."

Porter's response was drowned out by alarms. His holowatch also alarmed. SPF 4613. Ish's stasis pod had failed. Porter pushed away from the table and ran from the mess hall.

Weber glanced at the monitor, shrugged, reached over to grab the lieutenant's coffee mug, and finished it in one quick gulp. "No reason to waste it."

Saber frowned but nodded.

Moving as fast as he dared through the corridor, Porter entered the service tube. He grabbed the smooth vertical sides of the ladder and used them as a slide to drop down a level. He repeated this action until he reached Sub Level 3. The alarms shut off just as he arrived at the stasis pod in question to find Doctor Cromer, Commander Fox, and Ensign Katz in place. The commander pulled on the pod, but it didn't budge.

"Porter, here." Fox pointed to the opposite side of the container from where he stood.

Moving into place, Porter asked, "What happened?" The code, SPF, on the alarm gave no indication of criticality. Of course, any alarm on a stasis pod was a cause for concern.

"E5." Katz didn't look up from the screen where he typed furiously.

Porter cringed. E5 was a critical malfunction. The device failed with no option for repair. The only hope was to get the passenger out of the stasis pod ASAP.

Porter watched Katz's fingers fly over the screen. Holograph technology and touch screens were good for most things; however, for fast, precise interaction, keypads were still more efficient for most humans.

"Try again, commander."

At Fox's nod, Porter tugged on the pod. Nothing happened. Porter pulled harder. Nothing. Porter took a deep breath, saw Fox did the same, and together they put their weight into it. Slowly, the pod left its vertical travel position and slid down the rail to become horizontal. When it locked into place, Porter jumped out of the way, and Doctor Cromer moved in. While she worked, Fox unhitched a gurney and placed it under the pod.

"Commander, grab the lever on your side and release it when I say." The doctor continued to work on the pod for a few seconds. After a whooshing sound, indicating the pod was clear of chemicals, she said, "Now." The hatch swished open, and the person inside fell about three inches, plopping onto the gurney.

The commander and lieutenant pushed the pod up the rail which was only marginally easier than pulling it down. Task complete, Porter got his first look at Ish. The kid didn't look good. He smelled worse. "Is he okay?"

"Let the doctor work."

Porter heard the commander's words, but he needed answers. He had never been at someone else's awakening before, but Porter was sure that tremors and sweating weren't normal. He wasn't sure about the smell, but since no one else reacted, perhaps it was normal. All he remembered of his own awakening was confusion and weakness. Although he knew it was possible, Porter hadn't believed anyone would be lost to a pod malfunction, especially not one of the two people he knew.

To take his mind off the crisis, Porter looked at the pods in this section of the ship. The stasis pods were not the sleek, glass pods originally designed for space travel back when space travel was considered a luxury vacation. These pods were built for one reason, to pack as many people as possible into the least amount of space. Each pod was a self-contained metal drum. Until the pod opened, there was no visual verification as to the status or identity of the person, just a name on the screen and a list of stats.

The doctor looked up from the diagnostic screen on the gurney. "I need to run a full diagnostic when he's conscious, but his vitals are satisfactory."

At the doctor's words, Porter let out a breath he didn't know he had been holding.

The commander, curious expression on his face, tapped Porter on the shoulder. "Why did you respond to this alarm?"

"I was Magistrate Rees' aide before we left Old Earth. Ish is her son. I was in the mess hall and saw the alarm. I wanted to check on him." When his alarm had identified Ish as having a pod malfunction, Porter's heart dropped. How could he stay away? He liked Ish, despite the boy's tendency to ask lots of questions.

"Glad you did." Fox turned to the doctor. "I'll update the procedures. Based on today's experience, one person lacks the strength to manually move a stasis pod if the power is off. Porter, since you know Rees, stay with him until he's awake. Katz, full report by end of shift."

"Yes, Sir," Porter and Katz replied in concert.

"Lieutenant," Doctor Cromer handed Porter a tablet. "Take the gurney to medical."

"Yes, Ma'am." Porter adjusted the tablet and used it as a steering wheel to drive the gurney and its cargo to the Med Bay.

Chapter 2

Ish screamed but only in his mind. No sound passed his lips. Unable to breathe in the vacuum of space, he flung his arms about. He had to escape. A buzzing in his ears congealed into a voice, and reality hit. He wasn't dying in space unable to breathe. Ish was on board the *Scorpius*, awakening from his long sleep. Relief flooded through him as he realized the breathing issues had been a dream. Ish opened his eyes but saw nothing save a few shadows. He shut them and hoped his eyesight would return soon. The smell of antiseptic assaulted his nose, indicating he was in a medical facility, probably the med bay.

"Ishmael?"

The female voice grated on his nerves. His mother was never hesitant. Where was his mother? Jacey Rees wouldn't miss his awakening no matter how busy she was. Opening his eyes again, blurry people moved around the room. When a hand touched his arm, Ish forcibly pushed the hand away.

Firm hands grabbed him, and a familiar voice cut through the sounds of the medical bay. "Ishmael Rees."

7

"Don't call me that." His raspy voice barely managed a soft whisper. Though he couldn't place it, he knew that voice. That meant the person talking knew not to call him Ishmael.

"Thought that might get your attention. It's ok, Ish. You're safe."

Ish opened his eyes and blinked a few times before they finally focused. Lieutenant Porter, his mother's aide, stood over him, holding him in place. Why was Porter at his awakening? Ish looked around, but the only people in the room were military and medical staff, and not many of them. "What happened? Where's Mom?"

"Your mother's fine." Porter released him and stepped back. "Let the medical team finish their tests."

"But –"

"She's fine and still in stasis. You'll get answers once the doctor clears you," Porter said.

Ish nodded and tried to relax on the bed. Now that he was fully awake, he knew what to expect. Anyone who made elite status and earned a seat on a population ship did, even a teenager like him. Ish had expected his mother to be here but knew he wouldn't get answers until cleared by the doc.

The tests reminded him of the assessments required by everyone on Old Earth. The assessments didn't guarantee an assignment on a population ship if you made elite status. It meant you were in the pool to be chosen for a ship assignment, and a chance to survive. If everything aligned in your favor, meaning you ticked off all the boxes a specific ship wanted, you were selected. In the case of minors like him, a family member, or sponsor already assigned to the ship was required to gain passage.

The tests went on forever. Long enough that Porter received a call and left for a while. Ish spent the time imagining what type of world they had landed on. They should be able to breathe the air without masks. Would there be diverse animals and plants like the vids of Old Earth? Would there be ample water? Would they be able to see the moon and stars at night?

After Ish proved he could walk without falling, Doctor Cromer said, "That's it. You're cleared for duty."

Ish, not quite seventeen-years-old when he went in the stasis pod, looked at the doctor and raised his eyebrows.

She laughed. "Sorry. So far, I've only awakened crews, civilian and military. Lieutenant Porter will return soon."

Ish nodded, but the doctor didn't notice. She turned to her next patient, a crewman, carried in on a stretcher, with her leg at an odd angle. Unsure if he should move or stay where he was, Ish remained on the diagnostic bed, hopeful to remain out of the way. He reached over and picked up a tablet, turning on the mirror function. The scientists were right. He hadn't aged. Sky blue eyes stared back at him. Ish grinned. He looked the same as when he went in the pod. His light blond hair hadn't grown at all. It wasn't supposed to, but who really knew? There had been no tests leaving humans in the pods for extended periods of time, before the population ships left Old Earth. The luxury ships, with stasis pods for pleasure travel, hadn't even taken their maiden voyages before they had been turned into emergency evacuation transports.

The luxury ships were designed to travel through ERBs stopping at locations that would provide the ultra-wealthy with experiences to brag about when they returned home. These ships became the only hope of saving humans.

How long had he been in the pod? What happened? As a teenager, Ish should have been one of the last awakened, but the doctor said she had only revived those needed to keep the ship functioning in space. Ish watched the door and waited for Porter. As they had prepared to leave Old Earth, Lieutenant Porter had been his mother's military aide since she had been elected as the magistrate for their new world. Ish appreciated

Porter's willingness to explain things and his relaxed approach to life. Porter wasn't one to tell a guy's mother about small issues like missing curfew by a few minutes because he was with a girl.

Porter walked in, winked at one of the med techs and crooked his finger at Ish. "Come on. The captain doesn't like to be kept waiting."

Surprised he would see the captain, Ish hopped off the bed and followed. As they walked, Ish searched his memories for information on the ship. This section of the ship was for the workers. The corridors were wide enough for two to walk abreast. No more. Monitors were found outside most doors with handprints allowing or denying entry. A few doors would swish open if one stepped on the plate in front of the door and the embedded ID in one's wrist provided authorization. There were also touch screen monitors that, if he remembered correctly, required the wave of the authorized, embedded ID, to activate. Some stations would require a passcode as well. The corridor sections had doors that could be closed and locked in place, but it appeared that the most used ones were locked in the open position.

Ish glanced at Porter. He had aged. Before they left Old Earth, Porter had been in his mid-twenties. Now, he looked more like a man in his thirties. How long had Porter been awake? Ish felt the steady hum of the ship's engines under his feet which confirmed what he had suspected. They were still in transit. "What happened?"

"Your pod failed. Mechanical issues. Doctor Cromer was able to save you, but it was close. You were without oxygen for a couple of minutes"

"It wasn't a dream."

"Huh?" Porter cocked his head to one side.

"I thought I dreamed not being able to breathe."

"Afraid not."

"But Mom's okay, right?"

"Yes, only your pod failed."

"Lucky me."

"Lucky is right. The Doc did an amazing job reviving you. It was close."

"We're still moving. When will we land?"

"Captain Dolan will explain everything."

"That bad, huh?" First, his mother isn't at his awakening, and now he's meeting with the captain.

"Look, kid, there's no problem. Only the Alpha Crew is awake. Minimal staff. Captain wanted to talk to you."

Yeah, it was that bad. Ish had only met Captain Dolan once when he stopped by to talk to Mom.

The duo climbed an access ladder and exited into another corridor. Ish stopped dead. He hadn't seen this part of the ship when they boarded. "Prime."

Porter grinned. "Yeah. Passengers on this ship would have had it good if it were still a luxury liner."

Good was an understatement. The corridors were double the size of the ones they had been in and the bulkheads were painted soothing colors. There were even murals lining the walls. No exposed monitors here, but Ish noticed cloth covered shells at regular intervals where monitors could be hidden. The cloth had been painted to match the murals giving the walls a seamless look.

Ish was surprised when they arrived at the small observatory. He never expected to be here in person, especially not with the ship still in space. Ish looked out the windows to the world the ship orbited. The atmosphere lacked the pollution of Old Earth and the view was stunning. There were at least four moons circling a beautiful planet. "Is that our new home?"

"Afraid not. It failed the suitability test."

Ish twirled around to face Captain Dolan, who had aged more than Porter. Ish had been so focused on the world and its moons, he hadn't even noticed the captain. Considering the room could hold no more than six people, he should have noticed.

Dolan smiled. "I thought you might enjoy the view before we head to the next system. It will take a few days to get there and ERBs don't provide great views."

"That's the truth," Porter muttered.

The captain walked over and stood by Ish. "Do you remember your training?"

"Of course." Ish rolled his eyes before he thought better of it.

Dolan grinned. "Good. We reached our optimum zone fifteen years ago, and we're still searching for a habitable planet. Alpha crew has four months left in our five-year rotation before we switch out with Beta crew again. Your new pod will be prepped for the same time."

"What am I gonna do until then?"

"Academically, you're in the top two percent of your age group on this ship. No small feat as academics constituted the major part of the selection process for those under twenty. You will be a test subject for teaching skills on whatever new world we populate. In addition, Lieutenant Porter will assign you to departments as needs arise. I'm sure he'll keep you busy."

"Gofer duty." Ish, like all civilians, had learned the military slang for some of the more mundane jobs.

Captain Dolan's lips twitched. "Perhaps you'll enjoy some of the work."

"Yes, sir." Ish didn't buy that for a second, but he suspected doing anything beat sitting around twiddling his thumbs. While waiting for Porter, Ish had envisioned sitting someplace like here, in the tiny space some overly romantic person

12

named the Upper Observation Lounge, watching the universe pass him by for the next few months.

"The lieutenant will go over your duties with you." The captain left.

Ish returned to staring at the view. The sun was behind him, and there were three worlds before him. Two of them looked barren. He wasn't sure how long he stared but assumed it had been a while when Porter cleared his throat.

"Get settled in. Review the ship's schematic tonight. Also, review the awakened crew. There aren't many so it'll be good to know everyone's name. Tomorrow you'll get to work." Porter handed Ish a tablet.

"What's my assignment?" Ish tried to keep the whine out of his voice but failed.

"That's not the enthusiasm I expect from my first student."

"Huh?" Ish had a feeling he was about to be the subject of a prank. Porter was renowned for his pranks.

"When we're not in orbit around a possible home world, I'm developing a training schedule for civilians authorized to fly the shuttles. You're an awakened civilian, you passed the aptitude tests, ergo, you are my first student."

"Are you kidding?" Ish's mouth dropped open. He looked around the room but no one else was in there. "Tell me you're not kidding."

"Not kidding. Here. It's keyed to your voice and contains everything you need to know, including your schedule for the next few days. We'll tweak as we go."

Ish took the digital and placed it on his wrist. He never thought to have one.

When Ish continued to stare at the device, Porter tapped him on the shoulder. "We aren't going steady. You will need it to work on the ship."

Taking his eyes off the device, Ish said, "Yeah, I know. Just never thought I would have one."

Laughing, Porter led the way out of the observation deck. "Well, I didn't expect you to have one either. Come on. I'll show you to crew quarters, which has four bunks to a room. You better not snore."

*****

Alone in the crew quarters he now shared with Porter and Katz, Ish changed the monitor to a mirror to check himself out. He had been given the standard, black and green crew uniform for civilian support staff. He looked like an adult, except for the panic in his eyes. He had no clue what to expect or how the others would feel about a kid being awakened. Ish adjusted the digital on his wrist. That piece of tech made him feel more like a member of the crew than his clothes. The digital was a voice activated wrist device that held as much data as a data pad, but only if Ish could remember the right commands. The digital had been dubbed wrist craft — a joke that stuck — but was fairly accurate as far as Ish was concerned. The amount of data available was amazing. Only a few members of the crew had them and he wondered why he was one of the lucky ones. He suspected it was because all members of the awakened crew — the elite of the military and civilian crew — had them, and because he was a kid. It would be an easy way to keep tabs on him. Ish grabbed the tablet he had also been given and went to the Med Bay for one final check before he began his first work shift. The medical check took a few minutes, and he was released.

Ish moved down the corridor, absently rubbing the newly implanted ID in his wrist. That ID was required to go anywhere on the ship and for him to get rations. Apparently, there had been an accident and tight restrictions had been placed on food allowances. Hoping he wouldn't be bored, or more importantly fubar something on his first day, Ish stopped in the mess hall where the offering was stew and fruit. It looked suspiciously like what he had eaten yesterday. The only new item was a small brownie looking thing the chef offered him. Adding the brownie to his tray, Ish turned to find a handful of people in a room that was set up to sit eighteen comfortably.

He was still getting used to the plants, mostly vines, bushes and mushrooms, that hugged the edges of the room. According to Katz, the plants helped relax the crew. Ish wasn't so sure. Old Earth had become so barren that he was sure there were more plants in this one room than Ish had ever seen at one time. It was a bit creepy. Katz also said that the hydroponics bay had to be seen to be believed.

Porter waved him over. When Ish sat down, he pointed to the man across the table. "You'll spend the morning with Petty Officer Weber."

"Welcome to the grind, kid."

Ish nodded and dug into his meal. He listened while the others talked about everything from work schedules to dreams of a new world. Weber hoped for massive, pristine oceans like Old Earth once sported. Katz, the tech wizard, waxed poetic about crops of all things, and Porter looked forward to exploring the land. The stew tasted the same as it had yesterday, but it wasn't bad. The thing he thought was a brownie wasn't chocolate, but it was delicious. Ish wasn't sure why the others complained about the food.

"Ready, kid?" Weber asked.

"Yes, sir." Ish wondered if Weber was going to call him kid for the next few months. It was irritating. Funny how Porter calling him kid didn't irritate him.

"Didn't you hear the lieutenant? I'm not a sir. Call me Weber."

Until Porter, Ish had never spent time around anyone in the military. He thought everyone was called sir. Ish added form of address to the growing list of things he needed to learn fast.

Weber took them down the corridor Ish had just used to get to the mess hall. "We're going to main engineering. Did you study the schematics?"

"Yes, er, Weber." Before leaving Old Earth, all civilians had watched the vid on the layout of the ship, but Ish hadn't paid close attention. As a teenager, the odds of him spending time working on the ship were too small to calculate. Last night, he had tried to memorize the main levels. Ish wished he had studied longer, but Porter told him to turn off his light and get some sleep. Never having stayed in a barracks, if four beds to a room counted as barracks, Ish complied. He expected to reference the schematic a lot over the coming days.

Living quarters for the awakened were on Level 2 and it had most of the off-duty services. The mess hall was really the Officers' Mess, but with such a small crew it was being used by everyone currently awakened. The command briefing room was on the main level, one level down. The main level was the only way to access the engines themselves, and Ish had expected to use the main ladder next to the mess hall, but Weber led the way to the aft access ladder.

Weber opened the hatch on the main level. "Ms. Isles, this is Ishmael, our new gofer."

"It's Ish." He shot Weber a stare but couldn't tell if Weber had forgotten or didn't care. Ish was pretty sure Weber didn't care.

"Welcome to the trenches, Ish. We're doing a walk-thru of engineering. With a skeleton crew we are expected to assist with physical inspections, so you can expect to perform some type of inspection at least twice a week." Saber Isles touched her tablet and a checklist appeared on Ish's screen. She also pulled three noise cancellation headphones from a container, handed them out, placed one over her own ears, and opened the hatch.

Headphones in place, Ish followed the lieutenant and Weber into main engineering. Taking his first look at the bowels of the *Scorpius*, Ish was amazed. The vids didn't do justice to the actual size of engineering. Of course, it took a lot of power to move through space and keep stable gravity on the ship, but still. Main engineering consisted of a huge, circular power core surrounded by a raised walkway. At regular intervals on the walkway, there were workstations. This was a work area and not designed for comfort. He turned when he felt a tap on his shoulder.

Isles reached up and touched the side of his headgear. "You have to keep the comm on to hear us. These cancel out all outside noise."

"Sorry." Ish felt a blush rush up his cheeks. He knew that. He just forgot. "Why do we need 'em? I didn't think the engines made much noise."

Weber tapped the side of his head. "We're using them as a comm. They're so we don't have to yell."

"Weber, take sections D-G. Ish, you're with me in section A. Once you get the hang of it, I'll assign you a section."

Ish nodded and began his first assignment onboard the *Scorpius*.

*****

After a couple of weeks, Ish realized he didn't have time to be bored, though he still feared a massive fubar. Maintaining the ship while searching for a new world was a lot of work. He ran errands for everyone, delivered food when any of the Alpha Crew was stuck at their stations for long periods of time, which was more frequent than he had expected, and served as a test subject for training on projected jobs regardless of where they made landfall. As a result, he trained for a host of assignments that he didn't even know would be needed on a new home world. Life Sciences even allowed him to run minor tests on vegetation from prospective worlds, and Katz was right. Hydroponics was a jungle as far as Ish was concerned. A guy could get lost in there. But, by far, the best was spending time in the shuttle simulator. He loved flying and hoped to be a certified shuttle pilot on their new world. Porter seemed to think it would happen.

Porter's change had been a surprise. The lieutenant was more serious now, forgoing pranks. In fact, Porter had become so serious that he hovered over Ish like a parent whose kid was leaving for the first day of school, and it wasn't just Porter. Everyone did. As the only minor awakened, Alpha Crew had decided that Ish needed supervision, and lots of it.

Refocusing on his task, Ish performed a perfect landing, leaned out of the simulator, and looked at Porter. "Another run through?"

"No can do. I gotta go. Another possible home world has been found." Porter closed his tablet. "Come on. You can help me in Tac 1."

Ish smiled. He loved being in the tactical stations, too. He wasn't sure what the original purpose of the room was. It was an odd mix of sleek luxury and cobbled together equipment to create tactical stations, complete with exposed cables.

Even though he only did gofer work regardless of assignment, Ish listened to the command crew discuss worlds to populate. A few times, while working in the command briefing room, he got to stay while Captain Dolan and Porter selected new coordinates; and once, he provided food to command and control (CC), and Commander Fox let him stay for a while. Ish found it all fascinating. Even the view of space from the command briefing room was somehow more impressive than the upper observation lounge, but that was probably his imagination. The basic luxury ship design meant a few of the nice-to-haves remained after the conversion to population ship. The most notable were the views of space.

18

Ish followed Porter into Tac 1 to find all five wall monitors on and the discussion in full swing. Linked up to Tac 1 were Tac 2, CC, logistics, physical science, and life science. Tac sounded packed, but it was only the two of them and Weber.

Weber and Porter had similar workstations, both had an additional three monitors, although Porter's station was one of the pilot stations. Ish slid into his normal workstation. Not nearly as robust as the others, Ish received data on two monitors and looked for warnings. He suspected both Weber and Porter would identify warnings first, but he was happy to be in Tac.

"That planet takes regular damage, almost like a strafing run from the military planes of old." Doctor Xu, the civilian head of Natural Sciences for Alpha Crew, tapped his console and the screen changed. "You can see the pattern here."

"What pattern?" Weber asked.

Ish stared at the screen, glad Weber had asked the question. There were a lot of red lines, but he couldn't discern a pattern.

Xu touched the screen again, and the red overlay changed colors. Stripes of red, green, blue, and yellow now covered the planet. "This is the pattern of impact. Red is the newest. Yellow the oldest."

The planet in question had more water than Old Earth did in its prime and contained three main land masses which were lush and green. It was beautiful from space. The only stain on the planet was the pattern of destruction in various stages of regrowth.

"There has to be a reason there are no large prey or predators on the planet. And I don't like the looks of those burns," Xu said.

Ish stared at the screen. The 3-D projection showed a lot of creatures, but nothing as large as a man.

"Bosh. It's a great planet," Weber muttered.

"Language." Porter cut his eyes to Ish.

Ish blushed. Porter was too overprotective. He was a teenager. Of course, he knew all the banned words. He wouldn't dare say them in front of these adults for fear his mother would find out, but he knew them.

Weber laughed. "Sorry Ish. I forgot there was a kid present. But, come on, the planet is perfect. The air is as close to Old Earth normal as we could hope. The samples the miners brought back show that nearly all plants are edible. There's a lot of natural resources, plenty of water, and no predators larger than us. It'll be a breeze to take over the planet."

"Until whatever causes the destruction returns," Xu retorted.

"Find the source of the reoccurring impacts." The captain's order stopped the chatter.

A few days later, Ish grabbed lunch and joined Porter. Before he took his first bite, Weber joined them.

"Well, kid. We're back to square one." Weber dropped into the seat next to Ish and gave the stew a disgusted look. "I really liked that planet."

Ish frowned. Being called kid all the time grated on his nerves, but irritation over the form of address argued with curiosity. Curiosity won. "Did Doctor Xu determine what causes the planet to burn?"

Porter nodded. "A creature wakes from hibernation and lays waste to the planet. It burns whatever it sees, plant and animal, and eats the charred remains. Put simply, every third generation of humans would be subject to a deluge of fire."

"Yeah, a large predator that hibernates for long stretches at a time, wakes up, flambés its dinner, and the planet. It doesn't even look like a dragon."

Ish chuckled, for once agreeing with Weber. Seems like a fire breathing creature should look like a dragon.

20

"If anything, it resembles an armor-plated rodent," Porter said.

Weber shrugged. "Yeah. One the size of a shuttle. And the creatures all wake on the same, reoccurring cycle."

"Doesn't matter, we leave orbit today. Another planet fails the suitability test," Porter said.

Ish sighed. This world has looked to be prime, as had the three before it. It had never occurred to him that finding a planet to populate would be difficult. He was already tired of the boredom that settles in traveling between star systems. Everyone got grumpy. Nothing to do but work, exercise, and sleep.

Chapter 3

"Lieutenant." Weber's eyes were glued to the console. "I'm picking up comm chatter."

"Population ship?" Lieutenant Porter turned and raised a disbelieving eyebrow in Weber's direction.

With relief, Ish looked up from one of the not-so-fun administrative chores that he was assigned. Both Tac stations contained a monitoring station with three monitors focused outside the ship and a pilot's chair, a three-monitor station for internal ship functions, a data gathering station with two monitors where Ish sat, and a four-monitor command station that was rarely used unless a senior officer was in the room. Five additional monitors covered one wall. It had taken Ish a while to become comfortable with all that data. Once he did, he was able to focus on just the pieces he was responsible for, knowing that between the three of them, everything was covered. Ish suspected his contribution was not essential but was grateful to be included. This room, like many on the ship, had been designed for some luxury purpose. Now it was a tactical room.

Even being in tactical couldn't turn monitoring and sorting data into fun. The solar system they had just entered had multiple planets, and moons, in the habitable zone. Was the message from one of them? Like everyone on board, Ish knew the procedures Old Earth leadership set in place. No other vessel from Old Earth should be within communication range of the *Scorpius*. That had been the point of flying toward different star clusters. Each population ship left Old Earth and moved toward their assigned cluster to make sure they didn't encounter a sister ship. Not all ships had the same objectives, and it would be a waste for two population ships to go to war over the rights to a world both wanted to populate. Did one of the population ships leave its course, either on purpose or by accident?

"No lieutenant. Language is unknown."

Task forgotten, Ish watched Weber even though there was nothing to see. Three times Old Earth had encountered alien signals. All before Ish was born. The first two were chance meetings but was the reason humans had translators and the needed algorithms for new languages. The third was the reason humans left their home. The third race, the Vruhok, had appeared and offered to help humans with their pollution problems in exchange for a portion of the saltwater in the oceans. Although the scientific community objected saying the Vruhok could find water in space with ease, the politicians pounced on the chance to fix the pollution problem in exchange for a small amount of water.

Too late, the world leaders discovered the scientific community was right. The Vruhok tanker ships showed up and syphoned off more than water in the oceans. The Vruhok were predators and Old Earth was not the first planet they had ravaged. It only took three Vruhok tankers to complete the devastation the wasteful humans had started. Old Earth was in bad shape before the Vruhok arrived. It was in worse shape after they left.

Porter drummed his fingers on his workstation and pursed his lips. He opened the comm and paged the captain. "Captain Dolan, Tac 1 picked up a message."

"On my way." The captain must have been nearby because it didn't take him long to arrive. "On speaker."

"Aye, Captain." Weber touched his screen, and unrecognizable sounds came through the speaker.

Ish didn't know much about languages, but it sounded okay to him. The language was not as guttural as Vruhok, but not as flowy as the Encho or Yonya.

"Run it through the translation diagrams." Captain Dolan tapped his console, opening a channel to the medical bay. "Doctor Cromer."

"Yes, Captain."

"Wake Doctor Theon Clark."

Ish searched for the name in the passenger database. Clark's primary designation was linguist.

"Ensign Kratz is in Tac 2 converting the visual data into a format we can see." Porter homed in on the coordinates of the transmission and displayed a three-dimensional image of the world in question. "Captain, I've located the planet. It's light on above ground water. It has one natural satellite, a moon that's double the size of the one that circled Old Earth, and several man-made satellites in orbit around the planet. I'll bet the moon's a sight to see from the planet when it's full."

"Our goal is a planet without an indigenous population. Especially one who has already built structures and modified the landscape," Captain Dolan said, mostly to himself.

Ish watched the captain, wondering what he would do. Alpha team was scheduled to sleep for another five years in less than a month.

The captain opened the comm to the science lab. "Doctor Xu?"

"Here, Captain." Xu, senior scientist on the Alpha Crew, didn't look up from his station. "I'm looking at the data from Tac 1 now."

"Good. Send Lieutenant Porter your best guess on the technical capabilities of this planet. We need to establish an orbit outside of their ability to see or track us. Porter, I want to see the flight plan before we approach."

"Yes, Sir." Porter hunched over his station, typing furiously.

Captain Dolan nodded to himself and opened a channel to the medical bay. "Doctor Cromer. How fast can you wake Beta and Technical crews?"

"Three days."

"Do it."

"Captain." Xu's voice came over the comm. "We're already within range of their ability to track us."

"How?"

"Their moon. They have what appears to be an unmanned station on the moon gathering data. I estimate there's a 75% chance the station tracked us in some way."

"Why 75%?"

"It's what we would do. I lack the data to extrapolate the intentions of this species."

"Captain." Katz looked into the camera. "I have long range images of the surface. No video, but I managed a few stills of the indigenous population."

"On screen."

Although the image was a bit blurry, Ish's mouth dropped open. Bipedal reptiles, wearing minimal coverings, appeared to be having a normal day. A large building that, on Old Earth would have been an office building, overlooked a lake. Behind that building were a grouping of round buildings. Again, thinking in human terms, Ish dubbed them homes.

*****

Ish gulped down his food and hurried down the hallway, dodging people. Seventeen additional awakened people meant a line in the mess hall. He entered the life science lab and grabbed a seat, nodding to Doctor Poulsen. Two more people entered behind him and Ish smiled. He wasn't the only one who hadn't anticipated the longer lines.

"Check your tablets." Doctor Xu briefed as he always did, without looking up from his workstation. "You have the info on this new world. Doctor Poulsen, the miners will return with the plant samples within the hour."

When Xu paused for a breath, Ish said, "I can transport the samples here." It would have been the next words out of Xu's mouth anyway. Ish was, first and foremost, everyone's favorite gofer.

"Good. You're assigned to Poulsen for now."

Ish nodded. He was always assigned to botany. Poulsen was easy to work for, but, just once, he would like to work with zoology or even geology. Anything but plants. He didn't pay much attention to the other assignments that were handed out. He doubted the assignments would differ from previous planetary searches.

As soon as the briefing finished, Ish made his way to the SLAB (Small Launch Automation Bay) used by the robotic miners. He always marveled that anyone named this bay small. It housed twenty-six miners, five eight-foot-tall robots, and four large drones. The primary bay door was large enough that a full-sized shuttle could fly through and land in the center as long as nothing blocked the path. Right now, the bay was full of portable decontamination tents and ground samples.

The miners were data gatherers programmed to retrieve samples for study. This time, with an indigenous population, their programming had been altered to include stealth. He expected to find Porter, pilot for the Alpha Crew, monitoring the miners, as usual. Ish pulled up short when he saw Ensign Botha, Beta Crew pilot, at the station.

She looked up and grinned at Ish's surprised expression. "Monitoring the miners is a junior officer task. Porter outranks me, which leaves me permanently with the short straw until a pilot is awakened that I outrank."

Ish nodded. He hadn't given much thought to rank. As things currently stood, he was the bottom of the heap, regardless of who was awake. "Any miners still out?"

"Three. Give it thirty minutes and you can transport the goods to life science in one trip. At least I assume that's why you're here. Porter said you were marking time as a gofer."

"Yep. Anything I can do for you while we wait?"

"You just being nice, or you mean it?"

"I'm the gofer."

"Well, I wouldn't say no to a cup of caffeine in any form available."

"Be right back." Ish double-timed it to the mess hall and returned with coffee.

Sighing at the smell, Botha shook her head. "You didn't have to waste your coffee allowance on me."

"I don't drink it. I prefer tea. Everyone knows it, so I figured you were hinting for my daily coffee allowance."

"I didn't know, and I'm not that greedy, but I am appreciative." She took a sip and placed her drink aside as the last miner arrived, passed through the biohazard check, and loaded its container of samples on the cart. "You're good to go. And Ish, thanks for the coffee. I owe you one."

Ish used his tablet to drive the cart out of the SLAB and smiled. He had thought she might not know about his dislike of coffee, but he expected her to give him an IOU like most of the crew did. He had been racking them up from all over the ship, glad the ship voted for the barter system. He was starting this life flush with favors owed to him.

*****

Grass, grass, and more grass. Ish looked at his assignment. Poulsen had given Ish every possible blade of anything that might be considered grass. Nothing for it but to get to work. In the Life Science lab, Ish had a flat worktable of his own complete with equipment to test his grass. Laid out in neat rows of sealed packages, Ish counted thirty-two separate samples, each requiring multiple tests. He would be a while.

Hours later, Ish grabbed his meal and joined the handful of people sitting in the mess hall. It had taken a couple of days, but long lines for food were a thing of the past as routines were established.

"How's it going, kid? Learn anything in botany today?" Weber didn't look up from his stew.

Knowing Weber was being sarcastic, Ish grinned. "Actually, I did find something today."

"Did you?" Weber looked up, surprised.

"Yep." Ish took a bite of his stew. He had officially joined the crew in being tired of the same type of food three times a day, but he took his time chewing.

"Just as I thought. He's got nothing." Weber finished his meal and left.

Porter laughed. "Spill, Ish. What did you find?"

"Ish found a plant to replace caffeine in our stores." Doctor Xu patted Ish on the back as he walked by. "We may be running out of coffee, but it looks like we can replace it with cari if we land here. It's stronger than our tea."

"Excellent." Porter's voice carried and people turned to stare. He grinned sheepishly. "I like coffee."

"Don't we all? Except for Ish, of course." Botha walked over with her tray and sat down.

"He may not like it, but Ish found a coffee replacement."

Botha grinned. "You're a handy little gofer, aren't you?"

Ish took another bite when Botha and Porter looked at their comms at the same time. Porter jumped up and crooked his finger at Ish. "You're with me."

Ish shoved the last bite of his lunch into his mouth and joined the lieutenant. The duo made their way to Tac 1, arriving at the same time Weber did. Weber slid into his seat and performed a check. Porter slid into his chair and did the same.

Ish manned the third station. "What's going on, lieutenant?"

Before Porter could reply, the captain turned on the vid from CC. He glanced at Ish and raised a questioning eyebrow at the lieutenant.

Porter shrugged.

Ish frowned. It appeared the lieutenant had planned to keep him close in case there was a problem. Ish was beyond tired of being treated like a kid. Then again, it was probably the only reason Porter had him tag along, and thus, the only reason Ish could be in on the action.

Captain Dolan shook his head. "Doctor Clark."

For once, Clark looked up from his workstation. When he saw new people on the vid, he said, "We're getting a direct message from the planet. They want to talk."

"How?" Weber asked.

Clark sighed. "They know we're here, and they assumed we can hear their message. We can now that Katz has made a few modifications."

"What do you need both Tac crews for?" Porter asked.

"You will monitor around-the-clock." Captain Dolan said. "Both teams have their new schedules."

*****

Ish sat in Tac 1 with Porter. Tac 2 was also manned. The command officers were spread throughout command and control, logistics, engineering, and the science labs. All other awakened crews were at their duty stations. Captain Dolan was in the linguistics' lab with Dr. Clark. Thrilled to be in Tac 1, Ish wasn't sure why he was there. If this was another attempt by Porter to keep an eye on him, Ish was agreeable. Tac 1 was his best hope to be in the center of whatever happened.

Like everyone else, Ish was edgy. Today was the day. Communication day. Dr. Clark had prerecorded a message to the Rapulii on the same frequency they used to contact the *Scorpius*.

"Wonder how long it will take the Rapulii to reply?" Ish asked.

"It took Clark's team three days to compose a basic response message." Weber slid into his seat.

Ish shook his head. "Not just compose, hopefully be able to respond to whatever they say, if they say anything."

"Quiet. Channel is being opened. I want to hear everything," Porter said. "Our comm is muted. We can hear, but not respond."

Ish leaned forward to stare at the screen and leaned back awkwardly when he remembered it wasn't a live feed. This would be a preprogrammed transmission.

"Sending message now." Clark's voice was followed by an audible click and a string of gibberish.

At least that's what it sounded like to Ish. Oh wait, Kurazi. That's the name of the planet. He understood one word. The second word he got was *Scorpius*, so he guessed the ship's name wasn't to be translated. That made sense.

Ensign Botha ran into Tac 1. "What did I miss?"

"Message still being sent. What are you doing here?" Porter asked.

"If it goes fubar, I'm to translate for you as best I can." Botha changed one of the screens and they watched the words dance before them.

Ish raised both eyebrows. Could Botha translate the alien language?

The words, spoken by Clark, were spelled out using Old Earth Orthodox symbols. The theory was that humans would learn the Rapulii language quicker using the symbols that they already knew to sound out the words. Looking at the jumbled words flowing by, Ish wasn't so sure that would work. Hopefully the digital would be uploaded with each new word translated.

The screen changed and the pictures the Rapulii sent were displayed with the Rapulii and human names underneath while the audio pronunciation for the human words came through the speakers.

Ish glanced at the others. Porter and Botha didn't take their eyes off the screen. Weber looked bored. An hour passed and the communication completed its fourteenth repeat. Ish leaned back and stretched. In retrospect, he should have realized the Rapulii would take some time to respond.

Weber huffed and asked, "How long we gonna wait?"

"Commander Shaw just sent our new work schedules. Expanded monitoring." At Porter's words, a new schedule popped up on Ish's tablet and he sighed. Porter and Weber might be in Tac more, but Ish might as well take a pillow and move into life sciences.

*****

"It's about time," Weber grumbled.

Ish pressed his lips together to keep from smiling and handed Weber his order. He purposely made Tac 1 his last food delivery in the hopes of remaining.

Porter took the food Ish offered, and said, "Hope you brought food for yourself. I have a job for you."

Ish grinned and slipped into the workstation he was beginning to think of as his.

"Of course, he did. Why he wants to be here is beyond me, but he always does." Weber turned back to his screen. Typing quickly, he said, "Recording incoming message. It's from the Rapulii."

Porter punched in a code. "Tac 2."

Ensign Botha's face came into view, but she remained focused on her screen. "Botha here."

"You looking at the signal from the Rapulii?"

She nodded and left the vid on but ignored everything except the signal. A few minutes later, Doctor Clark slid into the workstation beside Botha to analyze the transmission.

With nothing else to do, Ish turned his attention to the task Porter had assigned him, but Ish continued to glance at the vid instead of his work, as if his attention would help Botha and the doctor translate faster. Alien contact. Ish had seen stills and watched the vids when Old Earth had been visited, but to observe communication with real-life aliens was exciting. Although, he supposed the Scorpius contained the alien life in this case. Either way, to be part of it all was prime.

"Report."

Ish looked at the vid when he heard the captain's voice. Captain Dolan had joined Clark and Botha in Tac 2.

"They want to talk," Clark said.

Chapter 4

Lieutenant Porter entered the conference room and took his seat at a workstation that allowed him to continue his duties during the briefing. He could have stayed in Tac 1, but he couldn't resist the opportunity. He wasn't the only one. This room was the original dining room and observation lounge for the *Scorpius'* previous life as a luxury cruise ship. It was huge and could accommodate fifty people in the lower tier. This was one of the luxury laden chambers and boasted eye-popping views the ultra-rich would have paid for. Even though traveling through space lost its allure months ago, Porter had to admit the view was magnificent. There was something about looking out the equivalent of a bank of windows, instead of a monitor, that moved the vista into the category of stunning. Three of the planets in this solar system were visible, with one being the focus of this briefing.

The upper tier, with the best views, now housed three polygon-shaped, military issue, conference tables. Tables that were butted together so that all participants could see each other with a hologram projector in the center. The only other person who didn't take a seat at the tables was Commander

Fox, who manned a tactical workstation. Fox always positioned himself for a fast response if an issue arose.

There were a few empty seats, but most attended in person, a rarity as most meetings were held via vids with everyone at their normal duty station. The last to enter, Captain Dolan and Doctor Clark arrived exactly on time, causing Porter to raise an eyebrow. How did they do that?

Before the captain claimed his chair, Saber Isles, who had been extolling the virtues of the populated planet, leaned forward. "Kurazi..."

The captain held up a hand for silence. "Before we discuss the already inhabited world, Commander Reddy, what's the analysis of the other planets in this solar system?"

Porter nodded. He doubted he was the only one in the room who didn't know specifics of the research from the various science departments. Glancing at the water world, Porter smiled at the thought of a pristine world with no pollution and an abundance of water.

Lieutenant Commander Reddy, science officer heading up both the life science and physical science departments, touched the digital on his wrist to the data pad and a hologram of the solar system appeared in the center of the three tables. "There are seven planets. The two gas giants are furthest away from the sun. The planet closest to the sun is tidally locked with rivers of lava. While it has an atmosphere, it's not habitable by our standards. Next out from the sun is a small asteroid belt, remains of a planet. That leaves three rocky planets in the habitable zone.

"The one closest to the sun is poisonous to us. Every sample the miners brought back from the surface contains significant oxalates or cyanide throughout each plant. The soil is more toxic than the polluted soil on Old Earth. The next planet is a water world, beautiful, with an excellent atmosphere and abundant plant and animal life in the water, but 93% of the land is covered by that water. The remaining 7% breaks down as follows: 3% at the poles, 1.2% rock or desert, 2.7% mountains, leaving .1% livable without terraforming. This does provide enough space for us to awaken everyone while we develop a water culture that we don't currently have the tech for but could probably develop. The issue is the hurricanes. The major land mass in a habitable zone has seen one hurricane and three tropical storms since we arrived. No moons in this system can support human life. That only leaves Kurazi, the populated planet, as an immediate option."

Captain Dolan nodded. "Shaw, we'll start with your report."

"Yes, Captain. Kurazi meets our needs for life support and growth potential. Winds run high and on a normal day hover in the 25-29 miles per hour range. Less than optimal above ground water, but there are huge underground lakes and rivers. We could pump enough water for drinking and crops." Commander Shaw, second in command on the *Scorpius*, changed the three-dimensional view of the solar system to focus in on the planet in question. "Of course, that would change the planet surface, and I outlined my objections in the document each of you received. Among other things, we will need to adjust our glutinous use of resources. The mountains are limestone and riddled with caverns, passages, and underground waterways. Detail scans are not possible. The metals in the ground interfere with our tech in many areas, but from what we can see, the underground system is incredible."

"Manufactured or natural?" The captain scratched his chin.

"Natural. The above ground scans identified three small settlements, one for each intelligent species. Perhaps the bulk of the population lives below the surface, or they keep their numbers low because of resources. More research is required."

The captain turned toward Fox. "Security?"

"Initial scans of the planet are promising. As expected, some dangerous wildlife but nothing we can't live with." Commander Fox, chief of security, didn't look up from his tablet. "From a security standpoint, the only issue is the three species who already inhabit this world. We would do better to find a world without intelligent life. It would eliminate a lot of issues, and it's what we voted for before we left space dock."

"We've been in space longer than anticipated," Saber Isles, civilian head of logistics, said. "We also have had losses in hydroponics. If we don't find a habitable world within six months, the awakened will have to go on reduced rations."

"We already are," Porter muttered before he thought better of it. Surprised when the lift opened, he watched Ish roll a cart into the lounge. What was the kid doing?

"Further reduced rations." Saber amended with a nod. "Thank you, Ish. Please pass out the plates. Everyone, the chef has provided a sample of what the food from Kurazi tastes like."

Ish passed out the plates, serving Porter last. When the lieutenant saw Ish's pleading expression, he pointed to the seat next to him. He couldn't hit a puppy. If someone on the command staff wanted Ish to leave, they would have to be the bad guy.

Commander Fox ignored Ish but was the first to comment on the food. "I've tasted worse."

When? Porter had never tasted anything so bitter and tried to hide his response. He failed. He offered a taste to Ish who shook his head. Obviously, the kid had tasted it before he left the kitchens.

"What did you have that was worse than this? Any seasoning, perhaps a few grams of sugar to sprinkle on top." Clark's face was scrunched up into an expression of distaste.

"Based on previous planets we've investigated, the odds of finding a world where we can immediately eat what grows there is high, but so far other issues have made planets unsuitable. Testing takes time. Here, we have that time. Initial tests are encouraging that most of the plant life is edible." She raised her hand to stave off the inevitable complaints. "Although, most plants will taste bitter to us. Think chicory, turnip greens, kale, and the like. Sugar — fructose and glucose — can be found on this world, but not at the levels we're accustomed to. We've only taken minimal samples using the miners, which we kept away from populated areas."

"No chocolate," Commander Shaw muttered.

Saber grinned. "Afraid not. We've found nothing resembling the cacao seed. Even fruits tend to be more bitter. Think grapefruit, not apples. We would devastate the plant life on this desert world if we tried to make large quantities of sugar."

"Enforced healthy eating. Once we adjust our thinking, we'll be healthier as a species. Besides, chocolate is nothing but empty calories," Commander Fox commented.

Porter frowned. He liked chocolate, too. Commander Fox had dedicated his entire life to becoming the best soldier he could be, and Porter had never seen the commander eat the occasional dessert the chef made. But, in this, Commander Fox was wrong. Chocolate was more than just empty calories. It was a reward after a hard day. A little taste of heaven and home.

When the captain nodded to Reddy, he stood and changed the image to show three species. The vids had already been viewed repeatedly by every awakened person on the ship, so no one was surprised. "There are three intelligent species on Kurazi. All three species are bipedal. The Rapulii didn't provide much detail, except to say the other two species would rather kill than talk."

"That sounds suspect," Dolan commented.

Shaw nodded. "It is. Aside from vids, a general physical description, and a warning that they are dangerous, the Rapulii did not send information on the Bugii or the Kurmii."

When the captain didn't respond to Shaw's comment, Reddy continued his briefing. "The Kurmii are cave dwellers with armored plating on most of their body. They appear to see the world through echolocation, but that doesn't make them slow. They move fast, covering ground twice as fast as the other two species. They are also the largest, and physically the strongest, of the locals. The Kurmii are one and a fourth the size of the average human, at least as big as our standard robots. As they live underground, we have limited direct observation of Kurmii life. They only come to the surface at night to hunt and they don't hunt every night. Based on our observations, they are carnivores and matriarchal. The hunters we've observed take orders from a female."

"It's possible the Kurmii have a female military command structure or some reason for their leadership role," Commander Fox said.

"True." Reddy nodded. "The Bugii are avian with what appears to be a more delicate body frame, probably because they fly. Their feathers are either dark blue or red. On average, Bugii are of equal height to humans, not counting when they fold each twelve-foot-long wing behind the back. When folded, the elbow of the wing reaches up to seven feet high. We've clocked the Bugii as a slow-flying species, but they still cover ground faster than our best sprinters run on foot. What we don't understand is why they only fly in the skies where they live. They've built their homes in caves high in the mountains, almost as if Bugii are hiding or protecting themselves from attack. We haven't observed any predators who would be more of a threat to them than the other two species. The Bugii are omnivores, as are the Rapulii. We've seen no indication that the Bugii and Kurmii have technical devices.

"The Rapulii, the ones who sent the message, are similar in size to us, and they are, as I said, omnivores. Aside from being reptilian in nature, we have the most in common with them. They have technology the others don't and appear to embrace the sciences more than the other two. The oddest thing is that their skin color appears to indicate their function. The Rapulii greens are warriors, similar in build to the Kurmii though smaller in size. This makes the greens the largest of the Rapulii. The blues are workers and technicians. Like most working groups, their muscle mass is related to how much activity their job requires, but the blues are at least a head shorter than the greens. Though the greens are larger, the blues and reds don't deviate in size as much. The reds rule," Reddy glanced at Fox, "but we have no indication as to why the stronger greens follow their rule."

"Yes, we do." Fox leaned forward.

"No proof," Reddy amended his words. "We have a vid of something, but we're not sure –"

"Let's see it," Dolan cut in.

"Aye, Sir." Reddy flipped the screen and ran the vid.

A blue Rapulii stood beneath the shade of a few yust trees, talking to a female red Rapulii. The yust tree had a long single trunk with limbs branching out in all directions covering the top third of the tree. The limbs were long and stringy with red needles. The blue backed away and held out his hands in a placating manner. The red female snarled and something that appeared to be lightning moved from the red female's hand toward the blue male. The blue crumbled to the ground when the lightning made contact.

Porter leaned forward to get a better look. So did the others who hadn't already viewed the vid. Reddy backed up the vid to the moment the lightning appeared and stopped it.

The captain raised an eyebrow. "I don't see the device. I didn't think they had such miniature tech."

"They don't." Fox tapped the console, enlarging the focus on the red. Although the leaves blocked a clear view of the entire scene, it was apparent there was nothing in her hand, except the lightning. "We need more data, but the hypothesis is the red created the lightning."

"And it appears only the females have this power," Fox said. "We've recorded three instances of lightning, all wielded by females. This was the best view."

Reddy pursed his lips together. "As I said, we don't have empirical proof." At the captain's nod, he moved on to the next detail, though most of the staff stared at the vid. "The Rapulii are the most advanced, technologically speaking, and the only species that we have observed communicating over a long distance.

"In addition, the planet hosts a wide array of insects, flying and crawling, many larger than what we are accustomed to." Reddy pulled up a three-dimensional vid of various wildlife. "Based on the data we collected and the transmissions we intercepted, here's a short list. The umak, or flies, weigh around five pounds. The ants of this world are called kemi, weighing on average eight pounds with pincers that slice through anything that fits within its grip, including the bones of other creatures. The snakes are ilan and range in size much like the snakes of Old Earth.

"There are two nice sized herd animals similar to dinosaurs, omuz and irhasi, that roam the plains foraging for food. Initial reports are positive for them being edible, as are most of the rodents and snakes. A large creature called a leri, is the most aggressive hunter on the planet. It has a mane like a cat, hunts in packs like a dog, and is built along the lines of a grizzly bear. The tuyu resembles a flightless bird. It runs on two legs using its long neck, and equally long tail, for balance. The much shorter arms have the vestiges of wings, with a few feathers on the neck, chest, elbows, and back. It has a short, thick beak that it uses to capture prey. Although there are yarasa, bats, that fly in the sky, no flying birds have been spotted, aside from the Bugii, of course.

"Both the Rapulii and the Bugii use an erkek, a reptilian, dog-like creature, for transporting bulky items either in a satchel on its back or by pulling a cart. We've been unable to get close to the above ground water because each species settled one of the three above ground lakes, but we don't expect to find much in the way of large marine life within the water as the Rapulii said they dry up during the summer season. I've sent out a detailed list of creatures and plants on this world for everyone's review." Reddy sat down and nodded to Shaw.

Porter rubbed his chin, noticing that everyone else looked as overloaded as he felt. Lieutenant Commander Reddy had thrown a lot of data at them. He made a mental note to review the vids later. It would take time to remember all of those names and connect them to the right creature.

"Thank you." Commander Shaw changed the presentation view to show a three-dimensional image of the planet and the satellites the *Scorpius* had deployed around the world. "Based on the satellite feeds, and Theon's translations of Rapulii audio signals, the Rapulii don't speak to the others at all, and we've seen no evidence that the Kurmii or Bugii communicate with each other, either. This makes the Rapulii information suspect. Why don't they communicate? Are they at war? Is that the reason their population is so small? Although in fairness, we've seen no war zones."

"Even with an indigenous population, this is the best planet we've found." Commander Fox leaned back in his chair and frowned as if he hadn't wanted to admit that. "We have yet to find a frequency the Bugii and Kurmii communicate on.

"Anyone have anything to add?" When no one spoke, the captain nodded. "This may be our best chance of survival. Doctor Clark, I need reliable translators for the Rapulii language. While linguistics translates, all departments continue to gather data on the planet and the solar system. If we decide to open discussions with the Rapulii, I need more data."

*****

"Did Commander Fox really say chocolate is empty calories?" Ensign Botha asked from her workstation in Tac 2.

Lieutenant Porter looked up at the vid from his station in Tac 1 and grinned. "Sure did. Commander Shaw looked downright depressed. How did you hear?"

"It's the talk of the mess hall," Botha said.

Ish laughed and checked his digital when it beeped. "Gotta go. I've been summoned to make food deliveries." When Porter nodded, Ish went to the mess hall. In no time, he maneuvered a cart of food before him toward the stops on his list, a list that had gotten longer since the awakening of the second team.

As he approached the destination of the final delivery, Ish hoped the translation team had made progress. Everyone waited for Doctor Clark to say he was ready to contact the planet. When Ish was close enough for the door to read Ish's implanted ID, it opened to Clark's lab. The three people in the room didn't look up or acknowledge him in any way. They never did. Apparently, they took a break at some point because the food Ish had brought earlier was gone. Ish moved the full trays to a table, loaded the empties on the cart, and turned to leave, bumping into Ensign Botha. The resulting clang was loud in the silence of the room and the translators looked up for the first time.

"Sorry." The blush that ran up Ish's cheeks irritated him. He hadn't expected to run into anyone, literally or figuratively.

Everyone was under strict orders to stay out of the translation team's way, but obviously her implanted ID had granted her access.

"My fault." Botha shrugged.

"Botha. Good. I want you on the spoken vids." Clark ignored Ish, but said, "Oh, food's here. Break when you can." Clark returned to his work.

Botha patted Ish on the shoulder and went to the station Clark had pointed to.

After returning the cart to the mess hall and helping the kitchen staff by loading the dishes in the sanitizers, Ish used his free time to take a stroll through hydroponics. When first awakened, he hadn't understood the draw of hydroponics, especially since he worked with the plants frequently. All food had been grown in hydroponic farms on Old Earth for decades. Now he got it.

Small plants were grown on seven-foot-tall walls. The walls had been organized to allow the chef's team to walk through and pick what they needed for a meal. Some paths were blocked by fruit trees or climbing plants. The result was a maze of plant life that was easy to work with. Doctor Cromer said that walking through the plants improved the health of the crew. Ish didn't know about that, but he felt more relaxed after his stroll.

Exiting the maze, Ish noticed a small table had been laid out with appetizers from Kurazi. Oh, yeah. The chef had prepared enough of the food from the planet for everyone to get a taste and it was tasting day. Off-duty personnel stood around the trays, eyeing the offerings.

"Try one," Weber said.

Ish shook his head. "Don't want to be greedy. Chief Janvier gave me a sample when he first worked on the recipes."

"Did Ish just turn down food? I think that's a first," Lieutenant Katz said.

"Have an appetizer." Ish pointed to trays.

"Nope, I've already had a taste. I agree that we should leave the samples to the others." Katz grinned.

Glancing between Katz and Weber, Ish asked, "Is Botha a linguist?"

Weber popped a Kurazi appetizer in his mouth. Even though it looked like he wanted to, Weber didn't spit out the food. That had been Ish's response as well. Bitter didn't begin to describe it, but with supplies running low, nothing was wasted. "Yuck. We need to look at that water world again."

"Botha?" Ish prompted, knowing if he didn't, Weber would ignore him.

"Not sure, kid. Most of the military had another skill that got them on a ship. Maybe that's hers."

"What's yours?" Irritated that Weber still called him kid, the question popped out of his mouth.

Weber shrugged. "Besides my tech skills and my winning personality, I'm good in the water. Diving is probably what got me on this ship."

"Not much water on Kurazi."

"Yeah, kid. Looks like I got the short straw." Weber frowned and walked away.

"Might want to watch what you say about secondary skills," Katz said. "All military gained passage on a ship by having skills in addition to their military training. Those skills had a high probability of being needed on a new home world. Weber's water skills, not just diving, would have been prime barter material on any water world."

"And on this desert world, they aren't worth much." Ish cringed. He didn't like Weber, but he hadn't meant to insult him either. No wonder Weber had been so interested in the worlds boasting a lot of water.

"Not sure. Depends on what the underground water is like. Perhaps the large caverns will provide options for him. Why ask about skill sets?"

"I saw Botha enter the linguistics lab."

"Aha. She speaks six, maybe seven, languages. Her strength is hearing the words. Clark raves about her hearing the small nuances of the Rapulii language. She's helping out with translations."

When Ish stared at him but didn't ask, Katz laughed. "My computer skills are gold no matter where we end up. This ship isn't giving up all tech for a return to nature."

A week passed while Ish continued to be everyone's favorite gofer and trainee. Sitting in the mess hall, watching their prospective future home through a vid screen, he was amazed at the small amount of water on the surface. Ish knew there was a lot of underground water, but the surface, even though it held more usable water than Old Earth before they left, still looked odd to him. He ate the stew in today's ration and considered the possibility of saving his dessert for a snack later. If they stayed on Kurazi, there wouldn't be much in the way of sweets once the fruit ran out. It had been months since Ish woke, and he had not been able to resist the lunch dessert yet. Tray empty, except for the sweet, his stomach growled. Today would not be that day. The rations the crew subsisted on seemed okay for the adults, but he was still growing. He wanted more food but knew better than to be greedy. Ish had already figured out he was the only one offered a daily dessert, probably because the chef had a son in stasis.

"Ready for another shift in Tac?" Lieutenant Porter asked when he and Ensign Botha joined the table.

"You bet." Wondering if this would be his last bite of chocolate, Ish bit into an actual brownie and swallowed. "Aside from general gofer duty and tac, I'm permanently assigned to Botany in the life sciences division. It's all about samples and testing. Good information and all, but when will I be searching for my own food? It would be nice to help with zoology or planetary science for a change."

"Somebody has to do it."

"Yeah, what are the odds adults will turn kids loose to forage for food?"

Botha laughed. "You're both right. Enjoy your shift. I'm off to grab some zzzs."

Thankful to be done with plants for the day, Ish followed Porter to Tac 1.

*****

"We still haven't heard from the Kurs or Bugs?" Petty Officer First Class Foss leaned back and rubbed her eyes.

Porter looked up with a frown. Weber was running inspections and Foss was filling in. "No and watch your language."

"Sorry, Sir." With a blush rushing up her cheeks, Foss focused on her screen.

Ish finished his task, glad he hadn't been the one to slip. Weber had dubbed the Kurmii, Kurs, and the Bugii, Bugs. It stuck, and unless Captain Dolan or Commander Shaw was around, everyone used the abbreviated form of their names. Ish had even heard Porter use it, but Porter was currently the senior officer in the observation lounge which might be the reason he corrected her.

For a time, the only talk in the observation lounge was the verbal exchange between Doctor Clark and a red Rapulii called Nufen. Ish kept one eye on the translation feed as they discussed rank on the *Scorpius* and status within the Rapulii structure. Ish was pleased to note that he caught the occasional Rapulii word. Sentence structure wasn't that different, and it helped Ish to fill in the blanks. Or maybe not. What did he know of languages?

"I'm done, lieutenant. Need anything else?" Ish handed the tablet to Porter. Task complete, his time in the lounge was over. He had helped prepare the room for the first live feed with the Rapulii, and he wanted to stay and be part of the meeting. Well, at least watch the proceedings.

Porter, sitting at the pilot's station again, didn't take his eyes off the screen as he took the tablet. "That's all." At Ish's sigh, Porter glanced up. Porter handed the tablet back to Ish. "How about you monitor the tac stations for me."

"Yes." Ish grabbed the device with enthusiasm. "I mean, of course, Sir."

"Sit next to Foss."

Ish rushed to her side.

Grinning, Foss pointed to the seat on her left.

As Ish sat down, the captain walked in. "You sure this is wise?"

Ish winced at the question, but Captain Dolan walked past him to stand by Doctor Clark currently standing at the main communications station. Ish grinned when Porter winked at him. He was staying.

Clark didn't look up. "I need to see Nufen in conversation with other Rapulii. It's possible when two Rapulii talk, they have some type of body language. There is something different with the second speaker. And Nufen won't speak over vids with more than just me unless a Sargu, the leaders of the Rapulii, is with him. All Sargu are females, but not all females are Sargu. I suspect they are like our political leaders and they want to be involved."

Nodding, the captain pointed to the center of the room. "Commander Shaw, you're up."

Shaw moved to where the captain pointed, a consolation to the fact that the Rapulii were matriarchal. "Floss, enable the video feed."

Ish tried to look invisible when, at Shaw's command, the petty officer's fingers flew over her console. The main command screen flickered and changed to show a female in front, with other Rapulii forming a semi-circle in the background.

The first live view of the Rapulii. Ish leaned forward and stared. He wasn't the only one. The female wore a red sash and a decorative headpiece of beautiful colored feathers. Based on the data they had on the Rapulii, the larger the headpiece, the more power the female Rapulii had. Perhaps this female was their leader, Shimgin. To the left of the female was a red Rapulii male. In the center, behind the two, stood a blue male Rapulii, a tech. In the back were three green Rapulii warriors. Ish eyed the warriors. They were huge, towering over the others.

The female scanned the room, looked past the female commander, and stared straight at the captain. Pointing to her chest, she said, "Shimgin."

Ish hid his smile as best he could. Shimgin was smart and didn't want to talk to someone who wasn't in charge, even if the captain was male.

The captain pointed to his chest, and replied, "Captain Percy Dolan."

Shimgin scowled. The red male spoke quickly, and Shimgin's expression relaxed.

Captain Dolan glanced at Clark who translated. "By listing three identifiers, she thought you were insulting her. The red male is Nufen."

Nufen and Clark had a quick conversation in a weird combination of Standard and Rapulii.

Ish watched Botha on one of the small vids. She was one of the handful of people who knew enough of the Rapulii language to follow without use of the translator. The ensign had worked hard to be on Clark's translation team, and she had been helpful according to the scuttlebutt. Most people, Ish included, were waiting for the translation earbuds, although he was pleased that he knew some of the nouns and even a few verbs.

When Theon and Nufen turned back to their respective leaders, Theon's wry smile was apologetic. "A small miscommunication. The Rapulii use only one word as an identifier. To use a second designation, or name, is an insult to whomever they are talking to. Three is unheard of."

"Why?" Foss asked

Captain Dolan shot the seaman an annoyed glare before asking, "Is my lapse forgiven?"

"Nufen is explaining to Shimgin that we use titles with names and that we have first and last names." Theon stopped speaking as a high-pitched cackling sound assaulted their ears. It wasn't quite a laugh, but somehow conveyed amusement.

The sound grew louder, and the humans faced the screen and the source of the cackle. The other Rapulii had joined Shimgin.

Shimgin pointed to herself and said, "Rapulii Leader Shimgin."

"Captain Percy Dolan."

When Dolan nodded to Shaw, she introduced herself as Lieutenant Commander Shaw, careful to give a three-name response. Theon Clark dropped the doctor title and referred to himself as linguist. When the crew introductions completed, Shimgin whispered to Nufen, who asked, "Who is the juvenile?"

Juvenile? Ish looked at Porter and then the captain. Receiving a nod, he stood and said "Ish Rees... gofer?"

"Ish is a trainee and works in all departments, doing whatever is needed." Dolan said.

Once the translation completed, Shimgin narrowed her eyes on Ish. "For a young male to receive such training he must be an exceptional member of your species."

Ish schooled his features into a polite mask. How did he end up the topic of conversation? And did Porter have to smile? No comments were made about Lieutenant Embry Porter or Seaman Zabel Floss. Everyone had been careful to keep a three-word name or title. Gofer was all he could think of.

Nufen turned out to be Ish's savior. With an expression that was either a grimace or a grin, Nufen bowed in Ish's direction. "Nufen, head gofer."

The tech, when prompted by Shimgin, said, "Ralim, senior tech."

The three warriors didn't seem concerned with the naming convention. They took turns stepping forward, saying one name, and stepping back. Once Tibiz, Griz, and Fiz were introduced, they melted into the background. Ish was pretty sure that was where they wanted to be. He sympathized with them.

The rest of the meeting droned on as each side provided lovely speeches that bored Ish and made him wish he had made fast his escape earlier.

Chapter 5

Sheer force of will kept Ish from bouncing on his toes. Ish stood with Theon Clark and Ensign Botha in the shuttle bay. He couldn't believe it. He was going to the planet. He would be one of the first to visit Kurazi. The captain had not been pleased, but Shimgin had been insistent. She wanted to meet the juvenile who had been at their first meeting. Ish was certain he would never be allowed to participate, or watch, another big meeting in any of the conference or tac rooms, but he would be one of the first humans on the planet.

Captain Dolan entered the bay and immediately shook his head, causing Ish to frown. Would he be kicked off the team now, in spite of Shimgin's demand?

The captain focused on Commander Fox and raised his hand in the signal for stop. "This conversation is over."

Ish relaxed. This wasn't about him, but an argument between the two officers that every awakened person had already heard. Fox thought the captain should remain on the ship while others negotiated.

Commander Vander Fox stood to his full height, which was an impressive six and a half feet. "Captain, you should send me."

Dolan waved Clark, Botha, and Ish onto the shuttle. Botha pointed Ish to the gear near the hatch. Ish nodded and took inventory, again. He was pretty sure he got the assignment to make sure he knew where every item was stored as if Ish hadn't been drilled repeatedly over each item and its use. Porter even made him pack all the gear. Porter and Botha supervised. As a result, Ish heard the repeat of the conversation the captain and commander had numerous times since this trip was scheduled.

The captain grinned at his chief of security. "Our first face to face with the Rapulii to negotiate the establishment of a human settlement on their world, and you think I should send a warrior?"

"Yes, Sir. You belong on the ship."

"I'm the captain. I'm the only one who can negotiate unless we wake up the politicians."

Ish grinned. That wasn't exactly true. The captain could wake the magistrate, Ish's mother, Jacey Rees, but Dolan had stated his intention to make sure the planet was viable, and in this case, that included determining if the Rapulii leadership would work with human males as equals.

"Anything but that," Van muttered. Louder he said, "At least take a security detail with you."

"Even with a security detail, we would be outnumbered. The Sargu, the Rapulii females who manipulate lightning and wind, are numerous. I doubt a security detail would be beneficial." Clapping Fox on the back, the captain boarded the shuttle.

*****

Botha initiated preflight as soon as she boarded. When the captain closed the shuttle door, the bay door lights flashed red and pulled back. She launched the shuttle with ease as she had done many times. The only difference was the destination. She was going to land on another planet. Silence ruled as they got their first unassisted look at the world they might colonize. It most definitely lacked above ground water, but otherwise appeared welcoming.

"Look at that." Ensign Botha pointed at the herd that scattered across the plains when the shuttle buzzed overhead. "The irhasi do look like brachiosaurs."

"Only superficially." Captain Dolan glanced out the viewport. "Their shoulders are only as high as we are tall. By comparison, the brachiosaurs of Old Earth were much larger."

"True but look at that herd. I bet the horns on those long necks and long tails can do some damage. I wouldn't want to be in their path," Botha said.

Ish forgot about the herd animals when Botha banked the shuttle and approached the landing site. The Rapulii were waiting in mass for their first look at a human or perhaps a human shuttle; however, only three others stood with Shimgin.

Seeing their prospective new neighbors in real life gave Ish goosebumps. In a one-on-one fight, without weapons, a green would decimate the average human. The headdresses the Sargu females wore made them at least as tall as a green. The crew had come to the conclusion that was the point. The feathers confused Ish. Where did the Sargu get the multicolored feathers? One hypothesis was the Rapulii traded with the Bugii for old feathers and dyed them. Ish, and most of the crew, found that theory lacking.

The Rapulii settlement was in a valley between two mountain ranges. The land was predominately rock. They controlled the largest body of above ground water on the planet, Remei Lake. It was also the only water source that retained above ground water year around. Doctor Xu theorized that the Rapulii used some type of pump to keep the water year around, but Ish hadn't paid attention to the details. The number of arches and rock formations around the lake led the ship's scientific teams to speculate that the valley was once a much larger lake or a sea.

As directed, Botha landed the shuttle south of Semelai, the arch near the bottom tip of the lake. Lieutenant Porter had dubbed it Claw Arch. The arch did look like a two-fingered claw reaching toward the sky.

Botha sighed when the shuttle was on the ground. That surprised Ish. The shuttles had been the main transportation between Old Earth and the population ships, meaning she had plenty of experience flying and landing the transport.

The captain asked, "Was landing on another world the same as landing on Old Earth?"

"Yes, Captain. I 'd been a bit worried about that. The wind didn't cause any trouble, and visibility is much better. No pollution."

Clark checked conditions outside. "Captain, wind speed is currently twenty-seven MPH."

"That's fairly normal for the area. Goggles and masks will keep the sand and such out of eyes, nose, and mouth" Botha passed out the equipment, and muttered, "Of course, we'll look like plonkers."

"Perhaps, but we'll be able to breathe." The captain walked down the ramp. Ensign Botha and Theon Clark walked a little behind with Ish between them. All four wore a small translation earbud. Not perfect, but better than nothing.

"Darken your goggles. The sun will be bright." When the others complied, the captain touched the access panel and opened the shuttle door.

The captain straightened his shoulders and walked down the ramp to stand on the soil of Kurazi. The others followed. When Ish's boot touched the soil, he realized he had been holding his breath. With his first real breath he found the air arid, but a pleasant scent surrounded him. Ish took another breath and recognized the smell from his time analyzing grasses. The sky was bright blue, like vids of Old Earth before the pollution took over.

The quartet walked over to Shimgin and Nufen. A total of four Rapulii stood between the Semelai and the Dekai. The Dekai was a double arch with one arch sitting atop another.

"Rapulii Leader Shimgin." Once again, Shimgin pointed to herself as she spoke.

Behind the mask, the captain grinned and matched her three-word title and name while pointing to his own chest. "Captain Percy Dolan."

The only unknown Rapulii was a young female. She introduced herself as Sargu Juvenile Zigmin. Ish was sure she was there to be his counterpart and to keep numbers even.

Once the three-word introductions were over, Shimgin provided what Ish assumed was a welcoming speech. Though he only caught one in three words thanks to the earbud he wore, Ish was sure he caught the intent. The whole time she spoke, her eyes returned to the shuttle again and again, as if it were more interesting than the humans in front of her.

Nufen directed the group to the only large public building above ground. It boasted three above-ground levels and was somewhat square in design, although each level was a bit smaller in circumference than the one below it. The other structures were round and multi-tiered. The Rapulii identified all other buildings as private residences or apartments. Ish was pleased that he had guessed the purpose of the buildings correctly.

Dolan and Shimgin fell in step together, following Nufen and Clark. Ish and Zigmin were next with Botha and Ralim bringing up the rear. The Rapulii crowd opened a path and watched the procession as if it were a parade. Females were in the front and males stood behind. Watching the Rapulii, he marveled at the lack of talking. The parade walked on a thin peninsula that led to a stone bridge. When they reached the bridge, the Rapulii on the peninsula divided into smaller groups and presumably went about their business. Crossing the bridge, the crew and Shimgin's entourage walked up a hill to the Dogu.

The Dogu was set up much like any office building on Old Earth, with the main floor divided into work areas for the techs. Ish peered down the steps wondering what was down there. Probably storage or maintenance stuff. Nufen led them up the steps to the second floor to a conference room overlooking the lake. The only surprise was that there were no coverings over the windows. Anything could fly in.

Dolan took the chair opposite Shimgin. Botha and Clark sat to either side of the captain with Ish to the left of Botha, opposite Zigmin. When Captain Dolan removed his mask and goggles, the others followed suit.

Ish took a deep breath for no reason. The mask filtered out the dust particles, not the air.

*****

Wearing her most impressive headdress, the one that made her taller than even the warriors, Shimgin watched the shuttle approach. How she wished she had newer feathers, but Margu were extinct, and their prized multicolored feathers were no longer obtainable. How inconsiderate of them. When the shuttle became more than a speck in the sky, Shimgin forgot all about the Margu, at least for the moment. This was what she wanted. The long-range images of the *Scorpius* in orbit hinted at the power of the human ship, but the Rapulii satellites were not strong enough to provide clear details.

The shuttle was impressive. As described by Nufen's human counterpart, the male Theon, the shuttle could carry eight plus a pilot and co-pilot. It could fly into space on short trips and enter the atmosphere of a planet. As she understood it, the shuttle worked underwater, but why would that be needed? While she knew the humans came from a world with more above ground water than land, she could not conceive of a single reason to corrupt precious water with emissions from a ship. No one would be that foolish.

Some of the Sargu thought she was the fool to desire an accord with the humans, but the sight of that shuttle removed her own doubts. Once Shimgin had the technology of the humans, none would oppose her. Not that anyone could now. She had never lost a battle. If she had, she would be dead.

Shimgin frowned as the shuttle landed and three males and a female walked down the ramp. Humans, with no scales, feathers, or armored plating, wore a lot of clothing. And that stuff on their head, hair they called it. Ghastly. At least the feathers of the Bugii served a purpose. But the oddest thing about the humans was that a male was in charge. Shimgin wanted the humans to land their ship near her home, and if that meant talking with males as equals, she would. She might need to remind a few Rapulii males of their place later, but that would be a pleasant diversion. A reward to herself for the tediousness of these talks.

Introductions complete, she had Nufen lead them to a meeting place. Making a show of her power, Shimgin sat with the view behind her, showing that she feared nothing, not even the possibility of a bolt of lightning flying through the opening behind her. Not that any Sargu would be foolish enough to attack her.

*****

Ish opened his eyes wide and told his mind to wake up. He tried taking notes, thinking it would make him look more professional. Ish gave up when he realized he couldn't catch the nuances of the language. His notes consisted of a list of nouns. He had filled in the human name for the item if he knew it. The talks droned on for a while, long enough that his focus turned to finding a bathroom. He wouldn't say no to food either.

"We have prepared food for you. Your Doctor Cromer approved all we prepared for human consumption."

Ish sat up straighter and refocused when Shimgin spoke of food. It had been hours since they entered the conference room. Apparently, Rapulii did not need breaks, but he sure did. Ish stretched, but before he could stand, food was brought into the room. What did a guy have to do to get a minute to himself? Ish grinned when Botha leaned back and sighed. He wasn't the only one needing a break.

The captain stood. "Humans require a pause every so often. After we eat, we will return to the shuttle for thirty minutes."

"That's nearly two kliki," Nufen said when Shimgin looked confused.

Shimgin nodded. "Acceptable."

Botha and Ish exchanged tentative smiles and accepted the plate of food handed to them. In addition to plant material, there was some type of protein.

Pointing to a slice of meat, Clark asked, "Omuz?"

Nufen shook his head. "Kemi. The plant is kurudi, and the drink is cari steeped in water."

Clark nodded. "Kemi are the house cat-sized, ant-like creatures with pinchers. Very high in protein. Kurudi is the widely found plant that we've nick-named brambles. Cari is a grass, the one that will serve as caffeine for us."

Dolan took a bite of kemi. He smiled and nodded.

Ish followed suit. The kemi tasted okay, but a little seasoning or sauce would make it better. He took a bite of kurudi and gritted his teeth to keep from puckering his lips at the bitter taste. He had hoped the plant would taste better prepared by the Rapulii. It did not. If anything, it was worse. He took a sip of the cari drink and smiled into the mug, enjoying the refreshing taste, and feeling proud that he had discovered its worth to humans.

After eating, Nufen escorted the humans back to the shuttle. Once inside the secure ship, and personal needs had been taken care of, the captain asked, "Impressions?"

"They are very generous with their offerings. We couldn't have found a nicer people," Clark said.

Ensign Botha shrugged. "Too good to be true comes to mind. Shimgin is offering more than we requested. There has to be a price to pay."

"Agreed. Politically, the meeting is going well. Shimgin is very accommodating, offering everything we could hope for: land, sovereignty, help building a settlement, and food from the Rapulii stores while we set up our own gardens and hunt. In exchange, the Rapulii leader wants a few medical and technological improvements."

"I don't buy it, Captain," Ensign Botha said. "Shimgin can't take her eyes off our tech."

Theon shrugged. "Can't blame her for that. Ours is better and she knows it."

"Ish, do you have anything to add?" Captain Dolan asked.

Ish looked up in surprise and decided to answer honestly. "I don't know much about this type of negotiation, but it seems like Shimgin is offering us whatever we want to get our ship on the planet. I would expect her to place more demands on us."

"You understand just fine. It's time to return." The captain led them out of the ship to the Semelai where Nufen waited for them.

*****

That evening, the humans joined the Rapulii for a formal dinner that included many more speeches. Ish sat by Botha and, like the others, followed Doctor Clark's lead. Afterward, Ish stood on a balcony overlooking the night sky with Botha.

Ish was amazed at how clear the stars were. To the unfiltered eye, the *Scorpius* looked like a bright star, making

Ish wonder how the stars on Old Earth should have looked from the ground. "I thought this moon was twice the size of the moon on Old Earth."

Botha placed her hands on the rail and looked up. "Physically, it is. But it's further away from Kurazi, so to our eyes, it looks about the same."

Joining them, Zigmin asked Botha, "Is this private time or may I speak with you in front of your chosen?"

"Private time?" Botha frowned.

Ish tilted his head to one side. "Chosen?"

"You dare speak?" A scowl crossed her face, but Zigmin smoothed out her expression and faced Botha. "You allow your chosen to speak?"

Confusion filtered across Ish's face. Before he could respond, Botha laid a hand on his shoulder and faced Zigmin. "Please explain private time and chosen."

Zigmin looked between them. "Ish Rees, gopher, spends much time with you. I thought it was your time and he was your chosen, Ensign Yareli Botha."

"My time?"

"It's your time of eketlii, yes? Why else would you keep a male so close?"

"The captain told me to stay with the Ensign," Ish muttered.

Zigmin glared at Ish, but said nothing.

Ignoring Ish's comment, and Zigmin's reaction to Ish continuing to speak, Botha's face screwed up as if she were doing a math problem. "Eketlii. That means... Wait. You think Ish is my... my what? Lover?"

Ish chuckled and tried to hide it with a cough.

"I don't know lover, but did you not choose him as mate during eketlii?"

Ish surrendered to the absurdity of it all, leaned on the balcony, and laughed out loud.

"Aside from the fact that we have a monthly instead of a yearly cycle of fertility, Ish is not yet an adult. In our culture, it is not an acceptable pairing." Botha glared at Ish. "Stop laughing."

Ish crossed his arms over his chest and pressed his lips together, though his shoulders continued to shake.

"Every month you select another male during eketlii? You must have many males to choose from."

Ish burst out laughing, again. Botha slapped him on the shoulder and changed the subject. "Call us Botha and Ish. We rarely use such formal address."

Zigmin clicked her teeth in what the humans understood to be agreement. "I was unsure if the informal use of a single identifier was true in private conversations. Rapulii also use only one identifier. Zigmin is acceptable to me. I wish to ask questions about life on your ship."

The two females walked away, deep in conversation, leaving Ish to his mirth.

*****

The negotiations lasted three days, culminating in a provisional agreement for the humans to settle on Kurazi. In exchange, the humans would provide medical and technological knowledge to the Rapulii. More details needed to be addressed, but Dolan would let the magistrate deal with those. As Ensign Botha piloted the shuttle back to the *Scorpius*, Theon pointed to a passing satellite the humans had deployed to gather data. "The Rapulii know of our intelligence gathering devices. They want access to the data. They suspect their own satellites are not as powerful as ours."

"We don't know much about the politics of Kurazi. We could give them access to data we shouldn't," Shaw said over the comm. "I'm specifically thinking about data on the other species. Since they are all intelligent, it seems odd that they don't at least exchange goods and services. We've seen no indication that they even talk to each other."

"Have we still heard nothing from the other two species?" Captain Dolan asked. Monitoring was ongoing, but so far, the Bugii and Kurmii were strangely silent.

Fox leaned into the screen, "Nothing, and I don't like it."

"Neither do I. The only two satellites the Rapulii have in orbit are directly over the mountain settlement of the Bugii and the caves where the Kurmii live." The captain leaned back in his chair. "We would expect such information if we were in their shoes. Scrub the data and send the Rapulii information on the unpopulated sections of the planet. Tell them we were looking for a suitable settlement and didn't focus our search where settlements already exist. The Rapulii satellites are tracking the Bugii and the Kurmii, scrub anything that shows the activities of the Bugii and Kurmii."

"Aye, Captain."

Chapter 6

Ish moved from side to side, waiting. What was taking so long? Still wired from qualifying as expert, with three handheld weapons this morning, Ish found the waiting unbearable. He met the minimum requirements with the bow and arrow, although his aim could be better. Ish already asked Botha, who rated expert with a bow and arrow, to work with him. It was the first IOU he had called in. Ish was beginning to view his early awakening as a benefit. The defective pod had resulted in privileges and experiences he could turn to his advantage.

Doctor Cromer smiled at him. "It'll be soon. You can hold her hand if you wish."

Ish nodded and moved forward, taking his mother's hand. He had expected her to be at his awakening. Instead, he was at hers. Based on what Porter told him, Ish's awakening had been hurried and right next to the stasis pod. This was a proper awakening. Jacey had been removed from the pod, cleaned up, and brought to the med bay where the awakening cocktail would be administered to allow for a gentle awakening. She looked so peaceful, like she was sleeping. He smiled. After all, Jacey Rees was, for all practical purposes, still asleep.

"When I give her the final med, she'll wake up. Expect your mother to be confused at first. Give her time to reacclimate. Speak, but understand that it will take her a couple of minutes to answer."

Ish nodded at the doctor's orders. "Let's do this." He remembered the confusion he felt at his awakening, so, when Jacey thrashed around, Ish hummed the song she used to sing to him when he was a baby, and it seemed to help. After a bit, his mom stretched, and her eyes opened, although she didn't appear to be able to focus. With relief, he looked into the same sky-blue eyes he had. Ish said, "Hey, Mom."

"Ishmael?" Jacey's eyes opened wider.

Ish winced. She never just called him Ish.

Jacey squinted and blinked her eyes as they adjusted. She looked up at her son and then at the doctor, "Why are... what happened?"

"Everything's fine, Mom. I was the first non-crew member awakened. It's been great. I've gotten to fly in the shuttle simulator, run experiments in the bio lab, and loads of other stuff. I've even been helping Porter in Tac. And we've found a prime world. I was with the captain for the first set of meetings on Kurazi. That's the planet."

Jacey's mouth dropped opened, but she said, "Guess you have a lot to tell me." Jacey moved to stand, but Doctor Cromer laid a hand on her shoulder to keep Jacey in place.

"Not yet."

"My son has been awake, obviously for a while. I need to catch up." Jacey stood, pushed the hand away, and immediately lost her balance.

Ish tried to steady her, but she lost consciousness and fell, taking Ish down with her.

"Mom?" Ish rolled to his knees and stood after the med techs lifted Jacey back onto the bed.

"It's ok." Doctor Cromer didn't look up from the diagnostics equipment. "Your mother never liked restrictions. She tried to move too soon. She'll be fine."

Ish watched his mom breathe. She didn't appear to be in pain, but he didn't like that she had fainted. Proving the doctor was right, Jacey woke and sat up within thirty minutes.

Once the doctor finished checking her out, Jacey turned to Ish. "Tell me everything that happened to you, including how you came to be awakened before me. Then you can tell me all you know about this new home world of ours."

Ish smiled in relief at Jacey's commands and launched into a discussion of all he had experienced since his awakening. Although he would deny it if asked, it was prime to have his mom awake.

*****

Theon stopped the captain and commander in the service hallway. "The Rapulii say the Bugii and Kurmii have no written language and that their verbal languages are mostly sounds, not words. They insist the Kurmii are not able to communicate as the Bugii and Rapulii do. Nufen has again expressed interest in learning how the ship works. He says Shimgin is most insistent."

"I understand, but she was warned we will use the ship for resources as we build our homes," Captain Dolan said.

Theon shifted on his feet. "Yes, sir, but she has repeatedly offered to supply housing."

"An offer we refused. We need the resources of this ship to create a home here," Commander Van Fox said.

"Yes, but I believe she expects, at a minimum, a tour before the ship becomes parts."

"Understood," Commander Fox said.

Theon nodded and turned toward his lab.

Dolan and Fox walked into the medical bay. Dr. Cromer saw them and switched on one of the displays. "Gentlemen, we're looking at two years to wake the entire ship's complement."

"Two years?" Van sputtered.

"It's simple logistics. That timeline includes having housing for each person as they are awakened." Saber Isles, head of logistics and coordination, spoke up from the console where she was currently crunching numbers.

"I understand, but two years?"

"Nearly five thousand people. It'll take two years," Saber repeated and pulled up another display. "That's if everything goes well, and there are no delays in building infrastructure. I have a modified wake up order for review. First, we wake the population needed to get us up and running on this desert world. Next, I recommend we wake the families of the civilian and military adults who are awake."

Captain Dolan watched as a small smile played on Van's lips. The captain imagined it would be great to have family awake soon. He had no family on this ship. His wife lost her elite status — and a place on this ship — when she contracted a new strain of influenza dubbed Elite Flu. It had been created in a lab for the express purpose of targeting those with elite status. She had died from the flu, but that was a rare occurrence. It had a low death rate, but anyone who contracted the sickness was immediately removed from a ship assignment because they became a carrier. It was assumed to have been created by a team that wanted to clear the deck so those with elite status, but unclaimed by a ship, would make the next round.

It had worked in that people were replaced on the ships. It had failed because no additional scientists were selected. Anyone who could have helped create the new strain was automatically removed from consideration. As it happened, most of those stricken with the virus were those with secondary skills. The military and scientists were already on their assigned ships, prepping for departure and not in the staging area on Old Earth. Dolan was pulled from his thoughts by Saber's voice.

"Once those with the necessary skills, and their families, are awake, the remaining family groups will awaken based on their lottery drawing before we left Old Earth." Saber leaned back and stretched her stiff joints.

"Agreed. Implement." Captain Dolan pointed to the private room off to the side. "Is she ready for visitors?"

"Yes, Sir. The magistrate has been reviewing logs since she could focus." Dr. Cromer pointed toward the room. Dolan peered through the glass to the person inside. As if she felt his gaze, Jacey Rees looked up and smiled before beckoning for the captain.

She was still in bed, but Jacey had two screens and a tablet in front of her. When Captain Dolan walked in, she scowled. "Dr. Cromer refuses to let me out of this bed until tomorrow."

"You passed out the first time you tried to stand, and your vitals are still low. Stay in bed for now. I doubt you'll get much chance to relax for a while once you're mobile."

Jacey snarled but turned to her tablet. "I've scanned your logs since the Rapulii made first contact. Why didn't you wake me then?"

"And what if we had decided the planet wouldn't suit?"

"You could have woken me a week ago." Jacey held Dolan's gaze and jutted out her chin.

"Could have," the captain agreed.

Jacey barked a laugh but nodded her understanding. "You wanted Shimgin to deal with a man. Can't say I blame you. Based on your observations, it appears they are willing to understand our customs. The Rapulii getting over the matriarchal thing?"

"No. The Rapulii accept that we rule equally, and they deal with human males as such. Few of the Rapulii males speak at all. At least not to us. But then, few of the Rapulii speak directly to us."

Jacey stretched her neck. "Orders from Shimgin, or do they fear us?"

"Unknown, but I suspect a bit of both."

"Tell me about the Bugii and Kurmii."

Dolan shrugged. "Not much to tell. We have been unable to contact them, and Shimgin insists a war will break out if we approach them directly."

"I don't like it."

"Neither do I. In three days, you'll meet Shimgin. She knows you're our magistrate and our civilian leader until elections are held. She thinks it's odd that we vote for our leaders rather than have a fight to the death if one wishes to replace the current ruler. She's very excited to meet with you."

"Won't that be fun?"

"That's what you're paid for."

"I get a paycheck?" Jacey smiled. Those traveling on *Scorpius* had agreed to a barter system as the initial means of payment. Everyone expected that would change, but for now bartering services was the way to go.

"No, but it sounded good." The grin dropped from the captain's face. "She wants our tech. Don't let her con you into an exchange."

Jacey nodded. The captain left, leaving her to study their possible new home. She needed to prepare for the next round of negotiations.

Chapter 7

Jacey sipped her cari and watched the sunset. It was beautiful. She turned back to the negotiations just in time to see an unknown Sargu use wind to send Weber into the wall. Before Jacey could move, Shimgin had shielded Weber and tossed lightning at the other Sargu, who crumbled.

"Kimrin, you idiot. Weber was being polite, not disrespectful." Shimgin stood over Kimrin with another lightning ball in her hand.

"Forgive?"

Kimrin remained on the ground but Jacey thought it was to lessen Shimgin's ire rather than because she was injured. When Commander Fox helped Weber to stand and nodded to Jacey, she returned her focus to Shimgin. "What happened?"

Shimgin pointed to Kimrin. "This fool forgot that your males are allowed to speak. She will not make the same mistake twice."

"Weber meant no disrespect. In our culture it is polite to speak when in close proximity to another."

Before Shimgin responded, Kimrin said, "The fault is mine. I should not have taken offense, but it is odd to be approached by a male. It will not happen again."

Shimgin nodded and Kimrin backed out of the room. "Come. We will continue our discussion. Nufen will see to your male."

*****

"Seriously, does the wind ever not blow?" Weber adjusted his scarf to cover his nose and mouth. He had pulled on his goggles as soon as they left the building. Three weeks on the planet and he still wasn't used to the wind and blowing sand.

"The wind is mild today."

Frowning at Colom's calm reply, Weber retorted, "Unlike you, humans don't have a second, clear eyelid, to protect from the sand. Likewise, we don't have a filter in our throats to keep out the dust particles."

"Yes, Nurita has blessed us."

Ignoring the reference to the Rapulii deity, Weber stopped at the shuttle door and held his wrist in front of the data pad. The door slid open.

"Impressive." Colom looked at Weber's wrist. "How does your wrist open the door?"

"It doesn't. The embedded ID does."

"You have something implanted in your skin?"

"Yep. Doesn't hurt and becomes inert if we die."

"There's no other way on the ship?"

"Passcodes from the command staff."

"What's going on?" Seaman Floss had been left on the shuttle. She pointed her weapon toward Colom.

"Easy, Floss. The magistrate sent me to pick up a couple of things. Shimgin asked if Colom could assist me."

Floss lowered her weapon. "Aha, sorry. They didn't tell me anyone was coming with you."

Colom bowed, keeping his eye on the weapon, and followed Weber.

"This is the cockpit. I'll only be a minute." Weber opened the storage bay and collected what he needed. When he turned, Colom was bent over the pilot's seat with his hands lightly touching the panel. "See anything you like?"

"Yes. This is a fine ship. The controls are nothing like ours. I would enjoy learning to fly such a ship."

Weber barked a laugh. "Me too, but it's not my job."

Colom nodded. "You have the same type of labor division that we have."

"Yes, and right now, the magistrate is waiting for me to get back with this."

"I understand. Your magistrate is the same as our Sargu leader."

"Not sure, but we need to get going."

Colom took a quick look around and followed Weber.

*****

The trio moved silently through the pass. At least the lieutenant assumed they were silent. The high winds on this world blocked out most sound. No one could explain the hearing capabilities the Kurmii had displayed, but she had no doubt if they were nearby, the Kurmii would hear them. The vids had shown they could hear prey from further away than a human could see in the daylight. She patted the vid for the Kurmii, pleased to have a mission. Since her awakening, she felt like she hadn't earned her keep. There wasn't a lot of work for a security force on a minimally staffed ship of experienced crew. Delivering a message in Rapulii — because Doctor Clark had no Kurmii to translate — might be a dangerous mission, but she was glad to contribute.

The hairs on the back of her neck stood up. Turning a slow circle, her goggles, set to night vision, took in the scene. The path included a dry creek bed that hadn't seen water in a very long time, sparse vegetation, evenly spaced monoliths, and cliffs overhanging the former creek bed on both sides. Exactly as described in the mission brief. She caught a small movement out of the side of her eye and saw a shadow. The lieutenant narrowed her gaze on the shadow and gasped.

"Ambush." Diving for cover with the rest of her team, the lieutenant reached for her comm. "Gamma..." The rockslide prevented further communication.

*****

"Captain, Gamma team started a transmission, but it ended abruptly. I can't raise them," Weber said.

"Had they made contact with the Kurmii?"

"Unknown, but I doubt it. The lieutenant would have reported it."

Doctor Cromer's face appeared on a vid. "Captain, life signs for Gamma team are gone."

"Malfunction?"

"All three implants at once? No."

"Shuttle."

Porter's voice came over the comm. "I heard, sir. Returning to Gamma team."

"Delta team life signs are gone," Cromer said.

"Shuttle, anyone who leaves the ship is to have personal vids on." The captain's hands tightened into fists. The decision to keep the vids off, knowing the Rapulii could track the signal, had been a bad one.

"Aye, Captain."

*****

Ish grabbed his food and joined Porter and Hardy at the table. "Any status on the negotiations?" His mom had been on Kurazi for nearly a month with the diplomacy team. He hadn't been worried at first, but since two security teams went missing last week, worry had become his constant companion. He couldn't get anyone to tell him what had happened either. That just made him worry more, especially since the full team didn't return from the planet surface.

Without being asked, Porter said, "Your mom is fine. The captain said things are progressing."

"As long as Weber keeps his mouth shut." Hardy sipped her cari and added, "I think I like this better than coffee. It has more of a kick."

"What happened?" Ish looked between the two. For them to volunteer information, something must have happened.

Porter glared at Hardy, who said, "He's gonna hear it somewhere." When Porter shrugged, she explained, "Weber spoke to one of the Sargu, Shimgin's second. I think her name is Kimrin. Caused a bit of a stink, but Shimgin was amused at his audacity rather than insulted."

"It's an insult to speak to a Sargu?" Both of Ish's eyebrows popped up. It hadn't been when he was on the planet.

"It's disrespectful for a male to speak to a Sargu who hasn't spoken to him first," Hardy corrected.

Ish considered that. Zigmin had spoken only to Botha and had been irritated by his speaking. Maybe that was what had upset her. Ish grinned, still amused by Zigmin's assumption that he and Botha were lovers. He had seen no difference between a Sargu and a normal female unless they were tossing wind or lightning, something they didn't seem to do very often. "Is there a physical difference between a Sargu and a normal female?"

"Only the clothes they wear."

"They all wear the same coverings in different colors." Ish felt like he had fallen down a rabbit hole. How would he keep from making the same mistake Weber had made? A mistake he had already made once. While they might excuse the first couple of offenses, Ish doubted that attitude would continue.

"Exactly." Hardy nodded. "Sargu adults wear various shades of blue, except for Shimgin, the leader, who wears red. Sargu juveniles wear lilac. All other females wear various shades of brown, gold, and yellow."

"How about kids, you know, anyone younger than a juvenile?"

"The Rapulii haven't mentioned them and none have been sighted," Hardy said.

"There have to be young," Ish said.

"True, but I hope we would protect our young in the same way." Hardy finished eating and left.

A few days later, Ish timed his work to be in Tac 1 at the correct hour to watch the shuttle return from Kurazi. He thought it would look less needy to watch from afar. Finally, his mom was coming home. Ish watched Botha land the ship in the landing bay and open the doors.

Jacey Rees was first to leave the shuttle. Though he had been waiting for her, Ish was surprised at the relief he felt now that his mom was back on the Scorpius and he could see her. Commander Fox, Doctor Clark, and Doctor Xu followed, with Botha and Weber bringing up the rear.

"Go on." Porter pointed toward the door. "If that were my mom, I would have been standing in the bay."

A blush crept up Ish's cheeks. He thought he had been subtle. Guess not. Nodding to Porter he left and jogged to the bay. He walked in, only to be grabbed from behind.

"There you are." Jacey enveloped Ish in a bear hug. "You okay? Any problems while I was gone?"

Ish frowned. What problems could he have on the ship? He had done fine without her for months. She needed to remember that.

Jacey kissed his cheek. "Meet me in our quarters after your shift. The captain and I should be done by then."

"Will do." Ish said as she walked out with the commander, then, because he knew it was expected, he turned to the shuttle. "Weber, need help unloading?"

"You bet, kid. You can take the new samples to life sciences."

74

"I'll grab a cart." Ish sighed. Weber still called him kid, but at least he didn't have to worry about his mother anymore. Ish and Weber left the shuttle bay together. Weber turned left and Ish, pushing a cart of samples, turned right. As he approached the first hatch, the explosion knocked him into the wall. Ish slid to the deck, unconscious.

*****

"I'm gonna miss this." Jacey Rees placed a slice of peach in her mouth and chewed thoughtfully. She sat across from Captain Dolan in the observation lounge. They were alone, sharing a single peach that Dolan sliced for them.

"As will I."

They talked about nothing much as they ate and watched *Scorpius* orbit around Kurazi. Both looked at the last bite of fruit, but neither touched it. Dolan pushed the bowl in front of her. "Go ahead."

"You should have it. You've been awake longer."

"Which means I've had more fruit. You take the last slice. That's the last peach."

Jacey grinned. "Why, Captain Dolan, you sir, are a gentleman." She speared the last wedge with her fork and bit into it, savoring the sweet, juicy slice.

He laughed. "That's what they told me when I was commissioned, except the term used was gentlefolk. And the name's Percy. Once we're on the ground we will be sharing duties for a while."

"Then you, Percy, may call me Jacey. Now, down to business. Shimgin wants our tech. We know that. Is there any chance we could have an outpost on Kurazi, keeping the Scorpius in orbit, while we create a home on Zucrii?"

"Isles is working on a plan. Scorpius wasn't designed to be maintained in orbit around a planet indefinitely. Parts of the ship were to be cannibalized from the remains of the ship to remain in orbit."

"That water world looks very inviting."

"As a vacation destination, maybe. We simply don't have the know how to create infrastructure on the water. Not at the level we would need. Xu and Lynn have been tracking the hurricanes on the water. They had to develop a new scale based on the windspeeds of the storms. With little land to slow down the storms, they are spectacular in both size and destructiveness."

"We both know when everyone is awakened, and elections are held, someone will see Zucrii as a wonderful opportunity to gather wealth, if they can figure out how to use the shuttles to go back and forth. We'll need a way to replace parts in the long term."

"That's a problem for whoever gets elected."

"Agreed." Jacey ran her hands through her short hair. "The problem you and I have are the Bugii and Kurmii. What happened with the two delegations you sent out?"

"They disappeared."

Jacey gave him a wry smile. "I gathered as much, and I understood the need to not discuss it while I was planet side. Now I want answers. What happened?"

"Both teams died. Hard to believe a rockslide just happened to hit delegations in two different locations at nearly the same time."

"The Sargu control wind." Jacey chewed her lip.

"True."

"No vids?"

Percy shook his head. "Didn't want to alert the Rapulii to what we were doing. The shuttle crew found no evidence of foul play, but we have no way to determine if Sargu were there. It's doubtful the Bugii could move those boulders without equipment, but the Kurmii are probably strong enough to do so."

"Unfortunate. Is this a showstopper, or will we keep the agreements I made with Shimgin to slowly move to Kurazi?"

The explosion rocked the ship. Jacey squeaked when Percy grabbed her, stuffed her in a corner, and used his body to protect hers from harm. When the shaking stopped, Percy stood and held out a hand to help her up. She ignored the hand and stood on her own, eyes flashing with anger. "You don't need to protect me..."

Jacey glanced past Percy to see that the Observation Lounge was a mess. Anything that wasn't locked in place had collided with either walls or other movable objects. Jacey gasped when Percy turned to check a panel. His back was a mess of shrapnel. "You need a doctor."

"No. I need a status on my ship." Percy gritted his teeth and tapped on the screen. "Tac 2, report."

"Explosion in Echo shuttle bay." Commander Shaw's face came up on the screen. "Fox and team are gearing up to inspect. Supply and maintenance were impacted, and twenty-three status pods are in danger of failing."

"I'm on my way to Tac 1." Percy took Jacey's arm to guide her from the room. "To answer your question, magistrate, I think we just ran out of time for other options."

Percy glanced to port and watched a hurricane, visible from space, that currently moved toward the largest land mass on Zucrii. Too bad that planet wasn't viable.

*****

"The explosion was no accident." Lieutenant Commander Reddy tapped the controls from his chair in CC, and a 3D image of the remains of Echo Shuttle Bay came into view. "As you can see, the blast radius expands outward from a small hatch in the shuttle that brought the magistrate back from Kurazi. The device, primitive from our point of view, was most effective."

"How? Why?" Jacey asked.

"Someone on this ship helped them," Commander Fox said. When the grumbling started, he held up his hand for silence. "I don't think it was intentional. Weber, when Colom went with you to the shuttle to pick up supplies, was Colom ever alone?"

Weber's eyes flashed. "No. Well, I didn't have eyes on him the whole time. I couldn't very well keep eyes on Colom when I dug around in the storage compartment."

"So, an unauthorized person had access to our shuttle and was able to plant a bomb?" Fox asked the question, but it was obvious to Weber that the commander made a statement.

Weber threw his hands up in the air and immediately dropped them. His left shoulder took the brunt of the fall after the explosion and it still hurt. It was the same shoulder that Sargu Kimrin knocked into the wall in the Dogu. At least that was the worst of it for him. Ish had to stay off his leg for a couple of days. "What would you have done? Collect the supplies Magistrate Rees asked for or guard a representative of our host? Colom moved around the cockpit, but I assumed Shimgin told him to look at everything he could. We would do the same if their tech was superior to ours."

"Yes, we would," Jacey agreed.

Weber nodded to the magistrate and calmed down. "Anyway, it was only a few seconds and Colom's okay. If he planted a bomb, it was on orders from above."

"Regardless, how can we trust the Rapulii now?" Fox said.

Reddy expanded the 3D view to show all ship impacts. "I'm not sure it matters. That explosion has made the ship unstable. In addition to losing one of our shuttle bays, there were impacts to supply stores and maintenance, as well as minor damage to life support and heavy loss of food in hydroponics. We've sealed all leaks and repaired external damage, but I wouldn't take this ship into an ERB ever again and I have concerns that we can remain in orbit for the two-year awakening schedule."

Doctor Cromer pressed her fingers to the bridge of her nose and leaned back in her chair. "The impacted pods housed children. We lost two when the stasis pods failed, both from the same family. Of the remaining twenty-one, we were able to stabilize twelve of the pods, thanks to Ensign Katz's quick actions. Their families owe Katz a huge thanks. We had to awaken nine. All are under the age of ten without awakened parents or sponsors."

Isles shook her head when the grumbling grew loud. "Don't worry. Magistrate Rees and I have just about settled sleeping arrangements and supervision for the children. If we haven't already contacted you, you're not part of our solution, unless you tell us you want to be."

As expected, the room went silent, while no one met Isles' eyes.

Jacey asked, "Are there any recommendations that don't include settling Rapulii?"

"Not now," Reddy muttered.

"Is Zucrii out of the running?" Weber asked.

"We don't have the tech to protect against the hurricanes," Reddy retorted. "And now we don't have the time to work on the issue."

"For now, no one from Kurazi will be allowed on our shuttles or inside the housing segments we land on the planet." Dolan looked at Lieutenant Porter. "Get ready. We're going to break the ship apart once the temporary housing is in place and the segmented sections of the ship suitable for landing will be moved to Kurazi. You will land the entire stasis pods section on the planet."

"That was always a last resort option." Porter's eyes skimmed the room.

"It still is." Reddy clapped Porter on the shoulder. "You might want to hit the simulator."

"Thank you, everyone. Fox and Weber, remain. Magistrate, I would appreciate you remaining as well. Everyone else is dismissed." Captain Dolan's tone did not invite discussion.

Weber watched the room clear wondering what he could have done differently. He didn't invite Colom. The magistrate did. Weber sat up straight and wondered what a court martial in space would entail.

Commander Fox looked up from his screen. "Is what you said about Colom true?"

"Sir?" Of all the interrogation questions running through his mind, that one had not occurred to Weber.

"You don't think Colom would act alone? You don't think the bomb was planted to destroy us?"

"No. If anything, the bomb was to make sure we stay." Weber looked at the wall and tried to remember the exact conversation. "Colom asked many questions about the ship. I didn't think much about it. They weren't technical questions about layout but more about traveling through space. What were our biggest concerns? Was the trip enjoyable? How does a shuttle dock with the ship and not lose breathable air? Stuff like that. Now, of course, the questions are suspect, but they sounded like questions I would have of the first space faring species to my world. I also asked questions of my own about their daily life and government. All this info is in my report."

"Yes, you gathered some good intelligence. Things I wasn't able to get Shimgin to discuss." Magistrate Rees patted Weber on the shoulder.

He winced when her hand touched the bruised area, but he appreciated her support. "Anyway, Colom would never act against Shimgin. He's too afraid of her. I got the impression they all are."

*****

"Ready for another delivery?" Weber asked.

"Twelve down, seven to go." Ensign Botha shrugged as she walked by. They, along with Ensign Katz, had spent the last four days together, locking six housing segments (HS) to the transport rover (TR) at a time, flying the cumbersome load to its designated home on the planet, and returning to the ship. They repeated that process three times every day. It was exhausting. Climbing into the TR, she checked her gear. "Ready to connect bolt 1."

"Connecting," Katz said.

Botha felt the slight bump and checked her readings. "Connected. Ready to connect bolt 2."

Once the sixth bolt was connected, Katz and Weber joined Botha in the TR.

"TR ready to depart." Botha was poised to begin her flight when, for the first time, CC stopped her."

"Stand by, TR. You have a passenger."

Botha looked at Katz and Weber, but they were as surprised as she.

"It's the magistrate." Weber hopped up and opened the latch and took her bag. "Welcome aboard, ma'am."

"I hope I didn't keep you waiting."

"No, ma'am." Katz verified Magistrate Rees was properly belted in while Weber stowed her gear.

Botha hid her smile. Scuttlebutt was Magistrate Rees had stood firm against Captain Dolan and Commander Fox, refusing to back down when they objected to her plan. She was amused, but not surprised, the magistrate was moving so soon. "Is Ish coming?"

"No. Captain Dolan and Commander Fox were quite insistent that he was useful on *Scorpius* and should arrive with the stasis pod section."

"Very good, ma'am." Botha notified CC they were ready, received permission to leave the ship, and headed to the planet and the location for this housing segment where the humans currently living on the planet waited for them. As she approached, Botha verified Lieutenant Hardy had prepped the site for the delivery. Commander Fox and Seaman Foss stood with her. The only three humans currently living on the planet shared a housing tube while prepping for the ship's complement to join them.

"Another prime landing." Katz grabbed his gear, and the magistrate's and left.

Once the TR was free of the HS, Botha and Weber performed preflight checks while waiting for Katz.

When Fox boarded the transport, Botha asked, "Do you need something, Sir?"

"Just to tell you all remaining trips will be fully loaded with passengers."

"Sir?"

"Katz is staying here to coordinate on the ground. Weber will remain on the ship and coordinate there. The majority of the passengers will be security."

"Very good, Sir."

When Fox closed the hatch, Weber said, "And so it begins. I thought I was ready to be off the *Scorpius* for good. Now, I think I'm going to miss the girl. I thought we would have years to go back and forth."

"We all did." Botha said as she finished preflight and received permission for the TR to return to the *Scorpius*.

*****

Hoping no one noticed, Lieutenant Porter wiped his sweaty hands on his pants. Even though this section of the ship was on a pre-programmed flight plan, he checked the course one last time. Decoupling from the main ship had been textbook; hopefully, the landing would be. As the *Scorpius* entered the atmosphere, Porter relaxed. He felt better now that he could see the lay of the land through the view screens.

He had flown repeated shuttle trips to the planet and had piloted smaller sections of the ship to the ground, but that was nothing compared to landing the pod section of the population ship. Though technically Porter would make a total of five trips to land the various sections of the ship, they would be united in a cluster, sealed together, and retain the name *Scorpius*. What would be left in space, especially after the explosion, would never fly again. Before its orbit degraded too much, it would be set on autopilot and sent into the sun to prevent a future catastrophic event.

Porter turned off the autopilot. It wasn't designed to land the ship but get close enough for the pilot to do his job. He adjusted course to land half a mile from Scorpius Valley, the human settlement. East of the Claw Arch, the settlement would be at the southern tip of Remei Lake, south of the Rapulii settlement.

"So, this is our new home," Commander Shaw murmured. "The arches around Remei Lake are impressive."

Porter barely heard the commander speak. His focus remained on his console, landing this section of the *Scorpius* for the first and only time. All pilots were trained in simulations to land the stasis pods section of the ship, but the one and only live landing would be on their new world, and then, only if necessary. Once landed, the stasis pod section would never fly again. There was simply no way to get it off the ground.

"Attention. Prepare for landing." The captain's calm voice helped to reduce the pounding of Porter's heart.

The ship landed with a small bump, and Porter leaned back in relief.

"Textbook landing. Prime," Ish switched his screens to external vid views, surprised at what he saw. "I didn't know the Rapulii would be here. And look, there are children." Even when he had been on the planet, the only juvenile he had seen was Zigmin. No young children had been present.

Through the vids, a large number of Rapulii were visible. Adults lounged or ate while Rapulii juveniles – a school outing perhaps – played on the hills overlooking the landing site. Ish was relieved to note that the children wore the same colors as the adults and suspected it was how he would be able to identify Sargu. Many of the Sargu wore decorative headgear similar to Shimgin's but not as ornate. Under the watchful eye of their owner, the erkek, reptilian beasts of burden smaller than an ox but larger than a dog on Old Earth, carried snacks. It looked like a massive picnic.

"They knew we were landing the largest section of the ship that we could, but we didn't invite them," Commander Van Fox said from his position on the ground. "A steady stream of observers arrived all morning. I asked Nufen and he used the term gezi. It means outing."

Captain Dolan's voice carried a bit of humor. "An alien species that they've only known for a short period of time lands a huge section of their spaceship with technology they don't understand in their backyard, and you didn't think they would be at the landing site?"

Commander Fox flashed a grin. "When you put it that way, I guess I understand."

"Shaw, you have command. Fox, I'm coming to you. Porter, excellent landing." Captain Dolan disabled his connection. Commander Shaw slid easily into her role and began issuing orders for power conservation.

Ish watched as standard shutdown began. He had spent the past couple of days reviewing the power save process and the reasons certain functions were turned off. The most obvious reason was power. If the ship lost its power reserves, anyone not yet awake, would die in their pods. And that was still the majority of the ship's complement.

Chapter 8

Dressed as he always was, in the civilian version of a military work uniform, Ish grabbed a plate of stew, flashed his wrist in front of the scanner to provide his ID, and asked for an apple. Once the steward verified Ish had not already had his allotted fruit for the day, Ish received a bright, red apple, and joined Porter and Botha at a table, weaving his way around the awakened children.

One of the children looked at Ish, wide-eyed and hopeful. "That's a mighty pretty apple you have, Ish."

Ish grinned, "How many times have you used that hustle today, Jacob?"

"You're the first." When the younger kids giggled, Jacob glared at them.

Ish set his tray down and sliced the apple quickly. He left one slice on his plate and gave the rest to Jacob. "Share."

"I always do." Jacob took the slices and proceeded to hand them out.

"Thanks, Ish." The response came from children with full mouths.

"Here Jacob, you eat this one." Ish handed over the slice on his plate. Ish noticed that, as usual, Jacob hadn't kept any for himself. It was the reason Ish shared so willingly. They received their daily allowance of fruit, but it seemed cruel not to share with kids who shouldn't be awake yet. None of them had awakened sponsors, but Ish heard the awakening schedule had been altered to awaken their parents or guardians soon.

"Thanks." Jacob bit into the slice.

Ish joined Alpha Crew.

"If you want to hunt today, get a move on. We leave in ten." Porter picked up a bow and quiver of arrows and laid them beside Ish's backpack. "I brought your gear."

"Really?" Ish eyed Porter. As far as he was concerned, Porter was the Mom Whisperer. The lieutenant consistently talked Jacey into allowing Ish to participate in activities that she vetoed when Ish asked. He had tried everything to get his mom to let him join a hunt. He had even taken to carrying his pack inside the ship in case he was allowed to leave the ship for any reason. Until today, she had not allowed him off the ship because their housing wasn't ready. Ish touched the bow. "Thanks."

"Our little gofer's all grown up." Weber dropped his hunting gear by an empty chair and went to get food.

Ish frowned at Weber's sarcastic remark, but he had more important matters to occupy his thoughts. While he wolfed down his meal, Ish asked Porter, "How did you do it?"

"I explained to your mom that you are fully trained, passed all the qualification tests, and we're about out of food. Anyone who can hunt or gather food, needs to."

"We wouldn't be if we used seeds from Old Earth?" Weber returned, ignored his stew, and peeled his orange.

"We can't cross contaminate. Our food can't leave this ship." Poulsen, from the life science division, sat down with his plate. Like Ish, he had given his fruit to the kids. "Aside from the possibility of introducing something more harmful to this world than us, our crops require too much water."

Ish shook his head. Weber knew this. They all did. Those traveling on the *Scorpius* agreed to a policy of protecting their new world when they found it. Humans needed to learn to live in harmony with the physical world. Ish finished his stew, which now had the added flavor, mostly bitter, of some local plants. He would have enjoyed that apple, but it went to a good cause. Nearly seven months of eating the same food every day and he had joined the rest of Alpha Crew in being tired of it. Although eating Rapulii food had the benefit of making the humans appreciate human food in any format. The offerings the Rapulii provided proved to be at least as bitter as expected, which was unfortunate as the humans slowly incorporated it into their diet.

Porter stood, strapped his quiver to his back and tossed the bow over his shoulder. "Alpha Crew, move out."

"Lieutenant Hardy, remember, irhasi is good. Omuz is better." Botha called out amid laughter. Hardy and Botha had the truest aim with a bow and arrow. As a result, the two had a friendly rivalry going. On Alpha Crew's first outing, Hardy brought down an irhasi with her arrow, and the chef had been pleased to have fresh meat to cook. The awakened had been equally pleased to eat something new. When Beta Crew went out the first time, Botha's arrow found a home in an omuz and the meat was excellent. The crews agreed that, while both meats were tasty, omuz was tastier, more like pork from Old Earth.

Although most of the awakened had been off the ship numerous times, this was Ish's first trip aside from the first ground meeting, and for that the captain had demanded Ish remain in visual view at all times. As the only awakened non-essential personnel, and the only minor, he had felt like he was trapped in a bubble. That eased up a lot when the young children had been awakened during the explosion. Another reason to share his fruit with them.

Ish followed Porter, pleased that his mom wasn't around. If she had showed up on the ship, he would have felt like a kid going to day camp. It hadn't escaped his notice that he was treated less like one of the guys now that his mom was awake. Ish wondered, not for the first time, when he would move to the housing segment with his mom.

When he walked out the hatch and his feet touched the ground for the first time, Ish stopped and looked around. He was on another world. Ish wasn't sure why he suddenly thought of that. He had been planet side for the initial meeting between Shimgin and the captain, but that entire experience had felt a bit surreal to him.

The ship landed on the planet a few weeks ago, but since Ish marked time as everyone's favorite gofer, and only saw the inside of the ship, it hadn't sunk in. He knew he was on another world, but today it seemed real. He would never return to space.

Ish looked up at the sky and immediately averted his eyes. How could he have forgotten how bright the sun was? "Ow, goggles. I need goggles."

"Oops. Should have given you these before we left the ship." Weber handed Ish a pair of tinted goggles.

Porter shot Weber an irritated look. "Wear the goggles for now. Your eyes will adjust. Ours did. The sun seems bright, but the physical science department assures us it's no brighter than Old Earth would have been if not for the pollution."

Ish adjusted the goggles and nodded. He looked around, relieved that some of the others also wore them. The sky was bright blue, like vids of Old Earth before the pollution took over. Plant life was sparse once they left the area around the lake, but they were headed toward some hills that had trees and undergrowth, so perhaps there was underground water nearby. Until Ish got closer, he wouldn't be able to identify the plants. The wind blew continuously, but it wasn't a cooling breeze. The wind was hot. Ish took a deep breath and coughed.

Porter tapped Ish on the shoulder. "Pull your scarf up over your mouth and nose. Otherwise, you'll eat sand."

Embarrassed, Ish followed the instructions. He should have thought of that himself. Ish became indistinguishable from the rest of the civilian hunters.

Porter pointed to a rock formation shaped like an hourglass. "Meet back here when you're done. No one returns to the ship until we're all accounted for."

"Yeah, we know," Weber muttered loud enough for Ish to hear.

Hardy tapped Ish on the shoulder. "I'm taking Ish and Ensign Katz with me into the hills. We'll search for omuz."

Porter nodded. "Call on the comm if you need help carrying anything out."

Watching the others break out into twos or threes for their own hunt, Ish stood a little straighter. For once, he wasn't being held back.

Katz led the way, keeping a running commentary. "We're headed southwest, toward the mountains. The Rapulii hunt north and east of their settlement, so we're establishing different hunting patterns. Don't want to decimate the herds."

Hardy walked over and touched a bush. "Culi –"

"No, Lieutenant. That's oprak. See the cluster of pod casings on the single stem. The pods inside are gold in color and good for stomach issues if you chew them. Bitter to the extreme but full of nutrients. The new growth is yellow with horizonal stripes, running up and down the casing. Old growth tastes more bitter but offers better medicinal value. It spreads out nearly twice as far as the roots which burrow down, not out." Ish corrected her without thinking.

"That's very detailed. You sure?"

"Yeah. The guys in life science ran tests on all of the plants in our landing zone. I worked mostly with grasses but saw the rest of the plant life. Trust me, culi is taller with a fatter leaf that points skyward. It has a casing that opens up to reveal burnt orange pods. The thicker the branch, the more bitter the taste. Culi retains its orange color."

"You're handy to have around." Switching topics, Hardy said, "If you see an omuz, aim for the eye socket. It's the easiest point of entry. The second-best option is the underside of the throat, but they tend to keep their head down to use their tusks to gouge with, so it's doubtful you'll get the chance to aim for the neck. If one charges you, hold your ground as long as possible and jump clear. They are fast, but they don't turn easily. Oh, and they're mean."

Ish glanced at her laser gun, knowing she wouldn't pull it unless she had to. The laser would damage the meat, and everyone was under orders to use the weapons that didn't require a charge or could run out of ammo. He was glad for the reminder on the omuz. He had listened to the briefings on the animals that would probably become their staple for meat, but now, at the start of his first hunt, it was nice to hear the basics repeated. The forest was cooler by a few degrees than the open plains and the trees helped to block the blowing sand. Ish took a deep breath.

"Ish, what's the red leafed plant called?" Hardy pointed to the plant in question.

Touching the soft leaf, Ish said, "It's mizi. We should take some leaves back. They have antibacterial properties that Doctor Poulson raved about. They want more to study."

"Do you know how to gather the leaves without harming the plant?"

Although his eyes were distorted through the goggles, Ish shot her a look with a whole lot of duh.

90

The look must have made it through the goggles. Hardy held up her hands. "Legit question. I don't know what percentage of the leaves or limbs can be taken without destroying the plant."

"Oh, then yes, I know the procedure." It was the first time Ish was pleased he had spent so much time working for the botanist.

"You gather, Katz and I'll hunt." Hardy walked away with Katz in tow leaving Ish alone.

Ish grinned and removed his pack. Although he would rather hunt, it was gratifying to work unsupervised on this new world. Finally, someone treated him as an adult. Even Porter treated him like a kid brother.

Setting aside his bow, Ish opened his pack and pulled out the tools he had only packed because the list said all hunters should have handheld horticultural tools with them as well. He had followed the recommendations exactly, glad he had prepacked days ago in case he was ever allowed off the ship for any reason. Ish carefully picked leaves from each adult mizi plant in the area. Once he had the mizi leaves in his pack, Ish realized he didn't know which way Hardy had gone. He thought about calling her, or maybe Porter, on the comm, but that seemed like a plonker move. There had been no chatter on the open lines since they left the ship. A bird-like whistle came from deep in the woods.

While deciding on a course of action, a rustle in the underbrush caught his attention. Not knowing what made the sound, Ish cocked an arrow, took a slow breath, and waited.

A tuyu ran out of the brush, and Ish lowered his bow. It wasn't high on the tasty meter, or aggressive toward humans, so there was no need to harm it. The creature ran on two legs using its long neck and equally long tail for balance. The little stubby arms had the vestiges of wings, but it couldn't fly. Though it had a beak, and a few feather-like plumes on the neck, chest, elbows, and back, life sciences said it wasn't a bird. Ish wasn't sure what it was, besides weird. The tuyu crossed the ravine and ran up into the trees on the other side, disappearing from view.

Katz walked into view carrying ilan with their heads chopped off. He had placed their future dinner in a liquid proof pouch. Katz stopped when he saw Ish with weapon drawn. "Didn't you hear the whistle?"

"I heard it, then a tuyu jumped out in front of me." Ish returned the arrow to his quiver, suddenly remembering that the military used Old Earth birdcalls for identification.

"The whistle is how we indicate our positions." Katz held out the ilan. "Toss these in your pack. Mine's full. Times like this I wish I was a tracker like my cousin."

Ish looked up in surprise. "Your cousin's a tracker and hasn't been woken yet?"

Katz grinned. "He's not on this ship. He earned a place on the Draco."

"Why weren't you assigned together?"

"We're both military and earned slots that way. The rest of our family didn't get on a ship, so we said our goodbyes and boarded our assigned ships."

"Weird that you have a cousin on another planet tracking dinner."

Katz looked up at the sky. "If he's lucky they've made planetfall and are living a good life."

Hardy stepped out of the bushes. "My quarry got away from me. I didn't even let loose a single arrow."

"At least we have ilan and plant samples for biology." Ish struggled into his now loaded pack and the trio walked to the meeting place. When they arrived Ish plopped down on a rock. "How long will we wait?"

"Not long." Hardy pointed to the left where the other hunters had topped the hill and were making their way down into the valley with an omuz tied to two poles. Each pole had a person holding each end.

"That's prime. Who brought it down?" Ish asked.

"The lieutenant," Weber said.

"I made the kill shot, but only because it ran in my direction. It was a group effort," Porter said.

Weber adjusted the pole on his shoulder and said, "We need to prep a miner or robot to carry these in the future."

"Not unless we get approval to use them. We can't depend on such conveniences," Porter said.

As they approached the *Scorpius*, a blue Rapulii walked toward them. Weber looked up and grinned. "Colom."

"Weber." The blue looked at the omuz and tightened his hold on the two erkek with him. Despite his grip, one of the erkek lunged for the omuz.

The man closest to the erkek dropped his end of the pole and jerked out of the way of the reptilian dog beast, leaving all of the weight on the other pole, which cracked, resulting in the full weight of the omuz tilting toward Weber, who fell under the omuz.

While the others lifted the omuz, Ish and Hardy pulled Weber from under the beast.

"He's free." Hardy said.

Dropping the omuz to the ground, the soldiers stepped back. Hardy, eyes on Weber's twisted leg, grabbed her comm, and said, "Alpha Crew needs medical assistance near the Semelai."

"Semelai?"

"Claw Arch. Learn the freakin' nouns," Weber yelled from the ground.

Ish raised an eyebrow at how fast the medical team showed up. They must have been on standby.

While the medical team worked on Weber, Colom bowed before Porter. "Apologies. Erkek enjoy the taste of omuz. We normally prepare the kill before returning to Remei and offer them some." Colom threw a tarp next to the omuz. "If you move the omuz onto the tapoleni, the erkek will drag it to your ship."

"Won't they turn and take a bite?" Hardy asked.

Colom bowed to the female and modified the leashes, turning them into a harness. "No. The harness will keep them facing forward."

Once the omuz was loaded and Colom led the erkek forward, one of the soldiers said, "We need trained erkek."

Porter nodded his agreement and watched carefully when Colom unhitched the tarp and left the harness on the erkek. "We appreciate your help."

"And I respectfully request you not mention my failure." Colom bowed again.

Porter cocked his head to the side. "Failure?"

"The erkek lunged toward your food. I should have had better control of my beasts."

"No harm done."

"Hey," Weber said as he was carried onto the ship. "The medic says my leg's broken."

"No permanent harm." Porter amended his statement.

Despite his complaint, Weber called. "It's all good, Colom. I'll see you soon."

Chapter 9

"Ishmael. You don't want to be late for your first day." Without opening his eyes, he reached out with his left hand to grab his tablet, the source of his mother's voice, knocking it off the edge of the bedroll. He lunged and followed the device to the floor. His first day in the new house was not starting off well. Yesterday, Ish moved from the *Scorpius* and his mom moved from temporary housing, the house segments from the ship where people stayed while housing was built. He still wasn't sure how he felt about the house. He had enjoyed helping out the crew and suspected he had been relegated to the ranks of kid again. Who knew he would miss being a gofer?

Groaning, he activated the comm. "It's Ish, Mom. New world, new name. You promised." He hopped up and checked his pack. The one he checked twice last night.

"Sweetie, I named you Ishmael because I love the name. I'm trying, but change is hard." Jacey's smile was evident in her voice.

"Try harder." He clicked off the comm. Why would a perfectly reasonable woman name her only child Ishmael? He spent most of his childhood being asked where Moby was.

Seriously, what had she been thinking? Shaking his head, Ish returned to his task. It was the work of a moment to throw on the assigned gear for the field trip, the same gear he wore working on the ship. Ish tossed on his backpack and looked at himself in the mirror. Ready for the day. He checked the time, grabbed a breakfast bar the ship's chef made from local ingredients, and ran out the door with his mouth full, mumbling, "Later."

Ish jogged down the path away from the handful of houses that were completed in the human settlement. Jacey had demanded to be one of the first housed outside the ship housing segments. Ish had been proud of her decision to lead by example. Of course, as they moved in, Commander Fox, head of security, moved in next door.

"You could have waited for me." Whisper, Commander Fox's daughter, dropped into a jog beside him and they passed the beginnings of the first human maintained vegetable garden.

Ish wasn't sure how he felt about Whisper. She must spend a lot of time studying as she seemed to know everything even though she had only been awake for a couple of weeks. Add to that, her aim on the practice field with a bow and arrow was excellent, and she was fearless in hand to hand, which made it appear she was good at everything. He didn't respond but waved at Weber who didn't look happy with his current assignment. With so few humans awake everyone did time doing manual labor that they weren't enthusiastic about. Ish was scheduled to work in the gardens tomorrow and he shared Weber's distaste for the task. Running tests in the lab was okay, but the act of farming was work. Hard, sweaty, demanding work.

When they passed the *Scorpius*, Commander Shaw's red-headed twins, Hartley and Haven, joined them.

Adjusting his goggles, Hartley said, "These goggles are irritating."

"Not nearly as irritating as the sand if it gets in your eyes. You'll get used to 'em," Ish retorted.

"New world. Loads to explore. And school is what gets me off the ship. Malefic." Hartley groused, pacing Ish.

"What better way to explore than with a school outing?" Whisper asked.

"For you, maybe. You like to study."

"Be nice." Haven, Hartley's twin, glared at her brother. "At least we're off the ship."

"You guys still live onboard?" Ish asked.

"Yeah. Mom will remain on the ship until everyone is out of stasis."

"Doesn't mean you have to, does it?"

Hartley barked a laugh. "According to Mom, that's exactly what it means."

"Bosh," Ish said. Although they would become adults within the next year, he was happy to be with others his age. It had been a while since he had fit in, at least in his mind.

"Yep."

The quartet were guinea pigs for the first combined class of Rapulii juveniles and human teenagers. Jacey thought that educating both species together would make the transition easier for everyone. Ish assumed the selection had more to do with who their parents were than anything else. Of course, most teenagers weren't awake yet, and the other kids were too young, so maybe they were all the humans had to offer.

The four teenagers continued past the Semelai rock formation with its two claws reaching skyward. The reptilian dog looking creatures, called erkek, were tethered waiting for their masters. Without a fresh kill to capture the erkek's attention, they didn't react to the kids. Turning left at the lake, and running under the double arch called Dekai, they slowed.

Across the lake, the Rapulii's only office building, the Dogu, resided. And behind that, the Rapulii lived. The quartet ran toward the Kaya Arch, which was a tall odd-looking arch with iridescent boulders crammed inside a hollow. Their destination, the Duvi rock formations, was before the Kaya but couldn't be seen until they topped the hill. The two nearly identical carved stones reached for the sky. It was a general meeting place. The Rapulii juveniles, their term for teenagers, arrived at the same time. They were all females, so they were all reds. Dressed in a type of uniform consisting of a sash with a sleeveless cape, all uniforms were light brown except for one female standing off to the side. Although her outfit was cut the same, hers was lilac in color.

"Why is that Rapulii standing alone?" Hartley asked.

"Don't know, but she's Zigmin, a young Sargu," Ish said. He waved to Zigmin and was surprised when she waved back, so were the other Rapulii.

"The one you met at the initial meetings?" Whisper asked. Ish nodded and she raised her voice. "I'm Whisper."

Hartley shrugged and said, "I'm Hartley, and this is my sister, Haven." The Rapulii gasped, and Hartley looked over at Ish.

Ish opened his mouth, but Zigmin beat him to it. "Surely you've each read the assignment. Human males speak. It's not an insult."

Haven waved but stopped when the Rapulii giggled. "Is waving rude?"

"I don't think so. It would've been in the briefings if it were." Whisper watched the juveniles for a second.

One Rapulii joined the humans and bowed. "I am Tobin. Your wave wasn't rude, but they are. They laugh at your name."

"Why?"

"Haven is our word for where we go to... um... take care of... um..."

"The humans call it a toilet," Zigmin said without moving. She had been the only one besides Tobin to refrain from laughter.

"My name means toilet?" A blush rose up Haven's cheeks. She glared at Hartley who laughed.

Assuming his name didn't mean anything embarrassing in Rapulii since no one commented during the first meetings, Ish said, "Ish." Although they didn't gasp when he spoke, he noticed that he received a lot of attention. Maybe it was because they heard he was at the initial meetings with Zigmin.

Introductions proceeded from there until only Zigmin had not introduced herself. When everyone turned to her, she grinned, showing teeth. "Zigmin."

"Good. Everyone is here. For those who don't know me, I'm Gwen." Gwen Hardy, a member of the command staff, joined the teenagers. She had exchanged her military uniform for the same type of unisex outfit the teenagers wore. An adult Rapulii in a light blue sash and cape stood with Gwen.

"Kimrin," the adult Sargu said, pointing to her chest. "Today we walk, identify plants and animals, and discuss their attributes. Zigmin, lead us to the Yolzi Path. There we start our studies."

Ish looked Kimrin over. This was the Sargu that tossed Weber. Seeing that would have been prime. A payback for all of Weber's kid comments.

The students followed Zigmin who jogged north past the half-moon shaped lake that the Rapulii called home. It was fed from underground. The Rapulii protected the water, with strict rules on building anything that might impact the precious liquid. It made sense. Remei Lake was the only above ground water resource that didn't dry out for at least part of the year.

When they passed under the Fusai, a series of ribbon arches, Ish perked up. Few humans had traveled past the ribbons on foot. The Rapulii walked or ran everywhere, and they professed no interest in travel outside of their settlement except for hunting. Most human exploration so far had been via satellite feeds or shuttle, and only the military was authorized to travel in the shuttles. The shuttles were only for official business and journeyed under stealth mode so that the Rapulii wouldn't be reminded of the advanced tech the humans had, pretending the huge sections of the *Scorpius* wasn't a reminder. Ish had only been in the shuttle simulators, although he was proud that he was the first fully certified civilian pilot. Still, he would love to fly a shuttle for real.

Once they left the valley, the wind picked up speed. Ish pulled his scarf up over his mouth and nose to block the sand being blown by the wind, as did the other humans. The Rapulii had secondary lenses over their eyes to block sand and their reptilian skin did not seem bothered by blowing sand. Shortly after passing the Osai, an arch that looked like someone making the hand signal for okay, they arrived at a fork.

Zigmin turned south entering the Yolzi Path, another valley between two mountain ranges. Ish looked at the path on the right. Even without trail markers, he knew it was the Kasak. A path that went north, to where the Kurmii lived. In the months since negotiations with the Rapulii began, humans had not met Kurmii or Bugii.

Zigmin slowed to a walk, still a bit away from everyone else. Wanting to talk to Zigmin again, Ish had decided she would not object to his speaking first since they were in class together, he jogged over and stopped beside her. "Have you been on the Kasak Path before?"

Surprise lit her eyes, and Zigmin shook her head. "Are all human males windblown? No one willingly takes the Kasak Path. Kurmii are not much better than animals and would kill any who enter their land. Kasak means forbidden. No one goes that way."

Ish didn't reply but he, like most awakened humans, had watched the vids of the Kurmii. They seemed intelligent to him, working as a group to hunt, and helping, even protecting, the injured.

The Yolzi Pass headed south between two mountain ranges. Trees were sparse. Ish had yet to see a lush forest, although the vids from the satellites indicated there was an actual forest near the Bugii. Those trees looked similar to the deciduous trees of Old Earth. Kurudi, the plant the humans called brambles, grew in various colors and were everywhere. No wonder it was a staple of the Rapulii diet. Mushrooms were supersized and most had more medicinal uses than culinary ones.

During a rest break, Haven joined them, laying a hand on Ish's shoulder, and wiping the sweat from her brow with the other. "How is it the wind is hot? A cooling breeze would be nice."

"No breeze would be better," Hartley retorted when he stopped by her side. "Does the wind ever not blow?"

"The wind is mild today, barely blowing small trees." Zigmin glanced back and forth from Ish and Haven.

Ish tracked Zigmin's eyes moving back and forth from him to Haven. "Before you ask, the answer is no." He was beginning to wonder if the Sargu viewed males as necessary for reproduction and nothing else.

Zigmin grinned and Haven shot him a confused look.

To distract Haven, and her overprotective brother, Ish said, "By the way, this was a decent wind on Old Earth."

"On Kurazi, twenty MPH is a mild wind. Doesn't this path go to the Bugii settlement?" Whisper dropped into step beside Zigmin.

"Yes, but they don't like us either. Bugii rarely kill on sight. Not that they could kill me." Zigmin preened a little.

"Then you have mastered wind properly. Two days ago, you nearly toppled part of a broken arch on a work crew. The techs will be relieved to hear of your newfound mastery." Kimrin spoke loud enough for all to hear.

Zigmin growled but didn't reply.

The other Rapulii seemed to be amused, but Ish wasn't sure how he knew that. None of them laughed, or cackled, as the Rapulii typically did. Perhaps the Rapulii didn't want to anger a young Sargu who might one day be in a position of power.

Kimrin clapped her hands. "Come. We have lessons to attend. Who can identify this plant?"

"It's culi. When you see it, you know there's water underground and not too deep. It's also edible. The botanists on the ship compared its nutritional value to kale on Old Earth." Ish spoke without thinking and was surprised when everyone, Rapulii and human, turned to stare.

"Wish I had been woken early," Hartley muttered.

A blush moved up Ish's cheeks. "I spent a lot of time in life sciences testing plants."

"What else do you know?" Kimrin asked. She pointed to a bush that was a bit taller than Ish. It boasted red leaves. "Identify this."

Ish looked where Kimrin pointed, glad he recognized the plant. "It's mizi. The crushed leaves have antibacterial properties for humans. The bark is bitter, at least to humans, but edible."

"What plant isn't bitter on this planet?" Hartley asked. When he saw Lieutenant Hardy's withering stare, he added, "But hey, we'll get used to it, and at least it's edible."

Three hours later, Ish had impressed the others with his knowledge of plant life, but Whisper outshined all with her in-depth knowledge of creatures. The students cooked a stew they made from plant cuttings and roots. Under Kimrin's direction, they divided into two teams to track, capture, and kill kemi, a house cat-sized insect that was an excellent source of protein.

Haven reached down to break the neck of a kemi her team had captured and lost her grip allowing one of the pinchers to brush Hartley's leg. "Oops."

Hartley jumped out of the way of the pinchers that could slice through skin and crush small bones. "Bosh! That overgrown ant —"

"Kemi," Whisper corrected automatically while Zigmin stepped in and killed it.

"Who cares? That thing could take a leg off." Hartley reached down and grabbed the now beheaded kemi. "Thanks, Zigmin."

"Thanks?" Zigmin looked confused.

"Yeah, you saved me from my sister's stupidity. Thanks."

Zigmin shook her head but managed a small smile. "Interesting."

"Don't you already know how to do this stuff?" Whisper asked Zigmin. "You've lived here all your life. You must know this stuff, right?"

"No, the techs do most of the gathering and cooking. Shimgin decided that we should learn since humans need these skills, but I doubt I'll ever do my own labor. I believe Ish knows more about plant life than I do."

Ish raised an eyebrow but didn't speak. How did Kimrin know this stuff if the reds weren't taught such things? Ish shook his head as he realized what had happened. Kimrin used him. She didn't say anything. She pointed and he answered. Keen to show off his knowledge, Ish hadn't realized what she had done.

"Why aren't any Rapulii males with us?" Whisper asked.

"You ask many questions," Zigmin said.

Ish added his own kemi to the stew. "You have no idea."

Whisper blushed.

"Males don't take classes with females. Not normally," Tobin said. "I heard this was a test to see if human males could keep up with females."

"I think I've been insulted," Ish muttered.

"You think?" Hartley laughed as he walked past. He carried his second bundle of grass to the bubbling pot. Before he could drop the grass into the stew, Kimrin slapped his hand away. "Imen bad. Never use. A little cari is okay, but not imen."

"It's grass. It's all the same." Hartley held up the green blades.

"No, it's not." Ish sighed and picked a few blades of the cari and held them next to the imen. "See? The yellow blades are longer and thinner. That's cari, our source of caffeine on this world. It takes on a brown color in the winter. The imen is a fatter blade and is light green."

"It looks about the same to me." Hartley tossed the imen aside.

Haven peered over Hartley's shoulder and eyed the plant. "Both blades of grass do look similar."

"It's different." Whisper picked up the bundle of imen. "This is taboo to the Rapulii, probably because it harms them in some way. Don't you read the daily notices, or watch the vids, from the science team?"

"Of course, I do. Well, most of the time. If I remember." Hartley had the decency to blush. "Sorry."

Whisper took the bundle of imen and walked it away from the fire before throwing it back on the ground. "Don't be sorry, be smart."

Zigmin cackled. "I thought your males were smarter than ours."

Ish rolled his eyes while Whisper hid her smile and kept her mouth shut for once. Haven laughed along with the Rapulii females.

On the return trip to Remei Lake, Tobin asked, "What was your home world like? Why did you leave?"

"We left because our planet could no longer support us. It was dying," Whisper said.

"Yeah, we had to wear full masks, not just these cloth coverings, most days to walk outside," Haven added.

"Why masks?" Zigmin asked.

"To breathe. The air was toxic, although some days it wasn't too bad." Ish dropped in step beside her. "The above ground water on our planet was contaminated, and most of our animal and plant food sources were gone. We were lucky to pass the selection process and garner a berth on a population ship."

"Some were left behind?" Tobin asked.

"Yes, there weren't enough population ships to take everyone," Whisper explained.

The return trip was more relaxed as the humans explained differences between daily life on Old Earth and their new life on Kurazi.

Chapter 10

Commander Van Fox walked in steady strides. No one would know he was nervous unless they knew him well. Walking beside her dad, Whisper recognized his apprehension for what it was, concern for her safety. For her part, excitement ruled her day. To be part of a team, even in a small way, was gratifying. With so few people awakened, she was charged with video recording the Dogu. Whisper had wondered why PC Weber, who was with them, wasn't recording but chalked it up to some military duty she didn't know about.

A blue Rapulii stood at the entrance to the Dogu. Like all males, he wore black leather slacks. As a tech, he wore a utility belt suited to his duties. He carried the equivalent of a handheld communication device on the belt as well as a couple of small data pads, indicating he was in charge of some activity. He bowed to Whisper but addressed his words to the commander. "Welcome, Commander Van Fox. I am Senior Tech Ralim. I will show you our facility and answer your questions."

"Just Fox will do." Fox nodded. "I am pleased to be here. Weber, from the negotiations, is my aide. I also brought

Whisper, my daughter, to record the tour for other humans to see."

"Then I am just Ralim." Ralim nodded and began the tour Shimgin authorized. As he completed the tour of level one, he waved for another tech to approach and said, "As you can see, Level 1 is for technical work. Each section supports specific tasks for our leaders. If it pleases you, Fox, Weber may stay with Colom. Colom can show him the workstations and the type of work done."

"That is acceptable." Commander Fox nodded to Weber who walked off with Colom.

"Now we go to Level 2, where the reds and Sargu work."

"How about down?" Fox asked.

Ralim looked at the steps before turning back to Commander Fox. "Downstairs is off limits to all but the nursery staff."

"Nursery?" Whisper leaned over the railing to look down. Seeing baby Rapulii would be prime. Though humans had seen a few young and juveniles, no infants or toddlers had been observed or recorded.

Fox tapped his daughter on the shoulder, and she straightened up with a blush.

"When a Sargu is in eketlii, I think you say fertile, she selects a male. Within a few weeks, she lay eggs, and the techs and warriors assigned to protect the eggs do so until they hatch. This has been the Rapulii hatching grounds since Natura blessed us with life." Ralim moved up the steps. "Come, the rest of the tour is upstairs."

Whisper sighed and followed. The nursery sounded interesting. Thrilled her dad asked for her help on the tour, she had expected to see something more interesting than a mundane office. The Dogu was just a workplace. Boring, even by her standards.

Once the tour finished, Whisper joined those in line for lunch. She mentally sighed when she was handed a plate of sautéed brambles, but the chopped meat on a tortilla looking thing with some type of green sauce held promise. She grabbed a mug of cari and joined the other teenagers on the rocks they had claimed as their eating place. In reality, the teens used the rocks to block the blowing sand from their food. The adults used a large tent for the same reason.

Hartley looked up with a frown. "I don't know what the green sauce is, but it isn't salsa verde."

"It's not all bad. The tortilla is... acceptable, and the meat is good. I think it's omuz." Ish took another bite and grimaced. "The green sauce is a bit bitter."

"A bit?" Hartley glared at his friend.

Haven laughed at her twin, but her face puckered up when she took a bite. "Bosh."

"That bad?" Whisper eyed the sauce with trepidation before she took a small bite. It tasted a bit like the breakfast smoothies her dad used to make. Not great, but she'd eaten worse. She took a bigger bite and chewed.

"The commander ruined your taste buds at an early age, didn't he?" Ish asked.

"Huh?"

"Before you guys were awakened, Commander Fox said chocolate was empty calories and we would get used to not having much sugar. Looks like he trained you early."

"Is that an insult?"

Ish shrugged. "Nah. Just an observation. He's the only one I never heard complain about the food on the ship. He doesn't complain about the food here either. I assumed he didn't let you have sugar on Old Earth, so you were used to the bitter life."

Hartley chuckled and Haven rolled her eyes.

Whisper thought about that for a minute. "I had sugar. Not much. Dad has always been a healthy eater, using food for fuel, not pleasure. I never gave it much thought."

"Another win for you, not that you need it. You already know more about this planet than most of the awakened." Hartley picked a bramble and sighed when he bit into its bitter stem.

"I watch the daily vids is all. Ish is the one with practical experience. I wish I had been awakened early. You learned so much." Whisper directed her last statement to Ish.

Hartley pushed his plate aside with one bramble uneaten. "Forget learning. I think everyone owes Ish. What bosh did you do on the ship that everyone owes you?"

"I was the gofer." Ish took a sip of his cari juice to hide the smile that threatened to take over his face.

"Dad said you were helpful, and not just as a gofer." Whisper grinned and added, "He also said you didn't like coffee and traded your daily cup for future favors."

In the middle of taking a drink, Hartley coughed. "You what?"

"Yeah. I've always preferred tea, so I used my coffee allowance to rack up favors." Ish frowned, unhappy he had been outed, but it gave him a chance to ask something he had wondered about. Commander Fox followed the rules and Ish had bent that one almost to the breaking point. "Was your dad angry that I sort of played the system?"

"Dad thought it very enterprising of you. He said the others were fools for wanting coffee so bad that they traded favors for it."

When Hartley laughed, Ish joined in.

*****

"At least we get to hunt today," Ish said. The last few meals had been the ultra-healthy kurudi and very little meat. He thought the name brambles was much more descriptive. All brambles, regardless of color, had thorns. As far as he was concerned, it was a tossup as to whether picking them or eating them was the worse activity. It was a favorite dish among the Rapulii, who said the different colors of kurudi tasted different. So far, no human admitted to being able to taste the difference between the various types of brambles. In general, the humans agreed that brambles, while filling, tasted extremely bitter.

"Yeah, maybe we can find something besides brambles." Hartley said. "Why does the healthiest and most readily available food have to taste so bitter?"

The humans ate communally to save on rations, and everyone was expected to forage for plant food if they couldn't hunt. Soldiers and hunters augmented the rations with the occasional omuz or irhasi, herd animals that were quite tasty and large enough to feed many. The irhasi were herbivores, with boney plates on the shoulder and back, horns on the head and a long tail and neck, reminding the humans of dinosaurs. Omuz were similar to hogs on Old Earth and stood waist high with adult humans. Though smaller, omuz were aggressive and more dangerous than the irhasi. The Rapulii had warned the humans that omuz resisted all attempts to domesticate them. As the teenagers progressed in their studies with the Rapulii, they captured and killed the smaller ican, ilan, and kemi for meals. Even the younger kids knew how to forage for edible plants, and that was something Ish never thought would happen. The two young men moved further east from the human settlement, tracking minor game. Big game was hunted to the west, but smaller creatures and foraging for plants could be done anywhere. They reached a hill, made up of mostly rocks and boulders, that had become a favorite hunting ground for the humans searching for small game.

"So, let's talk about bartering. What's the best return you've gotten so far? You know, in exchange for your daily cup of joe."

"No contest. Ensign Botha helped me improve my proficiency with a bow and arrow."

"Nice. She's really good. Almost always brings in an omuz or irhasi. What's her secret?"

Ish didn't look at Hartley. He liked having an edge over his peers, but this wasn't about showing up a friend on a ball court. It was about survival. "It really is all in the stance. Watch." Putting his bow and arrow aside, Ish proceeded to demonstrate. "Practice with just your feet first. You need a shooting line."

"Shooting line?"

"Yeah. Botha used the straight lines in the gym for my training, but we can use..." Ish looked around and picked up one long fallen branch and two short ones. He quickly cut away the extra limbs and created a plus sign in front of Hartley. "The long line is the shooting line. Line up your feet, shoulder width apart. This is a closed stance."

"Yeah. I know. Next, you're going to show me an open stance, right? And you're going to tell me to stand up tall and look at the target before raising the bow."

"Yes, but I'm also going to show you what Botha showed me."

While Hartley practiced what he had been shown, Ish glanced at the hillside, riddled with caves. He always felt like he was being watched here, but no one would be in the caves. The caves were off limits because the Rapulii said there were dangers, including the chance that a Kurmii was lying in wait and would attack.

Once the mini lesson was over, Hartley said, "Come, fellow hunter, we must quest for food."

With a final glance at the caves, Ish laughed and followed.

111

"This looks like a good place for ilan." Hartley pointed to the imprints in the sand made by the ilan slithering across the ground. He moved in closer, holding his staff like a spear, planning to trap the creature's head so it couldn't bite. All ilan had a poisonous bite, but it would take multiple strikes to kill a healthy teenager or adult. While it might not be deadly, a single bite was painful and resulted in flu-like symptoms that could last for over a week.

Ish followed Hartley's lead. Working together, the boys pulled back the rock.

"Bosh." Hartley's curse echoed Ish's thoughts. They both jumped when they realized they had found not one ilan but a nest. They let the stone fall back into place, and the hunt was on as some of the ilan slithered away from the rock.

"Got one." Ish trapped one under his staff.

"Me too," Hartley said.

The boys chopped off the heads and skinned the ilans before placing them in their travel pouches. With a little effort, the boys killed seven more. Nine ilan to add to the dinner stew would be a good haul for the day, and they were both proud of the accomplishment.

Hartley tossed his pack on his back. "Let's head back to camp."

Ish nodded. Camp was the name given to the communal eating and meeting area for the humans. Excluding homes, no structures had been built for human use. The ship was still the location of all closed-door meetings held by their leaders.

As the boys approached the camp, another hunting party approached from the open fields to the west. They carried an omuz.

Whisper left the hunters and ran up to them. "You won't believe it. I killed an omuz with an arrow. Okay, it took me three arrows, but Lieutenant Porter said I did well."

Hartley rolled his eyes.

"That's great," Ish said. He tried to keep the envy out of his voice but wasn't sure he succeeded. Her hunting and tracking skills far exceeded his, and everyone else's except for a few of the soldiers. Though Ish was good at plant identification, Whisper was always one step ahead of the survival learning curve the rest of the teenagers endured. No one would be impressed by the ilan when her omuz was carried into camp at the same time.

"What do you guys have?"

"Oh, just a few ilan to add to the stew." Ish shrugged.

"Nice. We'll have ilan tonight, and tomorrow we can eat omuz. We've all done well today." Whisper walked happily between the boys.

Ish shook his head. She was completely unaware that her kill lessened their accomplishment.

The guys dropped off the ilan with the cooks and joined Haven and Whisper. They watched the omuz being lowered into the pit to cook.

Haven looked over and smiled. "Can you believe Whisper took down an omuz? I show up with a few kemi, and she brings in a feast."

Whisper said, "You were supervising the younger kids as they foraged for plant food. I'm impressed you were able to hunt while doing that. And the guys found ilan, so we have that tonight as well. The omuz will have to cook for a full day before we can eat it."

"Gives us something to look forward to. You can hunt with me anytime." Porter patted Whisper's back.

Whisper beamed at the praise. Both girls watched the lieutenant walk away.

Ish also watched the lieutenant leave. Ish was happy for Whisper, but it would have been nice to have his contribution acknowledged. Besides, he wasn't sure why, but Ish didn't like the way Whisper stared after Porter.

*****

"Hey, Tobin. Where're you going?" Whisper caught up with the Rapulii on the bridge crossing over Remei Lake between the Rapulii buildings and the twin towering rock formations called Duvi. They had established a tentative friendship in the combined educational class.

"Just running an errand. I'm on my way to the Dogu."

"I've only been there once before. Can I come?" Whisper asked.

Tobin shrugged. "I'm not authorized to bring visitors into the building. Your dad has a position of power. You can get in with him. To be honest, there's not much to see, just offices."

Whisper nodded, a little disappointed. She had hoped for a more interesting visit if she tagged along without a camera. Maybe even get a peek at the babies. Then again, she couldn't bring visitors onto the ship, so it made sense that the Rapulii would have the same type of restrictions. "After your errand, we could gather food."

"Yes, I would enjoy that. I'll meet you at the Semelai." Tobin took off at a jog.

Whisper roamed around the arches, wondering if they were all named. So far, only a handful had been identified by name and they seemed to be landmarks more than anything else. Waiting for Tobin, she crossed the bridge again and sat at the base of Bench Rock, named by the humans. Soothing water surrounded her on three sides. Bench Rock was huge, with three nearly flat tiers where one could sit. It had become another hangout for the teenagers and juveniles. Or more accurately, teenagers and female juveniles. None of the male juveniles had joined to chat, so far. Not that they were around much. She assumed they were raised apart since they didn't study with the females. For now, Whisper was alone. Considering the hour, most of the humans would have chores to complete before they could meet up. She had been up early for target practice with her dad, and her tasks were done.

Whisper looked across the lake to where the Sargu lived. Movement caught her eye. She pulled out her data pad and zoomed in, using it as a binocular. Zigmin was fighting with two Sargu adults. Lightning and wind encircled all three. When the two adults, working together knocked Zigmin into the hillside, Whisper jumped off the rock and ran across the bridge. She ran past the Dogu and the dormitories where the non-Sargu reds lived. She stopped at the base of the Sky Arch, the largest arch in the valley, and stood beside Zigmin. "Stop."

Zigmin turned a confused face toward the human. "Are you windblown?" The adult Sargu looked equally confused.

Whisper blushed as she realized she wasn't stopping a fight. It was a training session. One of the Sargu was Kimrin. "Sorry. I thought... er, I thought..."

"You thought I was being attacked, and you came to help?" Zigmin's skin flashed iridescently, and her face contorted into a snarl. "Think you that I'm weak!"

"Whisper, why interfere?" Kimrin asked, effectively cutting off Zigmin's anger. "Even if it were a fight, it would be an internal Sargu matter."

Blush deepening, Whisper said, "I'm sorry if I broke your laws, but when humans see two people attack another, we tend to step in. Helping the underdog and all that."

The other adult cocked her head to one side. "What is underdog?"

"When outnumbered or weaker than her opponent, that person is an underdog?" Whisper turned to Zigmin. "I don't mean that you're weak, but when two adults attack a juvenile, most humans will run to help."

"You came to help me? What would you have done to be of assistance?" Zigmin's anger gave way to curiosity.

"I'm not sure. I didn't think that far ahead," Whisper admitted.

"You should. We Sargu are powerful. It would be deadly for you to interfere with a real fight amongst Sargu, even if one is a juvenile."

"Zigmin is right. You would have died if this had not been a training battle. We will cease training for today. I am Figlin." She bowed to Whisper. "You are a brave, but foolish, juvenile. This protective instinct among humans is interesting. Kimrin, why did you not mention it?"

"I answer only to Shimgin." Zigmin straightened her back and jutted out her chin.

Figlin wasn't intimidated by the display. She grinned and left. Snarling, Kimrin also departed.

Zigmin turned on Whisper. "You are windblown. If you had been killed, it would have caused problems between the Sargu and the humans. You don't want that."

"I don't want problems between our people or my death," Whisper agreed. "Do Sargu always refer to themselves as Sargu and not reds?"

"Of course, we are Sargu. Until humans arrived, we used the terms techs and warriors, not blues and greens. Only the non-Sargu reds were identified using color."

Whisper blushed. Humans really needed to improve their interspecies relationship skills. She looked across the lake. Squinting in the sun, Whisper saw Tobin looking for her. "I gotta go. Tobin and I are going to search for food. Wanna come?"

Zigmin shook her head. "No, I have tasks to attend."

"Okay, bye." Whisper left at a jog.

"Bye," Zigmin said. She watched them. The Sargu didn't have friends, not even among other Sargu. If Zigmin allowed anyone to get close, that person would stand the best chance of killing her or being the tool another Sargu would use to control or destroy her.

Zigmin watched Whisper say something. Tobin laughed. Zigmin remembered the trip when Ish talked with her in such a manner. Zigmin watched them until they were out of sight. Even with the danger involved, a friend might be nice.

*****

"I can't believe you stepped into a training fight between Sargu." Tobin added brambles to her pack that also included ican and ilan.

"I didn't realize they were training." Whisper regretted telling Tobin. If this story got back to the camp, it would make the rounds, and she would never hear the end of it.

"You're obviously windblown."

"Uh?" It was the second time today someone called her windblown.

"Windblown. Haven," Tobin tried and failed to hide her smile at the name, "said it meant balky."

"Aha, I see. No, I'm not windblown, at least not about this," Whisper amended. "If you saw two Sargu attacking Zigmin, would you try to help?"

"What could I do against lightning and wind?" Tobin asked.

"There is that." Whisper peered into Tobin's pack when she added more brambles into a full pouch. "I thought you hunted only for yourself?"

"I do, but since humans gather for all, I thought I would give some to you for your community pot and maybe take some to Nufen." Tobin's skin lightened a little.

Whisper stared. She thought only the Sargu had skin that flashed iridescently. There was still so much to learn about their new neighbors. "Nufen? Is he your friend? Do you, I don't know, like him?"

"Like him? You really are windblown. Why would I like Nufen? I owe him a favor. This seems like a good way to repay him."

Whisper smiled. Tobin protested rather strongly. Since she didn't know anything about Rapulii courtship, Whisper remained silent.

Chapter 11

"Ishmael? I know you came this way. Where are you?" Whisper's voice echoed around the arches.

"Hiding from you, oh great hunter," Ish muttered. Once again, Whisper had brought down the main meat dish for the next day's meal, not that anyone was keeping score. Well, no one but him, Hartley, and well, everyone. He knew he shouldn't be jealous, but he was. Ish moved further into a series of arches around this set of caves. Everyone knew he hated his name and preferred to be called Ish. He suspected she did it to annoy him. Ish had noticed she only slipped when she was peeved with him.

"Come on, Ishmael. I saw you come this way."

Ish ducked into one of the caves. They had been warned not to enter any cave since the Kurmii lived in caves and they were killers. At least that's what the Rapulii said, but Ish hadn't seen anything like a Kurmii in the caves. Of course, so far, he had only gone just inside the entrance of the few he had checked out.

Ish activated the light on his wrist device and panned around the cave entrance. Though normally used to access data, the device also served as a light and video recording device, and so on. He pulled up the 3-D map and wasn't surprised that all he got was a view of the topography above the cave.

The cave itself was relatively small, and he moved to the left where an indention indicated there might be a path deeper into the cave. It was also cooler in the cave, a welcome respite from the heat of the Kurazi sun and the sand blowing in the wind. After checking the area, Ish turned off his light and waited in the dark. He could see the cave entrance and would know when Whisper arrived and when she left.

"Ishmael, I just wanted to talk," Whisper said from the cave entrance. "Fine, enjoy your solitude. I'm sure you already know all and don't need the information I was going to share with you." She walked into the sun and disappeared down the path through the arches.

Why did her comment make him feel petty? Ish waited for a few minutes before he turned his light back on. When he did, he screamed. Or would have if a Rapulii male hadn't covered his mouth to keep the scream quiet.

"No harm."

Ish took a good look. The male was not yet an adult, or he was a very young adult, but he was more muscular than any red Ish had seen. Not as big as a green, but definitely more muscular than any red, and most of the blues, in the village. "You speak?" The question wasn't as odd as it sounded. Ish had only seen a couple of males speak. While he assumed the others did, he thought there was perhaps a taboo against males speaking in public. Of course, they weren't in public, were they?

The red grinned. "Don't you?"

"Yeah, stupid question." Ish stood up. "So, why hide here?"

The red stood tall but was about Ish's height. "Who says I hide?"

"So, if I go out and tell everyone I saw a male Rapulii in these caves, you'd be fine with that? They'd be fine with that?"

"No tell."

"That's what I thought. Who you hidin' from?" When the red didn't answer, Ish changed tactics. "I'm Ish."

"You're Ishmael. I listen."

"If we're gonna be friends, call me Ish. What's your name?"

'No name."

"You gotta have a name, so I suspect you're not going to tell me your name?" Ish held up his hands. "What have you got to lose? If you keep me here, and I'm not sure you can, Mom and the soldiers will hunt for me."

The Rapulii glared at Ish, and said, "You think I'm weak?"

Ish rolled his eyes. "I think we are evenly matched, size wise. Unless you have skills superior to what I've observed in other red males, I give me a fifty-fifty chance in a fight, although Mom will be furious if I fight a Rapulii. Same thing if I'm not home by dinner. You don't want my mom, angry and searching this cave for me."

The Rapulii almost smiled. "I've heard the word mom used before. What is mom?"

"Our people have a mom and dad. Well, normally. My dad died when I was young. I know you guys are raised by the blues and don't know who your parents are. That's weird to me."

"Having a mom and dad is weird to me."

Ish grinned. "Yeah, I guess it would be."

"Lifen."

"Lifen, nice to meet you. So, do you know your way around this cave?"

Lifen grinned. "Come."

Surprised they were going deeper in the cave, Ish said, "I thought you guys didn't like the caves because of the lack of sunlight."

"Most don't. I have found ways around that."

"Really?" When Lifen didn't explain, Ish changed tactics. "So how do you speak Standard? I speak a little Rapulii, but I'm still learning. I'm at the baby talk stage." Ish was pleased that he could speak and keep up with Lifen's fast pace in unknown territory.

"I listen."

Ish nodded. Guess Lifen wasn't a big talker. He followed Lifen down the path deeper into the cave. Ish used his light at first but when it started to flicker Ish sighed. "Well, we better turn around. I need to recharge the batteries."

"Use this." Lifen pulled a glowing root from his pouch and handed it to Ish.

"Nice. How long does it last?"

"A fresh cut root will light the area for the entire planet rotation cycle."

Lifen took Ish to a cave room with a river.

"Wow. Does this feed Remei Lake?" Looking around Ish thought Weber would be happy to see the size of the underground river.

Lifen's eyes blinked fast. "It's flowing southeast, toward Incekis."

"Incekis? Long, thin lake that's dry part of the year?"

"Yes. How do you not know your location in relation to the planet?" Lifen asked.

"How do you know?" Ish crossed his arms in from of his chest.

Lifen tilted his head to one side. "The magnetic pull?"

"Huh? You saying you always know which direction true north is?"

"I do not know this true north. I feel the pull of the magnetic field on my world."

"All of your people can do that?"

Lifen huffed. Something all Rapulii did when explaining something they thought humans should already know. "Yes."

"Guess Mom didn't think I needed to know."

Lifen nodded his understanding. "Parents like Sargu. Tell only what they want others to know."

"Yep." Ish checked the time. "I gotta go. If I'm late Mom will kill me."

"Maybe parents not so good."

"What?"

"Do parents frequently kill their offspring?"

Ish grinned. "It's an expression. She won't kill me for real, but I may wish I were dead if the lecture goes on too long."

"I think I understand. Your language is strange." Lifen jogged back to the entrance with Ish. "You may visit again."

"I'd like that. Later." Ish checked to make sure no one saw him leave the cave and then he took off at a run, already planning his next visit to see Lifen.

"Later," Lifen repeated, wishing he could run outside in the warmth of the daylight. He climbed to one of the higher cave entrances and spread out on a ledge where he basked in the sun, safe from prying eyes.

*****

"The back entrance is great," Ish said.

Lifen grinned when his friend approached. "Did she follow you again?"

"Yeah. Whisper knows something's up and she's determined to find the truth. Too bad she's a stickler for the rules. She's wicked good with weapons and fun to be around."

"You sure she would tell?"

"She would feel it was her responsibility to tell her father. He's our chief of security."

That doesn't sound good."

"It's not. By the way, I did some checking. The Rapulii think you're dead."

The grin dropped from Lifen's face.

"I had to talk fast, too. Zigmin demanded to know how I knew about you. I said I overheard something about a young Rapulii red who went missing and was curious."

"Why do you care?"

"Come on. You never talk about why you live here in the cave. You never speak of anything except the present. What's the deal?"

"The deal?"

"Why are you here?"

Lifen shook his head. "Just am. And I'm moving. Don't look for me again." He turned and took the left fork in the cave, moving swiftly. He should have known better than to trust anyone, especially someone not of his world. Although, Ish seemed kinder than the Rapulii. It had been nice to have a friend who could tell him what the Rapulii were doing.

"Wait up." Ish jogged to catch up. "You think you can make a statement like that and I'll leave? Man, you don't know much about friends, do you?"

Lifen stopped walking and faced Ish. "I don't have friends."

"What?" Ish scratched his head. "I won't tell. Promise, but you need to explain why."

"No, I don't." Lifen moved down the passageway again, this time at a jog. He should have known better. While Lifen had an understanding with those he saw occasionally, he never spent more than two-three days with them at a time. He had spent way too long in these caves, because he enjoyed talking with Ish and hearing what was going on in the Rapulii village.

"Wait up." Ish threw up his hands in defeat. "Fine. Don't tell me, but don't leave. You're the first Rapulii friend I've made. The males don't talk much. Neither do the females for that matter."

"They say what Shimgin allows."

Ish raised an eyebrow. "Shimgin is a dictator? Makes sense. Even I've noticed when she's around no one speaks unless she nods at them."

"So, you promise you won't tell? If Shimgin finds out I'm alive, she'll kill me for real, not that non-lethal death by lecture your mom seems to be fond of."

"I won't tell. You gonna explain why Shimgin wants you dead?"

"Maybe one day."

Ish would have slapped Lifen on the back, but he moved aside. Ish had noticed that the Rapulii continually moved to stay out of range of any touch. Maybe it was a Rapulii taboo he didn't know about. Shrugging, Ish said, "That's good enough for now, but one day I want the truth."

Lifen shrugged.

"I don't have a lot of time. I came to tell you my class is taking another field trip. I'll be gone for a few days. Kimrin is taking the class into the mountains. We're going to camp somewhere off the Yolzi Pass."

Lifen's eyes widened. "Be careful. Many accidents happen there."

"We'll have Kimrin and three greens with us. The Bugii and Kurmii won't harm us. We'll be fine. Gotta go."

Lifen watched Ish leave. His friend worried about the wrong species. The ones watching the class were the ones to be afraid of. Lifen went to a part of the cave he hadn't shown Ish and gathered his meager belongings. It was time to travel.

Chapter 12

"Yolzi Pass again. I had hoped to see something new, a different trail or something." Ish wiped sweat off his forehead but didn't slow his jog. Zigmin led the way again. He had tried to keep the pace she set, but he had fallen behind and was now running with Whisper and Tobin. Hartley and Haven were further back with the others. At least the winds, hot as they were, helped remove the perspiration.

"We will. I heard Kimrin say we would camp further down the trail, on this side of Bentepe. The Bugii live on the other side," Tobin said. She and Whisper had developed a friendship and they were normally together.

"I hope to see the Bugii flying. Can you imagine the freedom?" Whisper looked up, but the sky was empty.

"Come. We're almost to the camp." Kimrin ran past the kids and caught up with Zigmin. Their conversation heated up quickly.

"Wonder what that's about?" Ish indicated Kimrin's discussion with Zigmin.

Tobin shook her head. "Nothing we want to know about. Sargu don't get along."

"Why? They're the same," Whisper said.

"Yes, they are Sargu. Born to rule. Other Sargu are competition. Shimgin has only recently allowed young Sargu to live," Tobin said.

Whisper shook her head. "Doesn't make sense. What about the older Sargu living in the settlement?"

"All are older than Shimgin. She defeated them all in combat and they bow to her will. Kimrin is the oldest of the new Sargu. Some say Shimgin grows weak. Others say it's a sign of Shimgin's power that she fears none. Not even Zigmin, who is expected to be the next ruler."

"She's that strong?" Ish asked.

"Yes. Have you noticed how Kimrin asks Zigmin to do things? The rest of us she orders, but not Zigmin. Even when she insults Zigmin, Kimrin is polite by Sargu standards. She knows Zigmin will rule one day unless there's an accident."

"Accident?" Ish repeated in the hopes Tobin would continue speaking. Lifen spoke of accidents, too.

"Many Sargu have strange accidents, normally when learning to use their powers." Tobin looked around, as if she were searching for something.

Ish looked around but didn't see anything. "Why are you nervous?"

"I'm not." Tobin's voice squeaked. "Maybe a little. The passage we just passed leads to Surasi. It's a water cave. I've heard the Kurmii are sometimes seen here."

Ish wasn't sure that was why Tobin was nervous, but he let it slide. "Excellent. It would be great to see both Bugii and Kurmii." Excited, Ish sped up and joined Zigmin when Kimrin left.

"Foolish male. He doesn't know what that means. To see Bugii and Kurmii could lead to war," Tobin said.

"He is foolish about some things, but in this I agree with him. I would like to meet Bugii and Kurmii, too. Either way, we should catch up with him." Whisper sped up and Tobin followed.

Once they reached the camp, Rapulii and humans went about the task of prepping the site. Sleeping under the stars was an exciting prospect and the kids laid out their rolls.

"What are they doing?" Whisper asked, pointing at the warriors.

Tobin looked in the direction Whisper pointed. "They spread territorial markers. The techs and warriors frequently travel here for minerals Shimgin and the other Sargu require. The markers keep the predators and herd animals away."

"How?"

"The animals have learned that when they see or smell those markers, they will be harmed if they come near. It is most effective."

"How about the Bugii or Kurmii?" Ish asked.

"Don't know. I've never seen either," Tobin admitted.

Ish turned to look at Tobin in surprise. "Seriously? You've never seen either species. How do you know they hate your people?"

"Shimgin told us. As have all of the previous Sargu leaders according to the elders."

Ish started to say something but Whisper shook her head slightly. For once Ish paid attention to her and didn't ask any more questions.

Later, when they were foraging for food, Ish caught up with Whisper alone. "Why did you warn me to not ask more questions?"

"Kimrin was listening. I don't know how the Rapulii react to anyone who questions their leaders."

"Good point. Thanks." Ish grabbed some kurudi branches. "I hope we find something else. This tastes awful." When he cut himself on the bramble, he growled and placed a seal over the cut. "I really hate these plants."

"I don't know how the Rapulii can stand to eat them," Whisper agreed.

Tobin joined them with some prepared kemi for the pot. "Great, you found pink kurudi. My favorite."

Whisper giggled when Ish rolled his eyes. They followed Tobin back to camp with their offerings for dinner. While they were adding their finds to the pot, Zigmin returned with five icans.

"Where did you find those?" Ish asked in appreciation. Ugly they might be, but ican would add some much-needed protein and flavor to the pot. They were good eating. Some of the humans called them rats but Ish didn't see the comparison. He thought they had more in common with the herd animals from Old Earth that he had only seen in vids. The only difference was the ican appearance. Each ican had two arms with claws that served as hands. The arms attached to the shoulder. The talons grasped and sliced with ease. An ican stood about 2 feet tall with four hooved feet on stubby legs. Horns ran from the skull to tail bone and varied in size. The reason most humans thought the ican was ugly was a protruding lower jaw that lifted up and covered the upper jaw with two small tusks rising up from the bottom jaws.

Zigmin added the icans she had skinned and prepped into the pot. "I hunt. I find."

"Cool. Maybe I'll hunt with you tomorrow," Ish said.

"If you think you can keep up, human." Zigmin turned and went to sit by herself.

Tobin said, "See. Sargu prefer to be alone."

Ish wasn't so sure about that. He watched Zigmin close her eyes. She could be meditating, but he had a feeling she was pretending so that it wouldn't look like she was lonely.

*****

Ish finished his morning chores and jogged over to Zigmin. "Where're we hunting today?"

Zigmin looked up in surprise.

Ish grinned. He noticed Zigmin's confusion when anyone approached her. He bet it was because she wasn't used to having friends. He planned to remedy that. "Told you yesterday I would hunt with you today."

"I doubt you can keep up." Zigmin's jaw clenched.

"Bet I can." Ish dropped into step beside her. "And if I can't, you can tell everyone how the weak human male couldn't keep up."

Zigmin narrowed her eyes on Ish. "Okay. Today we're going to find ilan."

"Great! They're even better than ican. Let's do this." Ish smiled. Ilans tasted great, but were hard to catch. The poisonous bite made most humans leery around the ilan. Still, he had hunted them before and felt secure in his ability.

Zigmin and Ish ran toward the Surasi. When they approached the cave entrance, Zigmin slowed. "I was told we would find ilan near the water inside. It's not too far inside the cave so we shouldn't encounter Kurmii."

Ish nodded and they both extended their hunting staffs and flipped them, so the two-pronged crook at the top could be used to trap ilan. Ish pulled his knife and opened the blade, prepared to kill enough ican to feed the group. He smiled when he saw Zigmin had pulled her hunting blade as well.

They entered the cave with their wrist lights on. As they moved further into the cave, Ish realized there would be no problem finding ilan. The ilan were everywhere. "This is bad."

Ilan rested on ledges of the wall. Some slithered on the ground.

"Yes, very bad. This is a nesting ground. We need to leave." Zigmin turned and stopped. Ilan had moved in behind them.

Ish calculated how many bites would be needed to kill him and shook his head. "I don't have a weapon for this."

"You don't need a weapon. You have me." Zigmin pocketed her knife and handed Ish her staff. She held out her hands and created lightning balls. The balls sputtered at first but became stronger. She unleashed one and ilan moved or burned. They walked a few feet, and she threw the second. More ilan moved or burned. Zigmin created two more lightning balls and they continued toward the cave entrance.

"You're doing great. Two more blasts and we'll be out of here." Ish used the staffs to bat away any ilan that got too close to their flank.

Zigmin grinned and created two more lightning balls. They sputtered but didn't become stronger. The lightning died in her hands.

Ish batted away another ilan. "What's wrong?"

"Used too much energy." Zigmin looked down at her hands. She tried again but the lightning didn't form into balls. It crackled for a second and dissipated. She looked around as ilan closed in around them.

A lightning ball hit the ground in front of them. "Run."

Zigmin seemed to be in shock and didn't move. Ish, recognizing the voice, grabbed Zigmin's arm, and ran as another lightning ball opened up a path for them. Once they were outside, Ish released her arm and turned to face the cave. He wasn't sure how long he waited, but Lifen didn't come out.

Neither did any ilan.

When he realized Zigmin was staring at him and not the cave entrance, he thought fast and asked, "Why didn't the ilan follow us? They do fine in the sun."

"Nesting cave. They are gathering to prepare for an ilan sphere, their time of mating."

"We interrupted an ilan orgy? *Eww.*" Ish tried to reenter the cave, but Zigmin stopped him.

Zigmin shook her head. "We can't go back in there. Who helped us?"

Ish kept his eyes on the cave entrance and feigned confusion. "A Sargu, right? Throwing lightning and all."

"No. That was a male's voice." Zigmin's voice was firm.

"A male can't be Sargu?"

"A few have been born, but they always die young. No male Sargu has ever lived to adulthood."

"Then you tell me. Who saved us?" Ish turned from the cave, faced Zigmin, and said, "I think we better say you did."

"Me? My powers failed. You can tell everyone how my lightning fizzled. It's what any Rapulii would do."

"You want to go back and tell them your powers failed and you think an unknown male Sargu threw lightning to save you. You sure about that?" Ish cocked his head to one side. "What would happen after that announcement?"

Zigmin hung her head. "I would be punished, maybe killed."

"Killed? I can see you being laughed at, but killed? No way."

"Yes, if the others found out a male saved me, they would laugh, and I would be exiled or killed. If exiled, it would be expected that I would die in short order. As a Sargu, I'm accustomed to others taking care of my needs while I study."

"So, my plan is a good one." Ish hoped she agreed so that Lifen would be safe. But boy did Lifen have some explaining to do.

"Why would you do this for me?" Zigmin asked.

"We're friends. Why wouldn't I?" Ish glanced at the cave again and asked, "Who told you the cave was a good place for ilan hunting?"

"Kimrin." Zigmin's eyes turned dark and her skin displayed iridescent shapes that shifted and moved as a Sargu's emotions changed.

"Then I think we better gather any ilan close to the entrance and serve them for dinner. Maybe she'll choke on it."

"Maybe she will." Zigmin's voice was guttural.

132

They approached the cave and found a stack of ilan prepped for the cooking pot.

"Thanks for the assist." Ish said into the cave. He grinned at Zigmin's confusion. "It only seems polite."

Zigmin looked at the prepared ilan and bowed toward the cave. "Thank you for your help and for preparing this feast." They loaded the ilan into their hunting packs and headed back to camp.

*****

Whisper served the last of the ilan and stew. "Maybe tomorrow we'll all go hunting for ilan. I can't believe you killed so many for our dinner."

"I don't recommend it." Ish accepted another slice, happy he was the one doing the biting. "If Zigmin hadn't been tossing lightning balls, I think the ilan would have eaten us for dinner. Lieutenant, you should mark that cave as off limits. Zigmin realized it was a nesting cave once we entered."

"I'm glad you both made it out of there. Zigmin, thank you for saving Ish."

"You're welcome." Zigmin repeated the phrase she had heard humans use when thanked for something. Her skin again flashed iridescent shapes which irritated her. It was something all Sargu did when embarrassed, at least until they learned to control their powers.

"I am most interested to hear how you tossed so many lightning balls in a row," Kimrin said.

"I suspect you are." Zigmin smiled showing teeth. Kimrin backed away.

Ish looked over and exchanged a smile with Zigmin.

When Ish was sure everyone was asleep, he crept out of camp and made his way back to the cave. The moon was full and huge in the sky, allowing him to see without using his wrist light. He took a moment to stare at the moon. Had he ever done that on Old Earth? Stepped outside at night and watched the moon? He couldn't remember. The scientist said it was twice the size of the moon orbiting Old Earth, but further away. It didn't look that large to him. Ish approached the cave but didn't go in. "You there?"

"Whom do you seek?"

Ish turned when Zigmin approached. "Why did you follow me?"

"I'm not windblown. What you did protected me, but it also protected whoever helped us. You grabbed my arm and ran as soon as he called. You recognized his voice, didn't you?"

"Don't know what you're talking about." Ish felt the blush creep up his face.

"You humans show embarrassment as much as we Sargu do."

"Some of us do," Ish muttered. His fair skin made it impossible for him to hide embarrassment. Always had.

"I'm not going to turn him in. He did save my life. The three of us have something in common. Even though our reasons are different, none of us want the truth to get out. I'll leave, but if your friend is smart, he'll stay hidden. Spies are everywhere." Zigmin turned and left.

Before the moon fell below the mountains, Ish returned to his bedroll. He breathed a sigh of relief when he crawled into his bedroll with no one the wiser. Except for Zigmin, of course. Lifen had not shown up and that worried Ish. Did Lifen get bitten? Were Rapulii affected by the bite of an ilan?

"Where did you go?" Whisper kept her voice low.

Ish groaned. The females in this group were way too smart. "None of your business."

"I don't know what happened, but I know you and Zigmin are hiding something. So does Kimrin. Be careful."

"Yes, oh wise one." Ish didn't hide the irritation in his voice.

*****

134

Next morning Kimrin assigned Ish camp duty. The student on duty was responsible for cleaning the camp and prepping the fire for the food the others would bring back. While the others hunted, explored, and learned, he cleaned. At first, he was irritated, even though everyone had to take a turn with camp duty. As the morning continued, his irritation changed to humor. Even the umak, the five-pound flies of Kurazi, didn't bother him much. Ish found it odd that they hung around campfires, like the flies of Old Earth, looking for food. The size of the umak allowed them to carry off smaller creatures, and they could easily steal food off a plate, or out of a pot, if not stopped. He carefully checked the protective net over the pot each time he walked past.

Kimrin stoked the fire, adding more branches and leaves to increase the blaze.

Noticing the bright orange-red palm fronds, Ish objected. "Hey, aren't those kabu leaves? You can't burn them around humans." He took a breath and giggled.

Kimrin added a few more leaves to the fire. "Aha, yes. The fronds of the kabu tree relax humans much more than Rapulii."

"Yeah, Mom will not be happy if she finds out I inhaled this stuff." Ish giggled some more.

"Your mother need never know. The fire will die down soon, and we will never speak of it again." Kimrin smiled and moved closer to Ish. "Until it does, you should sit. Wouldn't want you to fall and injure yourself."

Ish giggled again and tripped. Shaking his head to sober up, he said, "Probably a good idea." He frowned when his words slurred.

Once Ish sat, Kimrin said, "Now you can tell me what really happened yesterday."

"Huh?" Ish tried to sit up and failed. This was trouble. He wasn't so drugged out on the leaves that he might tell Kimrin what happened, but he didn't trust her, and now he had two friends to protect. Ish breathed deep to clear his head and realized Kimrin had been stoking the fire the entire time. He breathed in more of the smoke and chuckled. "We told you, Zigmin to the rescue."

"Zigmin is too young, too new to her powers, to do what you said she did."

Ish used his staff to swat at a umak and tried to stop the giggle but it came out anyway. "She's powerful. No doubt about it."

Kimrin shook Ish. "Look at me. She. Couldn't. Do. It. What really happened?"

Giggling again, Ish grinned up into Kimrin's face. "If she didn't, then I guess it was me after all. A human male rescued a Sargu."

Kimrin released her grip and Ish fell to the ground. As she stomped off, Kimrin called over her shoulder. "Sober up. This camp better be clean when I return."

Ish didn't move from the position he had landed in, still giggling. His thoughts turned to Whisper-the-irritating. She was nearly a head shorter than he and a know-it-all who was better with weapons and hunting then he would ever be. She also had hair and eyes the color of chocolate, a pert little nose, and full lips that were kissable. Ish shook his head which made him dizzy. Apparently, the kabu leaves caused hallucinations. He lay there for a second, finally admitting to himself the feelings he had for Whisper. When did that happen? Ignoring his brain, he pulled himself up off the ground and tried to attend to his chores.

By the time the others returned from hunting, Ish was moving slowly and no longer giggling. If this was a hangover, he never wanted another one. At least he didn't black out. The only bright spot was he remembered everything and knew he didn't give Kimrin the information she desired.

"There are kabu leaves in the fire," Whisper hissed. "What did you do?"

"Nothing." Ish turned and threw more wood on the fire to hide the leaves. "Kimrin tried to trick me."

Tobin looked at the leaves and left.

Whisper snorted. "Looks to me like she was successful."

"Here, chew this." Tobin returned and handed Ish a root.

"What is it?"

"Cari. Not the leaves you humans like to brew and drink. This is the root. Chew it and you'll be better quicker."

Ish looked at Whisper, who shrugged. Knowing the root wasn't poisonous to humans, he bit into the root and only force of will kept him from spitting it out. Ish looked back at Tobin. "Thanks, but why is everything on this planet that's good for us taste bitter?"

"Bitter? Cari root is much better than the leaves," Tobin said in surprise.

"No, it's really not, but I do appreciate it. I'm already feeling less lightheaded." Ish walked away to tend the cooking fire, chewing on the root. When he passed Kimrin she looked shocked that he had the root. Ish grinned but didn't speak.

The grin dropped from Ish's face when Kimrin glared at Tobin. He had been intent on showing Kimrin that he could play her game, and win. Ish didn't think about the consequences to anyone who helped him.

Chapter 13

"Ish? You ready?" Zigmin stood before him ready to hunt.

Ish looked up and smiled. The Ilan Sphere Incident, as he thought of it, had cemented his friendship with Zigmin.

"What are you hunting today?" Whisper asked.

Ish frowned. What was Whisper up to?

Zigmin adjusted her pack. "Ican. Heading further south on Yolzi Pass."

"I heard there are irhasi further south. I'd love to see them. Can I join you?" Whisper smiled in expectation.

So that's her plan. Ish smiled back. "You're leaving Tobin to hunt alone?" The other Rapulii would not hunt with Zigmin. It seemed to be some type of pecking order thing.

Whisper shook her. "Tobin's on camp duty. If I don't go with you, I have to hunt alone."

Ish and Zigmin exchanged a look, before Zigmin said, "Come. Shimgin will be unhappy if we lose any humans."

Whisper glanced over at her friend tending the pot.

Zigmin followed Whisper's eyes, and added, "I warned Kimrin that Tobin was not to be harmed for giving Ish cari root. She was helping a human, as Shimgin commanded. I also mentioned that if Tobin is injured, I will tell the Sargu court that Kimrin was jealous of a non-Sargu."

Confused by her statement, Ish shrugged. He didn't really understand Rapulii customs, but perhaps he needed to address that particular gap in his knowledge. Ish glanced at Whisper and noticed her satisfied smile. Maybe he could ask her about Rapulii customs.

Zigmin ran at a fast pace, slowing when she reached an overlook. "From here we will see the irhasi if they are in this valley. Irhasi forage over great distances. We may not see them at all."

"We will. There they are." Ish pointed to the edge of the plains where the white-barked kabu grew. The leaves of the tree were a favorite food of the irhasi. A nice sized herd nibbled at the leaves, rearing up on their back legs to grab leaves higher up in the tree. Humans had been warned that burning the leaves caused inebriation, which Ish now knew firsthand. The Rapulii found it merely relaxing.

"I don't know much about irhasi, but they look nervous." Ish watched the way the herd moved back and forth. Here again Ish thought the humans got it wrong. Although the irhasi looked a little like a brachiosaurus on Old Earth with a long neck and a tail to match, that's where the comparison ended. Irhasi were small with shoulders that stood at an equal height to the average human, though the neck could extend much higher. Some type of hard shell ran from the shoulder to the backside. The tip of the tail had an oblong, rounded tip that was very useful for bashing things. Irhasi were plant eaters with a strong herd mentality. The more the lead irhasi moved the more nervous the herd became.

"Look." Zigmin pointed to three leri.

Equal in size to the irhasi, leri resembled a larger and beefier cat from Old Earth. Built more like a bear than a cat, the leri worked together, like wolves of Old Earth.

"Why are the leri herding the irhasi up this hill?" Whisper's voice trembled.

"Don't know. We better run." Ish turned to run down the other side of the hill, but Zigmin grabbed his arm.

"No. The caves. Irhasi won't enter the caves." Zigmin grabbed Whisper's arm as well and they ran.

Ish balked at the cave entrance. "Do you remember the last time we were in a cave?"

"Yes." Zigmin didn't look back as she led the way into the cave.

Ish followed her but turned his light in a wide arc. When he didn't see any ilan, he relaxed. A smile crossed his lips when he noticed Zigmin had done the same. "I didn't expect them to be so large." In the distance, Ish had thought the irhasi horse-like. Something a human could sit on the back of. Now that he was hiding from a stampeding herd of irhasi, they were bulky and dangerous looking.

Whisper turned to face the entrance and watched the irhasi race by. "I didn't expect to see them up close."

"Be careful what you ask of Nurita. She provides, but not always in the way you wish," Zigmin said.

Ish nodded "We have a saying. Be careful what you wish for, you just might get it."

"Exactly."

"So, Nurita is your goddess, right?" Ish asked.

"Yes."

"And Dotaru is your god. Which one rules? I have heard many Rapulii say, 'May Dotaru give you all that you deserve.'"

"Doesn't anyone read the daily Kurazi fact?" Whisper muttered.

Ish snorted. Every day a member of the command staff, normally Whisper's father, posted a new fact about the planet they were on. Many of the facts Whisper had suggested of late, based on her conversations with Tobin. "Just you."

Whisper released a sigh of long suffering. "Nurita is the goddess of the sun. Dotaru is the god of the moon. He rules

140

the underworld. It's a curse, not a blessing. If you want a blessing, try 'May Nurita nurture you.'"

"That makes sense." Ish nodded. As the last of the herd went by, he asked, "Will the leri enter the cave?"

"They could, but we interrupted their hunt. They will continue after the irhasi and ignore us. The irhasi will feed them longer." Zigmin's voice was uninterested as she moved in a circle checking out the cave.

Ish grabbed Zigmin's arm and turned her to face the entrance. "Explain it to the leri." Two leri sniffed at the cave entrance.

As one, the three kids backed up. Zigmin took a deep breath and said, "A staff to the eye is about all that will stop them. Aim true if you must throw your staff. Your knives are not long enough to reach a vital organ before they sink teeth and claws into you."

"No worries." Whisper unzipped her jacket and pulled a gun out of its holster and took a solid stance. "Dad prepared me."

"I need one of those," Ish said. Whisper's Dad teaches her to shoot and gives her a weapon. Even though he qualified with every hand-held weapon in the Scorpius's arsenal, all his Mom did was lecture about protocol. That needed to change.

Whisper grinned at Ish's statement. "I'll take the one on the right."

"I've got the left." Zigmin had dropped her staff and now had a lightning ball crackling in each hand. "Aim to scare them off. No reason to kill."

"Agreed." Whisper turned off the safety and settled her stance.

Ish did the only thing he could do. With his staff in his right hand, he picked up the two staffs the girls dropped with his left. He settled his stance, prepared to throw the staffs if needed. In other words, he stood there like a worthless dolt.

Zigmin's lightning ball landed in front of the leri on the left. It jumped back but didn't leave. The same thing happened when Whisper fired her weapon. Both leri continued to advance.

"Forget scaring them. Aim true," Whisper said. She fired again and the laser curved at the last second. She glared at her weapon. Laser fire didn't behave in that manner. "What was that?"

Zigmin's lightning also curved away from her target. "A Sargu is using wind to protect the leri. They're savasleri." Zigmin created a large lightning ball between her two hands and she sent it toward the cave entrance with all of her strength. The lightning continued on its course this time as Zigmin added her own wind to the trajectory. Her strength wavered. The lightning flew straight up, hitting the cave ceiling resulting in a cave in.

Ish pulled both females back as rocks and debris rained down upon them. He pushed them further into the cave away from the falling rocks. Once the cave-in stopped, and the three quit coughing, Ish said, "I get the feeling someone is trying to kill us."

"Not us. Me. Many juvenile Sargu die while learning to control their powers. I have been expecting an attack for some time. If I died out here, no one would be surprised. I didn't think they would be willing to kill two humans just to kill me."

"I am not collateral damage," Ish said.

Whisper looked around, and said, "You sure about that? We look like acceptable losses to me."

"What is collateral damage? Acceptable losses?" Zigmin asked.

"Both phrases mean the same thing. Removal of anyone who interferes with the successful completion of the mission," Whisper explained.

"Then, yes, you are collateral damage." Zigmin frowned. "I wonder if Shimgin ordered my death or if Kimrin is making a power play?"

Ish scratched his head. "That's it? No anger, just curiosity?"

Shimgin shrugged as she had observed the humans do from time to time. "I am Sargu. I am the most powerful of the young Sargu. Anyone who views me as a threat will plan to kill me before I replace her. It's a compliment."

"No. Attempted murder is many things, but compliment is not one of them." Ish pulled up his arm to turn on his holowatch. Nothing happened. He checked a few of the functions and found that simple functions — lights and data stored on his device — worked, but the same could not be said for communications. His holowatch wouldn't be useful now. He looked over at Whisper. "My comm's busted. Will yours cut through this rock or do we have to dig our way out?"

Whisper wiped dirt off her face and checked her wrist. "No signal. We dig."

"I was really hoping your comm would work." Ish moved to the cave-in and reached for a rock.

"Not there." Shimgin blocked his path.

"Why? It's as good as any."

"A Sargu might be waiting to finish the job if we come out this cave entrance. We need to look for an alternate exit."

"What about the Kurmii?" Whisper asked.

"I'm not sure they would be worse than the Sargu, present company excluded," Ish said. When he saw Zigmin's confused expression, he added, "That was a compliment."

"Interesting." Zigmin waved her light around as did Ish and Whisper. All three found the passage at the same time.

Whisper's expression brightened. "Hopefully, this opens to the pass."

"It goes in the opposite direction." Zigmin walked toward the trail.

Ish nodded. "Rapulii, and the true north thing. Handy trick that."

"You know? We were told not to tell humans." Zigmin followed Ish over the skinny ledge with its sheer drop, impressed that he was unconcerned. "Aha, your helpful friend."

"What friend?" Whisper peered over the side of the sheer drop and immediately hugged the wall. She had always been nervous about heights.

"Doesn't matter." Ish reached the end of the narrow ledge and stopped to wait on the others. His eyes cut to Zigmin warning her to be quiet.

Zigmin moved past him. "I'll lead. Both of you cut off your lights to conserve power. It may take a while to find a suitable exit and return to camp."

"What's the difference between leri and savasleri?" Whisper asked.

"Something else we were ordered not to tell humans," Zigmin said.

"Who gave that order?" Ish stopped to fill his canteen with water from a small waterfall.

Zigmin and Whisper followed suit, leaning over the water with their canteens. "Shimgin. She wants humans to be unaware of certain facts."

"What facts about the leri do we not know?" Ish asked. "I'm pretty sure we need to know now."

Canteens filled, Zigmin continued deeper into the cave. "Some leri, called savasleri, are bonded to a Sargu and obey only that Sargu."

"So, savasleri are guard dogs," Whisper said.

"Big, powerful, guard dogs. I suppose savasleri are trained to kill," Ish said.

Zigmin nodded. "Always. They will not contain a threat if sent by their master. Savasleri kill. They eat what they kill so it is not uncommon for the missing to never be found."

They were silent for a while, moving through the cave, climbing obstacles that couldn't be avoided. Some areas were so small they had to crawl. Spelunking through the cave was hard work, especially since Zigmin had to stop frequently to shine her light on an obstacle as a warning to the others.

During a break, relaxing on a rock, Whisper looked at the underground stream. The path followed the stream. "At least we won't run out of water."

Zigmin shook her wrist when the light flickered. "It's time for someone else to lead."

"That would be me." Ish moved to the front and turned on his light. While in the lead, he kept his eyes peeled for the root that could light their way but didn't find any. He should have asked Lifen where it grew and how to find it. Now that he thought about it, the odds were small that the root grew in a cave at all.

Whisper brought up the rear. When Zigmin stumbled for the third time, Whisper stopped moving. "We need to take a rest break."

"Why?" Zigmin asked.

Whisper stood her ground and chose her words carefully, knowing the Sargu would not appreciate being called weak, but understanding that without the sun, Zigmin grew weaker with every step. "Basic survival. We have no clue how long we'll be walking and what we'll find when we get out of this cave. We need to take regular rest breaks."

Before Zigmin could argue, Ish said, "She's right. Her dad's our chief of security. We should listen."

Zigmin nodded. "I attended the lectures of your Commander Fox. Though male, his words have value. Okay, we rest, but we rotate guard duty."

"Agreed. Two-hour shifts. I'm up first," Whisper went to a rock where she could see both directions of the trail without moving her head and got comfortable. Ish and Zigmin tried to get comfortable on the ground.

Ish groaned when Whisper woke him. He rubbed the sleep from his eyes and asked, "Two hours already?"

"Yep. All quiet. Nothing to report. Dad said you qualified with this weapon. Don't shoot me, 'k?" Whisper handed him the weapon, dropped to the ground where Ish had been. She fell asleep immediately.

Ish shook his head. Whisper even slept on command. He palmed the gun, checked the safety, and walked over to the same rock where Whisper performed sentinel duty.

At the first soft clunk, Ish cursed his imagination. The shuffling sound that followed forced him to acknowledge something else was in the cave. While inching along the wall toward the sound, weapon at the ready, he wondered what nest he was walking into now, ilan or leri, maybe even kemi. Ish rounded a curve and came face to face... with Lifen.

"Man, am I glad to see you," Ish whispered, lowering his weapon, and dropping the light below Lifen's eyes. "How did you know?"

Lifen kept his voice low as well. "I've been watching. I saw Kimrin unleash her leri on you earlier. Once the area caved in, I knew your only hope was to find the other exit from this cave. I know these caves, but it took me some time to get here."

"You mean savasleri, don't you?"

"Yes, well trained by their Sargu mistress."

"Speaking of Sargu. Got anything to tell me, friend?"

"Are you going to introduce us now?" Whisper asked. Zigmin stood beside her.

Lifen dropped into a fighting stance and created lightning.

Zigmin held her hands out to show she hadn't created lightning. "We both know I owe you my life. No harm to you."

146

Lifen didn't move and didn't drop his lightning. "I've never trusted the word of a Sargu before."

"Neither have I," Zigmin replied indicating his lightning balls. "We have much to discuss, you and I."

After watching Zigmin for a few seconds, Lifen released his lightning. "Perhaps we do."

"Now that that's settled, I'm hoping you know the way out of here and perhaps know where we can get food. I'm Whisper, and you are…"

Lifen's skin displayed iridescent shapes similar to, but not a match for, Zigmin's. "Lifen. I should warn you that Shimgin ordered my death, and Kimrin believes she executed that order. If they learn I'm alive and that you know of me, they will kill you to keep that secret."

Ish waved his light around to show the cave walls. "Thanks for the honesty, but I'm pretty sure we're already on the kill list."

"True." Lifen turned to Zigmin and said, "I know a way out, but we will exit in Bugii territory. They allow me passage because I have agreed to their laws. You will have to make the same agreement, or they will kill you."

"If they can." Zigmin stood tall.

"They can. Unless you throw focused lightning from a distance when they are unaware of your presence, the Bugii can kill you."

"What? That's not what the records say."

"No, but it is truth." Lifen's voice was firm.

"Has any of my training been truthful?" Zigmin whispered, mostly to herself.

Lifen answered anyway. "Not much. Your training in the use of powers is not complete either."

Lifen's response held an openness Zigmin had never heard from a Sargu before. She watched him, wondering what else he could teach her.

"I'll take the last watch. I need each of you rested for the trip out of here." Lifen herded them back to the area where they had been sleeping.

"What about you?" Whisper asked.

"I sleep in small bursts. I'm rested enough to guard you while you sleep and lead you out of here."

Zigmin settled in beside the humans. Once she heard their steady breathing, she walked back to Lifen and asked, "How have you learned to control your powers? I know Shimgin didn't train you."

Lifen shrugged. "Hardly. Others are more generous with their knowledge than the Rapulii."

"You mean the Bugii?" Zigmin asked. When Lifen didn't respond, her eyes widened, and her skin flashed iridescent again. "You can't mean the Kurmii." Still he didn't speak. She stared at the fire for a while and finally asked, "Will you teach me?"

Lifen eyed Zigmin. "I would know you better before I give you knowledge you could use against me. Know this, you have great power within you. You need to decide how you will use it."

Zigmin nodded. She wasn't surprised he didn't trust her. Giving voice to what she was truly concerned about, she asked, "Have you ever met a nice Sargu?"

Lifen sighed and shook his head.

"I was afraid of that." Zigmin walked away and laid down away from the others. Sleep did not come easily.

Lifen guarded the others and listened for danger. Mostly he watched Zigmin pretend to sleep.

Chapter 14

Whisper smelled the feast before she opened her eyes to a delightful sight, kemi roasting on the fire. She watched the smoke twirl upwards and out a vent of sorts. She hadn't noticed the vent earlier. "Won't the smoke give us away?"

"No." Lifen followed Whisper's eyes. "The fissure does not go outside but to an upper level of this cave. The Kurmii or Bugii might see it, but they know we are here. Our fire will not draw unwanted attention."

"You're handy to have around." Whisper joined the others and grabbed a bramble off the fire and bit into the roasted kemi stuck on one end. "Thanks."

"I thought this trip was to train you to feed and protect yourselves." Lifen's voice held a teasing quality as he selected his own bramble.

"As you said last night, we haven't received proper training." Zigmin finished eating the bramble once her kemi was consumed. She noticed that Whisper picked her kemi off the bramble. "You don't like the taste of bramble?"

Whisper blushed when she noticed Zigmin watching in confusion as she bit around the bramble. "It won't hurt us to eat it. In fact, the bramble is beneficial to us, but brambles taste bitter to humans."

Zigmin's gaze went from her bramble to Ish and Whisper. "Roasted over the fire gives it a wonderful flavor."

"Not really," Ish retorted.

Whisper held up her hands in surrender. "Dad says brambles are very healthy, and we need to get over the fact that we don't like the taste since it's one of the most readily available food sources. This one bramble provides many of the nutrients we humans need every day."

"Yeah, but your dad considers chocolate a waste of calories. His taste buds died long before we left Old Earth." Ish made a face but bit into the bramble.

Whisper nodded her agreement and bit into her own bramble. Munching slowly, her face screwed up in a pucker. Too bad this planet didn't have a natural sweetener that grew in large quantities. Some form of sugar would surely help the taste.

Once they finished their meal, they cleaned up the area, Lifen handed out glow roots.

"Great, you found some. I've looked but didn't see any." Ish took his root and waved it around.

Zigmin glared at the root and back at Lifen. "How did you learn of this?"

"As we discussed last night, the Bugii and Kurmii."

Whisper looked at her root and asked, "Are the Kurmii more intelligent than we've been told? Dad studied them extensively, and he thinks they are."

Lifen didn't speak. When he picked up the pace, Whisper grabbed his arm and immediately flew into the wall.

"Watch it!" Ish moved around Lifen to check on Whisper.

Lifen backed away from the others. "Never touch me or sneak up on me. Not even to save me. When I was still with the Sargu, they only touched me to beat me. It became a defensive reaction. I can't control it."

Whisper stood up with Ish's help. "It's okay. I'm alright." She punched Ish and said, "Stop glaring at him. Lifen didn't mean it."

"Why can't you control?" Ish asked. "You have a lot of control over your powers in all other aspects. If you trust us, you should be able to control this. You don't want to go through life without ever being touched."

"Who says I trust you?" Lifen moved down the path at a fast clip.

Zigmin rushed to catch up, careful not to touch him. "If you don't, why help us?"

"You need help. I won't leave someone else to die the way I was left, but that doesn't mean we're friends."

"I guess we should be grateful for your protection."

Lifen faced Zigmin, and said, "Yes. You should be." He turned and scrambled over some rocks. "We're near the exit. Just remember, these Bugii are friendly."

Zigmin slowed and motioned for the others to move in front of her.

When she saw sunlight, Whisper released a breath she didn't realize she had been holding. Once outside, she looked up at the sky and gasped. Bugii were everywhere. Young Bugii flew in the air playing some type of game. Others sat near the water, working, and preparing food with the adults. Erkek, the four-legged reptilian dog-like creature the Bugii had also tamed to carry for them, moved as directed by chirps and clicks. The line of horns on the head and back of the erkek provided protection from leri attack.

"I've seen vids, but it looks different in person." Ish bumped into Whisper because he was looking up instead of where he was going. He grabbed her to keep her upright but neither paid attention. The sight was amazing. The Bugii were bipedal with two arms. Two huge wings spread out from the back of the Bugii's shoulders. Minus the feathers, wings, and beak, the Bugii would be fairly human looking or at least as human looking as the Rapulii.

Zigmin pointed to the Bugii flying toward them. "What do we do?"

Lifen raised his hands out to his side, proving he had no weapons, and that he had not created lightning. The others followed suit.

A raven feathered female, carried by two males, landed in front of the teenagers. The males were younger, and they had the appearance of warriors of some type. Ish noticed the older female's feathers were thinning and wondered if she was old. For all he knew, it was molting season or something. Did Bugii molt?

"Sulka, you honor us." Lifen bowed. Though Ish and Whisper were quick to follow his movements, Zigmin didn't move at all until Lifen huffed. Then Zigmin nodded and bowed as well.

"Are these the ones you hoped to save from the Sargu?"

"That one is a Sargu." A male raven, who looked to be about the same age as Lifen, landed beside Sulka as he spoke. His blue feathers were twice as thick as Sulka's.

"So am I, Opalo." Lifen's voice was calm, but his eyes darkened, and his skin flashed iridescence.

"No insult. A statement. I won't allow a Sargu to send lightning balls at Sulka."

Sulka smiled. "I'm not unable to care for myself."

Opalo flapped his wings a few times, sending gusts toward the four travelers. Lifen braced but the others barely remained upright. "You have attained an age where others should do for you."

"Yes, I have, but old doesn't mean weak." Sulka flapped her one good wing once and blew them into the cave wall, including Opalo. She raised her voice and added, "These juveniles shall spend the night with me. Let this generation of outsiders see the Bugii for who we really are."

Zigmin looked at Lifen wondering what that meant. Lifen shrugged.

"Er, we need to get home," Whisper said. She had been pleased that the Bugii spoke the Rapulii language and was able to follow the conversation, but she had more immediate concerns. Surely the cave-in had been reported. Her father would demand to inspect the area and bring equipment to clear it up. Maybe they should have stayed there.

Sulka tilted her head to one side. "You are here. You will learn before you leave."

"Learn what?" Zigmin asked.

"That which you need to learn," Sulka said. She tucked her large wings into her back to make walking easier. Folded, the wings were nearly a foot above the height of her head. One wing hung at an odd angle.

Whisper watched everything, as she had been taught. First observation, the Bugii were thin. Made sense. Fat birds would not fly very well. She only saw red- and blue-feathered Bugii but knew there were a lot more colors. According to the Sargu, the other colors of feathers belonged to a subset of Bugii, called margu. The margu were extinct. Whisper had wondered how the multi-colored Bugii died out. The Sargu had many headdresses made from many colors of feathers, but birds were rare, and small, on this planet. The feathers on the Sargu headdresses were the same size feathers as those on the Bugii in front of her. She found that fact suspect.

*****

Ish accepted the bowl and watched the Bugii. Meals were silent experiences. Based on the number of Bugii present, meals were also communal. The juveniles delivered food to the old and visitors first, the adults second, fledglings third, and finally eating themselves. Ish wasn't sure if the Bugii always ate together or if they were doing so to keep an eye on the Sargu and humans.

"Why do the young erkek have their tails wrapped?" Ish asked.

Opalo followed Ish's eyes and laughed. "The young have to be trained to watch their tails or they slice everything."

"Slice?" Whisper asked.

"The tail horns are more spikes than horns. They draw blood easily." Lifen pulled up his pants leg and showed scars that formed a group of lines on his calf. The lines matched the pattern of horns on the unbound adult erkek. "That was one experience. I hope to never have another."

"The Rapulii have erkek without spikes on the tail. You should trade for some of theirs." Ish savored a bite of stew and smiled. Chewing the plants in the stew, Ish wondered why it didn't taste bitter. He looked over at Whisper and watched as she chewed and smiled. Obviously, she thought the stew was tasty as well.

"We feel no need to modify the erkek for our needs," Opalo said.

"Huh?"

"The Sargu remove the spikes from the tails of the erkek so that they do not hurt us." Zigmin took a bite of stew and frowned. "What is that taste?"

"It is from the milk of the irhasi," Lifen explained. "I didn't understand the taste at first. The Bugii say it is sweet, but I find it distasteful."

"They have milk?" Whisper asked.

"Humans will want to learn to milk the irhasi. This stuff is great." Ish smiled and stuffed his mouth with more stew.

Lifen grinned at the face Zigmin made. "It took me a while to accept the taste as well, but it won't harm us."

Zigmin looked back at her human friends. "They taste very differently than we do."

"So do the Kurmii and the Bugii. They seem to favor this sweet taste."

154

After the meal, Opalo flew up to Sulka's home and tossed a rope down. She lived in a cave on the side of a vertical cliff that was dotted with caves. Ish checked out the rock.

"Let's do this." Ish ignored the rope and moved to some handholds. He loved to free climb and was a fourth of the way up the cliff when he noticed Whisper was still looking at the rope. Ish quickly returned to her side. He remembered from their training on Old Earth that Whisper was a bit afraid of heights. "You got this."

Whisper nodded and grabbed the rope to start her ascent. Luckily, the climb was without incident. Lifen moved with the assurance of someone who had made the trip frequently, but Zigmin moved at a more sedate pace. Bugii flew below the climbers with a tightly woven net made of vines, ready to catch anyone who fell.

Sulka's home was nothing like Ish expected. It looked very similar to a human home, except it lacked a kitchen. The cave entrance was large and showed an open area for sleeping and another for working. There was a closed off room to the left, and he suspected it was for private business. There was a passage going further into the mountain. When some Bugii entered Sulka's home from that passage, Ish concluded that all the caves on the side of the mountain connected together.

Sulka spoke. "It's time you hear the tale of the Season of the West Winds."

Zigmin sputtered. "We know that story. Even the humans know it."

"No, child. You know the story told by the Sargu. Listen and learn what the Bugii young are taught."

Zigmin rolled her eyes, another expression she had learned from the humans. She dropped down beside Whisper and waited for the story.

Sulka got comfortable. "I'll start with the creation story. Nurita, goddess of the sun, and Dotaru, god of the moon, were happy for many seasons as they chased each other through the sky. One day Nurita, desiring progeny, created the Bugii to rule the air and the Rapulii to rule the ground. Dotaru, impressed by Nurita's creations, created the Kurmii. Dotaru gave his creation rule over the underground water and equipped the Kurmii to live in the caves.

"Over time the Rapulii settled into a matriarchal society for only the females can create life. The Bugii selected two co-leaders, one male, one female, and they ruled together as a united voice. The Kurmii also settled into a matriarchal society as the females produced life and communicated over longer distances due to their ability to create a lower frequency sound that carries further."

Zigmin huffed over the Kurmii communication statement. Whisper nudged her and Zigmin's body flushed with an iridescent blush.

Sulka's eyes lightened, but she made no comment. "At first, the three species lived in harmony. After many planet cycles around the sun, the three species began to argue, each one pushing their own laws on the other two. Nurita and Dotaru, tired of the constant bickering, separated the three species using the mountains to keep them away from each other. The Kurmii moved north by night and settled in the Kuzey water caves. The Bugii flew west and settled in the mountain caves of Bentepe. The Rapulii stayed at Remei Lake and settled into the hills around the arches. Eventually, the Rapulii built homes above ground. For many planet cycles, the three species didn't communicate, except for rare meetings in the Dialogue Hallow, a centrally located place where the leaders of the three species could meet."

Ish looked over at Lifen who shrugged. Back at the Rapulii settlement, Lifen had shown Ish many cave passages. One went to an open chamber that had statues representing the Rapulii, Bugii, and Kurmii. Ish had debated with himself the

156

value of telling his mother about the cave but didn't want to explain why he had been in the caves and who was showing him around.

"Incekis Lake, the Bugii primary water source, dries up for at least part of the Season of the West Winds. When the Bugii tried to access the Kuzey controlled underground waters, tensions between the two groups heightened. Eventually, the Bugii and Kurmii developed a trade agreement. In exchange for access to the Kuzey underground waters during the west winds, the Bugii provide the Kurmii with food during the shorter nights of the west winds when the sun stays longer in the sky." Sulka finished her story and watched Zigmin closely.

Zigmin shook her head. "I don't believe that. Kurmii are not intelligent. You can't have an agreement with them."

"Will you believe only what you are told by the Sargu?"

"I don't believe them either."

Sulka nodded. "Then there is hope for you. I meet with Kabrov, the leader of the Kurmii tonight. You will come. Meet her. See for yourself."

"She's not going alone." Ish stood. "We stay together."

Lifen also stood. "Sulka will not allow Zigmin to be harmed, but we should all go." Turning to Sulka, he added, "The humans will need to tell their leaders this truth."

"The human leaders are going to tear the mountains apart trying to find us," Whisper said.

Ish nodded.

"Right now, Kimrin or Shimgin is telling your parents that you guys are dead from the cave-in," Lifen said.

"We have to let them know we're okay." Whisper stood, ready to leave.

"It will take you three days to hike back to your ship alone if you can find your way without our help. Stay. We will help you on your journey, and you will be home by tomorrow night."

Ish stared at the red-feathered Bugii who spoke from the doorway. She commanded attention, much like his mother and Whisper's father.

Lifen bowed. "Lenta, co-leader of the Bugii, I present Zigmin, a Sargu juvenile like me, and the humans, Whisper and Ish."

Zigmin held her hands out to the side, showing there was no lightning, and bowed slightly.

"A pleasure," Whisper said, holding out her hand. When Lenta made no move to shake the proffered hand, Whisper blushed, and let her hand fall to her side.

"Nice to meet you." Ish followed Lifen's example and bowed.

Lenta inclined her head.

*****

Ish looked over the side of the cliff. "There's no Bugii waiting in case we fall. No safety net for the climb down?"

"We aren't climbing down. Not that you need anyone to protect you on the cliffs." Lifen tossed Ish his staff.

"How are we getting down?" Zigmin asked.

"Oh," Whisper grabbed her own staff and handed Zigmin hers. "These caves connect. They feed down to the underground caves of the Kurmii, don't they?"

"Yes. Now come. Sulka awaits." Lifen moved toward the back of the cave.

Whisper touched the smooth walls. "This isn't natural. The Bugii must have carved these connecting tunnels."

"You are partially correct." Sulka waved them over with her right wing. "All passages are natural, but over time we have enlarged them to make it easier for us to travel with our wings folded."

Whispering so that only the humans would hear her, Zigmin said, "We're heading north. Further away from Remei Lake, but closer to our base camp."

"Correct. A small group of Kurmii lives at the southern tip of the Surasi. They are our closest neighbors." Sulka spoke normally, and her voice echoed off the cave walls. "Even whispers carry in this area."

"Good to know," Zigmin muttered, irritated that she was caught being helpful. For Sargu, helpfulness was not encouraged. In fact, the opposite was true. The phrase, the smart Sargu will flourish while others perish, was popular for a reason.

The passage continued north as the elevation lowered. Hiking down the mountain, the travelers reached a fork. The left fork was dark, but the right fork was an exit into the sunlight. Assuming that was the way they would go, Zigmin moved ahead.

"No, we go left," Sulka said.

Ish scratched his head. "The right fork goes to sunlight. We'll be outside."

"Yes, and Kimrin might be looking for you," Opalo said. "Left we are protected from prying eyes."

"Explains why we never see Bugii hunting." Zigmin nodded her head as if puzzle pieces were falling into place.

"Yes. Forgive us for making it harder for the Sargu to kill us." Opalo spat the words.

"You blame the Sargu specifically. Not all Rapulii?" Whisper asked.

"Of course. The only Rapulii that can kill a Bugii without a weapon is a Sargu."

Zigmin glared at Opalo. "Rapulii have other weapons besides Sargu powers."

Opalo laughed. It was a shrill sound resembling a whistle. "Yes, but Sargu are the only ones who hunt us."

"Enough talk. We are near the meeting place," Sulka said.

"Any taboos we need to know about?" Ish asked.

"What is taboo?"

Whisper glanced at Ish before answering. "A taboo is something a culture doesn't approve of. For example, humans shake hands when they meet. Something the Bugii don't seem to do."

"Aha. Bugii don't shake hands because it is a common tactic of the Sargu to create lightning while shaking hands. It instantly kills a Bugii and appears to have no ill effects to a Sargu."

Zigmin's skin flashed iridescent again. "The punishment is death for a Sargu to do so."

"Perhaps that punishment only applies if the one killed is a Rapulii." Sulka's voice remained soft.

Zigmin didn't reply, but she thought Sulka might be right. Were all Sargu so evil? Would she have to become evil to survive?

Sulka led them into a large chamber with a lake. The lake was oblong and huge.

Whisper recorded the conversation, as she had throughout the trip. So far, no one had told her to turn off the device. Of course, it might be because they didn't know what the device did. Kurmii warriors stood in a loose formation around a central figure who was thinner and a bit shorter than the warriors, but not by much. The large and muscular warriors looked similar. All Kurmii had something akin to armor plating covering most of their bodies. Their face has the same plating covering the area where human eyes would be. The Kurmii were the strongest of the people of Kurazi. Whisper knew that the current hypothesis was that the Kurmii used some type of echolocation to see. Made sense, as the only light came from the Bugii and humans.

Sulka said, "Kabrov is in the center. Do not move to touch her in any manner, or her warriors will kill us. All of us." She glanced at Zigmin. "One day you may be able to kill this many Kurmii warriors before they kill you, but today is not that day."

Ish grinned. Was Sulka's statement a Bugii saying or had she learned it from listening to humans? If the latter, how had she been listening? He should remember to tell someone about that possibility.

Kabrov and Sulka exchanged a greeting, then Kabrov turned to Whisper. Lifen translated. "You may use your recording device. Your leaders must hear this conversation and know these truths."

Whisper blushed, surprised when Ish came to stand by her as if he was protecting her. As if. Her combat training was superior, but strangely enough, she appreciated his support.

Whisper tried to keep up with the conversation, but the meeting was tedious, and it was hard to stay focused. Good thing they allowed her to record their words. Lifen translated the clicks, chirps, and squeaks emitted by Kabrov. When Sulka talked, Whisper understood. After the first hour, Zigmin seemed to catch on and listened directly to Kabrov's speech, only occasionally turning to hear Lifen's translation.

When Kabrov turned and spoke to Zigmin, Whisper sat up a little straighter. Lifen moved closer to Zigmin's side though he continued to translate.

"What are your intentions?"

Zigmin's skin flashed iridescence. "I don't know. I have learned much this evening but must proceed with caution. The information you and Sulka have provided, if true, will change the Rapulii to our very core. Even the story of how we came to be will have to be rewritten."

"You don't believe?" Kabrov asked.

"Strangely enough, I do." Zigmin's eyes moved between Sulka and the Kurmii leader. "But if I'm to start a civil war amongst my people, I will be sure of my facts."

"Spoken like a true leader." Sulka nodded in approval.

"I do not lead the Rapulii." At least not yet.

"You will." Kabrov and Sulka replied in unison, but in separate languages.

Kabrov turned her eyeless face to the humans. "I will meet with this Captain Dolan of the humans. Bring him to me on the morning of the third sunrise. Do not tell Shimgin of this."

When Lifen translated, Whisper and Ish looked at each other.

Ish said, "We will tell Captain Dolan. I suspect he will want to meet with you as well." He looked expectantly at Lifen. When he didn't translate, Ish asked, "You gonna help me out? I don't speak Kurmii."

Lifen smiled at his friend. "The Kurmii can hear and understand your language as well as the Rapulii and Bugii languages. Their vocal cords can't make the proper sounds to reply in any language but their own."

"Oh." Ish blushed. "Captain Dolan will need a translator."

"I will come." Lifen performed a half-bow.

"Are you willing to be known now?" Ish asked.

"Doesn't matter. You will have to speak of me when you explain this journey. Shimgin will find out I'm alive."

"She'll kill you," Ish said.

"She'll try," Lifen agreed.

"I will stand with you." When everyone turned to Zigmin in surprise, she stood in a wide stance and said, "Nothing left for me to lose. I am outcast. I must learn a new way of living that include Bugii, Kurmii, and humans."

Sulka's feathers fluttered and her eyes brightened. "And we will help you."

Chapter 15

"You have failed." Shimgin didn't ask. Even with the low quality, long distance vid equipment her people possessed, it was obvious from Kimrin's stance in front of the vid and the hesitant tone of her voice that Zigmin was still alive. The humans were right. To have something done right the first time, do it yourself.

"Someone is helping them. Wind blocked the leri from entering the cave Zigmin and her human friends ran into. When I pushed Zigmin's lightning away, it caused some of the cave ceiling to fall."

Shimgin's skin flashed iridescent symbols, something that hadn't happened in many years. She needed control. Focusing on her body, Shimgin stopped the iridescent changes in her skin and asked the only question that mattered, "Which Sargu?"

"Unknown."

"Not acceptable." Shimgin pushed wind, fueled by anger, tossing a glass into the wall, shattering it. "Surely, you have some insight."

Nothing she wanted to share. Not surprised by Shimgin's expression of rage, Kimrin shook her head. If the Sargu was who she suspected, her life was forfeit, because Shimgin was right. Zigmin had help. The powers of the second Sargu felt familiar to Kimrin, but she hoped it wasn't him. Lifen should have died three years ago, as she reported to Shimgin at the time. Left near death at the base of Guntepe alone, the Bugii should have finished the male off or left him to die. That the Bugii would actively help an injured Rapulii was not something Kimrin had considered. It was, however, the only way Lifen could have recovered and survived.

"Zigmin tried to kill my savasleri, I pushed the lightning away, and the result was a full cave-in. Even if they survive, they will die before they escape and find a trail home. They carried only packs for gathering food and their staffs."

"They better die." Shimgin cut off the communication. She had thought Kimrin the perfect second, not smart enough to run the show but smart enough to know that fact. Kimrin followed orders to the best of her ability, which Shimgin had recently observed wasn't impressive. Zigmin had to die. She was far too smart and too strong. Eventually Zigmin would learn to use her powers without proper training. The same way Shimgin had.

Shimgin looked out over Remei Lake, watching the water ripple under the wind. She would tell the humans nothing at this time. Better to wait and see if the kids survived. This debacle could still be salvaged. If nothing else she would kill Kimrin and lay all the blame at her feet. It would be an irritant to have to train another second, but Shimgin certainly had experience in such things. And she did have a young Sargu she could groom for the job. In fact, that training had started a long time ago.

The vid beeped. Shimgin flipped a switch, and Ralim's fuzzy face appeared on the screen. Shimgin snarled. She wanted the superior tech of the humans and was tired of waiting. She had grown accustomed to the clear images the humans had on the few occasions she had seen them.

"The tests are complete." His voice was soft and deferential, as was the voice of all techs.

Shimgin grinned. It was time she had some good news. She didn't speak to Ralim before cutting the link. He wouldn't expect her to. Shimgin left her office and headed for the labs. She wanted to see this for herself. Walking down the center of the hall, she smiled as Rapulii — Sargu, reds, and techs — moved quickly out of her way. She loved the expressions of fear on their faces. The ones they tried to hide. The warriors didn't move, but they were always against the wall, ready for battle if she so ordered.

Shimgin entered the labs and walked straight to Ralim's station. He had the info she wanted, and he was the only blue she knew by name. The blues were interchangeable as far as Shimgin was concerned. Why bother with names? Of course, she didn't know most reds by name either. Excluding other Sargu, learning names was a waste of time. Shimgin glanced at the greens. She knew none of her warriors by name.

Ralim stood when Shimgin approached. He handed her the information before she asked. Knowing that this data meant death or subjugation for the humans, he had hidden the data as long as he dared. While he wished the humans no ill, he wished himself, and his people, healthy more. He still didn't trust the humans. When they first landed, Ralim had dared to hope they would overthrow Shimgin, but so far, the human leaders worked with Shimgin, not against her.

"You have deleted the information?" Shimgin asked the question but knew the answer. Ralim always followed her protocols. If the humans became an obstacle to Shimgin's taking control of the ship, she now had a poison that would kill the humans but not harm the Rapulii.

"Yes, Shimgin." Ralim bowed again to hide his eyes from her. He was sure if she looked into his eyes, the Sargu leader would know he had just lied to her.

*****

Commander Van Fox looked up from his tablet and stretched his arms over his head. Jacey Rees stood in the open door of his office. "Can I help you?"

"Do you think the kids are okay?"

Fox paused and took in Jacey Rees' worried expression. "Should be. They have Rapulii warriors with them."

"Ish didn't send me a message again last night. It's been three days since he last called." She still stood in the doorway as if she didn't want to invade Van's space.

"He's a teenager. Probably got involved doing something interesting and forgot."

Jacey flashed a smile. "I'm being silly, aren't I?"

"No, you're being a mother. We've been on this world for a few months, and your son is in the first group of teenagers to go off with the natives of this world for an extended period of time. Relax. I'll bet you hear from him this evening."

Jacey nodded and left.

Van rechecked his comm. He hadn't heard from Whisper for the last two nights. Van knew about the ilan sphere and knew Ish hadn't told his mother. Understandable, since no one was injured, there would be time enough to tell Jacey when the kids returned. Van shook his head. The kids probably did something thrilling, were exhausted, and fell asleep before calling. Nothing to worry about. The problem with the scenario was both Ish and Whisper were responsible, adhering to all protocols, one of which was to call in at least every two days.

Ish missed three check-ins. That was one too many. Van's thumb hovered over the call button, and he considered calling Whisper. No. He set the comm aside. The kids were told to call

166

every two days on an alternating schedule and to not draw attention to the tech. If there were a chance of being overheard, they would skip that check-in. The human leadership didn't want the Rapulii to think they didn't trust their new neighbors. Van didn't like the silence on the radio, but both Ish and Whisper were trustworthy, which was one of the reasons they were selected for the combined classes with the Rapulii. They were the only teens given comms.

Van picked up the comm and called Dolan's office. "Morning, Porter. I need to speak to the captain." Before the *Scorpius* took flight, it was decided that the captain would maintain military control until everyone was awakened and a general election could be held. Jacey Rees was the civilian head, and the two of them were expected to work closely together. Considering they landed on a planet with an indigenous population, that had turned out to be a good decision.

"Yes, sir. It will be a moment. He's talking with Shimgin."

"That's fine." Van fiddled with a pyramid containing three images of his wife and daughter on the day Whisper was born. His wife had died shortly after the birth from complications. Whisper was his whole world. Everything he had done, his focus and dedication, were all to protect Whisper and get her to a new world where she could live a good life. He had great faith in Whisper's abilities. Van had trained her from the time she could walk, and she was more responsible than most adults. If Whisper hadn't called, there was a good reason. It could be that they were sleeping in the open with the Rapulii and unable to call without being detected. Perfectly reasonable deduction. Unfortunately, it was also perfectly reasonable to deduct that the kids had found unexpected trouble. And that was the reason he called.

If something happened to Whisper, the captain would need to be prepared. Someone would have to deal with the PR nightmare Van would unleash.

Chapter 16

"Get some rest. We leave at dusk," Lifen said.

"Cut it," Ish retorted.

"Cut what?" Lifen reached for his knife.

"Stop ordering us around."

Lifen cocked his head to one side. "I do not understand. What do you want me to cut?"

"Uh?"

"It's an expression. It means stop." Whisper patted Ish's shoulder and turned to Lifen. "Ish is angry that you issue orders. You should ask. It's polite."

"Why?"

"Why what?" Ish asked.

"Why be polite?"

"I can answer that." Zigmin looked up from where she was preparing to rest. Sitting up partially, she said, "Humans expect a certain level of respect. If necessary, orders are given, but even leaders ask or suggest most of the time. You don't order a peer, you ask. It is assumed that if the request is reasonable, it will be carried out. I have observed that those in the military give and receive orders much as all Rapulii do."

"Are you saying Shimgin doesn't order the humans?" Lifen's voice was incredulous.

Zigmin grinned. "She only speaks to Captain Dolan and Magistrate Rees. She considers them her equal. I have observed that they are all careful to never order the other."

"That makes no sense. If someone will follow my requests anyway, what difference does it make if I order or ask?"

"It's polite." Ish, Whisper, and Zigmin replied in concert.

Whisper added, "We follow now because you understand the environment better at this moment. When we meet with our leaders, you will need to follow our lead."

Lifen looked at Zigmin, who nodded.

"That will be interesting to see," Ish said. He plopped down and closed his eyes, but he couldn't relax. Sleep eluded him. He hadn't called in three days. Mom would be frantic.

*****

Under cover of darkness, the Bugii flew the kids through a vast cave in the southern mountains. It took two Bugii to carry each Sargu and human. They exited in a valley northwest of Guntepe, the highest peak on the planet.

Once he adjusted to the fact that he was at the mercy of the Bugii who carried him, Ish relaxed and enjoyed the flight. The moon wasn't full but would be in a few days. There was plenty of light, especially when compared to the smog that had covered the Old Earth sky. The view was incredible. He glanced over at Whisper, who looked a little green and had a death grip on each Bugii carrying her. It was petty of him, but he was pleased he finally found something he did better. Although flying as a passenger was pretty lame as an accomplishment.

Once the Rapulii and humans landed on solid ground outside the cave, the Bugii, except for Opalo, returned back the way they had come.

"Do we walk back home from here?" Ish asked. Made sense, although the trip home would take a while. The Bugii wouldn't want to draw the attention of the Rapulii by flying them closer to home.

"No. Lenta said I was to introduce you to someone." Opalo opened his wings wide. A gesture the humans had learned meant the Bugii meant business. From this position, they could become airborne immediately, send a strong wind at an opponent, or use their wings in close quarters fighting. "I do not agree, but I do not rule. Understand that two of the Bugii you are about to meet are my mother and sister. If any harm comes to those here, I will blame you."

"You know I mean no harm. The Bugii have been good to me." Lifen bowed and held out his hands.

"No harm." Zigmin made the same movement.

"No harm." Whisper nudged Ish who nodded his agreement. "No harm."

"Come. Meet my family." Opalo tucked his wings and walked toward Guntepe, the largest mountain on the planet.

Ish caught up with Opalo and asked, "We can't fly?"

"The Rapulii imaging machines would see."

"They won't see us walking?" Ish asked.

"No, we have a lot of tree coverage here, and their images are not that good."

"Interesting. How do you know this?"

Opalo's eyes cut to Ish. "If I answer that question will you tell me how good your technology is? We know you have small ships you call shuttles that have been searching the planet and that your orbiting recording devices record much more than the Rapulii ones."

Ish opened and closed his mouth.

"You have my answer."

Ish looked over at Whisper and shrugged. He was surprised to know that the Bugii knew about the shuttles, and he received strict orders to not discuss the shuttles or satellites. Not that he had much knowledge on either anyway.

When they approached a small cave entrance, Opalo turned back to the others. "You enter where none but Bugii have ever been."

"Thank you for this honor." Zigmin bowed low with hands extended. The others copied her bow.

Opalo nodded, turned, and walked into the cave. The others followed. Ish looked up and came to a swift stop. Whisper bumped into him. Neither noticed. They both stared overhead.

Lifen tapped Opalo on the shoulder. "For three years I called the Bugii friend and never did I receive a hint of this."

Opalo shrugged. "That was intentional."

"They live." Zigmin's voice was full of wonder.

They live indeed. Ish watched Bugii of all colors flying. In addition to those with red or blue feathers, there were Bugii of various colors. Some had feathers that spread the color spectrum. The margu were not extinct after all. One of the margu young screeched and dove, landing in Opalo's arms. His wings encircled the child.

"Opalo! It's been so long. Why have you not returned before now? How long can you stay? How is Sulka? Did she come with you? Humans look funny, don't they? Who are..." When the young margu looked at the Rapulii, she cringed and screamed, "Sargu!"

Zigmin and Lifen cringed and stood with their hands out to show that no lightning had been created. Whisper and Ish flanked their friends.

The other young Bugii scattered, but the adults remained calm.

"All is well, Shea. These are my friends. These Sargu are nice. Lenta told me to bring them here to meet you."

"Me?"

"Everyone. I promise we'll talk later. Please let Kole know I am here with guests," Opalo said.

Shea took another look at the Rapulii and humans before she flew toward the cave ceiling. Mid-flight, she slowed and circled a male raven adult before she continued on to join a margu adult female.

The male Shea had talked to flew down and landed in front of Opalo and tucked his blue-black wings. "Did you think I would not notice your arrival?"

Opalo lifted and lowered his tucked wings, signaling his amusement. "I thought to introduce you first, and they cannot fly to your receiving area."

"I can see that." Turning to the others, he said, "I am Kole, co-leader of the Bugii."

A margu adult female landed, extending her wings around Opalo to embrace him. "My son."

"Maa." Opalo's eyes lightened, indicating both pleasure and embarrassment.

Kole whistled, which sounded like a sigh.

Shea had returned with her mother and landed by Whisper. "Are you not cold without feathers?"

"Shea!" Maa exclaimed.

"Her question is valid." Whisper smiled. "In truth, I'm hot. This planet is warmer and more arid than the one we left. We change our clothing based on the weather since our skin is not much protection from the elements." Whisper held out her arm and pushed up her sleeve so Shea could see her skin.

Shea touched Whisper's arm and clicked her beak. "You don't even have enough hair to protect you. No wonder you wear so much clothing. Why are you here? Can I visit your ship? I've always wanted to –"

"Enough." Kole tapped Shea on the shoulder. "You may ask your questions later. First, I need to speak with our new friends."

"Come, Shea, we will prepare a snack for Opalo and his friends." Maa held out her hand.

Shea reluctantly went to her mother, asking, "Why does Opalo get to stay? I have questions that need answers."

"Opalo stays because he is their sponsor while they are here. And while I'm sure you have many questions, yours must wait."

Kole smiled as Maa guided Shea away. "Don't worry, Lenta has already provided background information. I don't have a lot of questions for you, but I do have information to share. We have protected the margu for many seasons. We will continue to do so. In the past, we have hidden. No more. We will meet with your leaders. Our goal is mutually agreeable ways to work together."

*****

Whisper recorded Kole's message to the human leaders and locked the message so it couldn't be accidently deleted. Now she began to worry about how long she had been out of communication with her father. She wasn't surprised when Ish voiced the same concerns.

"Mom is probably having a meltdown. How are we getting back to Remei Lake?" Ish asked. He was long overdue for a chat with his mother. She would be frantic and might never let him out of her sight again. Jacey Rees could be a bit overprotective.

Whisper nodded. "Yes, our parents will be worried." Surely her dad would understand. It had only been three days since her last communication. She wasn't that overdue.

"We can avoid the Rapulii space machines, but the human machines are much more powerful." Kole looked at Whisper and Ish. "What will be the human reaction if we leave carrying you?"

"They need some warning." Ish looked at Whisper. It was time. "My comm broke in the cave-in."

"Whisper pulled out her comm. "I should be able to contact dad now."

174

"You could have called for help?" Lifen asked.

"Not in the caves. The metals keep the signal from reaching out. Once out of the cave, I waited for the satellite to be in range to bounce the signal to Dad. I also waited for a moment alone. And I was told to learn all I could."

Ish snorted. It sounded like laughter. Sporting matching grins, Lifen and Zigmin waited for their friend to continue.

Whisper blushed. "Once I realized we would meet the Bugii and the Kurmii, I thought I should gather data."

Ish cleared his throat.

"Fine, I wanted the adventure," Whisper admitted.

"Can you call him now?" Kole asked. His eyes lightened, indicating his amusement.

"Yes." Whisper opened the comm, put it on speaker, and keyed in the code.

Her dad answered instantly. "Are you safe? Are the others?"

"We're fine. At least Ish and I are fine. Hartley and Haven were at the base camp two days ago, but I haven't seen them since then. We're with two Sargu juveniles and the Bugii right now, but we met with Kurmii last night."

Van didn't speak for a second. Finally, he said, "Stand by one."

"Dad is prepping to receive my report." When Kole nodded, Whisper looked over at Zigmin and Lifen but didn't voice her concerns.

"We understand, you must tell your father of us." Zigmin turned to Lifen.

Lifen made a clicking and whistling noise before he said, "I don't like it, but I understand. My life just got complicated."

"Full report." Van's voice was clipped.

Whisper heard her dad settle in to listen. With no clue as to who else was in the room, but knowing he was recording the entire report, Whisper took a deep breath and relayed

175

their experiences as best she could. Ish only interrupted a couple of times to add a detail or two, mostly to explain Whisper's bravery as if she downplayed her part. When Whisper finished, the comm was silent for a few seconds.

"Ish, do you have anything else to add?"

"No sir, Whisper's report was complete."

She blushed at the praise.

"Although, it would be best if you didn't mention Lifen or Zigmin to the Rapulii yet," Ish added with a nod to his friends.

"We will not speak to the Rapulii, and more importantly, to Shimgin. Not until I can talk to your new friends," Van said. "Is Kole willing to speak with me?"

"Yes, I am."

"In the interest of diplomacy, I am informing you that when our comm is active, we can track locations. We know your location. I wish to send a shuttle to pick up our children. And the Rapulii juveniles if they wish to leave with us."

"I suspected you would be able to track us when I told them to contact you. Will Shimgin be able to trace this shuttle of yours?"

"No. We only fly in stealth mode," Commander Fox said.

Whisper chewed her bottom lip.

Noticing her concern, Kole adopted the same wording that Van used. "In the interest of diplomacy, I am informing you that we can track your shuttles in stealth mode. You may send one shuttle."

"Thank you. Our captain or magistrate can be on that shuttle if that is agreeable. Will we be able to meet with the Kurmii at Guntepe or do we need to make other arrangements?"

"It is a short and secure walk to meet with the Kurmii from here."

"Excellent. The shuttle will land in fifteen minutes. That's one kliki." Humans had adjusted to the differences in seconds,

176

minutes, hours, and days on this world, but they still used the same names for the unit of measure.

"I look forward to our meeting," Kole commented, obviously comfortable with the human and Rapulii units of measuring time. "I also look forward to seeing this shuttle and not just tracking it."

A few minutes later, the shuttle landed just inside the cave and dropped its shield. Whisper jumped up and ran to her father when he exited the shuttle. "You came."

"Yes." Hugging his daughter, Commander Fox faced the only adult Bugii with the children, and said, "I'm sorry the captain couldn't come himself. Shimgin called for him and hinted that there was a problem. We will not return until we know if she will say Ish and Whisper are missing or dead."

Kole's eyes lightened. "The Rapulii emphasis on protocol is stricter than the Bugii. We will not take offense."

Van smiled and tapped his comm. "All clear."

Jacey didn't run, but she walked fast and gave her son a tight hug. "Ishmael. I'm so glad to see you."

"Ish, Mom. The name is Ish."

Jacey smiled and kept her arm around her son as she turned to face Kole. "We have much to discuss."

*****

Sulka hugged Opalo. "Be on your best behavior. You will be the first Bugii many humans will meet. Represent us well."

Opalo nodded and preened a little. It was very gratifying to be able to travel with the humans and learn about their ship.

"I want to go with you." Shea stomped around Opalo and continued the same rant she started the moment Opalo received approval to go on an adventure with the humans. "Why do you get to go and not me? I never get to go anywhere. I can't even go to Bentepe."

Whisper looked over in surprise. "Why not?"

"If Shimgin knew margu still existed, she would declare war on the Bugii," Zigmin said. "I am sorry you can't go, but you are safer here with your mother."

Shea smiled. "Opalo is right. You are a nice Sargu."

Zigmin's skin flashed iridescent in a Sargu blush but didn't respond.

Whisper looked back at Shea. "When we have agreements in place, you can visit us, and I'll show you around the ship."

Shea eyed Whisper speculatively. "Promise?"

"Promise." Whisper crossed her hand over her heart.

"What was that thing you did with your hand?" Shea moved closer.

"When humans make a promise and cross their hand over their heart, it's a stronger promise."

"Like a double promise?"

"Yes, you could say that." Whisper nodded.

"Double promise." Shea mulled that around. "I like it." She grabbed Opalo and said, "Whisper made a double promise. I get to go."

"One day. Whisper said one day. Today is not your day," Opalo said. Making an awkward cross over his heart, which was a bit lower than a human's, he added, "I also double promise that when it's safe for you to visit, I will take you to see Whisper and the human ship myself."

Shea's eyes lit up in pleasure. She jumped and flew, making huge circles in the air above her brother. "May Nurita nurture you on your travels and bring you back to us in good health."

Chapter 17

Theon sat in the captain's quarters surrounded by human, Rapulii, and Bugii teenagers. His full attention on Opalo. "Speak normally. I will ask questions in Standard. You answer in Bugii."

"Will I translate?" Lifen asked.

"Not unless I ask. I want to hear the cadence, the flow of the words. Opalo, if you're agreeable, I will record you."

"I am agreeable," Opalo said in Standard.

Lifen nodded and leaned on the wall, watching Ish play a video game. Zigmin and Whisper joined him.

"Who is in your immediate family?" Theon leaned back and closed his eyes.

Opalo replied with a series of chirps, clicks, and a few sounds that resembled words.

Theon's eyes popped open. "I didn't catch everything, but did you say, mother and sister? You mentioned someone else, I think."

"Yes, my grandmother. I thought this was the first time you heard the language of the Bugii. How did you do that?"

"Root words."

Ish looked up from the game. "Huh?"

"Root words," Whisper explained, "are words from a common background language. For example, many Standard words are rooted in Latin even though no one speaks it anymore."

"Exactly. Latin is the language of origin for French, Italian, Spanish, Portuguese, and Romanian." Theon sat up, excitedly. "At some point, your people," he pointed to the Rapulii and Bugii, "had a shared language. I would love to hear the Kurmii speak. I bet they also share some of the same clicks and chirps."

Lifen nodded. "They do. I was surprised how easy it was to learn Kurmii after learning Bugii." When the others stared at him, he shrugged. "I didn't realize root words made it easier for me. I was simply grateful for the ease of it all."

"Can you say any of the Kurmii language?"

"A few words." Lifen let loose with a series of clicks, chirps, and other sounds.

"Something about high water level," Theon said.

"Yes, I said, 'the water is elevated this year. We are blessed.'"

Ish watched Theon stare into space. "What are you thinking?"

"I might be able to translate both Bugii and Kurmii faster than expected." Theon clapped his hands together. "Let's get to work."

Whisper opened her tablet and typed. After what was obviously a conversation with someone else, she sent a file to Theon's data pad. "Dad said I could share my recording of the meeting between the Bugii and Kurmii."

"You have a recording of them speaking?" Theon opened the file and went to work.

*****

"Happy birthday to me," Ish muttered as he opened a protein bar. When he saw Whisper's face, he added, "No, I don't want a cake or a party. I want freedom."

"Birthday?" Lifen asked.

"It's the anniversary of their hatching day," Zigmin explained. "They celebrate it."

"Interesting."

"Sorry I brought it up." Ish stuffed the bar in his mouth.

"Is that why you're so sad?" Whisper asked.

"No. It's great to be a legal adult and all... but come on. We had a great adventure, and we're locked up on the ship. The only interaction we've had with anyone else was interviews with authorized personnel. All three of them. We can't even see our friends." Ish dropped into the seat beside Lifen, careful not to touch him. The captain's quarters on the landed section of the *Scorpius* was a tight fit for two humans, two Rapulii, and one Bugii, even though it included a conference room set up for meetings allowing four to sit together. An extra chair had been brought in, making the table a bit snug for five.

Lifen raised an eyebrow. "So why are we stuck here?"

"No one knows we're back. They still think we're missing. Haven and Hartley were picked up and returned to camp, but they're in lockdown. I doubt they know anything. They can't talk to anyone either."

"I know that life. It's not fun, but at least they have each other," Lifen said.

Zigmin cackled, and her skin flashed iridescent. "Do you remember your hatch mates?"

Lifen's eyes narrowed for a second before a small smile stretched his lips. "Oh, yeah. Better to be alone."

"Your siblings couldn't have been that bad," Whisper said.

"Who do you think turned me in as a Sargu?" Lifen asked.

"Brutal," Ish said.

Lifen huffed. "You have no idea."

"How do you know who your siblings are?" Whisper asked.

"Not siblings the way you think of them," Zigmin explained. "Hatch mates are all those hatched together. Normally around fifty. They are called siblings or hatch mates, depending on who is talking."

Whisper looked over at Opalo. "How about you? More siblings than just Shea?"

"Our family units have parents and grandparents as you do. Our females have multiple hatchlings at one time. I had three hatch mates. Shimgin killed them all."

"Were they margu, like Shea?" Zigmin asked.

"Yes. It was during the last saime congress."

"Saime congress?" Whisper asked.

"The last time every saime gathered for a meeting. Now we are one saime, with part of our people hidden to keep them safe." Opalo explained. "I would be dead as well if I hadn't been a simple blue. When Shimgin attacked, only the margu were targeted."

"I get that Shimgin's evil, but why has she helped us. You have to admit the Rapulii have been good to humans." Ish shook his head. It didn't make sense.

"You do remember the ilan sphere?" Lifen asked.

"Don't forget the leri attack," Zigmin added. "Shimgin is setting a trap. I don't know what she wants, but she wants something."

Lifen cackled. "You don't know? What about that big ship that can fly into space and the considerable tech on that ship? She may control wind and fire, but the tech the humans have can destroy her, and she knows it."

"Won't work. *Scorpius* was a one-way ticket. Once on a new world, the ship was designed to be dismantled for parts to make life easier. Even if the ship wasn't damaged, and it was, the ship cannot be connected again." Ish grabbed a snack and chowed down.

182

"I'll bet Shimgin thinks she can make it work again." Lifen dropped to the floor and leaned back on the wall. "At a minimum, she wants the tech for her exclusive use.

Ish looked up from eating. "You don't have to sit on the floor. It's tight, but we have enough chairs."

"I'm fine." Lifen was still adjusting to being with others all the time. Excluding short visits with the Bugii and Kurmii, he had been alone for years. Besides, the floor of the ship was more comfortable than the caves he had been living in, cleaner too.

*****

Whisper turned on the vid to check out the news. Holt, the only reporter awakened, jumped on what he called a lack of shared information to provide a thirty-minute news feed daily. Problem was, there wasn't much to report. He and the cameraman hadn't been awakened to provide news, but to teach desert survival. Both had extensive knowledge of surviving some of the less habitable arid climates on Old Earth. Although she hadn't been allowed to attend his class yet, Whisper read the reviews, and it appeared Holt taught a stimulating class. It had to be better than his reporting.

"I'm standing outside the cave-in on Yolzi Pass. It looks like Commander Van Fox, chief of security and father of one of the missing teenagers, has found something." Holt motioned for his cameraman to get closer. The camera didn't move.

"Holt, I told you to stay back." Commander Fox's tone was a warning. One the reporter either didn't hear or ignored. Whisper shook her head.

"The people need to know about our new world. Hiking here we barely escaped a pack of leri who were tracking a brachiosaurus herd."

"They're called irhasi." The cameraman said outside of view.

Holt frowned. "Irhasi. Point is, this world is dangerous."

Van turned but didn't entirely hide his disgusted look. He breathed deep and stretched his shoulders.

Whisper grinned. The pretense of the search was wearing on her dad. He hated to waste time, and a pointless search was nothing but wasted time, but he doomed himself when he admitted that, if Whisper were really missing, he would lead the search. That admission made him the distraction. While he posed for the camera crew, the captain was meeting with the Kurmii and the Bugii working out agreements. Whisper wondered how long it would be before her dad flattened Holt.

"Stay back until we see what's under this mess," Van ordered.

"Commander, I got something." Lieutenant Porter raised his hand without looking up.

Fox ran over to see what it was. Holt was right on his heels.

"Is that a leri?" Holt leaned in for a better look before turning back to the camera. He didn't hide his glee at the scoop. "It looks like a leri. The huge dog-like creature must have been caught in the cave-in. Could it be the children were chased into the cave by leri?"

In the background, the camera picked up Porter's voice again, "Commander, another leri but so far no sign of Whisper, Ish, or Zigmin."

Holt continued his speculation, "Perhaps the kids were eaten by the leri."

Whisper winced. Could Holt be any more of an idiot? There was nothing to prove. Holt was the only reporter currently awake. He was the news media at this time.

"Commander, how do you feel about finding the leri in the cave-in?

Commander Van Fox executed a perfect right hook for the camera. Holt fell to the ground, dazed, as the cameraman zoomed in on his face.

Whisper grinned. The answer was yes. Holt could be a bigger idiot. She finished watching the news vid of the search, apparently done after Holt was able. Holt still managed to put a scowl on her face. "Ridiculous."

"You've been glued to the screen for an hour. What's up?" Ish asked.

"Have you checked the news today?"

"I haven't checked the news since we were forced into hiding on the ship."

"You should." Whisper left the common room.

Ish shrugged and sat down to watch the vid. When Commander Fox knocked out the reporter, Ish grinned. Yet another reason to like Whisper's father.

Chapter 18

Shea flew low to the ground. She had waited long enough. It had been days since Whisper and Opalo made their double promises. It was time for her to see the world. Whisper had experienced more of the planet than Shea, who had been here twelve years before the humans arrived.

While performing her chores this morning, she had overheard Maa and Kole talking. Opalo and his new friends were hiding on the human ship. It couldn't be that hard to slip onboard and visit. And think of the exciting stories she would have to tell. None of her friends back at Guntepe had ever been away from the mountain either.

Like all margu young, she had studied the lay of the land. They analyzed maps of the planet and even watched a few videos, although she didn't know where the images came from. They were grainier than the ones Whisper had shown her. After watching the video Whisper left, Shea was sure she could find her way to the ship. She planned her trip carefully, sticking to distinctive landmarks that could not be confused with anything else.

Shea approached the ship from the west, as far away from the Rapulii as possible. She took refuge on the ledge of an arch and watched the ship's entrance where two guards stood. She waited for an opening, her chance to board the ship.

*****

"What did you do to end up here?" Seaman Floss leaned forward with a smile.

Weber wasn't fooled. Floss was fishing for details. Their peers expected her to discover the secret of his downward spiral. Too bad, he didn't have the answer, and even if he did, he wouldn't share.

"Nothing. Finished inventory yesterday, filed my reports, and this was my next assignment." Everyone knew he went to see Commander Fox after he completed an inventory, but nothing else. When Weber was assigned to guard duty yesterday, he knew there had been a rush to find out what rule he broke. So far, no one knew. Not even him. Weber had inventoried the food stores and found that rations were missing. Combined with the fact that he had heard noises in the captain's quarters, and the captain had moved into his own house, Weber was sure someone was hiding on the ship. When he told Commander Fox about both instances, instead of being praised for what he observed, he was reassigned to guard duty. Guard duty! As if he were still a Seaman and not a Petty Officer Third Class. Since landing on an arid world, Weber had been ignored by the senior staff. Knowing his secondary skills were useless on this world, he worked to make friends with the Rapulii. They would be his ticket to wealth on this new world.

"Did you see that?" Floss pointed skyward. A colorful blur swooped up to one of the arches.

Lieutenant Weber didn't look up from the vid. Guarding the main entrance of the ship was a nothing task. Even if an unfriendly got past the guards, they couldn't enter the ship without an eye scan. Security got tighter after that. Even the human civilians who had been awakened were not authorized

187

to go back on the ship unescorted. There were still over three thousand humans yet to be awakened. Those humans could do nothing to protect themselves.

"Hey. Look up. Do you see anything up there?" Floss pointed toward one of the numerous arches. "I know I saw something."

Weber zoomed in on the area with his tablet and hid his grin. "Whatever you saw has left. There's nothing there." He closed his tablet, relieved that Floss wasn't authorized a tablet while on duty. He waited impatiently for the next shift to show up.

Once his shift was over, Weber made his way to the Dogu, the Rapulii office building. He always felt a sense of belonging when he passed the Semelai, but he wasn't sure why.

The Dogu stood three levels high, and it was the only building made of metal. The first level housed blues doing technical work. He had a friend there and was a frequent visitor to level one. Tapping his tablet, he smiled. That was about to change.

Walking to the entrance, Weber said, "I'm here to see Colom."

The blue nodded and waved him in.

Weber nodded, pleased that he had already established ties to the building. He had known it would come in handy someday but was surprised it was so soon. When he reached Colom's workstation, Weber said, "We need to talk, in private."

"In private. What have a human soldier and a Rapulii technician to discuss that is private?" Shimgin asked. A click ended the question. Humans understood the click to mean the Rapulii was pleased.

Weber ignored Colom's warning cringe and said, "I was going to show Colom a vid I captured while guarding the ship today. I think it might interest you as well."

Shimgin cackled. "And why would I wish to see your vid of our desert?"

"I captured an image of a flying creature, one your people said was extinct." Weber held up his tablet.

Shimgin's eyes narrowed, and she placed a gentle hand on Weber's arm. "Come human. Don't bother my technician. You may show me this wonder."

Weber followed Shimgin up the steps to the third level, the Sargu level. Shimgin waved her hand, and a small electronic light went out. Weber preened as he walked into Shimgin's private office. Of the humans, only the captain and magistrate had been here.

After the third time through the vid, Shimgin asked, "How do I know you didn't tamper with this image?"

"I couldn't adjust the image without it being tagged as such. I'm no coder or artist," Weber answered truthfully.

Shimgin nodded. "Speak of this to no one." When she saw his frown, she added, "I need to research before we announce your find. This is very important to my people. I will give you full credit for this wonderful discovery, and Captain Dolan will know of your intelligence in coming to me first."

"I want more." Weber clicked off the vid. "A position of power."

"Of course, you do. We Rapulii assign jobs based on ability, and it is obvious your talents are underutilized. If your leaders don't have a worthy position for you, I will make one."

Weber grinned. "I look forward to hearing from you."

As Weber left, Shimgin didn't try to take the vid. No reason. She knew which arch the margu had hidden in. What she didn't know was where the margu had been until now, and why a margu young watched the human ship. One thing Shimgin did know, if there was a young margu, there were others. She needed to get control of the human vessel. Whoever controlled that tech, controlled the world. Her world.

Shimgin watched from her window as Weber left the Dogu and return to the human settlement. He might prove to be a beneficial human, even if he was a male.

*****

Shea remained on the ledge until dark. At first, she enjoyed looking around from the safety of the cradle of the arch. The one she had hidden in was one of the smaller arches. If it had a name, she didn't know it. From her vantage point, Shea could see the Semelai, with its claw reaching to the sun. The Suzai towered over the Sargu above ground dwellings. Across the water, Osai reached out from the side of the hill. Dekai, a two-tiered arch, was unmistakable, as were the twin stone structures called Duvi. In the distance, Shea saw the Fusai, a grouping of tall, thin rock structures that looked like they could blow away in the high winds common to the planet. And there were many more. All arches and stone structures her grandmother had described and drawn pictures of. It had been fascinating at first, everything she could have hoped for in an adventure. Now, with the sun setting, she was hungry, tired of watching the ship waiting for something to happen, and more to the point, she didn't have a plan. How could she gain access to the ship when guards were always on duty? In addition, Shea observed that the humans stared into a light before entering the ship. It had to be some type of authorization or tracking light.

The humans were very concerned with making sure no one visited their ship. This adventure was not going as planned. Shea looked around. If she was going to hunt, it had to be now, just after sunset and before the moon rose. Tonight, the moon would be full. It would be as bright as an overcast day. At least that's how full moons were explained. It rarely rained, and there were few overcast days, not that a margu was ever allowed outside to see overcast days. Regardless, she needed to hunt in the shadows of dusk. Shea dropped off the ledge and spread her wings. She should have packed more food.

Knowing she couldn't start a fire to cook with, she captured, killed, and ate a raw kemi. Raw wasn't bad, but she preferred her kemi cooked. Shea slid one of the pinchers in her pouch in case she needed the serrated edge to cut something. She wasn't sure what, but she knew Opalo always carried something sharp for cutting when he flew. Shea grabbed a few brambles to snack on and spread her wings to fly back to her ledge. Strong wind knocked her down. It was blowing so hard she couldn't breathe. Without air, she passed out quickly.

Chapter 19

"You fool. How did you lose the data?" Shimgin screeched. Figlin cowered but didn't speak.

"Have you no common sense? Answer me."

"The data storage device was corrupt. I was unable to create the potion." Figlin shrank lower to hide her expression.

Shimgin sputtered and anger threatened to overcome her. Sheer force of will kept her skin from changing colors like a juvenile. She had entrusted Figlin with the only copy of the data on the poison. "Since you are incapable of running a simple lab, you shall take over the nursery."

Other Sargu watched the exchange with interest. The punishment was harsh. Figlin was the oldest living Sargu and had been respected by the others for her vast knowledge. Perhaps her time was at an end.

"As you wish, Shimgin." Figlin bowed and left.

Shimgin watched the fool leave. She had handed out the most degrading punishment she could think of, but it was a complication. Figlin would have to be gone before the next hatching which would be in a few months. A slow smile spread across Shimgin's face. It had been some time since Shimgin had killed. Figlin would be the next object lesson.

*****

As the oldest living Sargu, Figlin moved slowly, but with confidence, through the Dogu. It had taken many sun rotations to get this duty. Sargu hated supervising the nursery in the basement level. The job typically fell to the youngest adult Sargu who frequently died during the assignment, killed by the Rapulii leader for endangering the young in some way.

Figlin craved the job. She suspected that only here could she find the answers she sought. It had taken time to get the assignment. If she had asked for the duty, everyone would have known something was amiss. Figlin had been careful, and most thought the task was a punishment, just as she had planned. Though pleased she delayed the creation of the weapon to use against the humans, it wasn't her primary motive. The information she sought could only be found in the nursery recordings.

Blues bowed as she passed, but Figlin paid no notice. Once in her new office, she walked over to the stack of reports she had demanded yesterday when she took over as the supervisor. It would take time to read every entry, but if her suspicions were right, it would be time well spent.

Days later, Figlin tossed the last report on the pile. All that time wasted. There was nothing in the birthing reports to tell her what she needed to know. She would have to search deeper in the records. Shimgin was hiding data. Now, where would she put it?

Figlin looked at the pile of records that had been brought to her. Perhaps that was the problem. She rose and walked into the records room.

The techs stood when she walked in. The oldest of the techs said, "Do you require more records?"

"Yes. I will look for myself."

Rushing to catch up with Figlin's long stride, he said, "Tell me what you desire, and I will find it."

The sneer Figlin sported stopped the technician in his tracks. "I will search for myself."

He backed away.

After hours of fruitless searching, Figlin looked at the massive rows of data she had yet to review. Sorted by year, the files were stored in containers that protected them from ruin. She would die of old age before she reviewed all the data. Figlin sighed. She needed to translate the code used for the hatchlings. Too bad they didn't have a computer system like the humans did. The human system provided quick access to data.

Tossing one file aside, Figlin grabbed another. She looked up when she heard a click. One of the warriors who guarded the nursery stood next to a container. "Why have you left your post?"

"You seek."

"Of course, I seek. Why else would I be digging through these files?" Figlin looked at the warrior. He had been guarding the nursery longer than any other. To be exact, they had been hatch mates. "Tibiz, what do you know?"

"You seek."

"What do you know?" She didn't have time for this.

"You seek here." Tibiz pointed to a container and left.

Figlin almost ignored the warrior, but her search technique wasn't showing results. Why not try his? She walked to the container, popped open the lid, and read the first file.

*****

Not sure this was a good idea, but with no way around the meeting, Weber left the human camp and walked toward a field of brambles south of the Sargu homes. He was surprised that Shimgin was early. He hadn't intended to keep her waiting. She wasn't known for her benevolence.

"You promised me information. Where is it?" Shimgin's teeth gleamed in the full moon.

Weber gulped and backed up. "Commander Fox has tightened up security. They say he and Magistrate Rees are fed up with the lack of progress on finding their kids and they are angry. I peeked at the lieutenant's tablet earlier today, and he has orders to do a door-to-door search of the settlement."

"What?" Shimgin screeched.

"No, not Rapulii." Weber held his hands up in a placating manner. "His orders are to search the human buildings."

"Search the humans?" Shimgin rubbed her chin.

"Yes, just in case the kids are hiding out with some of their friends."

"Do human children often run away?"

"Not really. Old Earth had become too dangerous. I would have thought this world was too unknown for the kids to think such a prank was funny, but who knows. They are teenagers."

"What does this search entail?"

"Just like I said, door-to-door search. Each human home will be searched."

"And the ship? Can you get me onboard?"

"Locked down tighter than ever. No guests. Not now."

"I need to get on that ship. Make it happen before I forget that you've been helpful in the past. Leave me."

Weber backed away. He didn't turn around and walk until Shimgin had left his sight. Staying in the shadows he returned to the quarters he shared with four others. His bid for upward mobility hit a snag.

*****

When Shea opened her eyes, she found herself in an unfamiliar room. The architecture of the room was like nothing she had ever seen. As she looked around, Shea considered the possibility that she was on the ship. "Opalo, you here?" She listened but heard no response. "Whisper? Where are you?" A tear ran down Shea's face as she whispered, "Opalo, I need you. Where am I?"

Shimgin picked that moment to enter Shea's cell. "I heard you calling for help. Who are they?"

"They are my... friends. You are Sargu, but I don't think you're a nice Sargu."

"Who is this nice Sargu you speak of? Tell me, and I'll have her come here so you will feel more comfortable."

"He's not..." Shea's voice trailed off as she realized she wasn't supposed to mention Lifen, ever. She had overheard Opalo and Ish discuss Lifen's exile and the fact that the Rapulii thought he was dead. "I mean she's not here. Or maybe she's back. I don't know. Let me go, and I'll find her."

"Tell me his name."

"Why do you need to know?"

"Tell. Me. His. Name." Shimgin bent down to stare the young margu in the eyes. "You're right. I'm not a nice Sargu. I'm Shimgin, ruler of all."

Shea whimpered. This was bad, very bad. "I don't think I should tell you."

Shimgin created a lightning ball. "I had wanted to wait until you grew some more, but if you're going to be trouble..."

"Zigmin and Lifen are my friends. They will come for me." Shea blurted out the words and was immediately sorry. Everything she said was the wrong thing to say. She wrapped her wings around her upper body, knowing that feathers could not protect her.

"He's alive!" Shimgin threw the lightning at the desk, cracking it in half. She turned and left the room muttering, "She lied to me. He is not dead."

When the door slammed, and she heard the lock slide into place, Shea opened her wings and looked at her multi-colored feathers. She had betrayed all margu and her new friends, all for an adventure. With tears running down her face, Shea whispered, "I'm sorry."

*****

Kimrin hurried down the path to Shimgin's private residence. Only once before had Shimgin extended such an invitation, so this was either good news or bad.

Shimgin met her at the door with a smile. "We have much to discuss."

Definitely bad news. Shimgin only looked that happy when she was going to inflict great pain. Kimrin entered, wondering if she would be alive at the end of the day. She harbored no illusions that she could defeat Shimgin in a battle of any kind. If she survived this day, Kimrin knew it would be because Shimgin wanted something and she thought Kimrin would be able to provide it.

Shimgin walked through the open living area and placed her palm on one of the knickknacks on a table. A door slid open in the wall. Kimrin gaped at the cave entrance. The Rapulii leader had secret access between her home and one of the caves. She didn't need to check it out to know that Shimgin used the backdoor as an escape route. No wonder the strongest Sargu always lived here. A concealed escape from enemies was most valuable. Even one that went into the caves.

"Come into my private office." Shimgin didn't slow down. She knew, as did Kimrin, that failure to follow orders would result in a deathblow.

Kimrin looked at the walls. They had been smoothed over time, so this was not Shimgin's creation. Many past Sargu leaders had used the cave. Perhaps this was the sanctuary that the Sargu leader was reputed to have. The passage opened to a room with three savasleri guarding three additional paths. There must be multiple exits, which means there were numerous ways into the leader's home. There was only one reason Shimgin would show her this information. Kimrin was going to die.

Doubting it would help, Kimrin created lightning or attempted to. Not even a flicker of lightning formed in her hand. She tried again with wind and looked down at her hands. Nothing.

Shimgin cackled. "Lightning and wind can't be created here due to the design of the room. We fight hand to hand."

That didn't up Kimrin's odds. She had never defeated Shimgin in battle. No one had. Even in practice, if another Sargu had been victorious, she would have dealt Shimgin a deathblow and become the new leader of the Sargu, until a stronger Sargu dealt her own deathblow.

Kimrin looked around for something to use as a weapon, but there was nothing. She watched Shimgin retrieve a dagger from beneath the folds of her cloak. Nodding, Kimrin settled her stance. In her haste, she had not worn her dagger today, but she wouldn't regret it for long. Curious about Shimgin's change in attitude toward her, Kimrin asked, "Why?"

"Lifen lives."

"How?"

"How doesn't matter. That he lives, in spite of the fact that I ordered his death, is all that is important." Shimgin sprang forward with the dagger raised in her right hand. While Kimrin focused on the dagger, Shimgin swept her left hand in an upward motion, delivering three deep cuts to Kimrin's abdomen.

Kimrin reached for her stomach with her eyes on Shimgin's left hand. The metal claws were a new creation. They had seen the design in the human archives of weapons, and Shimgin had admired it. Kimrin fell to the ground as Shimgin's dagger found her heart.

Gasping her last breath, Kimrin said, "May Dotaru give you all that you deserve."

"I'm sure he will." Shimgin cackled. That silly curse had never concerned her. She rather liked it and would rather thank Dotaru for her success than Nurita. Dotaru, the god of the underworld, was a myth, but if he did exist, he would be pleased with her plan.

Looking at the bloody metal claw, Shimgin grinned. It had performed well in its first use. She wiped the blade and dropped the dagger back into its sheath. Her grin dropped as she surveyed the mess. She would have to remove the body and clean the room herself. No one knew about this sanctuary, and Shimgin intended to keep it that way, even if it meant she did her own housework.

Eyeing her savasleri, Shimgin gave a command, and they pounced on Kimrin's dead body. Satisfied that her pets would do most of the cleanup for her, she left them to it and went to check on her guest.

At first Shimgin had been angry that the Bugii and humans had befriended each other. But time had tempered her reaction. Time and the realization that she could use the margu to unite the Sargu when the time for attack came. While all would follow her or die, they would follow better with a reward for their efforts. New margu feathers would bind them to her plan.

She didn't clean the claw and blood dripped from its prongs, leaving scarlet drops where she walked.

Chapter 20

Shea checked her pockets and pouches, but the kemi pincher was missing. She wiped her tears and looked up when Shimgin entered the room. Attached to Shimgin's left hand was a bloody piece of metal, reminding her of a leri claw extended to attack. It was scary. Shea had never seen such a weapon or heard the warriors speak of such a thing.

Shimgin tracked Shea's eyes, and her own eyes lightened. "Does my new jewelry interest you? I used it for the first time, and the results were gratifying."

"Who..." Shea's voice trailed off as she realized she didn't want to know who was dead. Had a Bugii died trying to rescue her?

Shimgin didn't notice Shea's hesitation. "Give me the location of your friends, or you will be the next to feel the sting of my claw."

Shea stood and faced her fear. "I will tell you nothing. Kill me, but I will not betray my friends again."

"I was hoping you would say that." Shimgin smiled and swiped the claw lightly on Shea's right leg.

Watching three scratch marks welted up, Shea frowned. Shimgin had been careful not to break the skin. The Bugii tended to bleed out, and though Shea was young, she knew Shimgin wanted the feathers of an adult margu more than she wanted to kill in this moment. The full plumage of an adult margu would give Shimgin the best feathers for a new headdress.

Shea looked at the welts and back at Shimgin with defiance in her eyes. "You already know. You did this just to scare me."

"Of course, I know. You were watching the ship. It's the only place those troublesome juveniles can be." Shimgin slowly wiped the blood off the three-clawed weapon. "You will tell me everything I want to know."

Shea gulped. She was afraid Shimgin was right. She doubted she could withstand Shimgin's way of asking questions for long.

*****

Zigmin watched Commander Fox verify the corridor was empty except for him and the kids before he led them to the shuttle.

"Why are we leaving?" Ish shifted his backpack and grabbed Whisper's. When she rolled her eyes, he grinned. Neither action surprised Zigmin.

"Shimgin is suspicious. We aren't ready to confront her, and she no longer trusts us. Also, the crew is getting suspicious about the captain's quarters. I'm taking you to a safer place. One where you will be with others."

Whisper eyed her dad. "What else?"

The commander's eye cut to Opalo. "Kole will explain when we get to Guntepe."

Once again, Zigmin exhibited no surprise at the lack of information. She had noticed human adults treated their children the same way the Sargu treated anyone weaker than them, especially as related to the flow of information.

Supplies loaded, and everyone strapped in, the commander flew the kids back to Guntepe. Zigmin enjoyed the flight and the views the shuttle's screens provided. No wonder Shimgin wants the tech the humans brought with them. It was far superior to anything the Rapulii had.

When the commander landed the shuttle inside the cave, Ish said, "That's new." Bugii and Kurmii, inside the cave, worked alongside humans. A command center of sorts was set up with human tech. All three species shared information.

The commander grinned over his shoulder. "Welcome to the Collective. We've been busy. We have agreements with the Bugii and the Kurmii."

"We could have been here?" Whisper glared at her father. "Instead of stuck on the ship, going crazy. Not sure what was happening except on those so-called news reports."

"We just got the agreements ironed out. You couldn't stay here when we didn't know for sure this would work. Now, you can, safe from Shimgin."

"Shimgin will not react well to this." Zigmin waved her hands toward the command center. "She will see this as a betrayal. She will attack."

"She was going to anyway. Shimgin realized over the past few days that she wouldn't get the *Scorpius* and its tech." Van completed the shutdown of the shuttle.

"She will attack," Zigmin repeated. "She can take out this entire settlement. If the other Sargu come with her, they will turn this place to dust. The Bugii and Kurmii are much more intelligent than my Sargu training led me to believe, but they don't have the raw power to protect themselves."

The commander didn't respond as he led the kids off the shuttle.

Zigmin moved to block his path, and her voice took on an urgent tone. "You don't understand. You haven't seen her power. Not really. The Sargu were under strict orders to downplay certain abilities and get along. The Collective, this collaborative effort between species that she doesn't govern, will anger her. If she withdraws her protection, the Sargu will kill."

"And we will fight them." Sulka came to stand beside the commander. "We are not as helpless as you believe, young one."

"You cannot fight the Sargu if they are working together to kill you. Some of the Sargu enjoy the kill. Each will view war as a chance to become more powerful and replace Shimgin if you manage to kill her." Zigmin's voice was hard.

"We cannot fight with brute strength against the Sargu. That is truth, but we can fight, and you will help. You and Lifen."

"What?" Zigmin stared at Sulka. Sulka spoke as if it had already been decided. Zigmin wasn't sure she was willing to attack the Sargu. They were, after all, the closest thing she had to family.

Sulka lowered her voice. "You are both Sargu. You are both strong. Shimgin wants you both dead. Why? Because she knows you, individually, are stronger than she is. Together, you will be unstoppable."

"Stronger in raw power, probably. Able to defeat Shimgin, maybe. But I am not trained. She hid things from me." Zigmin pointed to the Bugii flying around. "I could drop one to two from the sky, but your numbers would overwhelm me. Every adult Sargu is better trained and, working together, can lay waste to this place. How do you expect me to defend you?" Zigmin took a deep breath. She had just admitted her weakness to these relative strangers. While she trusted Ish, Whisper, and even Lifen, she wondered if the adults were like Sargu adults, twisting the truth to serve their own purpose.

"Lifen has spent years learning to wield the powers. He will train you."

Lifen looked up when he heard his name. "I will?"

Sulka nodded. "Yes, two Sargu are better than one."

"What about me? What can I do?" Ish asked.

"He means what can we do?" Whisper came to stand beside him. "We can't just sit and wait."

Opalo had not spoken since they landed. He had been staring at the young Bugii flying around. "Where is Shea? I don't see her?"

Sulka's wings drooped.

Opalo glared at her and repeated his question. "Where is she?"

"We aren't sure."

Opalo looked from Sulka to Commander Fox. "You knew. You knew, and you didn't tell me."

"I told him not to," Kole said. There was no trace of embarrassment or regret in his voice.

"How could you?" Opalo's wings rose and spread out. The speed of the movement sent wind in all directions.

"Our best soldiers are searching for her. They tracked her to an arch near the human ship but lost her trail." Sulka tapped Opalo's shoulder with her wing. "Had you known, you would have revealed yourself in your quest to find her."

Opalo opened his wings again and shot into the air, heading straight for the cave entrance. He dodged the Bugii warriors and continued toward the opening with the warriors in pursuit. The young Bugii left the warriors in the dust.

Lifen turned to Sulka. "Can they stop him?"

"Only if they can catch him. Opalo is the fastest flyer in the saime."

Everyone watched as Opalo widened the distance from his pursuers.

"I hope he forgives me." Lifen pressed his hands together and pulled them apart as if he were holding a ball. Wind circled in his hands. Lifen tracked Opalo's movement and released his wind just as Opalo reached the cave entrance. Opalo dropped from the sky with the wind still circling him.

204

When Opalo would have crashed to the ground, Lifen changed the wind, and Opalo landed softly, still surrounded by Lifen's wind. Opalo tried to fly again, but the wind held him in place.

Opalo glared at Lifen. "I trusted you. I called you friend."

Zigmin winced at Opalo's use of past tense, noting that Lifen didn't drop his wind.

Instead, Lifen said, "If you fly into Rapulii territory, the Sargu will kill you immediately and claim your feathers. Your sister is young and will be kept alive and healthy so that she can grow into her full plumage before they kill her."

"That will take years. We can't leave my sister in the hands of the Sargu for years."

The Bugii warriors landed at the same time the Kurmii warriors arrived on foot. Lifen dropped his wind. The Bugii immediately grabbed Opalo, holding his wings at an odd angle so that he could not fly off again. One of the Kurmii warriors wrapped his arms around Opalo's waist. Zigmin assumed Opalo could not fly with that much weight holding him down.

"I will find your sister and return her to you." Lifen spoke the words as a vow.

"Will she still have her feathers when you so kindly bring her back?" Opalo spat the words.

Lifen didn't respond as he walked away. His steps echoed in the silence of the cave, and Bugii scurried out of his way.

"Lifen." He stopped walking but didn't turn around or speak when Sulka called his name.

"Thank you for saving my grandson from a foolish mistake. Don't make one yourself. We will meet at the reflection chamber in two kliki. Don't go after Shea until we have a plan, a real plan." Sulka spoke loudly, and her voice carried.

Lifen resumed his walk but angled toward the section of cave Sulka had indicated. He would stay long enough to hear their plan, but he knew his time with the Bugii was at an end. His actions had reminded everyone of what he was. He hoped the Kurmii, who had their own tricks and were not much afraid of Sargu powers, might still accept him. The human reaction was unknown. Since Shimgin had gone to great lengths to keep the humans in the dark about the true powers of the Sargu, their response was not predictable.

"They knew you were Sargu and you had this power," Whisper said as she caught up with him.

Lifen huffed, and his skin flashed iridescent. "They knew, but I had been careful not to use my powers near them. Most of them thought I was weak because I'm male."

"Now they don't." Ish dropped into step with his friends. "That was something. The focus of your wind was amazing. It only touched Opalo."

Zigmin glared at Ish. Didn't he know his comments were not helpful right now? "Yes, few Sargu can control the wind so completely. Had I tried that, I would have taken down the nearest Bugii warriors too, and I would not have been able to cushion their fall. Sulka is right. There is much you can teach me."

Lifen waved his hand as if waving away her statement. "I won't be here long enough to teach you."

Zigmin moved to stand directly in his path. "You don't get to do that. You tell me I have this great power within me that I don't even know about. Now I see for myself that there is much you can teach me, and you think I'm going to wave as you leave. No! You will stay and train me. If for no other reason than because the Bugii need our help."

Lifen got right in her face. "Look around. They don't want me here."

Zigmin didn't take her eyes off Lifen. There was no need to look. She knew the Bugii were staying away from them. The young had been called from their flights. The cave looked

206

empty and sad compared to the happy and noisy ruckus when they arrived.

"Some don't," Opalo agreed as he joined the others. "But I do. I was angry with my people for lying to me, and with Commander Fox, for not telling me Shea went missing. I took that anger out on you. I'm sorry for what I said. I know you would never harm Shea or stand by while she was harmed."

When Lifen said nothing, Opalo continued, "I didn't know Sargu could control the wind so well. I thought they could only use it to flatten Bugii."

"That's what most Sargu can do," Zigmin said. "Our training is focused on lightning as it is considered the most powerful gift."

"Speaking as one who has felt that wind, I'm not sure I agree." Careful not to touch Lifen, Opalo pointed toward the reflection chamber. "Come, let's go hear this great plan the leaders have made to rescue my foolish sister."

*****

"We have intel that says Shea is with Shimgin, in her private offices on the top floor of the Dogu." Commander Fox raised his hand for silence.

"No one other than a Sargu can enter Shimgin's private office. There is an alarm of sorts. If you don't have the power of wind to turn it off before the second soft beep, it will turn into a true alarm using sound and lights to track the intruder," Zigmin said. "The alarm also tracks outcasts. Lifen, though considered dead, is an outcast. I'm sure my ID," she pointed to her necklace, "has been tagged, and I'm also an outcast now."

"You sure?"

"What?"

"What do Shimgin and the other Sargu know?" Kole asked. "They know you disappeared with two humans. If you were to go back now and say you escaped alone, would they believe you?"

"No, too dangerous. Shimgin wants her dead. Zigmin would be walking to her death." Lifen stood and crossed his arms in front of his chest. "Zigmin's death should have happened in the ilan cave. If she returns saying she survived the leri attack and a cave-in, Shimgin will kill Zigmin just to make sure she doesn't get any stronger."

Kole raised his wings. "But she might have time −"

"No, she won't. Shimgin kills any who might be a threat. She knows Zigmin is a threat. Zigmin will be killed." Lifen shook his head. "Do you remember how you found me? A juvenile about Zigmin's age, beaten, left to die from exposure or to be killed by you. The Sargu could not imagine that the Bugii would show kindness to a Sargu, even one near death. That was their mistake. Don't let yours be a belief that the Sargu will show kindness to another Sargu. They won't."

"What if someone is with her?" Whisper asked.

"What do you mean?" Kole asked.

"If Zigmin arrives in the center of town, with Ish and me by her side, could they kill her easily? Would we have time to search for Shea?"

"Possibly, but it's not worth the risk," Lifen said. "Instead of Shimgin having one hostage, she would have three, plus Shea. And that's assuming she allowed any of the three of you to live."

"Shea is young. We can't leave her with Shimgin." Zigmin's voice rose.

"I'm not suggesting we do. What I'm saying is that you are not the one to show up on Shimgin's door. I am." Lifen turned to leave.

"No," Zigmin said.

Hands clenched in fists, Ish blocked Lifen's path. "Bosh. That would be trading one martyr for another."

"No martyrs." Sulka's voice captured everyone's attention. She stood and opened both of her wings, showing her crushed and improperly healed left wing. "We need a plan that works. Not a plan that is one step above a hope."

"Agreed." Commander Fox used his tablet to create a three-dimensional view of the Rapulii settlement. "I propose a distraction using trained military personnel. We keep the Sargu busy." His eyes cut to Zigmin. "If you are with a strike team, can you protect the others while you're in the Dogu?"

"If all Sargu are engaged elsewhere, yes."

"What about the greens and other reds?"

"The greens obey any Sargu over another red. Their allegiance is tied to the strongest Sargu in their field of vision," Zigmin said. She didn't tell them that Shimgin could give the greens an order that no Sargu could override. She glanced at Lifen, hoping he would keep quiet. Lifen didn't speak but met her gaze with a bland expression. Zigmin almost smiled. He knew she was lying but would keep the secret.

"Will all Sargu engage, or will some remain back to protect whatever makes the Dogu so important?" Commander Fox asked.

Zigmin shrugged. "A couple of the younger Sargu will remain behind to order the greens. They will not be the strongest, and they will be less trained than I am."

"What she says is true, if Shimgin follows protocol. I don't think she will," Lifen said. When Zigmin glared at him, Lifen shrugged. "Shimgin wants power. The human spaceship is a great power. If Shimgin has Shea, and it makes sense that she does, Shea will be in the most secure place Shimgin has. It will be four or five years before Shea's full plumage comes in. I don't think the Dogu is Shimgin's most secure location."

"Are you talking about the sanctuary? It's nothing but a myth." Zigmin eyed Lifen, and asked, "Do you have proof?"

"I've lived in the caves near Remei Lake for three years. I know all caves and all passages, except for the area directly behind Shimgin's home. It is guarded by savasleri."

"What are savasleri?" Commander Fox asked.

Lifen's skin flashed in iridescent colors. "Leri trained by Sargu to kill on command. Ish and Whisper met Kimrin's savasleri the other day."

"The ones we found at the cave in?" When Lifen nodded, Fox scratched his chin. "I thought they were normal leri. How are they different."

"A leri becomes a savasleri if they imprint on a Sargu when they are cubs. The savasleri remains completely loyal to that one Sargu. Shimgin has gone to great length to keep the humans in the dark about some things," Zigmin said. "All adult Sargu have savasleri and have kept them hidden. Normally the Sargu ride their savasleri everywhere. They've been walking since you arrived and some of them are not happy about it."

"Neither was I at first. Since the humans arrived, I've had fewer passages to walk." Lifen turned back to the commander. "Even before you arrived, Shimgin's savasleri guarded the area behind her house. Why have them guard nothing?"

"I agree. You will go with a force through the caves to check Shimgin's quarters while Zigmin accompanies a force to the Dogu." Commander Fox's eyes narrowed on the two Sargu in the meeting. "Is there anything else we need to know about Shimgin's ability to wage war?"

Chapter 21

Though he wanted to pace, Lifen kept his body still by force of will. How had he ended up on a team? He took a deep breath and made sure he didn't twitch. Whisper sat across from him and smiled. Though her smile should have been reassuring, her forehead was wrinkled. Lifen associated that human expression with worry. He returned her smile, remembering how Whisper got assigned to the team. She used the fact that Shea would recognize her as a friend and not be afraid. Once Sulka backed Whisper's statement, the others could do nothing but agree. Commander Fox had not been happy, but he didn't forbid it.

Under cover of darkness, and in stealth mode, Porter flew Gamma Team to the base of the Suzai. As Lifen had instructed, Porter landed inside one of the cave entrances on the far side of the mountain near Shimgin's home. Once the shuttle was secure, Lifen led Gamma Team, a task force of humans and Kurmii warriors, through the underground passages to the hills the Sargu called home. There were no Bugii on this team because the natural corridors were small, and their wings would have made it difficult to traverse the terrain with any speed.

"Remember, low profile." Whisper's voice was soft in Lifen's ear. "No Rapulii, especially no Sargu, are to see you."

"Got it," Lifen growled. How many times were the humans going to say that? Commander Fox and Kole had decided Lifen was to be the last line of defense. The longer the Rapulii had no proof of his continued existence, the better, from their point of view.

"Silence," Porter hissed.

Nodding, Lifen continued toward his destination. He was impressed with the ability of the humans, even Whisper, to keep up. He had mistakenly thought the humans were as physically weak as most Sargu. Naturally, the Kurmii warriors were up to the hike, even though the Kurmii jogged bent over to protect their heads. When Lifen arrived at his destination, he held up a fist as Porter had shown him. Everyone settled down to wait. This location, chosen because the human comm signal could reach Porter through a cave opening, was too small for even a human toddler to enter. It wasn't, however, too small to prevent noise from entering or escaping. In order to protect the surprise, they would have to remain quiet and still. Commander Fox would signal the lieutenant over the comm when the battle commenced.

Lifen wanted to be on Alpha Team. They were going to fight the Sargu directly. But, if there were a chance his being here saved Shea, he was willing to postpone his vengeance. If someone else killed Shimgin, he would be disappointed, but he could live with that. As long as she died, he would consider it to be a good day, and it would solve a concern. He couldn't kill Shimgin without starting a Sargu war, but if Shimgin died by Zigmin's hand, she would be the new Sargu leader. Zigmin would be an adult soon enough, and Lifen could provide additional muscle and power to keep the internal fighting to a minimum. That would be the best outcome.

Porter touched his comm and looked at Lifen. He mouthed the word, "Go."

Lifen nodded and jogged toward the passage to Shimgin's house. He didn't slow as he created a lightning ball. Lifen rounded the corner and threw the ball, killing the first savasleri before it could call out. The second savasleri sounded the alarm, but Lifen threw a second lightning ball, silencing it as well. Both had on the full battle armor of a combat trained savasleri.

Two Kurmii warriors moved in to drag the leri out of the way. Lieutenant Porter moved to take the lead, and Lifen stopped him. He held up three fingers and then removed two. There was one savasleri remaining.

The lieutenant nodded his understanding. Porter motioned Lifen back into the lead.

Lightning ball in hand, Lifen moved further in the passage. A massive explosion shook the ground, and dirt floated down on their heads from the cave ceiling. Lifen looked back at Whisper. There was no reason to be quiet now. "Bomb?"

"Yes, hurry." Whisper's worried expression motivated him more than her words.

Lifen moved into a small cave room and stopped. His lightning ball sputtered and dissipated. Three savasleri guarded three doors. Three! In the past there had not been five savasleri in this area. Lifen tried to create another lightning ball. Nothing happened. He couldn't form wind either. "This place is shielded. My powers are blocked, probably by something in the walls."

The nearest savasleri attacked.

Lifen fell back out of reach of the claws as the lieutenant fired a hefty laser gun, dropping the savasleri that attacked Lifen before killing the other two creatures. Lifen looked up at the Porter. "You have a weapon worthy of the name."

Lieutenant Porter grinned.

"Come on, let's check these rooms." Whisper walked up to the first room and reached for the door.

Lifen scrambled to his feet and moved in front of her. "Let me check for Sargu traps first."

Another blast shook the ground. "Then get on with it. The battle is in full swing. No telling how much longer the diversion will last." Whisper shook more debris from her hair, and muttered, "Or the ceiling."

Lifen inspected the door, opened it slowly, and peered inside. He shook his head. "No Shea, but a nice weapons cache. No traps inside."

"Gather what you can carry. Destroy the rest." Porter pointed a couple of men into the room.

After inspecting the second door and disabling the trap, Lifen opened it to discover that it went to Shimgin's home. This time Porter sent a tech and two warriors in. "You know what to do. Be quick."

Door number three had seven Sargu traps, and it took Lifen a bit of time to enter.

"Hurry," Whisper hissed.

"Saying it does not make it so," Lifen retorted.

Porter placed a hand on Whisper's shoulder. "Let him work."

She nodded but continued to bounce on her feet, leaning over Lifen.

"Stand back. There may be another trap I can't see from here."

Whisper said, "Just open it."

Porter pushed her behind him. "I promised the commander you would be safe."

Whisper glared at the over-protective lieutenant's back.

Lifen opened the door and was blown backward. Porter went to check on him.

Whisper's mouth dropped open. Over-protective lieutenants had their place after all. Whisper peered into the room. "Shea?"

"Whisper? Is it really you?" Shea's voice was small and scared.

Without a thought, Whisper ran into the room. "Yes, it's me. We need to get you out of here."

"Shimgin tied me to this post."

"I'll untie it."

"No," Lifen stumbled in, tripping on a desk that was broken in half. "It's another trap. Let me."

Porter walked in the room, speaking into his comm. "Beta Team to the Collective. We've got Shea. She's alive."

Leaning heavily on the bed, Lifen bypassed the Sargu version of a booby trap and released Shea. She immediately jumped into Whisper's arms. "Where's Opalo?"

"We weren't sure where Shimgin held you. He's with another team, searching the Dogu." Whisper hugged Shea, careful of her wings.

"I've caused a lot of trouble." Shea hid her face in Whisper's shoulder.

"You got Shea?" Lieutenant Porter asked Whisper. When she adjusted Shea's position in her arms and nodded, he said, "Let's go. The place is rigged to blow." Porter held out his arm to Lifen who had fallen back on the bed. "I know you don't like to be touched, but we need to move fast. May I help you?"

Lifen tried to stand and stumbled. He shook his head and reached for Porter's arm. "I believe that is wise."

Gamma Team ran down the passages toward the shuttle. Whisper ran in the middle of the pack, carrying their precious cargo.

*****

At the same time Gamma Team flew to their position, Ensign Botha flew Beta Team north of Fusai, the set of arches the humans called The Ribbons. Beta Team, including Zigmin, Opalo, and Ish, would attack the Dogu once the assault on Shimgin and the Sargu began.

"Don't get killed." Botha whispered to Ish.

He grinned and opened his mouth to respond, but the grin faded when he saw her expression. He had the knowledge of the caves to get them where they were going and Opalo had been vocal that he had to help find his sister. Ish hadn't considered how that impacted anyone else.

"You and your friends are not adults. I don't want to lose kids on my watch."

"You're not that much..." Ish's voice trailed off. She had rotated through the pods and aged more than he had. "I'll do my best."

"That's all I ask. Now, lead us toward the coordinates."

The team, led by Ish with his superior knowledge of the caves, jogged easily through the open passages in this portion of the caverns and waited for the signal.

When the first explosion sounded, Ensign Botha nodded to Zigmin who led Gamma Team into the Dogu.

"Traitor." Two young Sargu, lightning in their hands, stood at the entrance.

"Move out of my way." Zigmin held wind in her hands.

"Will you kill us with wind?" One of the Sargu juveniles asked as a cackle bubbled up.

"No, you fool." Zigmin unleashed the wind and knocked the two Sargu into each other. When they connected their lightning joined, and both were knocked unconscious by the jolt.

Botha shot darts into both. "That will keep them unconscious for a while. Where to?"

The blues working the night shift looked up from their work when the fight started. Ralim had been working late on a project and saw the team of humans, Sargu, Bugii, and

Kurmii. He turned to his staff and said, "Return to your assignments. Regardless of which Sargu wins this battle, we have quotas to meet and tasks to complete." He nodded to Zigmin as the blues returned to work.

Zigmin smiled. Ralim might come in handy later.

"Two warriors guard here. The rest come with me." Zigmin fell easily into giving orders as she had been trained. The Kurmii seemed okay with that strategy as she ran up the stairs. Zigmin sent Kurmii and humans to check every room, searching for Shea. Opalo and Ish remained with her.

When the green Rapulii warriors saw her approach, they dropped into a fighting stance. "By order of Shimgin, the traitor Zigmin shall not pass."

Zigmin stopped moving with Opalo at her side. Commander Fox and Lifen had been right. Both had suspected Zigmin would be unable to order the Rapulii warriors. "I don't wish to harm you." The Kurmii warriors moved up beside her. "But I will if I must."

The Rapulii warriors looked surprised but held their ground. Zigmin had suspected as much. The Rapulii could fight Kurmii, and Bugii were considered an easy kill. When Ish and Botha moved up with weapons drawn, the warriors narrowed their eyes on the trespassers. Human firearms could take down large herd animals with one shot.

"Fire," Botha said. She and Ish fired darts into the greens. Botha tapped her comm, listened for a moment, and smiled. "Shea is with Beta Team. Let's finish this. Where to now?"

"We continue up." Zigmin took to the stairs again.

On the third level, Shimgin greeted them. "Foolish juvenile. You could have had it all."

"I could have died to cement your power." Zigmin didn't bother to create lightning. Shimgin was too powerful.

"Yes, that would have been nice. You will not find Shea here."

"We didn't think we would. She's in your sanctuary, right?" Zigmin's smile widened. "Or should I say she was."

Shimgin created lightning and threw it straight at Zigmin.

Zigmin dove out of the way of the lightning as Botha fired darts at the Rapulii leader. Shimgin stopped the darts in midair, and they dropped to the ground.

Zigmin jumped to her feet and created lightning. "The time for darts is over."

"I agree." Opalo flew straight at Shimgin.

Zigmin growled. She couldn't throw lightning at Shimgin with Opalo in the way. She dissipated her lightning balls.

Shimgin laughed when Zigmin gave up the advantage. The Sargu leader used wind to toss Opalo through the window and out into the night. The last Zigmin saw of Opalo was his silhouette rolling in front of the moon. Hopefully, he would regain control of his wings before he hit the ground.

Zigmin looked around. The Kurmii warriors were busy fighting the Rapulii warriors, and she could hear fighting out in the streets. Lifen and Whisper would need more time to get Shea to safety. Zigmin stood, lightning balls in both hands, and faced Shimgin. "Let us see which of us is stronger."

Shimgin created her own lightning but didn't move. She would let the young one wear herself out with posturing. Besides, Zigmin had not yet killed. She would hesitate.

Zigmin threw one lighting ball and held wind in the now empty hand. "You shouldn't underestimate me." Using wind, the way Lifen had taught her, Zigmin threw the second lightning ball and used the wind to increase its speed. Shimgin barely jumped out of the way in time.

"You fool. You lack the training to defeat me." Shimgin held her own lightning.

"Yes, your training was abysmal at best." Zigmin threw another lightning ball.

Shimgin used one of her own to block the incoming lightning. "Why would I train a traitor?"

Zigmin snorted. "You never train anyone fully. Your time is over."

"My time has just begun." Shimgin created a single large lightning ball, infused with wind, and threw it right at Zigmin.

Zigmin used wind to block as best she could, but the lightning engulfed the top of the stairs. She and Ish fell over the rail.

Botha unleashed all the darts in her gun. Shimgin dropped them effortlessly to the ground before she tossed the ensign out the same window as Opalo.

Zigmin bounced down the stairs, hit the landing, and rolled to a stop. She immediately jumped up, prepared for Shimgin to deal a death blow. The explosions rocked the building. Zigmin ran up the stairs, but Shimgin was gone. She had no comm to call anyone. She ran back down and grabbed Ish. "Do you have a comm?"

Eyebrows swished together, Ish checked out his new wrist com. It had not survived the fall, or maybe the lightning caused it to fail. Either way, it was the second one he had busted. "Botha does."

"She was tossed out the window." Zigmin pulled Ish to a standing position. "We need to go."

Ish shook his head and motioned for Zigmin to lead the way.

Zigmin turned and, using the Kurmii language, called the warriors back to her. She caught movement out of the side of her eyes and saw Ralim watching. His eyes were full of disappointment. The remains of Gamma Team ran down the steps and out into the night. Their only hope was to make it to Kasak Path and the Kurmii.

Opalo met up with them with Botha in his arms. "Guess we lost, uh?"

"Your sister is safe. That's a win," Zigmin said. "Head for Kasak Path."

Ish must have regained some of his strength since he grabbed her arm. "Shuttle."

"No pilot." Zigmin knew the shuttle was stashed in case it was needed, but without a pilot, it was useless. Botha was in no condition to fly.

Ish pulled her along. "I'm a pilot."

"Oh." She hadn't thought of that.

"We'll meet you at the shuttle." Opalo flew with Botha in his arms.

"Good thing she's petite, and Opalo is strong," Ish said.

While Zigmin secured Botha in one of the seats, Ish completed preflight checks.

Ish yelled, "Someone secure the hatch." The sound of a lock falling in place was his answer.

"I'm not a pilot, but I'm good at weapons fire." A soldier dropped into the second chair. "You fly us to the Collective, and I'll keep the enemy off our back."

Ish nodded. He had been worried about that and appreciated having someone in the co-pilot seat, especially a military man. The uniform calmed him, though he had no idea why. The guy admitted he wasn't a pilot. With a deep breath, Ish lifted off for his first non-simulator flight with a shuttle full of passengers and no senior pilot by his side.

When the shuttle approached the Collective's bay, the soldier leaned back without firing a shot. "Good flight."

The soldier issued orders to the military while Ish landed and shut down the engines.

Only after the flight did Ish's hands shake. The soldier was kind enough to not mention it.

*****

Commander Fox checked his comm and nodded to Kole. "Execute rescue diversion. Remember, low profile. We are a group of disgruntled humans who have taken up arms with the Bugii and Kurmii to overthrow the Rapulii and our leaders."

To that end, they didn't use any of the miners or robots from the ship. Fox had set the charges himself, excluding Shimgin's home, and zero civilian losses was the plan. Minimal structural damage would be an excellent add-on. The goal was to come out of this mess with a world where all four species could coexist. That would be difficult if innocent Rapulii were killed.

Alpha Team was mostly human, with a few Kurmii and Bugii warriors tossed in to make it look like an uprising. The first set of charges exploded, and the resultant confusion was all that Fox could have hoped for.

Red and blue Rapulii came out of their homes, saw the combined fighting force, heard weapons fire, and immediately returned to their homes and hid. The greens ran to their assigned posts as expected. Warriors were, after all, warriors. The Sargu, who lived away from the other Rapulii, came out and attacked. Riding savasleri or directing them in battle, the Sargu were efficient in the way they threw lightning and wind. They might not trust each other, but it was obvious the Sargu maintained a readiness to repel any attack on their settlement.

"Keep your eyes on the lightning. It doesn't move naturally." Fox issued the order via comm to all three attack forces. Although Zigmin and Lifen had said as much in the briefings, seeing the effect was unnerving. Humans dove out of the way, and the lightning followed them. It was as if the lightning, once sent toward an individual, followed any path they took.

Wind and lightning ruled the night. Lightning was volatile when a Sargu threw wind after a lightning ball and caused the ball to career in unpredictable directions if the Sargu wasn't in full control. The Bugii warriors had been ordered to stay out of the line of fire. They had no experience flying near the types of weapons the humans detonated, so the Bugii performed triage, flying as many of their injured Collective colleagues away from the fighting as they could.

When the second charges exploded, many Sargu abandoned their positions to secure their personal possessions.

"Keep the Sargu occupied. Don't let them regroup," Fox ordered through the comm. Seeing movement with his peripheral vision, Fox turned and saw Nufen standing in an alley with some of his fellow non-Sargu reds.

"What is your purpose?" Nufen asked.

"We are only after Shimgin and any Sargu who get in our way," Fox explained. "She took something that belongs to the Bugii."

Nufen cocked his head to one side, nodded, and returned down the alley. The other reds followed him.

Fox grinned. Maybe the other Rapulii weren't fond of the Sargu either. When his comm beeped, Fox yelled, "Shea is safe."

The Bugii co-leader nodded but continued to dodge the green warrior one of the Sargu had ordered to attack him. Kole flew straight up, and the green grabbed his foot. Kole's foot was released when a Kurmii warrior tackled the green. The Kurmii warrior shook off the lightning that engulfed him and continued to pummel the green. Kole soared only to be hit by lightning. Lucky for him, the lightning was weak. He fell to the ground and groaned as he rolled to his feet. Though dazed, Kole continued to fight.

Fox moved to help Kole, but wind tossed both males into the base of the Duvi arch. Fox hit his head and was unconscious before the third and final set of charges exploded.

Chapter 22

As soon as their shuttle landed, Whisper handed Shea to Lifen. "Let them see you were the rescuer."

Shea narrowed her eyes. "Did someone blame you for my capture?"

"No." Lifen's skin flashed iridescence.

"You don't lie well." Shea's comment caused a few to laugh. She tightened her hold on his neck, and said, "Return me to Maa and Sulka."

Lifen winced as he was still sore from the battle, but he did as Shea instructed. He didn't have a choice. She wouldn't let go. He exited the shuttle with Shea in his arms. Sulka ran to Lifen, thanked him, and grabbed Shea. The rest of Beta Team followed him out just as the Alpha Team was unloading the unconscious Commander Fox on a stretcher.

"Dad!" Whisper ran to the commander's side. "What happened? Will he be alright?"

"Yes, he was knocked unconscious, but is otherwise unharmed," Kole said.

"Medic!" Ish called from Gamma Team's shuttle. "I don't think we should move Ensign Botha again without someone looking at her."

Lieutenant Porter's head swerved around. "Who flew?"

The soldier who wasn't a pilot tapped Ish on the shoulder as he walked by. "Ish can be my pilot anytime."

"Can't wait for the debrief." Porter chuckled when Ish blushed.

Dr. Cromer ran to the shuttle as Opalo ran from the shuttle to his sister.

"Shea." Opalo pulled Shea from Sulka's arms and saw the welts from the claw marks. "Are you alright? Who did this?"

"I wasn't harmed, at least not much. I knew you would rescue me." Shea tightened her grip on his neck. "I didn't mean to cause any of this. I wanted to see the ship."

"A few injuries, but no deaths." Kole walked over with a tablet. "How many Sargu know you exist?"

"Shimgin is the only one I saw." Shea winced. Opalo hugged her tighter and wrapped his wings around her, glaring at Kole.

"Opalo, she must answer questions. We must know what the damage is." Sulka said.

"Shea!" Maa flew down and grabbed her daughter.

"But perhaps we can wait a few minutes," Sulka added as her eyes grew lighter.

*****

As her wind sent Zigmin tumbling down the stairs a second time, a larger explosion shook the ground and Shimgin fell. Looking toward the sound, she saw her home was under attack. She ran across the bridge from the Dogu to the Sargu residences. The Sargu leader's residence was nestled in the mountain protected by the ground on three sides. Only the front room faced open land. If what Zigmin said was true, her private space had been invaded. She ignored the damage and cries for help from other Sargu. Rounding the hill, Shimgin saw her home. Destroyed. Lightning formed in both hands. The humans, the homeless beings she had allowed on her planet, had ruined her home. She slowed and stepped through the rubble that had been the grand entryway to her residence, past her sleeping quarters, finally reaching her sanctuary.

Three of her most accomplished savasleri were dead. Killed by human weapons. The door to Shea's prison was open and empty. The weapons cache was destroyed, and Shea was gone. Shimgin screamed. It was a primal sound that echoed through the cave passages. She checked on the remaining savasleri guards but knew they would be dead. They were. Killed by lightning. What other Sargu worked with Zigmin? Could it be Lifen? Had he managed to convince the Bugii to take him in? Were they so easily manipulated?

Shimgin stormed from her home, once again ignoring the cries for help. This time she noticed the damage. Only Sargu homes were hit. The humans thought to take out all Sargu. No wonder the Bugii helped. The humans needed to improve their aim. Not a single charge inflicted any real damage, except for the attack on her home. She entered the Dogu and walked straight to Ralim's desk.

"Move the satellite from the Kurmii lands to the human ship." Shimgin stood over the tech.

"As you command, Shimgin." Ralim licked his lips and said, "But we will not see the Kurmii if they attack."

Shimgin grabbed the tech's arm. "Did we see them attack today? No. They used the underground passages in the caves to move from one place to another. Do it."

"Yes, Shimgin." Ralim made the necessary changes so that all activity outside the *Scorpius* would be monitored. The Sargu satellite could not penetrate the hull of their ship.

"Someone is to monitor this screen at all times. I will be notified immediately if the humans move. Any movement at all. And get me the charts of the Caves of Kurazi."

"Yes, Shimgin."

She turned and left. If the humans wanted a war, she'd give them one. She was done with the one world, one society pretense. Sargu were created to rule, not coexist, and she was the most powerful Sargu of all.

*****

"We allowed you on our world. Welcomed you into our settlement. Taught you about this world. And you repay us with treachery and lies." Shimgin glared at the human sitting calmly before her.

"The attack was the work of a few, disgruntled humans," Captain Dolan said.

She wanted to pace, to burn off the restlessness, but that would show weakness. Forcing herself to remain seated, Shimgin said, "Fox led them."

"Commander Fox has not been the same since his daughter disappeared. Those who committed this crime have been excluded. To use your own words, they are outcasts now."

"And living with my enemies. The male juvenile, Ish, was with Zigmin when she attacked. You must share the tech of your ship. We Rapulii need to be able to defend against your weapons."

"Without the ability to recharge their weapons, the outcasts no longer have the use of those weapons." Percy opened his arms in a non-threatening gesture. "We are not blaming you for the fact that a Sargu outcast fought with the dissidents. Will you blame us for the actions of our dissidents?"

"Now we get to the problem. I'm not sure your dissidents are outcasts. Leave me." Shimgin turned from the captain.

Percy left the Dogu quickly, returning to the ship's command center. "Stop the awakenings. Double the guards. All military personnel will be fully armed at all times. Slowly move the civilians back to the safety of the ship, under cover

226

of darkness if you must. No Rapulii can suspect what is going on, not even those we might consider friends."

"Commander Reddy, you have the bridge. Send the magistrate to my briefing room." The captain turned to his first officer. "You're with me." Once in the briefing room, Dolan connected to the newly formed Collective, a camp where humans, Bugii, Kurmii, and two Rapulii worked together. When Fox came into view, Dolan was all business. "I need a plan to protect our people. Shimgin declared war."

Shaw sighed. "No hope for a peaceful outcome."

"We attacked her. She believes we're working with the Collective. Dissidents, she called them. Turns out, she's right. Peace is not a choice she will make."

*****

"How's it going?" Whisper joined Ish on a bench in the reflection center.

"It's not." Ish watched Lifen and Zigmin practice. "I have no powers to master. No tasks to complete. I'm too young to be truly helpful in the command center and too old to sit around doing nothing. I'm amazed I wasn't assigned to the little kids in school." Ish pointed toward the makeshift school with a combined class of Bugii, Kurmii, and human children.

"Come with me." Whisper stood.

"Where?" Ish followed but wasn't hopeful it would be somewhere good.

"The Kurmii warriors are teaching a basic defense class. Thought I would check it out."

Ish shrugged and followed. After a morning of training where they learned lightning didn't impact Kurmii and wind had to be strong enough to move their massive weight, they joined Lifen and Opalo in the search for food. Using the human camp as a blueprint, the Collective gathered food for all to share.

"Gathering food is what started this mess," Ish said to Whisper.

"True. And just think of all we've learned."

"But think of all the problems it's created," Ish retorted.

"Gathering food for so many is hard work, but I wouldn't call it a problem," Lifen said.

"I was referring to the fact that we started a war." Ish cut more brambles.

Opalo nodded, "And since Shimgin is looking for us, we bugii can only fly under cover of darkness now and only in emergencies at that."

"At least you can fly," Ish muttered. When Lifen tapped him on the shoulder, Ish pushed him away. "You have powers. Opalo flies. I got nothing."

"Nothing?" Lifen asked. "You can pilot a shuttle. You climb like an ubuk. The Bugii don't even worry about you falling. You are well known and well liked. You can do many things."

Ish blushed. "I'm well-known because Mom's the magistrate and I was the first civilian awakened because my pod failed. And what's an ubuk?"

"They aren't that rare, but perhaps humans haven't been where they live. The ubuk looks like a thin limb with grasping appendages."

Ish nodded his understanding. "You mean those twig looking things? I've only seen vids. Where do you find them?"

Whisper sighed, "You never watch the daily educational vids, do you?"

"We established that a long time ago," Ish said, his eyes focused on Lifen. "Where?"

"They live in the kabu tree. You rarely see them if the winds are high because a high wind can blow them away and they might starve before they find another kabu tree.

"When isn't the wind high on this planet?" Ish asked before he turned to Opalo and asked a question that proved he occasionally watched the vids. "Why is it taboo for Bugii to use kabu bark?"

"The same reason humans shouldn't inhale the fumes of the burning leaves."

Ish winced, remembering the time Kimrin got him inebriated off the burning leaves. To change the subject, he asked, "So I guess we're picking brambles again."

"That's all I see. I wish we had some of the irhasi milk." Whisper sounded as forlorn as Ish felt.

"Do the kurudi really taste so bitter to humans?" Opalo asked.

"Yes." Whisper and Ish replied in concert while they picked more brambles for dinner.

Opalo fluttered his wings in amusement. "Most Bugii prefer them soaked in irhasi milk to sweeten them up, but we can't move our irhasi here until the danger is past. We shall suffer together."

Chapter 23

Chief Petty Officer Third Class Weber glared at Lieutenant Popov. "You aren't going to tell us what happened last night? Those were our bombs and our weapons fire. You think we didn't notice?"

"Those who need to know have been briefed." Popov turned back to Seaman Foss. "Pull up the new duty roster and make sure everyone knows their assignments. Physically check with each person. No transmissions that might be intercepted."

Foss nodded. "That will take all day, but at least I'll get to walk around."

"What's my assignment?" Weber leaned over Foss but didn't see his name.

"You're to report directly to Captain Dolan at his home. Now," Popov said.

Weber sauntered out. It looked like Shimgin finally told the captain how things were going to change. Excellent. He cruised down the path while his current peers worked hard. His time had come. When next he saw them, Weber, regardless of his new title, would be in charge. Yeah, it would be nice to be the one giving orders for a change.

Weber walked up to the captain's home, and the door swung open before he could knock.

"Go on. The captain is waiting for you." Commander Shaw pulled the door wide and waited for Weber to walk in before she shut it.

Weber smiled to see the commander waiting on him. That felt good. Though he could see the captain through the open office door, Weber rapped on the door jam. No reason to advertise he knew what was coming.

Captain Dolan looked up and pointed to the seat in front of his desk. Weber nodded and dropped into the chair. Being part of the ruling class was going to be a joy.

"Can you explain why you have met with Shimgin twice in three days? Think carefully before you answer. Treason is a real possibility for you."

"What?" Weber's thoughts scattered.

"I was clear. What did you talk with Shimgin about?"

"I... well, I..."

"Stuttering won't help." Dolan leaned back in his chair and watched Weber squirm. "I'll help you. You ran to the Dogu, but instead of talking to Colom, your tech friend, you talked to Shimgin directly. Shortly after that, a young Bugii was captured. Yesterday, you again met with Shimgin. I hope she paid you handsomely for your services."

"She didn't pay me at all," Weber muttered.

"Tsk-tsk," Dolan said. "That's too bad. I doubt she'll keep any promise she made."

Weber didn't reply, but he was beginning to believe the captain was right. "I can explain. I wasn't sure what I saw, and I wanted to ask Colom. After all, we were told there weren't any multi-colored Bugii left alive. Shimgin overheard me and dragged me to her office, demanding to see the vid. I showed it to her. I didn't know what else to do."

Dolan leaned his elbows on the desk and held his hands so that his fingertips touched. "And if that was all you did, and you reported up the chain immediately afterward, that would have been, if not acceptable, at least understandable. But you kept the conversation private and met with her again. What did she want?"

Weber weighed his options and decided the truth was his best chance to get out of this mess. "She wanted me to get her on the ship. I refused. Said it wasn't possible. I didn't do anything wrong."

"The only reason we're having this conversation is that the young Bugii is safe now. If you had come to me, or anyone in the chain of command, we wouldn't have ended up in a firefight last night to save her. You endangered not only the Bugii but the human population as well."

The captain stood. "Lieutenant Popov, take Weber to the brig."

Weber looked up in surprise. He hadn't heard her arrive.

"Yes, sir." Popov grabbed Weber and pulled him to a standing position, contained his hands behind his back, and marched him out of the captain's house.

Weber struggled to keep up with Popov's gait. He noticed the stares and snickering as they walked past the work crews and back onboard the ship. This was not the outcome he had expected.

*****

Shimgin threw lightning from the High Seat of Dogu. Only the Sargu leader could open the door on the roof of the Dogu where the High Seat provided a three-hundred-sixty-degree view of the Rapulii lands. She threw the lightning ball as far as she could, grazing the top of the Dekai, the Double Arch as the humans called it. It now sported a new defining characteristic, a scorch mark. Let the other Sargu focus on that for a while.

That fool, Weber, was nowhere to be found. She couldn't ask about him, or Dolan would suspect something was not as it should be. Captain Dolan acquired the most annoying facts. Though male, he was not to be underestimated.

Shimgin left the roof and returned to her office, surprised to see one of the blues waiting outside her door.

"Where's Ralim?" Not only was he the only blue Shimgin knew by name, but he was also the only one she didn't mind speaking with, at least most of the time.

"He did not believe this was important." The blue bowed low as she approached. "Perhaps he is right, but I heard you tell him to report any anomaly at the human settlement."

"What did you find?" Shimgin closed in on the blue. Even if the anomaly proved to be nothing, she could kill him to burn off some of her anger so either way, this blue would serve a purpose today.

The blue became nervous, dropping the tablet. He shook as he picked it up.

Shimgin clicked her teeth. "Come. Place the tablet on my desk. I can't see anything with you shaking like an ubuk in high winds.

Following instructions, the blue tapped the screen to make the image larger. "As you can see, everything looks normal. Watch now. A shimmer will glide across the screen."

"You interrupted me for a shimmer on the vid?"

"Wait. See how the humans suddenly appear from behind the shimmer?"

Shimgin's mouth dropped open. She hit the replay button and watched it in slow motion.

The blue cleared his throat. "This has happened repeatedly."

Shimgin grinned. The humans had some type of stealth ability that she could steal, and she would still be able to kill a blue. "What's your name?"

"Colom."

Shimgin rubbed her chin. Weber had mentioned his blue friend's name was Colom. This might be an improvement. "Colom, you just got promoted to Senior Tech. Take over Ralim's desk and tell Ralim to report to me."

Colom bowed and backed out of the room. He wasn't sure he wanted the promotion, but he didn't have a choice. Unlike his human friend, Weber, Colom knew it was not a good thing to be known to Shimgin. Ralim had held the job of Senior longer than any other blue under Shimgin's rule. Colom doubted he would break that record.

*****

Ralim left as soon as he saw Colom waiting for Shimgin. Did Colom think he could curry favor with Shimgin by telling her? Once Shimgin realized Ralim had withheld knowledge, his life was forfeit. He walked out the main entrance, not because he was so bold, but because there was no other way to escape the Dogu. No one questioned him. He was, after all, Senior. At least for the next few minutes. They assumed he was on Shimgin's business. As Senior, he frequently moved around the settlement during his shift. And thank Nurita for that.

He headed for the caves. Since the day he became Senior, Ralim had prepared for the day Shimgin would kill him. Once the humans landed, he expanded his plans. He patted his pocket where the small storage device resided to make sure it was still there. The weight comforted him. Ralim's only goal was to get the information on the device to the humans before Shimgin killed him. He held no illusion that he would live to see the next sunrise. If he made it to the humans, and gave them the information, Ralim expected the humans would kill him, thereby saving Shimgin the trouble.

Using the map of the caves Shimgin had asked for, Ralim entered the caves and headed west. He stopped in the Dialogue Hallow. It was a piece of history he never expected

234

to see. Just past the expanded cave, he turned south toward Guntepe, a Bugii stronghold he had discovered but kept hidden from Shimgin. He had tracked the shimmers and knew the humans traveled between their ship and Guntepe.

Ralim continued on his journey. If he didn't find any humans before he arrived at Guntepe, Ralim knew the Bugii would kill him, but he suspected they would be kinder about it than Shimgin would. And hopefully, they would give the humans the storage device. He slowed when he heard human speech.

Ralim shrank back against the cave wall, tucking himself into a crevasse as best as he could, defeated. This was his best chance to turn over the device to the humans, and he automatically hid. And that turned out to be a good thing. A Rapulii male, red in color, walked with the humans. These humans were friends of Rapulii. It wouldn't do to give them the device.

The male cackled at something the human said. Slowly the male red turned and peered into the dark looking directly at the crevasse Ralim was hiding inside.

The red palmed lightning, and said, "Come out. I know you're there."

Ralim stared at the lightning the male controlled with no effort. Unheard of. All male Sargu died before reaching adulthood. A birth defect according to the records. Ralim took a second look. The male was barely an adult.

"Tech, don't make me come after you." The male Sargu raised the lightning, using it as a light, but not releasing it.

Ralim stepped slowly out of the crevasse holding the storage device in his palm. It would never get to the human dissidents, but he could stall a little longer. "No harm. I have something for the humans."

"You could not harm me," the red said.

"Lifen, be nice." The human female, who was also not yet an adult, looked closely at the blue. "Aren't you Ralim? I met you once. I'm Whisper, Commander Fox's daughter."

Ralim took a hard look at the two humans and recognized the commander's daughter. He would have noticed her sooner if Lifen hadn't been holding lightning. The human male was Ish. Both were listed as dissidents. What were they doing with Lifen? Ralim was present when Kimrin had told Shimgin the male Sargu had died three years ago. Ralim nodded to Whisper and held out the hand with the storage device in it. "Yes, I am Ralim. Your father will find this useful."

"Convenient," Lifen said. "Shimgin's Senior shows up with useful information right after we attack Shimgin."

"I agree it is suspect," Whisper said. "I'm going to get Dad. You guys stay and guard Ralim."

No one spoke. Fidgeting under Lifen's stare, Ralim was surprised when Whisper returned quickly with Commander Fox and Kole, co-leader of the Bugii. They must have been nearby.

Ralim bowed and held out the device again.

Commander Fox didn't bother with niceties. "You must know how suspicious this looks. Why would you show up now? There were many times since our ship landed that you could have shared this."

Ralim appreciated the directness and replied in kind. "Today, Shimgin discovered that I had hidden information from her. I'm dead as soon as she finds me."

"In response, you led her here?" Lifen's lightning ball tightened in his hand and crackled from the pressure.

"She does not know where I am, but I have no means of proving that to you. I have been tracking your stealth movements between here and the ship for a few days. Only I could track the shuttle when it was veiled. I deleted the data and that code before leaving the Dogu. Today, another blue saw the same anomaly and, he too, deduced that your shuttles were using stealth technology. He told Shimgin. This device will show you how I tracked your ships. Your techs should be able to create a better design for your veil. It also contains all the data I could gather on Shimgin's plans."

"What do you think we will do with you?" Fox asked.

"Kill me," Ralim admitted. "I hoped you would be kinder about it than Shimgin."

Lifen cackled. "You have my assurance that, if you need to be killed, it will be quick. But consider this, the Bugii healed my wounds and accepted me in their homes, and I'm Sargu. If what you say is true, and you mean no harm to the Bugii or the humans, your death serves no purpose."

"I would be amenable to living." Ralim bowed again.

*****

"How accurate is Ralim's data?" Commander Fox asked.

Zigmin looked up from the screen and stretched. She had hunched over the screen for a while. "Based on what Lifen and I know to be fact, extremely. As Senior, Ralim could have acquired all the data presented, but it would have been dangerous. I don't know why he would chance losing his position."

"Because Shimgin is evil," Lifen retorted.

"Of course, she is," Zigmin rolled her eyes. "But he was Senior. Why give that up? Doing so for the greater good is a human concept, not a Rapulii one, regardless of station."

"True, but Ralim's been Senior longer than any before him. He had to know his days were numbered," Lifen said.

"For now, mark all data that can't be verified. Briefing in the reflection center in thirty minutes." Commander Fox walked away.

"Have you noticed how frequently 'in thirty minutes' is used by humans? It must have some significance we don't understand." Lifen scratched his head.

"Not really. It's more of a round number, easily thrown out." Ish stood from his console. "Later. I gotta fly."

Opalo also stood. "May I come? I can help with the loading and unloading."

"Sure, but it's just a supply run. We'll be the only ones onboard, and there will be lots of supplies to load and unload."

"A welcome change from looking at these screens." Opalo followed Ish.

Lifen and Zigmin completed their task and arrived in the reflection center at the same time the commander did. Before the meeting started, Lifen said, "We found something. Shimgin has a weapon, a poison that can kill humans but won't harm anyone else. There also appears to be an antidote." Lifen looked over at Ralim.

Ralim blushed, his skin taking on the same type of iridescent markings that humans at first attributed only to the Sargu. "I could not hide the info from her, but we did create an antidote that Shimgin doesn't know about."

"Deliver that data to medical," Commander Fox said.

*****

"Ralim, can we talk?"

Ralim looked up in surprise. He had not noticed the new arrivals while he watched the hustle and bustle below him. Commander Fox and Kole approached with Lifen and Zigmin in tow. The four were without guards, alone and relaxed, so Ralim remained relaxed as well. He had been at Guntepe for less than twenty kliki, and Ralim had learned that he could relax. As strange as it seemed, the Bugii were kinder than the Rapulii, or at least the Sargu, excluding the two Sargu before him. He still wasn't sure what he thought about Zigmin and Lifen.

"What do you wish?" Ralim stood.

"Keep your seat. We want to talk about the future," Commander Fox said, joining Ralim on the overlook.

Wondering if he had outlived his usefulness to the humans, Ralim asked, "What future?"

Lifen sat on one of the rocks. "Will the techs follow your leadership?"

Ralim didn't speak for a few minutes. He had no intention of telling Lifen about the underground movement he had started a few years ago. Under Ralim's leadership, certain advances had been hidden from the Sargu. Eventually, he said, "Why would they?"

"Someone has organized the techs. I've been listening and watching for three years. I'm amazed Shimgin hasn't noticed." Lifen smiled slightly.

Ralim raised an eyebrow as the humans frequently did. "Shimgin rarely notices anything she isn't expecting. Perhaps you are a different type of Sargu."

"I hope I am."

Ralim leaned forward. "What are your future plans? Will you challenge Shimgin?"

"I don't want to lead the Sargu," Lifen said.

"Then you doom the Rapulii to continue under Shimgin's rule." Ralim leaned back, amazed that he had dared to talk to a Sargu in such a manner. "Zigmin does not yet control her powers enough to be a true threat to Shimgin, but from what little I've seen, you do."

"You've been watching us?"

"I watched you and Zigmin train this morning." Taking a deep breath, Ralim admitted, "Under your rule, I could see my people being treated better."

Lifen shook his head. "The Sargu will never accept a male as their leader."

"Says who?" Zigmin, silent until now, joined the discussion. "Ralim is right. You are the only one strong enough to stand a chance against Shimgin one-on-one. If you won, the other Sargu would follow, at least for a time. They would wait for the wind to scatter and see what the damage is. Sargu will look for an angle, but if the new Sargu leader has agreements with the humans, Bugii, and Kurmii, the other Sargu will wait to see how things play out. I don't believe all Sargu are evil. I can't believe that."

"You're not evil," Lifen said, giving voice to what he knew concerned her.

"I hope not, but you've seen how the Sargu treat everyone. Surely, if they can see another way, they will want to embrace it."

"Perhaps," Commander Fox said, "Perhaps not. Some would react badly to losing power."

"If you don't lead the tech resistance, who does?" Lifen waited for a response that didn't come. "It has to be you. You were Senior for years, much longer than anyone else managed to hold the position. No one else would have been in the position to keep things from the Sargu, especially Shimgin."

Ralim remained silent. There was nothing to say.

"How about this?" Lifen leaned in close. "I also know the reds have their own resistance and I'm pretty sure I know who leads it. If they come forth and support a change, will the blues?"

Still Ralim didn't speak.

Kole sat beside Ralim. "I understand. You've worked for years to keep the techs safe, and it's scary to even consider what you're being asked to do. But consider this, what are you waiting for? Did you ever think there would come a time when the possibility of freedom was in your grasp?"

"Even if I believed in the possibility of this utopian future you speak of, I am no longer in a position to be of use. As soon as I left, the resistance, as you call it, severed all ties with me. They know Shimgin wants me dead and have redefined rules

240

for coordination. They will not answer to any request from me for communication. If, as I suspect, the new senior is Colom, he remains faithful to Shimgin. He has no hope for a better world and is trying to survive in this one." Ralim looked at Lifen. "If the non-Sargu reds come out in support of you, and they see proof that you are the better option, many techs will join you. You need to set up agreements with the non-Sargu reds."

"Do you have a contact?"

Ralim leaned back. "Until I trust you, I cannot help. You said you know who it is. Talk to him... or her."

Lifen grinned. The person he suspected was male.

Chapter 24

In the shuttle, the duo prepped for takeoff. Since Ish's first flight in a combat situation, he had become the supply pilot. Opalo frequently flew with Ish on these runs, and he was now able to help with preflight tasks. He wanted to be the first Bugii to pilot a shuttle.

"Why this route?" Opalo's eyes narrowed on the screen. The flight plan veered east and approached *Scorpius* from the hills at a very low altitude. In the past, Ish plotted a straight approach between Bentepe and Remei Lake.

"Based on Ralim's data, the Rapulii satellite has trouble focusing on low altitude flying. Besides, it is focused on our ship, not the surrounding area. He purposefully set it up that way."

"Yeah, and if Shimgin figured out what Ralim did, she has already corrected that flaw, although they can't do anything about the low altitude static. I guess it's a good plan," Opalo admitted.

"Thank you. I certainly thought it was when I submitted it." Ish grinned.

"Your leaders have shown great faith in you."

"Not really," Ish admitted. "There are only four of us cleared to pilot the shuttles who live at the Collective. Ensign Botha, Lieutenant Porter, and Commander Fox do the people flights and the commander doesn't have a lot of time. I'm lucky they allow me to fly at all."

"At least you get to fly." Opalo's eyes lightened, which Ish had learned meant the Bugii were amused. Beaks, instead of lips, prevented many facial expressions the humans relied on.

"Supply shuttle, you're cleared for departure." Lieutenant Porter's voice came over the comm. "And Ish, be careful. Your mom's a bear when you go missing."

"Roger Command. Careful it is." Ish frowned. He was never going to get out from under the cave-in story. Ish thought it would be nice if people knew what he had done, but some of the guys ribbed him about letting the girls do the fighting. Like he had a choice. Whisper had a weapon, and Zigmin was a weapon. Ish pulled to the cave entrance, set the ship to stealth mode, and flew into the night.

Opalo cocked his head to one side. "What is bear?"

"A bear was a large, fur-covered, land animal from Old Earth. They were between the size of omuz and an irhasi. The mother bear was extremely aggressive in defending her cubs, er, offspring."

"Interesting. And this is what your mother becomes when she can't find you?"

"It's what most human mothers become when they can't find their children."

"Protective as a leri. That is what we Bugii say about our females when defending their children."

As they crossed the open plains south of the ship, Opalo noticed Ish staring at him. "What?"

"You fly, like for real fly. Why are you so interested in looking out the viewport?"

"I never thought I would see so much of the planet, especially the arches around Remei Lake. They're amazing. Besides, flying in the shuttle is different. I can't explain it, but it seems more thrilling to fly when I'm not in control. That sounds odd, now that I've said it aloud."

"We're all odd about something." Ish banked the shuttle and started his approach through the hills to the *Scorpius.* "Bosh. We've got trouble. Supply Shuttle to Command. Sargu are placed strategically throughout the hills. We're turning back."

"Incoming lightning on our starboard. Multiple directions," Opalo said.

"I see it." Ish changed course, but the lightning followed the shuttle, bathing it in electricity, disabling system after system. "Command, we took a direct hit. We're visible. Systems failing. We're going down."

"I'm tracking you. *Scorpius* is sending help. Hang..." Lieutenant Porter's voice cut out as the comm system fell to the lightning.

The shuttle, visible in the night sky even without lights, crashed with a single thud. Ish was surprised that they didn't bounce or roll. "You okay?"

"I'm alive. Leg hurts but wings seem fine."

They grabbed their survival gear and headed for the door. Before he opened it, Ish said, "We have no vid. We don't know who's out there."

"Does it matter? You told me on our first flight that there is a manual lock for this transport outside. Without power, we can't keep whoever's out there from entering unless we go out and lock it. If it's Sargu, they have us. If it's your people, we have to move quickly before the Sargu reach us."

"Yeah, I know. Just thought I would mention it." Ish manually opened the door, and they stepped onto the ramp.

Three Sargu rounded a stand of trees and stood before the boys, each palming a lightning ball, and sporting a smile.

Ish pressed his palm into the wall pad, using the motion of his fingertips to set the shuttle to distress mode, locking the ship tight so that only a member of the command staff could use their palm print and code to unlock the door. The wall pad had its own shielded power source. He couldn't prevent their capture, but he could protect the shuttle, preventing Shimgin from gaining access to the tech she wanted so desperately. At least he could do that much. When Ish got out of this mess, he would recommend that the entire fleet be converted to allow a manual lock of the door from the interior.

Both males backed away as the Sargu approached. When the Sargu realized they couldn't open the door, one of the Sargu threw lightning at a tree, causing it to go up in flames. Another grabbed Ish. "Open it."

Ish hoped he had the strength for whatever happened next. He took a deep breath and said, "I can't."

One of the other Sargu said, "Place his hand over the pad."

Hauled back to the door, the Sargu forced Ish's palm over the keypad. It flashed red, and the computer's non-emotional voice said, "Invalid. Only the *Scorpius* command staff may enter a locked shuttle."

Ish grinned. "Guess Shimgin won't be happy, huh?"

The Sargu glared at Ish and looked between themselves.

*****

Commander Shaw completed the brief to the security team on the *Scorpius*. Just as she keyed in the code to open the hatch, the captain's voice came over the comm. "Stand down."

"Sir?" Shaw looked up to where she knew the camera was.

"Sargu have the shuttle surrounded. They've already taken the boys away."

"Bosh. We can catch them." A mother herself, Shaw didn't want Jacey to have to deal with the fact that Shimgin captured her son.

"Not without injuring many civilian Rapulii," Dolan said. "The ship is secure. Ish saw to that. The Sargu are guarding it, but they can't get inside."

*****

"Where is my son?" Magistrate Rees stormed into a conference room on *Scorpius*. Captain Dolan and most of the command staff were with him. They were linked to the remainder of the human leaders at the Collective by vid.

"I should not have allowed Ish and Opalo to do the supply run alone," Commander Fox said.

Jacey waved away the concerns of Fox. "I don't care about blame. As much as I hate to admit it, Ish is an adult and must contribute. What I want to know is where is he now? Does Shimgin have him?"

Lifen moved into the screen. "Probably. Unless another Sargu is making a play for leadership, they will take Ish and Opalo to her. With the current unrest, it is unlikely that a Sargu would choose this time to fight for leadership. They will wait for the outcome of this uprising before making a move. Sargu play a long game."

"Understood. What will Shimgin do to them?"

Lifen's skin flashed iridescent, but he didn't flinch as he focused on Ish's mother. "If the most expedient way to get information is to torture them, she will."

"I have a team ready to go after them," Commander Fox said.

"I'm sure you do, but I doubt we can surprise Shimgin again. What are our options?" Rees asked. Much as she wanted to send in the troops to save her son, she knew it was a bad idea.

*****

246

"Well, this was not where I expected to end up this morning," Opalo said dryly.

"Yeah, this isn't good." Ish didn't stop moving when he spoke. "You're the one I'm worried about. You have your adult plumage, right?"

"Yes, but my feathers aren't prized. I suspect Shimgin will want information more than she'll want to kill me for my blue-black feathers." Opalo tilted his head and asked, "What are you doing?"

Ish looked up from checking the walls and blushed. "Trying to find a way out of here."

"By touching the walls?"

"Yeah, it's stupid. In stories and vids, the captured always find a way out of a cell. I have no clue how to do that, but I hate just waiting." Ish eyed Opalo. "So, you're thinking Shimgin, too?"

Opalo waved his hands around the room. "Looks like we're in the Sargu holding cells. If so, only a Sargu can open or close these doors."

"Yeah, I figured." Ish cut his eyes to Opalo. "Any ideas on what she will do, torture wise?"

"No. Excluding Lifen, those who have been through it have not survived. Lifen closed up whenever Shimgin's name was mentioned, so I quit asking a few seasons ago."

"Disappointing. That would be good information to have right about now." Ish tilted his head toward the door as it opened.

Shimgin walked in. They stood tall and faced the Sargu.

Shimgin's lips twitched in amusement. "I have no desire to harm you. I need information."

"I don't believe you." Opalo flapped his wings to push wind at Shimgin.

She didn't budge. Her clothing didn't even blow in the wind. "Do you think I'm unable to control wind? Foolish juvenile."

The wind Opalo pushed with his wings swirled between him and Shimgin while she spoke. With no warning, the wind rushed back at Opalo, knocking him into the wall, sending shooting pain throughout the vein and bones of his flight limbs.

His right wing hung limply at his side. Opalo groaned and rubbed his head where it had connected with the wall. He didn't know Sargu could control wind created by someone else. It made sense, but he had never heard of such a thing. Surely their leaders would have told him if it were so. Of course, that might be information shared when a Bugii attained full adulthood. That day was a season away for him.

"Watch it." Ish stood between Opalo and Shimgin. "You will not hurt my friend."

"Think you that you can stop me?" Shimgin asked.

"If I have to." Ish's voice was calm though he was shaking inside. The tension in his shoulders gave lie to his words. Him and his stupid mouth. He had no clue how to stop Shimgin.

Shimgin cackled and unleashed more wind. When it finally died down, Shimgin was gone, and both males gasped for breath.

Opalo's wing hurt, and he was sure he wouldn't be flying for a while. He checked the joints of his tender wing. "Next time, don't goad the powerful Sargu into proving she is stronger than we are."

When Ish finished gasping for breath, he said, "Don't mouth off to a Sargu when trapped in one of their holding cells. Good advice. Wish I had thought of that earlier."

Chapter 25

"We have to do something." Zigmin paced between the cooking supplies and the shuttle. The first person that had ever been kind to her was in trouble. She had to help Ish and Opalo as well. Interesting, her first friends were human, Bugii, and another Sargu. She glanced over at the Kurmii and human fighters engaged in combat training. They were also comrades.

"I agree, but we need a plan that will work. Shimgin won't be unprepared this time." Lifen palmed a lightning ball, practicing the art of keeping the ball small and carrying it around.

Zigmin followed Lifen's example and created her own lightning ball. She had observed that maintaining lightning without using it required concentration and reduced stress. Perhaps that was Lifen's experience as well.

"You have both grown much in the past few days." Sulka approached them but stood back a little.

Lifen and Zigmin dissipated their lightning. Both understood that the Bugii had understandable issues with Sargu tossing lightning around, even if they were allies. The fact that Lifen was barely an adult and Zigmin was a juvenile didn't help. A Sargu who didn't have full control of the powers she, or he, wielded, could accidentally cause more damage than an adult Sargu.

Sulka winced, but raised and lowered her right wing, indicating amusement. "You have powers you have not yet tapped. To help your friends, my grandson, you will have to use all that you have."

"What powers?" Zigmin asked.

Lifen narrowed his focus on Sulka, and said, "How do you know? What do you know?"

Sulka wrapped her right wing loosely around her body. "I witnessed the last battle between Sargu and margu. I was injured during a small skirmish the day before, and one of my wings was damaged. I could not fly from the caves at Bentepe to help."

Zigmin and Lifen were careful to not stare. They had noticed that Sulka never flew but hadn't asked how the ability was lost. It was rude by Bugii and Rapulii standards to ask for personal information that was not offered.

Sulka's right wing wrapped tighter around her body, but the left remained where it was, useless. Her voice was sad when she said, "I have not been able to fly since that day."

Zigmin, under the pretense of scratching her face, wiped away a tear.

Sulka observed her movement and said, "Do not shed tears for this limitation Nurita saw fit to give me. I made peace with my restrictions long ago, and I am otherwise strong and healthy. One day I will be in the safety of Nurita's wings and will once again be able to fly."

Zigmin nodded. Sulka had a wonderful way of looking at the world.

"What powers are we not using?" Lifen asked.

"So far, you have only used wind that you created. You can take someone else's wind and use it against them. For example, when Bugii fly, we create wind by flapping our wings. You have the ability to pull the wind out from under us."

Zigmin gasped. "That's awful. Any Sargu that would do so should have a swift journey to Sidir."

Sulka's wings loosened as she said, "Indeed. I believe you will find that all Bugii agree with you. Dropping us out of the sky is an action that should be met with eternity in Sidir."

"What else?" Lifen asked. He and Zigmin would need more than a little wind to defeat Shimgin and any Sargu who followed her.

"I have seen Sargu send lightning in multiple directions at one time."

"Not possible. You must have seen wrong." Zigmin was emphatic.

"I have excellent vision."

Zigmin gulped. Bugii hunted by sight. To say a Bugii couldn't see well was a huge insult. "Forgive me. I mean no disrespect, but I've never seen any Sargu do that. Not even Shimgin."

"How often does Shimgin fight multiple opponents at the same time? Think you that she doesn't keep some things private?"

Of course, she does. "Okay, how do we do that?" Zigmin asked.

"I'm not sure," Sulka admitted. "I know what I saw, but I don't know how to tell you to do it."

Lifen, who had been quiet for some time, spoke up and said, "I might have an idea."

"You do?" Zigmin's tone indicated she didn't believe him.

"The last beating Shimgin gave me, before Kimrin was told to dispose of me, was because I shot lightning at Shimgin and Kimrin at the same time."

"And you didn't mention this before now?" Zigmin's skin flashed.

Lifen's skin also flashed. "I don't know how to recreate the event. Every time I try, I fail. I knew that they planned to kill me and say I had a tragic training accident."

"How have you tried to recreate it?"

"Focused on two points, like I did that day, and send the lightning."

Zigmin thought for a moment. "How did you feel when you were successful?"

"Uh?"

"At that moment, right before you sent lightning at both of them, how did you feel?"

"Terrified. I knew Shimgin and Kimrin were going to kill me. If this only works when terrified, it's not very useful."

"Being terrified allowed you to tap into the ability, but I don't think it's the cause. Don't you see?"

Lifen growled at his friend. "No. Explain it, She Who Knows All."

"Now you're being snippy," Zigmin said, borrowing the phrase from Whisper. "I've watched you. When you're angry, and I suspect terrified, your focus is impressive. Everything except the objective falls from your view. You don't notice anything else. Perhaps sending lightning in multiple directions from a single ball requires that type of focus."

Lifen scratched his head. What Zigmin said was logical. He created a small but powerful lightning ball in his palm. Lifen focused on just the ball, falling into the sphere. In one swift movement he sent it flying through the air toward three archery targets the Bugii used for practice. All three exploded from the force of the lightning.

The Bugii who had aimed at the targets looked over and turned their bows and arrows toward Lifen. Sulka motioned for them to wait and stay where they were.

"That's it. That's exactly right," Zigmin exclaimed. Without thinking, she hugged Lifen. She jumped back, skin flashing iridescently, when she realized what she had done. "Sorry."

Lifen looked at her in shock, but replied, "It's okay. I rather liked it."

Sulka, careful not to touch Lifen, patted Zigmin on the shoulder. "You should both practice this new skill. It may be needed soon. See you at the reflection center for the midday meal." Sulka walked over to the archers to explain what had happened.

*****

Ralim walked around the Guntepe cave. In awe, he watched Rapulii, Bugii, Kurmii, and human work together. The four species were very different, but it didn't seem to hinder progress. Everyone was respectful. Ralim had often wondered what respect looked like. The Sargu ruled by fear.

He had often imagined life with Rapulii, Bugii, Kurmii, and now humans coexisting in peace. It would be like this. Though few spoke to him, Ralim saw Bugii lift a wing in acknowledgment and humans smile slightly. Even though they knew Ish and Opalo were prisoners, no one blamed him. This was an enormous improvement in his daily life.

For seven years Ralim had been Senior. As Shimgin's go-to tech, he was feared by many of the techs because they assumed, incorrectly, that Ralim held some sway with her. Foolishness. No one was safe around Shimgin, especially her Senior.

"Takes some getting used to, doesn't it?" Lifen shortened his stride to walk beside Ralim.

For the first time in his life, Ralim didn't guard his tongue. "It does. Have your friends been found?"

"No." Lifen watched the Bugii young fly. Lifen didn't speak though it was obvious he wanted to.

Ralim asked, "Is there something I can do to help?"

"There is, but it might be distasteful to you. Be assured if you are not comfortable answering questions, you do not have to. You will not be killed or tortured for the information, especially since you may have none."

"I doubt anyone here will be as distasteful in their demands as Shimgin. Let me hear these questions."

Lifen led Ralim to the command center. The leaders were gathered around a vid with much clearer images than anything the Rapulii had. Ralim wasn't surprised. He knew the humans had more tech than they had shared with Shimgin and that their communications systems worked better than the ones developed by the Rapulii.

"Good. You're here." Commander Fox got right to business. "We have questions about Shimgin. If, in good conscience, you cannot answer a question, say so. No one wants you to betray your people, but we are asking you to betray the Sargu leadership."

Ralim grinned. The expression felt foreign on his face. "So Lifen explained. I will help if I can."

"Where would Shimgin place Ish and Opalo?" Fox asked.

"The cells on the third floor of the Dogu. Cells that only Shimgin can open." Ralim glanced at Lifen. "The cells where you were held."

Lifen nodded. "I suspected as much."

"There is an escape route unknown to any Sargu, part of the original design and known to a small select group of techs and non-Sargu reds who do not agree with how the Sargu rule. If they are there, I could release them."

"What?" Lifen, skin flashing iridescently, turned on Ralim.

"Had we rescued you, we would have been unable to hide you. And you are, after all, Sargu. We discussed options and determined we couldn't chance it." Ralim looked Lifen in the eye, ready for the attack. He expected Lifen to engulf him in a lightning ball.

254

Lifen returned Ralim's stare. "That was not a happy place, and I could have used an assist. As much as I don't like it, I do understand."

Surprised that Lifen remained calm, Ralim turned back to the commander. "It would be dangerous, and the escape would not be simple. We would have to enter the settlement from the caves and leave again through the same caves. I don't know the cave system between here and the arches well, but I believe I can return the way I came."

"I know the way. I can lead you." Lifen said.

Jacey Rees, magistrate for the humans and Ish's mother, leaned into the screen. Her face filled the vid. "Don't be hasty. Take the time to flesh out a real plan that will rescue them. I want my son back, but I don't want deaths that could be avoided with a little planning."

Ralim stared at the human leader. Never had a Sargu considered the losses before ordering any tech to complete a task.

Chapter 26

"We've got to get out of here," Ish said for the third time.

"Agreed. What's the plan?" Opalo didn't look up from massaging his wing. He knew Ish didn't have one. Neither did he.

"Still working on it." Ish gritted his teeth. If he hadn't mouthed off, Opalo would be okay... or not. Ish had no experience dealing with deranged rulers, and Shimgin was a ruler who was most certainly deranged. "How bad are you hurt?"

Opalo let go of his wing and stood. "I'm fine. A little sore."

Ish raised his eyebrows. "Lying now?"

"Not lying exactly, hoping." Opalo shrugged with his functioning wing. "There's nothing to be done. If the wing does not heal properly, I'll never fly again. Let's not worry about that right now. We need to escape."

"Still working on a plan." Ish turned toward the door. "Hear that?"

"Tapping and scratching at the door." Opalo moved toward the door. "No, not the door, this section of wall."

Ish placed his hand on the door. "I feel vibrations."

"Yeah, it's getting stronger." Opalo listened for a moment before pulling Ish back. "The vibrations are an old style of communication. It's said that was how the ancestors of all three species communicated over distance."

Ish nodded his understanding. "Sort of like Morse Code on Old Earth."

"I do not know this Morse Code, but the language of the ancestors is known to all. We need to move back." Opalo tapped the wall before pulling Ish back.

"Yep, that's your version of Morse Code."

A section of the wall slid away, revealing Nufen and another red. Nufen asked, "Can the humans defeat Shimgin and the Sargu?"

"Probably, but we have laws about harming others. My leaders won't start a war if they can help it," Ish said, hoping he wasn't speaking out of turn. He didn't have the authorization, or the necessary training, to be able to make agreements or discuss strategy with anyone.

"We thought as much. When the humans attacked, the bombs were carefully placed. A few injuries, no deaths, and our dwellings were left intact, except for Shimgin's. We wish to join you."

"Who wishes to join?" Ish asked.

"Non-Sargu reds. I believe many of the techs will join us. Warriors only obey the Sargu. We are unsure of them."

"Why haven't you guys risen up before if you wanted the Sargu gone?" Ish asked. And how did he end up in the middle of a discussion on overthrowing the ruling government of this world? He was still trying to work up the nerve to kiss Whisper. Not exactly hero material.

Nufen and Opalo glared at Ish. Opalo said, "You've met Shimgin. Now imagine fighting twenty or so Shimgins with our weapons. Ours are not as powerful as yours."

Ish winced. That would be bad.

"We go now." Nufen was insistent. "We help you escape, get you as far as the caves where you escape unseen, and you set up a meeting with your leaders."

"Deal." Ish was relieved that the reds didn't want to go to the Collective. He didn't think the location should be shared until the reds were vetted.

Ish and Opalo followed Nufen into the passage. It was tall enough for Ish to walk upright most of the time. To descend a flight of stairs, Ish had to lean back at an angle to protect his head. Opalo had a harder time of it as he had to bend back further because of his wings.

Opalo asked, "How is it Shimgin doesn't know of this passage?"

Nufen grinned. "When the Dogu was built, a small group of non-Sargu reds and techs modified the design to put in a few small passages. While we fear the Sargu, it was hoped that one day we would overthrow their rule."

"Couldn't you have made it a bit taller?" Opalo asked. Back on level ground, he bent over to keep his wings from scraping the ceiling and walls, all of which were rough. His efforts were not sufficient, and it made his injured wing ache terribly. It certainly made Opalo appreciate the passages his ancestors had expanded in Bentepe and Guntepe.

"We thought we would be saving Rapulii. We did not envision rescuing Bugii." Nufen stated a fact. There was no apology in his tone.

Ish heard before he saw the underground waterfall. "What's this?"

"We are under the Remei Lake you see above ground. The larger part of the lake is beneath us. We have installed pumps to move the water aboveground. This spillway is how the overflow returns to the lower lake."

"The upper lake isn't natural?" Opalo asked.

"Yes, it's natural, but it would dry up for part of the year without the pumps."

Opalo stopped moving. "You could have shared this knowledge with us. The Bugii could also have a lake that never dries."

"I suppose but talks between our people have been nonexistent."

Opalo huffed but continued walking, asking questions about water pumps.

After a while, Nufen slowed. "Silence. Warriors will now be able to hear us if we make noise. None of us can defeat them in battle without weapons."

Ish narrowed his eyes on the Rapulii. "Where are these weapons?"

"Shimgin keeps all weapons. She issues only when necessary. Your people destroyed the entire supply."

Ish blushed. The cache had been taken during Shea's rescue. Any weapons Porter's team couldn't carry were blown up. "Sorry about that."

"It is fine. We can't use them, but neither can Shimgin or her supporters. The destruction is helpful in its own way." Nufen listened at the wall. "Now quiet. No more talking."

The next section of passage was long and flat, but no taller. Eventually, Nufen stopped and turned to the other red. "Go. Verify it is safe to open this door. Tap three times before opening."

The red nodded and took off down another passage.

"Where's he going?" Opalo wasn't sure he trusted these Rapulii rescuers. He had thought to get out of the cell and into the relative safety of the caves before overpowering them. That would be harder to do if they weren't together, especially if he didn't know where the other red was or what he was doing.

"He will exit the passage into our dorm and walk back by the roads. That way we won't accidentally open the door when someone could see us."

Opalo nodded begrudgingly. The logic was sound. The wait was long enough that he became restless and his thoughts returned to traps. Three raps sounded, and the door opened.

"Move quickly. Run to the caves." The urgency of the red's voice was catching.

"Come. I know the way." Ish ran between the buildings and dove for one of the cave entrances Lifen had shown him. "We're underneath the Sky Arch, I mean Suzai."

"Okay." Opalo looked around. He didn't know where he was. His one and only trip into Rapulii territory had been as part of the attack force to rescue Shea. He had never been in this terrain before, not flying solo, and definitely not on the ground inside a cave. The maps and images all Bugii studied did not do justice to the size of it all.

Alarms sounded.

"What's that?" Ish asked, sure he already knew the answer.

"I think Shimgin knows we're missing." Opalo looked at Nufen for confirmation.

"Yes, I must return before she becomes suspicious. I will be here, in this part of the cave, three days hence at sunset. If Captain Dolan or Magistrate Rees is not here, I will assume we cannot work together."

"Wait." Ish thought frantically. "If they can't make it, is there someone else you will speak to?"

"Commander Fox. No other. I trust Theon, but I do not believe he has the power to make an accord with us."

Ish nodded. "I'm sure one of the three will be here in three days at sunset. I know they will want to meet with you."

The reds ran out of the cave. Ish and Opalo sprinted down the larger cave passage heading west.

260

Ish slowed to a jog when they reached the underside of the Ribbon Arches and pointed to one of the rock stacks Lifen helped him erect. The stacks helped Ish learn his way around. "We're at the edge of Rapulii territory, underneath Fusai."

Opalo stopped to check his wings. Both were battered and bleeding from the escape. "Will they follow us past here? I'm leaving a blood trail that a fledgling could follow."

Ish shrugged. He had been worried about the blood but saw no reason to mention something they couldn't do anything about. "I'm hoping..." His voice trailed off when they heard the cries of the savasleri. "Guess the Sargu are tracking us."

"Yes, we should run."

They picked up the pace and ran down the tunnel. Drops of blood followed in Opalo's wake. Even if the savasleri couldn't smell the blood, which they could, it was a perfect trail.

*****

"Captain, alarms are going off all over the Rapulii settlement." Saber Isles didn't look up from her feeds.

"Yes, we can hear them. Cut the sound. No reason to scare the non-combatants."

"Sorry, Sir." Saber pressed a few buttons, turning off the sound throughout the ship, except for her console, where she lowered the volume. Here she would listen to any announcements. "Captain, warriors are rounding up all the humans they can find. The only ones left in the settlement are the military personnel left behind so Shimgin would see humans moving about. Also, according to Rapulii internal communications, Ish and Opalo escaped."

Captain Dolan leaned back in his chair and smiled. "I wonder how they managed that?"

Commander Shaw didn't look up from her console. "Captain, I can't find a human heat signature anywhere.

Wherever the greens took the prisoners, we can't track them. I can't find Ish or Opalo either."

"Hopefully, the boys made it to the caves, where not even our sensors can penetrate. Ish knows them better than most Rapulii. It's their best chance of escape. Tell Commander Fox the rescue team goes after the boys now. It no longer matters if we still have some questions. Commander Shaw. Take another team and remove our people still in the city. Deadly force if necessary."

"Aye, captain." Shaw left quickly.

*****

"This is it?" Shimgin's skin flashed in iridescent colors. "Where are the rest of the humans?"

"Unknown. These were all we could find." The tech showed no expression and kept his eyes averted.

Shimgin threw lightning at the wall, creating a new window. The humans didn't flinch. Soldiers wearing civilian garb had stayed behind to allow others a chance to escape. Shimgin kicked one of the soldiers in the ribs. "Take five to the medical wing for testing." At least they would serve as test subjects.

"Find the human and the Bugii. Torture these if you must. Find those juveniles." Shimgin stormed out of the holding cell. She needed the friends of Lifen and Zigmin to control them. They might be young, but Lifen and Zigmin were the strongest Sargu she had ever seen. Zigmin had more raw power than the previous Sargu leader and Shimgin had killed that leader while she slept, otherwise Shimgin would never have become the ruler. Shimgin could not have Lifen and Zigmin working together. She could lose everything.

Nufen watched Shimgin leave and turned back to the prisoners as another red raised a whip. Nufen grabbed it and pulled, knocking the red off balance. "No."

"Shimgin said —"

262

"No torture. They don't know where the juveniles are. It's a waste of time." Nufen looked at the soldiers, finding one he recognized. "You are in command of this group. Yes?"

A male, dark of skin, nodded. "Reddy, lieutenant commander."

Nufen ordered the guards out of the room and dropped into a squat in front of Reddy. "We talk."

*****

Ish and Opalo ran for a while with the sound of leri chasing them.

"Shouldn't they have caught us by now? The savasleri are faster than we are." Ish had always been a runner, and it was coming in handy now.

Opalo, breathing heavily, said, "Leashed, so the Sargu can keep up. That's what my training said."

"We can't return to the Collective with Sargu following us." Ish picked up speed.

"Where?" Opalo asked. He was too tired to form a complete sentence. He hadn't realized how much he used his wings. He rarely ran anywhere. If he survived this, he would start jogging like the humans to build up his leg muscles. His legs should be at least as strong as his wings. Right?

"There's a room ahead with three exits. Four if you count this passage. The south one goes to Bentepe, and the north one goes to the Kurmii. We'll go west. I don't know where it goes, but I'm not leading the Sargu to our allies."

Opalo nodded but didn't speak while he looked around. He sucked in air and hoped his lungs would quit burning. What he saw was something he didn't expect to ever see. He had always assumed it was a legend. The Dialogue Hallow was huge, with large flat boulders placed in a seating arrangement. Three stones stood tall. At the top, each stone had been carved into a statue. Each sculpture was bathed in light with no readily identifiable source of illumination. One Bugii, one

263

Kurmii, and one Rapulii. Opalo looked at Ish. "You have been here before and didn't mention it?"

"Yeah. Lifen thought this was where the ancestors of all three species used to meet. Makes sense," Ish said. "Each had their own passage that could be guarded by their warriors.

"It's called the Dialogue Hallow. I never expected to see it," Opalo said.

Before they reached the center of the room, the savasleri, leashes trailing behind, entered the room.

Ish sighed. "Guess the Sargu released them."

The guys scrambled up the nearest set of boulders. The handholds were small, and they struggled to climb, but the snarling savasleri provided excellent motivation. After a few failed attempts to jump to where the guys were, the savasleri stopped trying to reach their prey and patrolled beneath the duo.

Just as Ish and Opalo began to relax, two Sargu walked out of the corridor from the Rapulii settlement, lightning already swirling in their hands.

Ish looked at Opalo. This was going to hurt. The Sargu hurled lightning balls through the room: one at Ish, two at Opalo. Ish screamed as the lightning engulfed him. Once it stopped, he crumbled to the floor of the ledge, unconscious.

Opalo, also screaming, was knocked into the ledge wall before he fell over the side. He felt his right-wing break, closer to shoulder this time, but unconsciousness overtook him before he could determine the amount of damage. Thankfully, he didn't see the savasleri close in.

Chapter 27

Lifen led the Collective's retrieval force into the Dialogue Hallow just in time to watch Ish and Opalo fall from the lightning the Sargu had sent at them. Gathering his anger, Lifen created a tightly focused lightning ball and threw it at the three Sargu, who were so surprised to see a male Sargu that they didn't react fast enough. His lightning broke apart and engulfed them.

While Lifen took care of the Sargu, Zigmin threw lightning at three savasleri wearing full battle gear. When the leri were dead, she said, "I guess Shimgin no longer cares about deceiving the humans."

"Savasleri make an excellent secret weapon." Lieutenant Porter tapped the saddle and reins.

"I need a stretcher over here for when I get Opalo stabilized," Doctor Cromer said.

"We need to be gone before more Sargu arrive. You can treat Opalo when we're back at the Collective." Porter didn't look away from the cave passage to the Rapulii settlement.

"Opalo is badly wounded. I'll let you know when he can be moved."

Porter issued commands to the soldiers and warriors before turning back to the doctor. "I'll do what I can, but if I tell you to move, you move. We only brought a strike force. I don't have enough soldiers to secure this area."

"I'll take point with the warriors at the Rapulii passage." Lifen jogged over to join the soldiers.

"And they can help." Zigmin pointed to the north passage where Kurmii warriors entered the chamber. Four stopped to provide muscle if the boys needed to be carried. The rest ran to block the passage to the Rapulii Settlement.

Porter breathed a sigh of relief. So far, excluding weapons fire, the humans had proved to be less than successful in hand-to-hand combat with the Sargu. The Kurmii were all but immune to Sargu powers and were physically stronger than any Rapulii.

Two kliki later, Porter leaned over Cromer. "Hate to rush you Doc, but we've been here a while."

"I know. I almost have Opalo secure." Cromer looked up at Porter, her eyes haunted. "I'm not sure I can fix this."

Porter patted her shoulder. "Do your best, that's all anyone can do."

Ish had been lowered from the ledge and finally awakened from the shock of lightning he had received. Leaning heavily on Zigmin, Ish walked over with his hair frizzed out from his head. "How bad is he, Doc?"

"Won't know for sure until we're back in my lab." Cromer made a few final adjustments and said, "Okay, let's move out. Gently. Keep Opalo level."

Two Kurmii lifted the stretcher with Opalo on it and followed the Doctor down the passage to the Collective. Lifen and the remaining Kurmii were the last to leave the chamber, frequently stopping to listen for Sargu and their savasleri.

Figlin, currently in charge of the Rapulii nursery, and a Sargu unhappy with Shimgin's leadership had crawled to a

266

lookout point over the chamber and stayed low. She saw everything from the time the male Sargu entered the Dialogue Hallow until the dissidents left with their wounded. The care for the wounded impressed her. As she turned back toward the settlement, Figlin wondered if the male had been Lifen. He was of the right age to be the powerful male Sargu that Shimgin and Kimrin said had died in training. If it was Lifen, how did he survive?

Figlin left her vigil and returned to the settlement. She didn't report to Shimgin. As far as Figlin was concerned, there was nothing to report. She wanted to recheck the nursery records. Seeing Lifen reinforced a concern she had had for some time. Tibiz, the warrior who had told her to search a specific container, had been wrong. At least, that's what she thought before she saw the male Sargu. The more she considered the puzzle, the surer she was that the male was Lifen.

Tobin waited until Figlin was gone before she emerged. She had grown to hate her life. She had stood by and watched as a friend was engulfed in lightning. Tobin trailed Figlin, no longer interested in learning what the elder Sargu was keeping from Shimgin.

*****

Ish gave a full report, detailing everything he had learned. He had spent the first part of the meeting assuring his mother, who had arrived at the Collective, that his battered appearance looked worse than it was. When Ish finished his report with Nufen's request for a meeting, Commander Fox nodded. "Good work. We'll be there."

Briefing complete, department heads left to make use of the knowledge, but Ish remained seated. Jacey would have stayed, but after exchanging a look with Fox, she leaned over and kissed Ish on the forehead, then she left as well.

When Jacey walked out, Commander Fox said, "You and Opalo should be proud of yourselves. You behaved well in a stressful situation. Now, tell me what's troubling you?"

Ish blushed. "If I hadn't shot off my mouth, Opalo might not have been hurt."

"This is war. People get hurt in wartime."

"My friend is injured because of me. It should have been me. Opalo shouldn't have to pay for my bad mistake. He may never fly again." Ish jumped up and paced.

"That attitude right there. Remember it. Hold it close. Next time you'll remember to temper your words, and that will make you a better leader one day."

Ish shook his head and walked out of the room. Platitudes were not what he needed right now.

*****

"How did you lose a blue feathered Bugii and a human, both males, who are barely adults?" Shimgin leaned over the table, looking each Sargu in the eyes, letting them feel her anger.

Figlin looked around and realized no one would answer. Kimrin normally spoke for all in these meetings, but she was suspiciously absent. Figlin cleared her throat. "One of the techs, during torture, admitted that he saw the prisoners escape into the caves. Two Sargu took three savasleri into the caves to search for them. They have not returned." And they never would, but it would be safe to send a search team into the caves now.

"Find them, the boys and the missing Sargu. I want answers." Shimgin's shriek echoed around the walls. She left walking down the hallway to another room with another issue that needed to be addressed. Fools surrounded her.

Opening the door, Shimgin said, "Have you gained access to the shuttle?"

"No Shimgin." The tech bowed low.

268

Shimgin growled and threw lightning, killing the tech. "Does anyone have a better answer?"

The remaining techs remained still and silent. Shimgin rolled her eyes, an expression she learned from the humans. "Leave me. Tell Colom to report to me now."

The techs looked confused for a moment before one stood, bowed low, and pointed to the tech she had killed. "Colom is there."

Shimgin peered closely at the dead tech. Yes, it was Colom. She had thought he had looked familiar. She looked back at the one who spoke. "What's your name?"

"Pilom."

"Congratulations, Pilom. You're the new senior. Now get that shuttle open." Shimgin stormed out the door.

Pilom stared at the door. He had attained the highest station a tech could hope for, but he wasn't proud or even thankful. The position was a death sentence, as Colom just proved. Pilom stood. "Come, we'll try to pull the door off."

As the techs followed him, one of them asked, "Will that work?"

Pilom shrugged. No tool they had would cut the door open. He didn't know what else to try.

*****

She was wind-blown. The humans would call her a fool. Tobin approached Shimgin's office and knocked. She had enjoyed getting to know Whisper, Ish, and even Zigmin. Hiding her status as a Sargu had been difficult, but she had always looked young for her age, and Shimgin had kept her hidden from the other Sargu. None knew that Tobin was Sargu, not even Kimrin, who was still absent. Tobin had been raised and trained to be a spy. When she heard her friends had disappeared in a cave-in, Tobin knew Shimgin had ordered Kimrin to do something despicable.

"Enter." Shimgin's shrill voice did not offer any hope that she was calmer than she had been earlier.

Tobin entered but didn't immediately speak.

"What have you found?"

"Two dead Sargu and three dead savasleri." Tobin didn't bother to name the dead. Shimgin wouldn't care. "Killed by lightning. Two different signatures."

"Two?" Shimgin stood, her voice dangerously calm.

"Verified." Tobin didn't move. That would only draw Shimgin's attention and she didn't want that. It was the best way to stay alive when near the volatile leader of the Sargu. Though her eyes faced the ground, Tobin kept Shimgin in her peripheral vision in case she needed to dodge an attack.

"Leave me." Shimgin didn't look up as Tobin closed the door.

Tobin walked away. Based on Shimgin's reaction, she knew Lifen was with Zigmin. Shimgin didn't seem surprised that Zigmin wasn't the only Sargu with the rebels. How could she help Whisper, and by extension Zigmin and the Bugii? There must be some way to warn her friend of the danger, but Tobin couldn't think of a single way to make that happen.

Chapter 28

Opalo had never felt pain like this. His right wing throbbed, and he couldn't change positions. He was strapped down to keep his movements as restricted as possible. His current plan was to change positions or at least move a little. To be fair, he wasn't sure a change would help, but the pain overwhelmed his common sense. Opalo was willing to try anything, and the effort required to move would at least give him a different type of pain to focus on for a short period of time.

The door whooshed as it opened.

"Who's there?" Opalo assumed it was medical personnel. Forced to lie on his stomach to protect his wing, he had been faced away from the door, so he didn't know who entered his room until they spoke. When Opalo didn't receive an immediate answer, his voice became frantic. "Who are you?"

"Just me." Ish's voice was soft, and Opalo strained to hear him.

Opalo relaxed when he realized that Ish had arrived but immediately got angry. It had been a full sun cycle. Everyone had come to visit except Ish. "Where have you been?"

"Reporting to the commander and a long talk with Mom."

"That did not take a full sun cycle." When Ish didn't respond, Opalo asked, "Did something else happen?" When the silence threatened to engulf the room, Opalo said, "By Salinu and Sidir, what I'm thinking is worse than what you aren't saying."

"Nothing else happened," Ish rounded the bed so that he could meet Opalo's eyes. "I'm sorry I caused this."

"What?"

"All this. The broken wing. The battered body. All of it." Ish waved his arms over Opalo's bandages and said, "If I hadn't provoked Shimgin you would still have the use of your wings. I don't expect you to forgive me, and I understand if you don't want to be around me anymore."

"You wind-blown fool. Do you blame yourself for the west winds?"

"I have no control over the wind," Ish retorted.

"You have even less control over Shimgin." Opalo tried to turn more to get a better view of Ish and winced. "I was already injured before she tossed me around like an ubuk. The two Sargu who tracked us with their savasleri are the ones who assured my injury would be bad. You are not to blame, my friend."

Ish let out a slow breath and smiled. "Wind-blown fool?"

"It's what we say to someone whose thinking is faulty."

"I like it."

Whisper chose that moment to walk into the room. "Finally. I was beginning to think Ish would never smile again." Lifen and Zigmin followed her.

Doctor Cromer walked in with medicine. "Only two visitors at a time." She looked at Opalo's crestfallen face and said, "Okay, fifteen minutes, then I'm kicking the lot of you out." Placing two tablets under Opalo's tongue, she added, "Don't chew. Let them dissolve under your tongue. These will kick in before your friends leave, and you'll be extremely relaxed. I'm going to run a few more tests and, once the drug is out of your system, we can discuss treatment plans."

Opalo said, "Lifen, come over here where I can see you."

When Lifen knelt so that they were eye level, Opalo said, "Don't let anyone try to avenge my injuries." Opalo's eyes cut to Ish.

"Consider it taken care of," Lifen replied with a knowing smile.

Zigmin provided a detailed account of the rescue followed by Whisper's status of all Opalo had missed. Listening to Whisper, Opalo's face relaxed, and he slurred his words together. "Feel good. Has my wing healed?"

Ish grinned. "Nope, but the drugs have kicked in."

"Drugs?" Opalo sighed and fell asleep.

*****

"Three surgeries?" Opalo looked between Sulka and the Doc. The pain was now bearable, and his head was no longer fuzzy. "Three?"

"Yes, both the Bugii and human medical staffs have reviewed the data." Doctor Cromer enlarged the slide so Opalo could see the issue.

Not wanting to look too long at the multiple breaks in his wing, Opalo asked, "Will I remain here the entire time?"

"You should be able to leave the med bay after the first surgery, which we would like to do later today. The additional surgeries will be as an outpatient. You will not be able to fly immediately, probably not before the west winds dry up Incekis Lake."

"That long?" Opalo turned his head into his pillow and groaned, hoping no one knew what he was doing. He felt Sulka's hand on his back, carefully staying away from his right side. When she didn't speak, Opalo turned his head to look at her.

"I know it seems like a long time –"

"It is a long time," Opalo growled.

Sulka locked eyes with her grandson. Speaking as only a mother or grandmother can, she tilted her head and said, "But it's not a lifetime."

If Bugii skin were capable of such a display, Opalo would have blushed like a human or a young Sargu. Sulka was right. It might take longer than he would like, but there was an excellent chance his injuries could be healed. Opalo would fly again. The Bugii lacked the medical knowledge to perform the needed surgeries, but the humans could. They were his only hope. "Forgive my impatience, Doctor Cromer. I meant no disrespect. I am grateful that there is a chance I can soar again."

"It's okay. I understand. I've thrown a lot of information at you, and you need to discuss everything with your family and healers. Three surgeries will take recovery time, and you will be restricted from certain activities." Doctor Cromer reviewed details and eventually left the room.

When they were alone, Opalo asked his grandmother, "Can the humans perform the same surgery on you?"

Sulka raised and lowered her right wing. "I haven't asked. I will be happy if you can soar again. But I'm too old, and it's been too long, for such a procedure to be successful."

"You think, or you know?"

"I think. Now rest, grandson. This surgery will probably be uncomfortable."

Chapter 29

"Pilom." Shimgin rode her savasleri up to the techs working on the shuttle door. She rode to remind the blues and greens that she was the master of numerous savasleri, for everyone knew that she had lost a few when the humans had attacked her home, just hers. Everyone else had been spared. The humans' foresight in appearing to be considerate of the lower casts had worked for them. She had already observed a lack of respect from those who should have bowed and scraped when she approached.

To add to her threatening demeanor, Shimgin played with a small lightning ball, bouncing it around in her hand. Shimgin was pleased when the blues backed nervously out of her way. Her eyes narrowed on the shuttle. She couldn't wait to access what the humans knew about technology. "Why am I not inside this lovely shuttle?" She pushed the savasleri to weave between the Rapulii, enjoying the way they tensed when the creature got too close.

"We hit another trap." Pilom bowed low. He had discovered that the door could not be pulled away. "The humans were very persistent in proactively protecting their technology."

"Then you should be equally persistent in breaking through. Failure will not be greeted with benevolence." Confident her conversation had fulfilled its objective, Shimgin's smile was evil as she rode toward her next victim.

Nufen turned toward Shimgin as she approached. He looked frightened. She took that as a good sign. She was done waiting for her minions to complete their assigned tasks.

"Shimgin, what do you desire?" Nufen bowed.

"The same thing I have desired for days. Have you discovered how the boys escaped my cells?" She stared down at him from astride the savasleri. "And where are they now? The Bugii was injured and could not have flown anywhere."

"I believe they went north."

"North? Into Kurmii territory? Why would they? The, what did they call it, the Collective, has to be south, closer to Bentepe."

"Yes, but Kurmii territory is closer. As I explained earlier, it is logical to assume that the Kurmii and Bugii have an agreement of some sort that benefits both. There have been too many satellite images of them passing each other without fighting. Even a few gatherings that looked like a meeting."

"It is not logical. It's foolish." Shimgin loosened the leash and let the savasleri move where it wished. Since she had not fed him today, Shimgin knew he would move closer to Nufen. She had offered her savasleri disobedient reds before. The one bright spot from her home being destroyed was that this savasleri had been guarding her office in the Dogu, and it had been saved. Under the pretense of checking the wall for a secret exit, Nufen placed a pillar between him and the savasleri. Shimgin's grin widened. "Someone helped them escape. Find the traitor and bring them to me." She clicked her heels, and the savasleri loped down the path to the Dogu.

Shimgin was still angry, but Nufen provided her with information she might be able to use. Could the Dialogue Hallow be in use again?

*****

Nufen walked to the underground passage with no real belief that any human would meet with him. Still, he walked. He brought no support. If the humans wanted him dead, any Rapulii who came with him would also die. Life could not continue as it had been. Shimgin would find the tunnels if she looked herself, but he would not expose them for her. The humans were Nufen's best chance to rescue his people from Shimgin's oppressive leadership. Past Sargu leaders had been cruel, but Shimgin was genuinely malevolent. May Dotaru give her all that she deserves, and then, maybe, just a little more.

Past Sargu leaders threatened more than they actually harmed. Shimgin enjoyed inflicting pain, and the number of non-Sargu reds had been cut in half. The techs had faced a similar plight over the past few years.

When he arrived at the appointed location, Nufen was surprised to see Theon Clark, his friend, with Commander Fox. Standing to Fox's left was another red male and Ish. Finally, he saw Ralim, whom Shimgin had supposedly killed. Nufen looked more closely at the red, and his mouth dropped open.

Ralim grinned. "Yes, Nufen, this is Lifen, whom Shimgin claimed died in a training accident because he couldn't control his powers."

"You must be the reason Shimgin wants to wage war now. Does she know you're alive?"

"I believe she suspects I live. I'm not sure she knows for sure."

"She will not hear so from me." Nufen bowed slightly toward Lifen, before turning to Ralim. "You are also said to be dead. Killed for failure to complete a task."

Ralim held his arms out to his side. "As you can see, I am not yet in the arms of Nurita."

"I find that pleases me. Shall I inform Pilom of your living status? He is now the senior," Nufen said.

Ralim grinned and said to Fox, "Good news. Pilom was my second in the resistance as you call it. Nufen can inform him of our agreements. The blues will join us."

Nufen raised an eyebrow at Ralim's openness. "You trust these humans?"

"Yes, and the Bugii and Kurmii too. Our future is brighter than either of us could have believed."

Nufen said nothing to this pronouncement. He wasn't sure he trusted the humans enough to discuss such things.

"Thank you for helping the boys. My first question is, who do you represent?" Commander Fox asked.

Nufen looked around nervously.

"Are you expecting trouble?" the commander asked.

"Always," Nufen retorted. "I will not give you names, but I represent a group of non-Sargu reds who feel as I do. That Shimgin is not good for the Rapulii. We want a more beneficial agreement for all Rapulii than the one we have with Shimgin."

"What is your current agreement?" Commander Fox asked.

Nufen couldn't keep the wry smile off his face. "We do as Shimgin commands, on her timeline. In exchange, she doesn't kill us, at least not often."

Ralim stepped in and said, "You will find the humans, Bugii, and Kurmii to be much more generous. The humans have strong beliefs about equality. They like it."

"That does sound promising," Nufen said. "Commander, your soldiers are not safe but currently have no life-threatening injuries. Shimgin has placed guards inside the holding cells so that they don't disappear as the boys did. Each shift has at least one guard loyal to me in an attempt to prevent torture. Shall we discuss the details?" Nufen asked.

"Indeed," Commander Fox said.

Nufen watched the human soldiers spread out, to serve as lookouts, and turned his thoughts to negotiations.

Chapter 30

Opalo eyed the cane with disgust. Ish had hand carved the staff from a branch taken from a fallen koyua tree limb, and Lifen had used lightning to brand a beautiful design over the entire cane. Their work was striking. It was a thing of beauty. What was disgusting was the fact that Opalo had to use the thing. He needed the cane in his left hand for balance. He was still a bit unsteady on his feet a couple of days after the surgery.

Doc Cromer had spent a significant amount of time explaining that he would have trouble walking because he wouldn't be able to use his wings for balance. To make sure he didn't pull his flying limbs and undo her work, both were taped tightly against his shoulders. Something about making sure the left wing didn't pull on his right. The doctor was insistent that neither wing could be used. Until today, he didn't know how helpless his grandmother felt. Opalo couldn't even depend on others to fly him to the high caves to sleep. Even that might cause the doctor's hard work to be undone. He would sleep with the humans in the far side of the cave, near the reflection center.

How had Sulka stood it all these years? She hadn't flown since she was a few years older than Opalo. Now Sulka was the most senior of the Bugii. According to Whisper, Bugii lived three times as long as humans. It was odd to imagine that when he had lived a third of his life, Whisper and Ish would die of old age. Over a year ago, when the humans landed on Kurazi, he thought they were like the Sargu because the Sargu embraced them. Now he counted Sargu and humans amongst his closest friends. Life was certainly strange.

Ish's head popped into the room. "You ready?"

"What's the rush?" Opalo was wrapped like an erkek still being trained to not bang things with its tail, and he didn't want to see anyone.

"Nothing, just want to get a move on."

"Uh-huh." Opalo scratched his chin. At least his arms were allowed limited movement. "You don't lie very well."

Ish blushed. "There's a bit of a celebration waiting for you."

Growling, Opalo turned too fast and wobbled until Ish grabbed Opalo's arm and handed him the staff. "You need to keep this in your hands anytime you're not sitting or lying down."

"And this is exactly why I don't want to see anyone." Opalo leaned on the staff. To his dismay, it did stabilize him. "I can't fly. I cannot walk without the aid of this cane. I don't want anyone to see me like this."

"You know you're going to be in various versions of restrictive casts for weeks, right? Unless you stay hidden here, everyone will see you."

"Fine. Let's get this over with." Opalo tightened his grip on the staff, and they proceeded down the corridor to the shuttle. Everyone he passed gave him plenty of room so as not to accidentally bump into him. He found that their consideration irritated him as well. Ish explained that shuttle's emissions had been modified per Ralim's instructions. They were able to travel between the ship and the Collective with ease. No more shimmers for Shimgin to track.

When they boarded a shuttle, and Ish started flight prep, Opalo asked, "Isn't this how we got captured the first time?"

Ish winced. "Yeah, would you prefer another pilot?"

"I was jesting. I am comfortable with you flying the shuttle."

"You mean joking, and that makes one of us," Ish muttered.

Opalo checked the board and tried to get comfortable sitting with his wings bandaged tight. "Is this your first flight since we were Shimgin's guests?"

"Yeah."

"Sorry for the bad joke." The rest of the flight was silent while Ish concentrated on not getting captured again. Opalo looked out the viewport and dreaded the welcome home festivities.

Once they landed, Opalo knew he had been right to dread them. He wasn't to the bottom of the shuttle ramp before Shea ran at him. Opalo planted his staff and tried to steady himself as best he could. Shea jumped and flapped her wings to rush Opalo as she always did. Opalo breathed a sigh of relief when Ish stepped in and caught her.

"We talked about this. For Opalo to heal properly, he cannot lift or catch anything for a while."

Shea eyed Opalo's bandages and fluttered her wings as Ish lowered her to the ground. "Sorry, I forgot. So, you really can't fly for a while."

"No." This was his life now. If his wing didn't heal, he would be like this forever. A lifetime unable to support himself. A burden to his family and saime.

Shea tilted her head to the side to look at her brother. "Don't be sad. You got to be on the ship for days. I still haven't seen the inside. What's it like? Did you walk through every room? Do you have to go back? If you do, can I come?"

Opalo couldn't help it, he laughed. "Easy, fledgling. Slow down with the questions."

"I'm not a fledgling. I'm a juvenile, and you know it. I can fly. I'm what the humans call a teenager. I like that better than juvenile, don't you? And you're a teenager too. Ish said so."

Opalo raised an eyebrow at Ish. "What have you been teaching my sister?"

"We use the term teenager to explain the years where you still live at home, but you have some freedom of choices, and you are expected to shoulder some responsibility. Shea is a young teenager, but she is a teenager by our standards. Like me, you're at the high end of the teen years."

"Uh-oh. Here comes Taiva. She drives me crazy asking about you all the time. Irritating." Shea eyed the newcomer, and when Taiva approached Opalo with the obvious intention of hugging him, Shea stepped in the way. "Don't touch him. You don't want him to heal improperly, do you?"

Ish pressed his lips together to hide his laughter. Opalo had been trying to get Taiva to notice him for a while. Now that she had, Shea decided to protect her big brother.

"Sorry." Taiva took a step backward. "How are you feeling?"

"I'm okay." *Much better if you had hugged me.* Opalo cut his eyes to Ish, whose unbecoming grin also annoyed him.

Whisper, Zigmin, and Lifen were next to arrive, followed by a large number of the saime. By the time he thanked everyone for their concern and get well wishes, Taiva was nowhere to be seen.

*****

Let me help you." Taiva reached out to take the basket of brambles Opalo held in one hand while he leaned heavily on his staff.

"I can do it." Opalo barked out the words and was immediately sorry.

At his harsh words, Taiva stopped in mid reach, her hands fluttered in the air in concert with her wings.

Opalo handed her the basket. "Sorry. I shouldn't have snapped at you. It's not your fault that I can't soar or that walking hurts, or that bending over to pick up the brambles for next meal hurts more than falling from the cliffs."

"You're still recovering. You are not expected to –"

"I'm not expected to what? Participate in daily life? Help in any way? Be useful?"

"If you're done feeling sorry for yourself, I was going to say you're not expected to bend over and grab brambles. That's a job for the young. You should be in the command center." Taiva emptied the contents of the basket into the food staging area.

Opalo was glad that Bugii didn't blush, or he would be bright red like Ish got when Whisper called him out on something. Finally, he admitted, "It hurts to sit too long."

Taiva raised and lowered her wings. "Perhaps you could help me. I'm going to walk into the fields to pick cari for first meal tomorrow. I don't know why humans love the drink they make with it, but they do."

"You're going to walk. Really?" Since he couldn't use his wings to express disbelief, Opalo raised an eyebrow as he had seen the humans do.

Taiva's eye lightened. "I'll fly if you don't go because it's faster, but I would much rather walk with you."

"A walk would be nice." Opalo's step picked up a little. Besides, the doctors did tell him to walk as much as possible every day. As they walked out to the fields, he tried to come up with a topic of conversation that wouldn't sound self-serving. Finally, he said, "According to Whisper, cari contains an ingredient very close to a substance from their home world called caffeine. It's a stimulant for them. They use it to wake up after sleep. That's why they crush the leaves and make a

284

hot drink out of it. The humans are pleased to have found it here."

Taiva smiled. "The humans do such interesting things. What else have you learned from our new friends?"

Opalo searched his memory for everything he had learned. If talking about the humans kept Taiva with him longer, he would provide all the knowledge he had.

*****

Ish caught up with Whisper on the practice field where she shot arrows with great precision at the replacement targets Lifen had made for the Bugii warriors. He had felt bad about burning the last ones.

"I'm done, if you want to practice," Whisper said after she released her last arrow.

"Nope, I'm good," Ish said. Whisper's command of weapons was impressive. It couldn't just be that her father was a security chief. She had natural talent, but he was willing to bet Commander Fox had trained her to fight from birth. She was proficient at hand-to-hand, skilled with small arms, and expert with a bow and arrow. Though he passed all qualification tests, he considered himself to be amazingly average at all those things.

"Then why come to the target range?" Whisper tossed her bow over her shoulder and collected her arrows, placing them in the quiver.

Ish pressed his lips together. No way was he going to admit he was looking for her. Realizing Whisper was waiting for his answer, and he had to say something, Ish said, "I'm tired of being cooped up here. At first, I thought it would be better to be here than to be on the ship, but now that most humans are on the ship, I'm feeling a little lost. It's not like we're allowed to really participate in the missions."

Whisper nodded her agreement. "I know. I want to do more. Lifen and Zigmin are preparing for battle, and we're still in training."

"How about we take a walk and look for food?" Ish asked.

"Anything but brambles," they said in unison and laughed.

"Okay." Whisper adjusted her bow and fell into step with Ish.

They walked in silence for a while through the valley north of Guntepe. There was a grove of yust along the base of the mountains making it possible for the duo to move under the tall branches which would hide them from Shimgin's satellites. When Whisper stopped and pulled an arrow from her quiver, Ish looked in the direction her arrow pointed.

Whisper looked at him, silently asking if she should. Ish nodded. The boar-like omuz would be a great meal if they could figure out how to move it.

Whisper pulled back her bow, took a deep breath, and let her arrow fly. She hit the omuz, the arrow going through its eye and into its brain. It died immediately.

"Great! You did it!" Ish grinned, pulling her into a hug.

Whisper smiled. Many humans, especially guys her age, didn't seem to be pleased when she outshot them, but Ish was different. He didn't seem jealous at all. In fact, he was genuinely happy for her. Whisper leaned up and kissed Ish on the lips. Okay, she brushed her lips over his. She had never kissed anyone. Before they left Old Earth, she, like everyone else, was too busy learning all she could to be sure she made elite status and got assigned to a ship with her father.

Ish pulled back in surprise, smiled, and kissed her for real.

Whisper enjoyed the feel of his arms around her and the kiss. Apparently, he had devoted at least some time to the art of kissing for he was quite good at it.

A throat cleared behind them. Ish and Whisper jumped away from each other and turned to see who had caught them.

Lieutenant Porter dropped his arrow back into his quiver and grinned. "We should get that omuz back to Guntepe. Looks like we'll be eating good tomorrow."

"Tomorrow?" Ish asked in confusion before he remembered how long it took to cook the omuz.

"Yeah." Porter pulled out his comm and said, "Command, Whisper took down another omuz. We need help getting it back to camp. We're in Sector 2."

"Nice," Ensign Botha replied. After a short discussion with the comm muted, she was back. "Four Kurmii are heading your way now."

The lieutenant sat down and got comfortable. "We'll have to wait for them. And guys don't do anything that I might have to report to my commander. I believe you know him, Ish, Whisper's father."

Whisper blushed. For once, Ish didn't.

Looking up at the sky, Ish said, "I know it doesn't snow here, but what's falling from the sky?"

Whisper and Lieutenant Porter looked up. Whisper held out her hand and watched a flake landed on her finger. "How odd."

Porter rubbed a flake that fell into his hand. It felt like a grain of sand. He tapped his comm and said, "Command, run an atmospheric test. There is an odd, coarse, white grain falling from the sky."

"Yes, sir." A few seconds later, Botha said, "Find shelter. It's the poison Shimgin invented to kill humans."

"Everyone's inoculated. Why hide?" Ish asked. Whisper passed out, and Ish caught her before she hit the ground.

"Fireman carry," Porter said. They adjusted Whisper's weight between them and headed for the nearest cave.

287

"Because the immunization was estimated to be ninety percent effective."

Ish did the math and said, "Ten out of every one hundred humans will die?"

"Doctor Cromer thought it was more likely that ten percent would become extremely sick, but death is a possibility." They entered the cave and placed Whisper gently on the floor.

Immune to the poison snow, the Kurmii ran up the same path Ish and Whisper had used earlier. The warriors gathered up the omuz and returned. Using a combination of Kurmii, Rapulii, and hand signals, Porter asked the Kurmii to remain.

"Will we even be able to eat that?" Ish pointed to the omuz.

"Good question. Guess the doctors will have to test it to see. If not, we will have to test all food now before we eat anything."

Ish sighed. If that were the case, humans might find this planet unsuitable. And that would be problematic, as some ship functions had already been disabled for use on this world, and what remained in space was no longer able to go through an ERB. There was also the more significant problem of getting enough thrust to leave orbit. Problem as in it wasn't possible.

Whisper's breathing became more labored, and Ish knelt by her side. "We need to get her to the Doc."

"Agreed." Porter tapped his comm. "Command, we need a biohazard cleansing ASAP. Whisper is having trouble breathing. How fast can you get that set up at our location?"

"Stand by," Botha said. Within seconds she was back on the comm. "A team is heading your way. If you move her to where the passage you're in joins the larger passage, the team will set up the cleansing there."

"Thanks, Command. Porter out." Porter pulled out of his backpack a small square that unfolded into a hammock. "We can use this as a makeshift stretcher. Should make it easier to carry her."

288

"No shuttle?" Ish asked.

"Can't risk the biohazard adhering to the shuttle and carrying the poison back to the base."

"How about us?" Ish grunted and held up his section of the hammock.

Porter took the lead and grabbed a section of the hammock. Walking down the passage, Porter replied, "We won't leave this passage until they have the biohazard unit set up to remove any particles."

The Kurmii, carrying the omuz, fell in step behind the humans carrying Whisper.

Chapter 31

Commander Fox ran to the makeshift med bay the humans had set up in Guntepe. When he saw no one was in bio gear, he breathed a sigh of relief. At least Whisper wasn't contagious. When he approached the bed, Doctor Cromer looked up and smiled.

"Come closer." Adjusting the equipment, Cromer said, "Whisper will be okay. Once she was through the bio cleansing, and I cleared out her lungs, she began breathing normally. She didn't succumb to the poison, but she is allergic to the dust. At this point, we don't know if she's an isolated case or if others will have a similar reaction."

Fox held his daughter's hand and watched her sleep. Whisper would always be his little girl.

"Doctor Cromer." The med tech tapped a screen and said, "As long as the poison snow doesn't contact human skin, it becomes inert. The poison is a combination of two repelling molecules. Individually, they are not harmful. Unless the poison is inhaled, and coats the lungs together, it breaks down into its separate particles."

"Poison snow?" Fox asked.

"Sorry, commander," The red-headed med tech blushed. "It's the name we gave it in the lab. The more important problem is the breathing issue. While it still holds true that the vaccine is ninety percent effect, we now estimate that forty percent of our population will have debilitating asthma attacks."

"What can we do?"

"The quick fix is that everyone needs to carry a breathing mask at all times." Cromer opened a cabinet and tossed the commander a mask. "A final solution will take time."

"Solution to what?" Whisper asked.

"Don't worry about that. Concentrate on getting better." Fox leaned over and kissed her on the forehead. "I was worried."

Whisper looked over the equipment she was attached to and frowned. "Did the falling specks do this?"

*****

Fox completed his task and looked up. Lifen had approached the command center and waited to be acknowledged. In Fox's experience, that attitude, regardless of species, meant the person wanted something. "What can I do for you?"

"I think I know a way for us to end this conflict with Shimgin and the Sargu."

"Do tell."

"If I challenge Shimgin, Sargu to Sargu, she must accept the challenge or the other Sargu will no longer follow her."

"Challenge? You mean a duel?"

"Yes, I believe so. I challenge the leader of the Sargu to a fight. The winner becomes the new leader of the Sargu or remains the leader."

"That has merit. Why would Shimgin accept your challenge?"

"No choice. Any challenge by any Sargu, even one who is not yet an adult, must be accepted."

"Why don't the other Sargu challenge their leader all the time?" Fox eyed Lifen. "There must be a penalty to be paid?"

Lifen shrugged. "Only the loser pays the price. No one else."

"What is the price?" When Lifen didn't answer, Fox shook his head. "It's a to-the-death match, isn't it?"

"Yes," Lifen admitted reluctantly.

"We aren't sending you in to die."

"I will win."

"You're sure? You know for a fact that you're stronger than Shimgin?"

"I was nearly as strong when Shimgin and Kimrin left me for dead. I should be strong enough now."

"Should is not a power word."

"I'm not sure I know what that means."

"It means you're hedging. You hope you're strong enough, but you aren't sure. Why do this?"

Lifen paced. "We have to do something. Shimgin, if left alone, will devise a way to attack us and she is extremely efficient. The poison snow failed in its intent, and we can't give her time to improve the toxin. She needs to be kept off balance. A challenge, especially one from a male who is supposed to be dead, will do that nicely."

"No." Zigmin ran into the command center.

Ish was right on her heels and said, "We've already had this discussion. No martyrs."

"Don't throw your life away." Whisper had moved slower, but the glare she shot Lifen showed her anger well enough.

"I should be insulted by the lack of faith my friends are showing in my ability to fight. Somehow, though, I find it soothing that you care for my safety." A small smile played on Lifen's lips. "I am quite sure of my ability to fight."

Zigmin got right in his face. "Shimgin won't follow the rules, and you know it. She will cheat, and she will win."

Lifen smiled for real. "Commander, let me know what you decide. I'm the best distraction with the highest odds of success, and everyone knows it."

When Lifen walked away, his three friends turned to Commander Fox and stared.

Fox held up his hands. "Yes, it's dangerous, but it's also a good plan. From everything we've learned from Nufen and Ralim, if Shimgin dies, the other Sargu will be more reasonable until they know 'which way the wind blows' as Ralim said. I'm not saying it's a go. I'm saying we have to consider it."

Whisper placed her hands on her father's desk and asked, "Would you consider it if I were the best person to take on Shimgin?"

"Yes. I would look for any reason to veto the plan, and protect my daughter, but I would have to look at it. If Shimgin wages a full-scale war against us, she and the other Sargu, working together, can destroy the *Scorpius*. We still have over three thousand humans who have not been awakened. If the ship loses power, they die. The only reason she hasn't attacked the ship is that she wants it in working order. If she thinks there's no hope, Shimgin will do her best to destroy it." Fox cut his eyes to Zigmin. "Could you, working alone, take out the ship's power?"

Zigmin shrugged. "It would be fairly easy. Shimgin made sure all Sargu, even those still in training, like me, know what sections of the ship to hit to do the most damage. Assuming the information she provided is accurate, I could do so without aid."

"Thought so." Fox turned his eyes on his daughter. "I don't wish to put your friend in danger, but with the poison snow a real threat, it might become the best option."

*****

Shimgin heard the noise outside and went to investigate. Had the humans attacked again? When she saw a 3-D larger-than-life image of Lifen atop the Semelai, she knew the humans had helped him project that image. Her skin flashed iridescent, moving in time to her anger. "You!"

"It has been a while, Shimgin. I'm pleased you remember me." Lifen smiled and held out his hands. His voice carried for all Rapulii to hear. "I am Lifen. My death was ordered three years ago. As you can see, Shimgin failed to kill me. Yesterday, I attained my majority. As an adult Sargu, I challenge you, Shimgin, for the right to rule the Sargu."

"You are male. You can't rule."

Lifen grinned. "Then you should have no trouble defeating me."

"Come to me now. Let us battle and be done with it."

"No," Lifen said. "I will meet you in three days, at the height of the sun. Down in the meeting chambers of the ancestors. Surely you can find the Dialogue Hallow."

"I shall be there." Shimgin turned and walked away, wanting to be the first to end the conversation. She also didn't want him to see her smile. How kind of Lifen and his human friends to give her the distraction she needed.

*****

As soon as the transmission ended, Lifen stepped off the projection device.

"Nicely done." Ensign Botha secured the communication gear. When she noticed Zigmin's expression, she pointed Ish, Whisper, and Opalo out of the room, leaving Lifen and Zigmin alone.

Lifen moved to follow them, but Zigmin grabbed his arm and turned him to face her. "She will kill you."

"You don't believe I will be the victor?" Lifen asked. He was as surprised as she had been to find out that Zigmin could touch Lifen without him reacting negatively.

"I believe you will play by the rules. Shimgin will break any rule she has to in order to achieve victory."

"I issued a direct challenge, Sargu to Sargu. There are no rules. We both will win by any means possible."

"Think about that for a minute." Zigmin got right in Lifen's face. "If you win, and that's a big if, you will be the new leader of the Sargu. The others may attack in mass to keep a male from leading the Sargu."

Lifen grinned. "I know, that's why I have a plan."

"You do?" Surprise etched Zigmin's face. "You've actually considered that you might be the next Sargu leader?"

"Of course, but I'm changing the structure."

"How?"

Lifen took Zigmin's hand. "Co-leaders, like the Bugii. You and I will rule together."

"You would trust me enough to share power with me?"

"Yes." Lifen moved in slowly, gauging Zigmin's response. When he was satisfied with what he saw, Lifen tilted his head and nipped her neck. "I trust you with all that I am."

Zigmin beamed, her skin flashing iridescently. For once she didn't notice.

*****

Three days later, Lifen walked toward the reflection center for breakfast. He wasn't hungry but knew that others would be looking for signs of nervousness or weakness. He would show neither.

"If we are to be co-leaders, I will walk with you this day." Zigmin dropped into step with Lifen.

"It will be dangerous. If I lose, all Sargu will attack anyone with me."

"I understand, and I know this fight is yours. But if we are to be co-leaders, I will be there to support you."

Lifen didn't reply. As much as he wanted Zigmin to be safe, his steps felt lighter.

Before they arrived at the reflection center, Ish and Whisper blocked their path. Lifen looked at his friends. "What's this?"

"If you are to battle today, your clothes should reflect your new status as co-leaders of the Sargu." Ish held out an outfit.

"Take it. Saber Isles, our chief of logistics, helped create something appropriate for co-leaders to wear." Whisper handed Zigmin a matching outfit. "Change quickly. We should eat before we go."

"The clothes are a good idea, but you won't be with them. Only Rapulii, Kurmii, and Bugii will be in attendance. Shimgin is calling this an internal matter. If we are there, she will say we interfered directly. She will claim we are behind the fight and might be able to rally supporters behind her." Commander Fox handed Lifen and Zigmin comm devices. "If the fight goes badly, use these to contact us. We'll use the security cameras to watch the fight, but we have no sound."

Sporting their new clothes with comm devices in their pockets, Lifen and Zigmin ate in silence except for those stopping to give Lifen words of encouragement. When it was time, the duo, and their entourage, minus the humans, walked down the passage to the Dialogue Hallows.

*****

Ish and Whisper gathered with the humans in the command center to watch the battle through the vids. Commander Fox's security devices would serve another purpose today.

"Commander," Porter didn't look up from his screen as he called to Fox. "A small Rapulii drone is heading south. Based on current trajectory, it will be at Guntepe in less than a minute."

"Understood." Fox shook his head. He had argued against giving Shimgin the specs for the small drones. It had been the first tech the humans had given the Rapulii, and it had seemed benign at the time. Now that Shimgin had a biological weapon to use against the humans, Fox no longer thought benign was the proper word. "Masks on. Ish, spread the word throughout the camp."

When Whisper turned to leave with Ish, Fox said, "No. You've already had a bad reaction to the Rapulii bioweapon. Stay here with Doctor Cromer."

Whisper rolled her eyes at her father but stayed where she was.

Ish ran for the front of the cave, waving his mask, and telling all humans to put on their masks. It was easier to yell without the mask on. Easier to be understood too. So far, Ish and Lieutenant Porter were the only humans known for a fact to not have an asthma attack from the poison snow. As he approached the cave entrance, Ensign Botha ran past him to a bunker. She took aim and shot the drone. Unfortunately, when the drone exploded its payload scattered over the cave entrance.

Ish turned and ran in the other direction. Humans in the back of the cave might not have gotten the word. When this was over, he was going to find out when an internal comm system would be installed in Guntepe, and Bentepe as well. As he ran, sounding the alarm along the way, he noticed the kids. When Ish approached the school, where Bugii and human young were being trained together, he saw three more drones. Shimgin had sent drones through the underground passages, and no one had noticed. Everyone who could see a vid was focused on Lifen.

"Put on your masks." Ish didn't wait for the children or teachers to respond. He dropped next to the nearest child to help, but it wasn't necessary. These children, young though they were, had been born on Old Earth, where a mask was required to walk outside most days. The human children calmly put on their masks as if it were a drill like they used to have on Old Earth. Jacob gave Ish a thumbs up.

The two human teachers, slow to respond because they were checking the children, passed out unable to breath. Ish put the masks on the teachers. "Everyone stay where you are until an adult comes for you." As soon as the children nodded, Ish took off running, further back into the cave. Anyone he found passed out, Ish placed their mask on them as well, but he wasn't sure it would help after the fact.

The Bugii saw his actions and helped the unconscious humans. Sulka used her right wing to tap Ish on the shoulder. "Go. Tell the commander about this attack. We'll see to your people."

"Thanks." Ish ran back to the command center. "Commander, three more drones came in through the tunnels. There might be more on the way."

Whisper grabbed Ish and hugged him. Without thinking, Ish leaned down and planted a kiss on her shoulder since her head and face were hidden behind a mask.

"Ensign Botha, secure the tunnels."

"Aye, commander."

"And Ish, put your mask on. Long term effects are unknown." Commander Fox turned back to his console without commenting on the attention Ish had paid to his daughter.

"Aye, commander." Ish grinned and put his mask on.

Chapter 32

Lifen walked into the meeting chamber of the ancestors with Zigmin at his side. He was not surprised when the Sargu glared at them. Aside from being a male Sargu who should have died years ago, he and Zigmin were wearing new clothing designed with the help of the humans and the Bugii. The unisex outfits the duo had on presented them as equals and were similar to what the Bugii leaders wore. The Kurmii saw no reason for clothing and considered it a waste of time as their body plates covered them well enough.

"What is this?" Shimgin demanded. "Lifen challenged. Zigmin has no place here."

"You have your Sargu supporters." Zigmin pointed to the other Sargu in the room, most of whom had brought their savasleri with them. Zigmin hesitated when she noticed Tobin, sitting astride her own savasleri. She had been a plant. Zigmin had trusted Tobin, who she thought was a simple red, and Tobin was an adult Sargu.

Tobin's skin flashed iridescently, and she looked embarrassed.

Zigmin hid her disappointment and pointed to her own chest. "Lifen has me."

Lifen spoke as if the exchange hadn't occurred. "Once the challenge is over and I'm the Sargu leader, Zigmin will be my co-leader."

"You are too weak to lead alone." Shimgin grinned. "The Sargu will not follow a leader that needs help."

"No, I will defeat you and any other challenger alone, if only to prove to the Sargu and all Rapulii that males are not weak. When it comes to policy and decisions, Zigmin and I will rule together."

Shimgin turned to Zigmin. "Will you follow the rule of a male?"

Zigmin jutted out her chin. "We shall rule together."

Shimgin cackled. "Even if Lifen were to defeat me, the Rapulii will not support a male Sargu. Their powers are too unstable."

"I will follow the rule of Lifen and Zigmin." Ralim walked into the chamber, with a large number of blues and non-Sargu reds following him. "As will my friends."

"Traitor. You die now." Shimgin created lightning and threw it at Ralim.

Lifen caught the lightning and extinguished it. The exclamations from the Sargu were loud. No one else had ever been able to dissipate Shimgin's lightning. It was one of the reasons she ruled. Her aggressive attacks were unstoppable.

Shimgin growled and threw another lightning ball at Ralim. She couldn't appear weak to the Sargu. This time she watched as Zigmin caught the lightning and dissipated it.

The Sargu looked among themselves.

"Enough." Lifen's voice carried to the furthest corners of the chamber. "Shimgin, I am here to fight you in accordance with the rite of challenge. You and me, with none interfering. A fight to the death. Are you backing out of this challenge?"

"I back down from no challenge." Shimgin grinned at Ralim before turning back to Lifen. "There's time enough to kill the traitor after I kill you."

"There can be no other kills after a rite of challenge." Lifen ground out the words that all Sargu knew.

"After I kill you, that rule may change."

Lifen nodded to Zigmin, and she went to stand by Ralim. Lifen rose to his full height and borrowed a phrase that Ish said often enough. "Let's do this."

At his words, Shimgin threw three lightning balls in fast succession.

Lifen created wind, circled the lightning balls, and combined them into one huge ball, tossing it back at Shimgin. Shimgin ducked, allowing the lightning to hit the wall.

Due to the size of the ball, the cave shook, sending debris raining down on those assembled in the chamber. Sargu used wind to keep the rubble off them. The blues and non-Sargu reds ran for cover. Ralim remained by Zigmin's side. A silent but obvious statement that he trusted her to protect him, which she did. Zigmin created a shield of wind, and no debris fell on them.

Shimgin called wind and increased its strength, sending it straight at Lifen. He flew back into the wall. Snarling, he created lightning and threw it at Shimgin. She jumped out of the way and looked up just in time to see that he had divided his lightning, sending it in five directions. One of the bolts hit her, knocking her back to the ground.

The observers were excited to see such a display from Lifen. Few of the female Sargu could break lightning apart, and none could perform the feat that many times.

Lifen prepared his next volley as Shimgin jumped to her feet. The downside of sending lightning in multiple directions was each new bolt weakened the lightning. Shimgin had been knocked to the ground and shaken, but not injured. However, she was mad. Shimgin created lightning, sending it in a high arc, and allowing it to spread out and land around Lifen in a tight circle. The close proximity of the multiple bolts was stronger than Lifen's divided lightning, and he fell to the ground in pain.

Shimgin moved in, gathering all the lightning she could, sending the ball straight at Lifen's chest. She smiled, knowing he would die. Then she would kill Zigmin, Ralim, and anyone else she felt like killing today. She had noticed Tobin and Zigmin staring at each other and no longer trusted her spy. Shimgin was so caught up in her plans, she didn't immediately notice Lifen grabbing her lightning and sending it back at her. She caught on in time and pushed it back toward Lifen. It didn't budge.

Lifen's eyes narrowed on Shimgin, and he kept his hands held out in front of him as if he was still holding the ball. Shimgin pushed back using a similar stance. The ball moved toward Lifen, then back at Shimgin. The back and forth went on for a few seconds with neither combatant gaining any ground.

Shimgin called out to the young fighter. "You cannot win. You are only a male. Inferior in every way."

"Not inferior," Lifen grunted. "Just different." Gathering up his lightning one more time, Lifen fed more power into the ball, pushing it toward Shimgin with all of his might. The ball pushed into Shimgin, knocking her into the wall, holding her in place. Lifen did not release the lightning until the light left Shimgin's eyes.

Lifen wanted nothing so much as to fall to the ground, but he turned and faced the Sargu. "Do any wish to challenge me this day for the right to rule the Sargu and all Rapulii?"

Aside from some rumbling by the Sargu, the chamber was silent for a few moments. Eventually, the other Sargu nodded to Figlin, and she stood. "Your plan for Sargu co-rulers is

302

unprecedented, but perhaps it is time for a change. Let us hear your plans."

Zigmin handed out documents to each Sargu. Lifen and Zigmin had prepared for this. When a challenger for Sargu leader wins the battle, their rule starts immediately. They must know what to expect or the Sargu fight.

"We are to align with the Bugii, humans, and Kurmii? They will not accept us." Figlin didn't look up from the document. "Some of us have hunted their kind."

"There is no 'their kind.' Not anymore." Lifen looked around the room. "We must unite as a planet. That is the only way for us to grow. For too many seasons to list, we have stayed within our own settlement. No interaction with the others except to kill them. While the Bugii and Kurmii have maintained trade agreements that have allowed them to grow, we Rapulii have stagnated. The Sargu have become idle, depending on the techs to provide for our needs, and the warriors to defend our lands."

Looking each Sargu in the eyes, Lifen said, "We have been left behind. The Bugii and Kurmii are much more advanced than we are, and the humans have more advanced tech than we could have imagined before they landed, and we have seen for ourselves some of what their powerful tech can do. Ralim and some of the other blues have managed to keep some advances hidden to prevent Shimgin from destroying the planet. For this, we owe them thanks. It's time for all Rapulii to be treated equally."

"Only the reds can reproduce. How can the others be equal?" The question was thrown out from the back of the room.

"The ability to reproduce is not the only service that makes someone useful." Figlin stood again. "Your words have merit Lifen, but we need to evaluate the full impact on our society. Your plan will completely redefine the life of the Rapulii."

"Not all changes will be made immediately." Zigmin spoke for the first time. "We will resume discussions tomorrow in the Dogu."

Figlin waited as the other Sargu left hurriedly on their savasleri. She dismounted and walked over to Lifen. "Many of us are pleased that you killed Shimgin, but not all. Some of the new rules will displease the majority of the Sargu. They will find it hard to accept a lower station than they are accustomed to."

"Where do you stand?" Lifen asked.

"Before the humans arrived, I would not have been pleased."

"What changed?"

"I have lived a long time and had noticed something odd that all four Sargu leaders that I have known had in common. A task they all performed. I finally attained a position where I could review the nursery records. I was appalled at what I found." Figlin handed Lifen a storage device. "Ralim should be able to find somewhere to read the data. I warn you, the blues and greens will not like what is on this device. I know I don't. I shall be at the Dogu tomorrow."

Lifen held the storage device in his hand and looked at Zigmin. "Guess this is our first item of business. Together, the new Sargu co-leaders, and their Rapulii supporters, returned to the Collective to find a thin layer of dust covering everything.

Ralim wet his finger and picked up some of the dust to taste it. "It's the poison snow."

The Rapulii ran to help.

Chapter 33

"Final count?" Jacey Rees took her seat across from Captain Dolan.

Doctor Cromer looked up from her tablet. "Thirty-seven negative reactions to the poison, but all but seven have recovered. There were two deaths. Both died because their lungs were coated in the poison snow, and they couldn't breathe even with a mask. We would have lost more if Ish and the Bugii hadn't placed masks on the unconscious. That was fast thinking on Ish's part. It prevented too much of the snow from coating the lungs."

Jacey beamed with pride in her son. "And the remaining seven?"

"I believe they will recover, but it will take time."

"Any chance the Sargu will attack?" Jacey looked at Commander Fox.

Fox shrugged. "I don't think so. They seem to be waiting to see which way the wind blows. Lifen was right about that. The Sargu want to see what Lifen and Zigmin do with their new positions."

"And the bombshell Figlin dropped?" Jacey asked.

"Hopefully, the Rapulii will survive the anger over what has been done."

*****

"Did no one suspect?" Whisper asked.

"No. The Sargu leader is always at the hatching, which occurs twice a year. She pronounces each hatchling healthy or not. She removes the unhealthy ones herself with lightning, burning them, and scattering the resultant ash. It has been so for generations." Zigmin shook her head. "I, and I assume the rest of the Sargu, thought we Rapulii had a high death rate. It was one of the reasons giving birth was so highly valued. At least we thought it was."

"But it doesn't make sense." Whisper didn't have words for the horror of what had been done to the Rapulii for generations.

"No, it doesn't, but here's the proof. The Sargu leaders, going back generations, have killed all female blues and greens. Then they sterilized the blue and green males. Since red is a recessive gene, each clutch by Sargu hatched enough blues and greens to keep the structure the way the Sargu leader wanted it. The Sargu leaders have killed more Rapulii than any war with the Bugii or Kurmii ever did or could have," Zigmin said. They fell silent for a while, continuing to review the data.

"I'm meeting her tonight." Whisper didn't look up from the screen.

"Tobin? It's too dangerous. She's Sargu."

"So are you."

Zigmin shook her head. "I chose a side, ours. She chose Shimgin's. Tobin was Shimgin's spy. You can't trust her."

"I have to meet her. I have to know."

"Then I'm going with you."

A few hours later, Whisper walked to the ancestor's meeting chamber, with Zigmin, Lifen, and Ish in tow. "This is ridiculous. Tobin is my friend."

"No, Tobin pretended to be your friend. She didn't tell you she was Sargu, did she?" Lifen asked.

"Did you tell Ish you were a Sargu when you first met?"

"That's different." Lifen was indignant.

Whisper turned and looked at her friend. "How?"

"It just is."

"Man, I agree with you on this, and that's lame," Ish said.

The four friends walked the rest of the way in silence.

Tobin stood alone in the chamber when they arrived. She had left her savasleri behind. She looked at Whisper. "I find myself surprised you came at all. I wasn't sure you would get the message, and, even if you did, I wasn't sure you would want to see me."

"Nufen gave me the message. I'm here because I want to know why." Whisper crossed her arms in front of her chest.

"I was Shimgin's spy, but I'm sure you already know that."

Whisper's voice raised in frustration. "But why? Why were you her spy?"

"I wasn't strong enough to say no to her. She trained me herself. Not even Kimrin knew about me."

"Interesting, but it doesn't tell us why," Lifen said.

"Who knows? Most of my assignments were searching for the resistance. Shimgin knew the techs and non-Sargu reds were up to something. She didn't tell me why she assigned me to the combined school, but she wanted daily updates." Tobin shrugged.

"You didn't tell her much," Lifen said.

"How do you know what I told her, or, more to the point, didn't tell her?"

"If you had told her everything you and Whisper talked about, she would have known Whisper was asking a lot of questions. Shimgin would have tried to use her."

"She did." Ish got in Tobin's face. "That's the reason Kimrin tried to kill us."

"No." Lifen put a hand on Ish's shoulder to calm him down. "I listened in on many conversations."

"What?" Whisper was indignant.

"Old habit. I listened to the Rapulii from the caves for the last three years." Lifen shrugged. "Fact is, if Tobin had told Shimgin what you guys talked about, she would have stopped Kimrin from making an attempt on your life. You would be much more valuable talking to Tobin. She didn't tell."

"Is that true?" Whisper asked.

"Yes, but it doesn't matter. If you hadn't been in a cave in, I would probably have told Shimgin everything to save myself."

"Not sure we could blame you for that," Ish said. When the others looked at him, he added, "I spent some quality time with Shimgin. I certainly didn't come out on top in those discussions, and we weren't tortured, just tossed around a little."

"I don't expect you to trust me. I simply want to apologize and to see if I'm to be exiled." When no one spoke, Tobin nodded. "I'm packed, and my savasleri is waiting. I will leave now." Tobin turned to leave.

"Wait." Lifen moved to stand in front of her. "You haven't been banished."

"I supported the previous leader, of course I'm..." Tobin hung her head. "I see. When is my execution?"

"What?" Whisper asked.

Tobin shrugged. "Lifen needs to establish his rule quickly. A public execution would stop some of the immediate problems."

"No, it wouldn't," Lifen said. "I don't intend to rule by fear. Besides, I have a job for you."

"A job?" Tobin looked into Lifen's eyes for the first time. Perhaps she would have a life after all.

*****

Lifen and Zigmin walked into the Sargu meeting together. No one spoke as they took seats at the newly installed circular table. A gift from the humans, taken from their spaceship and presented to the new leaders.

Zigmin broke the silence. "Has everyone read the information we sent?" Heads bobbed up and down. "I won't bother to ask if anyone knew, because even if you did, you wouldn't be stupid enough to admit it. This genocide stops now."

Lifen stood. "Zigmin and I will be at the next hatching which coincides with the next full moon. We will also have other observers. Nufen will represent the non-Sargu reds. Ralim will represent the techs, and Tibiz the warriors. If any Sargu has a problem with this, speak now."

When no one spoke, Lifen said, "Figlin will continue to supervise the nursery for now. The humans have already installed security devices so that the nursery will be guarded onsite and remotely from now on. In addition, the greens have orders from me to protect the nursery with deadly force. Orders they appeared quite amenable to carrying out. My first proclamation as co-leader of the Sargu is that any Sargu who attempts to harm any hatchling will die."

"Was it wise to admit to the techs and warriors what was done to them? We did not do this, but the Sargu leaders did. They might blame us." The question came from a sargu sitting almost directly across from Lifen.

Lifen locked eyes with her. "I understand your reluctance, but it's too late. I have already informed the leaders of all

Rapulii sects. They know. We will no longer keep secrets that impact the well-being of our fellow Rapulii. We will unite."

Lifen exchanged a look with Zigmin. They would have to keep an eye on most of the Sargu for some time to come. Thanks be to Nurita that the humans could help them. Truth be told, Lifen was certain if they didn't have the non-Sargu Rapulii, Bugii, humans, and Kurmii at their backs, the Sargu would have already assassinated the new co-leaders of the Sargu.

Chapter 34

Lifen looked out on Remei Lake from the office he shared with Zigmin. Some of the Sargu had embraced the changes, but most still had reservations. So far, there had been no overt attacks, but it was only a matter of time. He saw Opalo standing underneath Dekai, the Double Arch, with the wind rushing through his wings. It was about time for Opalo to try his wings, wasn't it? He wished he had time to check on his friend but being the co-leader of the Rapulii took a lot of work.

Tobin, in her new job as administrator for the Rapulii co-leaders, entered the office. "The Rapulii council is waiting. It's time to review the latest changes. The techs and warriors were in the room with Zigmin when the Sargu arrived. It's a bit tense in there already. After that, Commander Fox wants to discuss some security issue, and Kole asked to speak with you about additional flight routes for the Bugii."

Shaking his head, Lifen stood and saw Nufen standing off to the side as he always did. Lifen had observed Nufen, and at first thought he was guarding Tobin because she wasn't trusted by the other Rapulii. After seeing them together for a while, Lifen realized that Nufen cared for Tobin. It would be interesting to see how they progressed.

Lifen had gone from always alone to never alone, and he still had a lot of work to do. He wasn't sure he liked his new position, and he certainly didn't feel qualified for the job, but who else could or would do it? He sighed and followed Tobin.

*****

Opalo stood with his wings open beneath Dekai, the double arch. It felt good to feel the wind in his feathers again, to be completely free of the wraps and the cane, although the engraved walking stick would always have a place of honor wherever he lived. It had served him well.

"You gonna stand here all day or you gonna test out your wings?" Ish asked.

Caught up in his musings, Opalo had not heard Ish's approach. "I thought I would walk further away."

"Okay, let's go."

"No, I go alone. I don't want anyone to see if I fail." Opalo waved his hands, indicating those who had stopped to see if today he would soar.

Ish shook his head. "Bosh, no way my windblown friend. If you fail to soar on your first attempt, you plan to have a pity party. I won't allow it. We'll cut through the underground passages to the other side of the hills behind the settlement. You'll go low to make sure you can, and then we'll come back, and you can do a big reveal."

"I don't know."

Sulka walked over and stood beneath Dekai. She had seen it once when she was a small child and had always wanted to soar to the top of the arch, toward the sun. Even without the injury, she would not have been able to make that flight until now. "You won't know until you try."

Opalo huffed. "You always say that."

"That's because it's true." Sulka turned to Ish. "Do humans have any similar phrases? Words of wisdom."

Ish laughed. "We have many. My Mom says, 'You only fail when you stop trying,' and she says it often."

"Much the same as my saying. Our people have many things in common."

"Fine." Opalo held up his hands in surrender. "Ish and I will go to the other side of the hill, and I will try to fly. If I'm successful on my first flight, you will agree to let the human doctors look at your injuries. Perhaps you will be able to soar again as well."

Sulka shook her head. "I'm too old."

"No, you're not," Ish said. "Doc Cromer thinks she can help you. Something about Bugii regenerative powers, how you heal so fast."

"Fast? I haven't flown in weeks." Opalo's stance was indignant.

"Your broken wing healed in half the time a human would heal from equivalent wounds to our bones."

"Fine. Let's go before I change my mind." Opalo headed for the caves. When they came out the other side, Opalo said, "Regardless of my success, you will ask Whisper out on a date. No more hedging."

"Blackmail? You're resorting to blackmail."

"You have preened around Whisper since the day we met. Stop making excuses and do that dating thing you humans talk about all the time. Everyone already knows you've kissed."

"What? How?"

"Well, maybe not everyone. I don't think Whisper's father knows. It appears to be taboo to mention such things to the father of the female involved. But word got around."

"Great," Ish moaned. Lieutenant Porter was not the soul of discretion Ish had hoped for.

"What's wrong with others knowing? The dating thing sounds like fun."

"There are consequences to dating."

"Indeed. You might discover that Whisper feels the same way about you."

"Fine. Soar already." Ish waved toward the sky. He would talk his way out of the dating thing. Ish was afraid that a date might ruin his friendship with Whisper, and while he wanted more, he wasn't sure of Whisper's feelings.

Opalo handed Ish the cane and opened his wings again. After a few seconds, he flew low, skimming the top of the kabu trees. The ubuks chattered from the safety of their nests. A couple of the twig creatures hopped on the top branches, almost as if the ubuks were cheering Opalo on to greater heights.

Opalo grinned and flew a circle around Ish. "See you on the other side."

"No fair." Ish turned and ran through the cave passages. He exited in time to see Opalo sail through the Suzai, the Sky Arch, and drop down to skim the water of Remei Lake.

Sulka was where they had left her. She waved at her grandson and clapped her hands. Opalo soared.

When Opalo landed, Sulka was the first to hug him. "I'm so happy for you."

"What about you? We should check with the doctors and see if you can be helped," Opalo said.

"It is enough that you can soar. I'm too old."

Ish listened to the conversation with interest. According to his calculation, Sulka could expect to live another fifty years, flying status had nothing to do with her aging. It wasn't fair. As Ish thought on that for a moment, a plan formed. Ish congratulated his friend and ran to the Doc's office.

*****

"Going hunting?" Ish dropped into step with Whisper. After considering Opalo's words, Ish realized he wanted to change his relationship with Whisper more than he wanted to maintain the status quo.

314

Grinning, Whisper asked, "What gave me away? The bow? Or the quiver full of arrows?"

Ish grinned. "A little of both. How about I come with? We could gather some food and eat near the mountains. I have some of Botha's cider."

Whisper responded with an answering grin. Botha had been the first to make a hard cider, and it had quickly become the drink of choice for the adults, even those who were new to adulthood. "A picnic? Sounds good. Anyone else coming?"

"No, just us."

Finally. Whisper forced herself to keep calm. Ever since that kiss she had waited for Ish to say something, anything to indicate he wanted to be more than friends.

"Where you going?" Shea ran up and jumped, knowing Ish would catch her.

"Hunting and a picnic." Whisper pointed to her gear.

"Great. Can I come?" Shea jumped from Ish's arms and flew circles around the couple.

Well, um, sure." Ish sighed.

"Great. Hey, Opalo, I'm going hunting with Whisper and Ish. And we're having a picnic, whatever that is. Wanna come?"

"That sounds like fun," Taiva said.

"Guess we're going." Opalo clapped Ish on the back.

Shea whispered not too softly, "Taiva invited herself. Some people don't know when they aren't wanted."

Whisper saw Ish's crestfallen face and smiled.

*****

Zigmin walked into the Sargu leader's office, the workspace she shared with Lifen. He had been adamant that they share the room and, with Ralim's help, had reconfigured the furniture so that both desks had equal command of the room. She smiled when Lifen didn't look up. He was bent over a tablet, scowling at whatever he was reading. Her smile dropped from her face when she remembered why she was here.

Instead of going to her desk, Zigmin stopped in front of Lifen's.

Lifen looked up, and sighed. "New problem?"

"Not exactly, well maybe, depends on how you look at it?"

"What?"

Zigmin watched as Lifen's full focus shifted to her. "There's another change we should make."

"Okay, write it up." Lifen relaxed. It wasn't a crisis.

"It needs to be addressed now."

"Why?"

"Because I want to raise my own young. I don't want the eggs thrown into a huge nursery waiting for hatching day. I don't want to look at the hatchlings and wonder which children I helped to create. The Bugii and Kurmii raise their own offspring like the humans do. I want that."

Lifen raised an eyebrow. "Okay, write it up, and we'll present it to the council. Any Rapulii who wishes to raise her own young may do so."

"How about the father?"

"I think that would be up to him, but sure, I have watched mated Bugii and Kurmii for years, and, more recently, the humans. I like the closeness of family units. I would like to know my offspring so other males might want that as well."

"That's good."

"Why is this so urgent?"

"I am entering eketlii. I choose you as the father of my young." Zigmin smiled.

Lifen, who fought Shimgin without fear, fainted.

*****

Sulka woke up from surgery in the medical bay of the *Scorpius.* Though she knew where she was, and why, she felt disoriented. She lay on her stomach, left wing strapped in

316

place. Sulka knew from Opalo's surgery that she would not be allowed to move until they taped up the other side. She couldn't see anyone, but she could hear talking. It was her human doctor.

"Did it work? Can I soar?" Watching Opalo regain flight had been wonderful, and Sulka was glad for her grandson. But to fly solo again, just her and the wind. That was something she had never dared hope for.

"I warned you," Doctor Cromer said. "Even if you can soar again, it might take some time to build up the strength of your wings again."

"I understand, but do I have hope?" Sulka hated the sound of need in her voice, but she had been so long without the ability to soar.

Doctor Cromer grinned. "There is hope. Today you rest, and tomorrow we will try some simple tests. For now, there are a few Bugii waiting to see you."

"I don't want the saime to see me like this." It felt like the only areas free from the tape Doctor Cromer was so fond of was her head, feet, and hands. Even her arms were restricted.

"Don't worry, after surgery, the rule is three visitors at a time and only immediate family at that. Maa, Opalo, and Shea are waiting in the hall. I'm pretty sure the entire saime has sent their wish that Nurita will bless you."

Sulka nodded. It was good to have friends. She just wasn't ready to face them with their expectations. Then she thought about her granddaughter. "I don't want Shea to be afraid." This ship was strange and scary to Sulka, and Shea was young. She didn't want her granddaughter frightened.

Cromer laughed. "Shea loves the ship. She's pestered every human she could to teach her the functions of the various parts of the ship. She even convinced Ish to teach her to fly the shuttle."

Before Sulka could speak, her family entered the room. Once they were sure she was okay, Shea began listing all that she had learned. Sulka didn't understand the reference to flying a simulator, but she could see Shea's enthusiasm for the device. Her granddaughter would be fine.

*****

Weeks later, Sulka stood outside, underneath the arch to the sun. Her wings felt good and strong, and the doctors had said she could try to fly, but she had not attempted it. Sulka found that she enjoyed the hope of flying and was worried that she would be devastated if she couldn't. She had spent many hours with a medical person called a therapist who had developed exercises for her to do every day. Supposedly, the exercises made her wings strong. She had been faithful to the schedule the therapist devised, but she didn't enjoy the exercises.

Although she no longer needed it, Sulka held the staff Ish and Lifen had gifted her. She treasured it. Sulka never expected to have a gift from a Rapulii. Humans were odd with their desire to offer help. She watched Opalo as he dove off the Highchair of the Dogu. It was now a lookout, and everyone was allowed up there. If she could soar, she would be able to land there, something she could not have predicted.

As Opalo made lazy circles in the air, Sulka spread her wings and flapped them. The first time she flapped her wings after the surgery, she was amazed at how good it felt to move both together. There was no pain, although her wings had been stiff. She had not been able to flap her wings in concert since the accident. Sulka flapped some more and using the wind, glided from the Semelai across the tip of the lake, turned back and landed on the dry land east of her starting position.

"Sulka, you did it." Opalo's enthusiastic voice was loud and echoed over the water.

"Shh. I don't want everyone to watch." She looked around and added. "I mostly glided. I didn't soar. I don't want to see pity in everyone's eyes if I can't."

"You won't know until you try." Opalo recited his grandmother's favorite phrase to her.

Sulka's wings raised and lowered in amusement. That her wings could work in concert again, pleased her more than she would have thought possible. It was time, and she knew it. "If you're going to recite my words back to me, we might as well fly." With those words, Sulka flapped her wings and jumped.

Staying low to the ground, she made a slow circle around the Semelai. Her wings felt good. Her left wing, which had ached since the injury, didn't hurt anymore. Flapping her wings harder, she turned skyward, flying between the Semelai and up into the sky. When those on the ground realized who was flying, the humans and Rapulii stopped to clap and cheer. The Bugii took to the air and joined Sulka as she flew circles around the arches and over the human settlement.

Whisper looked up from milking an irhasi. Once the humans learned that irhasi milk was a sweetener, irhasi moved up in status from edible herd animal to desired milk source. They had made great strides in domestication. Lifen had said the humans' success was because they were so focused on getting the milk. She was pretty sure he was right. Whisper stood and pointed to the sky. "Sulka is flying."

Ish whistled and waved. Sulka and her followers did a low fly-by over their heads and turned toward the sky. The Bugii soared.

Whisper hugged Ish. He reached for her chin, turned her lips toward his, leaned down and kissed her. Though they couldn't fly, their hearts soared.

From the Author

Thank you for taking this journey through one of the worlds of my mind. If you enjoyed the book, tell a friend.

If you would like to get notifications of new releases and special offers on my books, please join my mailing list by going to **https://nrtucker.com** and providing your email when the mailing list offer pops up. This list is not sold or used for any other purpose.

Books by N. R. Tucker

Farseen Chronicles

Deceived
Enthralled
Betrayed
Revealed
Destined
Vowed
Prized

Finding Earth

Drifters Rising
The Maiden Voyage of the Okar Lane
The Caves of Kurazi

More information about the worlds of N. R. Tucker's mind – flash fiction, character lists, glossaries, and maps – can be found at

https://NRTucker.com

www.ingramcontent.com/pod-product-compliance
Lightning Source LLC
Chambersburg PA
CBHW020335180626
46812CB00001B/215